DERRINGER

DERRINGER

WILLIAM W. JOHNSTONE
and
J.A. JOHNSTONE

PINNACLE BOOKS
Kensington Publishing Corp.
kensingtonbooks.com

CHAPTER 1

General Grenville M. Dodge sat beside a small fire on the bank of Lodgepole Creek drinking a cup of coffee. His column of one hundred and fifty cavalry had totally routed a party of about forty Arapaho warriors who had been raiding settlers between Crow Creek and Fort Laramie. They had been fortunate to attack the Arapaho camp while the warriors were still asleep in their blankets. The forced march to catch the Indians was the suggestion made by the general's personal scout, Sergeant Jesse Derringer. It was Derringer who found the Indians' camp at the base of a line of mountains after they raided a small settlement north of Crow Creek. The few Indians who had escaped the attack disappeared into the steep mountains of the Black Hills, so Dodge decided to have breakfast before starting the march back to Fort Laramie.

"You send for me, General?" Jesse Derringer asked when he approached Dodge.

"Yes, I did, Sergeant," Dodge replied. "Did you get something to eat?"

"Yes, sir, I ate," Derringer said. "What can I do for you?"

Dodge smiled in response to Derringer's submissive attitude. The general would be willing to wager that he was the only person on the planet who commanded much respect from the burly sergeant. "Now that the horses have had a chance to rest, I'm going to go on a little scout up into those mountains to see if those Indians kept running. You wanna go with me?"

"I reckon I'd better," Derringer said, thinking that wasn't the smartest idea the general had ever had. "You want me to mount up a detail of fifteen?"

"No, I was thinking about just the two of us," Dodge said. "I feel pretty sure they're not planning to attack us. You said you were sure they headed for home, didn't you?"

"Yes, sir, but I didn't know you were plannin' to go ridin' up into the mountains by yourself." He paused for a few moments before asking a question. "This have anything to do with the railroad?"

"As a matter of fact, it would be interesting to see if there's any place the railroad could go through this line of mountains. It would sure cut off a lot of miles of track if it could, and they're too damn high to climb."

"I expect it would," Derringer said. He knew how interested the general was in the construction of the cross-country railroad and that he had already been involved in planning the path of that track. The general had told him it would shorten the route a hundred and fifty miles if the tracks were brought this way from

Council Bluffs, if they could go straight across this line of mountains. It was by coincidence that they followed the raiding party to the base of the very mountain range that was blocking Dodge's preferred path to the West for the Union Pacific Railroad. Since they were here by chance, it would seem a shame to leave without giving the general the opportunity to estimate the possibility of somehow getting past this mountain range.

"Jesse," Dodge said, "when we leave here, we're going straight back to Fort Laramie. I don't know when I might get a chance to get back to this place again."

"That is a fact, sir," Derringer responded. The general addressed him by his first name only when he was asking a favor, instead of giving a direct order. "I expect we oughta go up those mountains and take a little look around." He felt pretty sure they wouldn't find any of those Arapaho warriors waiting for them. "I'll get the horses."

They followed the path the fleeing Arapaho warriors had taken to ascend the mountain, since it was obviously the easiest way up. All the way to the top, Derringer kept a cautious eye on the trail left by the Indians. They had made no real effort to disguise their retreat and once they reached the top of the ridge, they varied their direction only to the extent of picking the easiest way down the other side. Only then was Derringer willing to dismiss them from his concern.

Dodge wanted to scout the ridge to the north first, so they made their way along it for almost a mile before they stopped when they found the mountains grew higher the farther north they rode. "Too steep to climb and too far to tunnel through," the general conceded.

When he looked at Derringer for a response to his comment, he found the sergeant staring at a large outcropping of rock ahead of them. Staring back at them, a lone Indian warrior stood motionless, as fully surprised as they were. When Derringer pulled the Henry rifle out of his saddle scabbard, the Indian turned and fled, disappearing in the rocks.

Derringer was immediately after him. "Stay here!" he told the general. "I'll try to see if he's alone!" He gave his horse a kick and worked his way through the rocks, where he found a trail on the other side, leading down the mountainside. He caught a glimpse of the Indian just before he disappeared again when the trail bent around a clump of trees. When he got to that clump, he reined his horse to a sliding halt because he saw the Indian he had been chasing pulling up before a camp beside a small stream. *A war party*, he thought, for they were wearing paint. He did a quick count of those he could see and figured there were about twenty of them. The one he had been following didn't dismount but was gesturing wildly and pointing back in the direction he had fled. "Damn," Derringer swore, and wheeled his horse around when he saw the warriors scrambling to get to their horses.

He started yelling to Dodge before he reached him. "War party! We've got to ride like hell!"

"Can we hold them off?" Dodge yelled back.

"Too many!" Derringer answered. "We've gotta ride like hell," he repeated. The general still waited until Derringer caught up to him before falling in behind him, preferring to have the rugged scout lead the way. They rode south along the ridge as fast as they safely could to the sound of war hoops from their pursuers. It began to look as if they might be trapped on top of this mountain ridge, so when they came to what looked like a narrow pass, Derringer didn't hesitate; he guided his horse down into the pass and followed it. To his surprise, it continued to gradually descend until it took them all the way to the prairie floor. "You all right, sir?" Derringer asked when he reined back to let the general catch up.

"That was a helluva ride," Dodge said. "They didn't even see us drop down in that pass, so I expect they're wondering where we went." He laughed in relief. "I'll tell you the truth, I thought you'd lost your mind when you dropped down in that gully. And I thought I was crazy to follow you. How did you know that narrow ravine was a pass that would take us down to the prairie?"

"It just looked like a narrow pass that would just naturally lead down to the prairie," Derringer lied. In fact, he had given up hope of outrunning the war party and was looking for some place where they might hold them off. But since it had turned out to be a safe way down to the bottom, he figured he might as well take credit for a smart move.

Dodge just shook his head, still amazed that they had escaped. "I'll tell you one thing, though. If we can save our scalps, I believe we've found a pass through which the Union Pacific can go."

"Well then, I reckon the scout was worth it," Derringer responded. "I expect we oughta get along back to the column now before those boys up there on that mountain figure out we ain't up there no more." He paused before suggesting another option. "Unless you wanna wait for that war party to find out we're down here on the plains, so we can lead 'em back to our camp. It ain't but about a mile from here and then they wouldn't waste all that war paint they're wearin'."

"I don't know what that war party was doing up on the top of that mountain," Dodge remarked. "Where were they going? There's no settlement south of these mountains."

"That's a fact," Derringer said. "I suspect they mighta been thinkin' about settlements east, back along the South Platte, and there's a few of them. Hard to tell what they're thinkin' now. They mighta run into those Arapaho we chased up on top of that mountain. If they did, then they know there's a column of a hundred and fifty soldiers right behind them."

"I know we put a stop to that Arapaho raiding party, but we're two and a half days' march back to Fort Laramie," Dodge said. "I swear, damn it, I can't leave now when we know there's a war party of twenty or more savages probably on their way to attack some settlement east of here."

"I reckon I could go back up there and ask 'em what they're plannin' to do, so we'd know what we oughta do," Derringer japed. "Since it ain't but about a mile back to camp, how 'bout we take you back to your command? Then I can come back here and keep an eye on this war party. There ain't no sense in makin' a hundred and fifty men worry about their commandin' officer when they could just have to worry about one sergeant."

The general couldn't help chuckling in response. "I'm sure Colonel Walsh is standing ready and willing to take command of the column in the event of my absence."

Derringer started to laugh but stopped short. "He might get his chance," he said when he saw the warrior suddenly appear in the mouth of the narrow pass. "It's time to go!" He gave the general's horse a smack on the behind just as they heard the war cries coming from the base of the mountain. They were off at a gallop with twenty-two screaming Cheyenne warriors in hot pursuit. "Head for the gap in that line of trees!" he shouted to the general. "I'm gonna slow 'em down some!" Dodge did as he was instructed and continued to gallop toward the gap in the trees that outlined the creek where his men were camped.

Derringer pulled his horse to a stop and wheeled around to face the war party chasing them. One particular brave was out in front of the rest of the war party and he was gaining on them. So Derringer drew his Henry rifle from his saddle scabbard. He waited for the horse to be still while he cranked a cartridge into the cylinder, guessing the warrior was at a distance of about one hundred and twenty yards and closing fast. Then he took dead aim and knocked the racing warrior off his horse. Thinking also to put the detachment of soldiers on alert, he fired twice more at the war party. It caused them to spread out and those with rifles answered fire. "That oughta do it," he said, wheeled his horse again and raced after General Dodge. *Now it's up to you, Colonel Walsh,* he thought. The colonel was already up to the surprise. He stepped out of the trees and signaled the general to come to him. Seeing him,

General Dodge headed straight for him and Derringer was not far behind.

As he rode into the cover of the trees, Derringer passed through a long line of soldiers lying in ambush and waiting for the command to fire at the charging party of twenty-one unsuspecting Cheyenne warriors. Derringer's first thought upon riding into the safety of the trees was, *That answers the question why they didn't run into the fleeing Arapaho on the mountain.* He and the general quickly dismounted and took cover while Colonel Walsh commanded the men to hold their fire. When the war party was about thirty-five yards away, he gave the order to fire and the trees erupted in a long line of rifle fire that decimated the hapless Indian war party. It was reduced to half a dozen in a few minutes' time and half of them were wounded. They promptly retreated as best they could. Walsh reported to General Dodge and asked if he wanted to mount a patrol to go after the survivors. Dodge gave him a "Well done," but said no. He thought the war party had been sufficiently discouraged from any raids they had sought to perform on any settlement. "We'll start back to Fort Laramie after the noon meal."

With six other soldiers Derringer walked out among the bodies left on the prairie. Their purpose was to make sure all the bodies were dead, so as not to prolong suffering. Those who survived the ambush would most likely come back to take care of the dead after the soldiers left. Derringer's purpose, however, was to identify the dead, and he found that he was right in thinking they were Cheyenne. He reported the fact to General

Dodge and Colonel Walsh. Walsh, known for his sense of humor, made a suggestion when planning future campaigns. "Instead of mounting patrols of fifteen or more men, why not just send you and Sergeant Derringer out as bait? And you can just lead them back to an ambush like you did today." Overheard by some of the soldiers close by, it became a running joke among the regiment.

The ambush of the Cheyenne war party happened in September of 1865. It turned out to be the last campaign of that nature for the general and the sergeant. During the following months, the general was called back to Washington to plan the building of the railroad while the sergeant was assigned to a cavalry regiment. In May of 1866, General Dodge resigned from the army and later that same year was appointed chief engineer of the Union Pacific Railroad. When news of the general's appointment finally got around to Sergeant Jesse Derringer, he was not surprised at all and he was happy for his old boss. He realized how much he missed the days when he was the general's personal scout and how little he liked serving in a regular cavalry company. So he decided to resign from the army, fully convinced he had no desire to retire from it. He preferred to find out what else was out there to see before he became too old to see it. It had been some time before the war since he had been back to the family farm near Omaha, so he decided to visit the old homeplace. His younger brother, Dan, and Dan's wife,

Shirley, had taken over the farm after his parents were gone. They had passed away while Jesse was serving in Dakota Territory.

Jesse's visit with his brother was a brief one, lasting only a couple of days. Although Dan and Shirley made a show of welcoming him home, Jesse was aware of a sense of concern from both of them that he was planning to claim his inheritance and move in with them and their two boys. He assured them that he had no desire to settle down on the farm, so he would be on his way again the next day. His statement relieved the tension immediately and they persuaded him to stay over an extra day. When he left, Dan asked where he was heading and Jesse simply answered, "West."

CHAPTER 2

William C. Cartwright, assistant construction supervisor, sat at his desk in the Council Bluffs office of the Union Pacific Railroad. He was studying a large map spread out across the desk when one of his clerks stuck his head in the door and announced that there was a gentleman who wanted to see him. Cartwright was not inclined to waste his time granting interviews to newspaper reporters, so he asked, "Newspaper reporter?"

"I don't know," the clerk responded. "He doesn't look like one. He was a rather direct gentleman, however, when he said it was important."

"Oh, he did, did he?" Cartwright replied. "Did he give his name?"

"Yes, sir. He said his name is Derringer."

"Derringer?" Cartwright responded. "The only Derringer I know about is no gentleman. Send him in here, Lewis. Hell, I sent word for him to come see me." He got up from the desk to receive him when Lewis withdrew his head from the door and opened it for Derringer to come in. "Sergeant Derringer!" Cartwright announced, grinning from ear to ear. He stepped forward to extend his hand to the tall, serious-looking man.

"Sergeant?" Jesse Derringer responded with a genuine look of surprise. "It's been a while since anybody's called me Sergeant. I mustered out of the army when there wasn't nobody left to fight. How did you know I was in the army?"

"I know that you served as a scout for my boss at Union Pacific, General Grenville M. Dodge, and I know he's looking for you."

"I heard that General Dodge was workin' for the railroad," Derringer said. "I didn't know he was lookin' for me, though. How did you know I was in Council Bluffs?"

"I didn't," Cartwright responded, "but the general remembered you had a home in Omaha before the war and he thought you might be passing through here sometime on your way there. So I gave your name to the bartender at the Whistlestop Saloon. And I told him if Jesse Derringer ever stops in, tell him I want to see him and it's important."

"Yes, sir, it sure surprised me when he told me that," Jesse said. "Mickey Deal's his name, ain't it? The last I heard about General Dodge was that he won an election for congressman, but he's workin' for the Union Pacific Railroad now." He looked around him and nodded, smiling. "I see they fixed him up in a nice office."

"Yes, but he doesn't spend much time in it," Cartwright was quick to reply. "My job is assistant superintendent of construction for the railroad across the country to connect with Central Pacific Railroad to form a transcontinental railroad. The general is in the field with the surveyors, mapping out the right of way for the tracks, so I'm glad you got here when you did. General Dodge wants me to offer you a job with the Union Pacific."

"That's mighty thoughtful of the general, but I don't know anything about workin' on the railroad," Derringer responded as he pictured himself swinging a pickax or driving a spike, and it wasn't the kind of work that suited him.

"Mr. Derringer, the general says you're the best damn scout he's ever had the pleasure of working with," Cartwright informed him. "He said that maybe you're the only man he trusts to fill the job he's got in mind. The railroad has given him the task of planning the route of the railroad from Council Bluffs into Dakota Territory. Right now, General Dodge is at Crow Creek Crossing where they're building a bridge across Crow Creek. After Crow Creek, they're faced with a rougher route to follow up across what the general's calling Sherman Hill. The general said that back in 1865, in the Black Hills campaign, your outfit had to escape from an Indian war party, and it was you who found a pass out of that mess. He said he thought at the time that it would serve as a pass skirting the Black Hills for the railroad, west of the Platte River."

"Yes, sir," Derringer remarked with a chuckle, "I remember that time."

"So how about it? Are you ready to go back to work as the general's scout? You'll go on the Union Pacific payroll starting today if you are. I can authorize some advance expense money so you can get what supplies you need right away."

"Well, I could say I'd have to think about it, since I had other plans," Derringer said, "but that would be a lie. So I reckon I'm your man." He didn't say as much to Cartwright, but when he mentioned the money in advance, it was a done deal. His financial state was down to pocket change. When he rode into town the day before, the thought that he would ever see General Dodge again never entered his mind as a possibility. And with winter coming on, he was expecting to be riding the grub line, hoping to sign on as a cowhand with some rancher.

"Excellent!" Cartwright responded. "That's going to make the general very happy. He's told me some tales about your time in the army."

"Is that right?" Derringer responded. "Well, I hope you didn't believe all of them."

"When did you get in town?" Cartwright asked.

"Yesterday mornin'," Derringer answered.

"Did you take a room in the hotel?"

"No, sir, I spent last night in the jailhouse," Jesse told him.

"Oh? Did you drink a little too much of the demon whiskey?" Cartwright asked.

"No, sir, I only had a couple of drinks, but the fellow at the end of the bar had way too much to drink. And I reckon it affected his eyesight, because he said he didn't like the way I was lookin' at him. He invited me to settle it with our guns, and when I told him I druther not, he said he was gonna shoot me down, anyway.

When he drew his gun, I grabbed his arm and he shot himself in the leg. The bartender sent for the sheriff, and I reckon we musta caught him at a bad time, because he took me to jail, even though Mickey and I both tried to tell him I didn't shoot that fellow. I didn't put up too much fuss about it, though, since I'm a little short of money and I couldn't afford a hotel room. I figured I'd at least have a place to sleep and maybe a meal or two, and they put my horses in the stable, too. So I figure I came out ahead on that deal."

Cartwright shook his head, not sure if Derringer was serious or not. "If you're broke, what were you thinking about doing next?"

"I was thinkin' about maybe robbing the bank, but I hadn't made a final decision on that yet, so I'm glad you have a job for me."

"I'll get you a room in the hotel tonight," Cartwright said, thinking Derringer was joking, but not willing to bet on it. "So you'll have tomorrow to take care of your horses and any needs you might have in personal supplies or ammunition. He looked at the clock on the wall. "It's about dinnertime," he announced. "Let's go to the hotel to get something to eat. Then I'll get a room for you for tonight and tomorrow night. Then you can hitch a ride on a train that's leaving at ten o'clock Wednesday mornin', heading for the end of the track."

"How far will that take me?" Derringer asked, since he was going to have to buy supplies for the trip. Cartwright said the general was at Crow Creek Crossing and that had to be about five hundred miles from Council Bluffs.

Cartwright took another look at his map. "Here's

where they were when he wired me two days ago. Based on the rate they've been laying track, about three miles a day, that ought to put them close to Crow Creek."

"Well, I'll be . . ." Derringer started. "How many days will I be on the train?"

Cartwright shrugged. "Depending on how many hours they travel a day, I'd say about two and a half days."

Derringer shook his head and grinned. "I expect it would take me the better part of two weeks to ride my horse that far. I reckon I won't need as many supplies as I thought."

As Cartwright suggested, they walked down to the hotel dining room for dinner. Jesse left his two horses tied at the hotel hitching rail. After dinner, they went to the front desk in the hotel to get Jesse a room. When that was taken care of, Cartwright took a roll of money out of his pocket and peeled off fifty dollars and gave it to him as an advance. "That oughta be enough to get you set to travel," he said. "Are your horses in good shape?"

"Yes, sir," Jesse replied. "I always take care of them, so they'll take care of me. I'll take 'em back to the stable. I just picked 'em up before I came to your office."

"Tell John Walker to put the fee on my bill," Cartwright said. "He seems to take pretty good care of my horses. I've got to meet with some people this afternoon, so I'm going back to the office. I may not see you tonight, so check in with me sometime tomorrow. All right?" Jesse said that he would, so Cartwright started back to his office with the air of a man who had accomplished an important item on his list of things to do. "Don't spend all that advance in the Whistlestop," he called back.

"Right," Jesse responded as he took his rifle and his saddlebags off the gray gelding. "I'll spread it around in the other saloons." Then he took his things up to his room before taking his horses back to the stable.

"Howdy," John Walker greeted him when he rode up to the stable again. "I didn't expect to see you back so soon."

"I got a job when I got outta jail," Jesse replied. "So I'm gonna need to leave my horses with you until Wednesday mornin'. But instead of the sheriff paying for 'em, this time you can charge General Grenville Dodge's account, or the Union Pacific's, whichever."

"Is that so?" Walker responded. "You goin' to work for the railroad?"

"I reckon so," Jesse shrugged.

"Doin' what?"

"Whatever he says," Jesse replied. "I worked for General Dodge for quite a while as a scout durin' the war and after that in the Indian Wars. Looks like I'm gonna start out doin' that right away, scoutin' for the railroad this time."

"So you'll be leadin' the Union Pacific Railroad across the country to join up with the Central Pacific Railroad?" Walker asked.

"I wouldn't put it that way," Jesse said. "General Dodge is the one who says which way to go. My job is just to take a look to see if there's anything he might stub his toe on ahead of him."

"That still sounds important, so you better be careful you don't run into nobody else like Stony Packer before you leave town," Walker said.

"Who's Stony Packer?"

"He's the fellow you shot in the leg yesterday that landed you in jail," Walker said with a chuckle.

"I didn't shoot that fellow," Jesse immediately replied. "He shot himself. I tried to tell that sheriff that I was just tryin' to keep him from shootin' me. Hell, he pulled the trigger, the damn fool."

"Tell you the truth, Warner Black ain't really the sheriff. He's just takin' on the job until we get another one," Walker said. "He's the blacksmith, and I expect the situation was a little bit unusual for him and he wasn't sure what to do."

"To be honest with you," Jesse confessed, "I didn't give him any argument that amounted to much because I figured I could use a bed for the night. He was pretty reasonable about it this mornin', though. Even got me a breakfast before he let me go."

"I expect there's a lotta folks that woulda liked it better if you had turned Stony's gun up at his head, instead of down toward his leg," Walker said. "Him and those two saddle tramps he hangs out with think they own the town, now that Luke Collins left to take the marshal's job in Omaha. It wouldn't be a bad idea to stay clear of those two friends of his while you're at it."

"It'd help if somebody would hang a sign around their necks with their names on it," Jesse said. "I really didn't pay much attention to who was with him yesterday."

"Travis Stacy and Rob Gentry," Walker announced. "Each one of 'em is worse than the other one."

"Well, now, right off, that don't sound too good," Jesse remarked. "I was hopin' to enjoy some of the town's hospitality before startin' out on a trip that's liable to take almost two and a half days on a train. And when we get there, there won't be a saloon to celebrate the journey."

Walker chuckled again. "Yeah, but you'll be part of history."

"That's right," Jesse replied, "the part they throw out of the chamber pot when they empty it. What time will you open up in the mornin'?" Jesse asked, changing the subject.

"Usually around five-thirty or six," Walker answered. "So I reckon that's when I'll see you that mornin'."

"I reckon," Jesse replied. "It's gonna be just like bein' back in the army again."

He left the gray gelding he called Clem and the sorrel he called various names with John Walker in the stable while he spent some of the money Cartwright had given him to replenish his stock of ammunition. Cartwright didn't say anything about food during the train trip, so he figured he'd better buy something he could gnaw on during the trip. He found a message Cartwright had left for him when he came back to his room. It was an invitation for him to join his party for supper in the hotel that night.

Jesse was surprised to discover it was a bigger group of men than he had imagined. There were surveyors, which he had expected, but in addition, there were land agents and speculators, as well as military officers and personal friends of the general. He was left with little doubt that the Union Pacific intended to build a solid town at Crow Creek Crossing. Jesse enjoyed the supper and a couple of drinks afterward, but he felt like a square peg in a round hole in a social setting with officers, politicians, and executives of the Union Pacific Railroad. So he retired to his room at the hotel after a polite good night to Cartwright. "Use tomorrow to get everything you think you'll need for a couple of days' ride to Crow Creek Crossing," Cartwright told him.

"Yes, sir," Jesse responded. "That gives me plenty of time to do the little bit I need to do." He took his leave then and Cartwright fully understood he was more comfortable elsewhere.

As he had told Cartwright the night before, he had very little to do to be ready. Much of his day was spent with his horses to make sure they were fit and ready to go on a long ride. As a consequence, he spent a great deal of time talking to John Walker at the stable and found the man one he would count as a friend. They agreed to meet after supper at the Whistlestop for a drink or two after John closed the stable and went home for his supper. "You sure the little woman will think it's a good idea to let you out for a drink?" Jesse asked. "Better not let her know I was in jail night before last."

"Ain't no problem," John replied. "I'm the one who

does the thinkin' in my house. Course she tells me what to think."

"I reckon I'll just have to wait to see if you show up," Jesse japed. "And if you don't, I'll take a drink for all the poor men who took that rocky trail called matrimony."

CHAPTER 3

"Whaddya have?" Mickey Deal asked when Jesse walked up to the bar at the Whistlestop Saloon.

"You got any corn likker?" Jesse asked. "I'd like a shot of that, if you have it, since that's what I was raised on."

"Sure, I've got corn whiskey," Mickey said, and poured a shot for him. He watched Jesse toss it back, then he held the bottle ready to pour another one. But Jesse held his hand up to stop him.

"I wanna wait a minute for John Walker to join me," Jesse said. "If he drinks corn, I'll just buy a bottle. That first drink was just to remind my belly what I came in here for."

Mickey chuckled and said, "Fellow told me you was General Grenville Dodge's personal scout and you'd be scoutin' the trail for the Union Pacific Railroad across the country."

"The general's the man who decides where the tracks

are going," Jesse said. "I just ride up ahead to see if there are any problems on the way he wants to go."

Two men farther down the bar took special interest in Jesse and the bartender's conversation. "Jesse Derringer," one of them said, loud enough to be overheard. "Derringer," he repeated, "like them little pocket pistols women like to carry in their purses or under their garters. I reckon the railroad didn't have enough money to hire a man-sized .45-caliber pistol, so they went with a lady-sized one instead."

Jesse didn't respond to the insult. He just looked at Mickey and gave him a tired smile. "Is that the same two that were with the fellow who tried to shoot me?"

"That's right," Mickey answered, almost in a whisper. "Rob Gentry and Travis Stacy. Don't let 'em draw you out. They're both fast with a six-gun, but Stacy's got a reputation."

"Is that a fact?" Jesse said, loud enough for the two men to hear. "Which one of you gents is Stacy?"

"I reckon that's me," Travis Stacy spoke up, and took a step away from the bar to give himself some room, a confident smirk on his face. "You got somethin' you wanna say to me, Pocket Pistol?"

"Mickey says you've got a reputation," Derringer said.

"That's what they say," Stacy said.

"A reputation for what?" Derringer asked.

"What the hell do you think?" Stacy replied.

"Well, I ain't sure," Jesse said. "Judgin' by your stubby little body, I'd guess maybe throwin' buffalo chips or something like that. I've seen a few fast guns and there ain't none of 'em as chubby around the belly as you are." He cocked his head as if just noticing something. "Are you by any chance the son of Maisie Stacy? She's a whore over in Omaha. Ol' Crazy Maisie they called her, said she'd entertain a buffalo if somebody would pay for the critter." He turned back to face Mickey again and planted his elbows on the bar.

"You son of a . . . !" Stacy roared, infuriated. "My mama ain't no whore!" He took another step back and the men standing close by the bar quickly moved out of the line of fire.

Jesse continued leaning on the bar. "I'll take your word for it," he said. "Mickey, pour me another shot of that corn likker. No, wait a minute, here comes John. Let's wait and see what he's drinkin'." He turned his back on Stacy as he called out to John Walker. "You're just in time, John. What do you usually drink?"

Walker didn't know how to respond. He looked at Stacy standing several feet away from the bar as if ready to draw his six-gun and fire. Then he looked back at Derringer, slumped over the bar, his back to Stacy as if unaware of the man waiting to face him. Finally, he spoke. "It looks like you're busy right now and I don't wanna get in the way." He backed slowly away into the circle of spectators that had expanded, anticipating the gunfight.

"Nah, you ain't in the way," Derringer responded, still leaning on the bar. "That's just young Stacy, hoping I'll play with him, but I don't do shoot-outs or duels. That's just foolishness for young boys that ain't growed up yet. I'll just take the whole bottle," he said to Mickey then, and grabbed the bottle off the bar. "Come on, John, and we'll sit down at a table."

Infuriated for being treated like a child, Stacy stepped in front of him and stopped him with a hand against his chest and drew his six-gun with the other one. Before the weapon cleared leather, however, Derringer's almost full bottle of whiskey exploded against the side of Stacy's head, dropping him in an unconscious heap. Startled by the unexpected turn of events, Stacy's pal, Gentry, saw fit to reach for his .45, only to look back and find Derringer smiling at him, his Colt already out and waiting for his next move. Gentry released the pistol at once and let it drop back into his holster. "That's the first smart thing I've seen from either one of you fellows," Derringer said. "If you're really smart, you'll let this be the last of anything to do with me. And from the look of that eye and the lump growin' on the side of his head, it might be a good idea to take him to the doctor's office before it gets any later. He's gonna be hurtin' like hell when he comes to, if he ever does. I'll help you put him on his horse, if you're ready to take him right now."

Gentry stared in total confusion as his partner lay prone on the barroom floor with blood oozing out of a lump the size of a hickory nut just above his eye. He couldn't think of anything to do but take hold of Stacy's shoulders when Derringer grabbed his boots and they picked him up. John Walker hurried to hold the door open for them, then helped them lay Stacy across his saddle. John held the horse while Gentry climbed on his horse and took the reins from him.

"This ain't over yet," Gentry said, thinking he had to say something in defiance.

"Well, it had damn sure better be," Derringer said. "'Cause I don't intend to put up with any more crap from you three fellows." He gave his horse a slap on the rump to get him on his way.

"I swear, Jesse," John Walker fretted, "you mighta made some real trouble for yourself with those three. It's a good thing you're leaving here in the mornin'."

"Yeah, I reckon so," Derringer agreed. "I don't intend to hang around here very long. I just wanted to enjoy a couple of drinks of likker before I go to bed. I didn't think I was gonna have to buy two bottles of whiskey to get a couple of drinks. I expect I'd best go back inside now and apologize to the bartender for makin' a mess on the floor. And maybe we can have that drink we were plannin' to have."

"Maybe you'd better let me buy you a drink," Walker suggested. "I'm only gonna have a couple before I call it a night."

"Nope, I invited you for a drink," Jesse insisted. "I'm gonna buy another bottle, we'll have a couple of drinks, and I'll take the rest with me to keep for medicinal purposes on the way to Crow Creek Crossin'." Since Cartwright had advanced him fifty dollars, he could afford to be generous. So they went back inside the saloon to find Mickey mopping up the contents of the original bottle of whiskey. "I'm real sorry about the mess, Mickey," Jesse said. "I didn't think that fellow's head was gonna be that hard. Can I give you a hand?"

"It ain't no problem," Mickey said. "I've just about got most of it anyway."

"There's a fellow outside sittin' up against the front wall said he'd give you a nickel if you'd wring your mop out over his mouth," Jesse quipped.

"I'd do that," Mickey replied, "but most likely he'd complain about all the broken glass in it." When he was finished, he set his mop and bucket behind the bar and got Derringer another bottle of corn whiskey. Jesse took it and a couple of glasses to a table and poured a drink for John and himself. They sat a while and had a couple more drinks, but both men were thinking about the early morning awaiting, even though Jesse didn't have to get his horses early. The train wasn't leaving until ten o'clock, but they called it a night. Derringer took his bottle, which was still half full, to carry on his packhorse in the morning.

"Well, I reckon I'll see you in the mornin'," John said as they parted, and he headed toward the stable while Derringer went the opposite direction, toward the hotel.

"In the mornin'," Derringer confirmed, and walked down the street toward the two-story building near the railroad tracks. Looking forward to a few hours' sleep, he failed to take notice of the man standing in the dark alley between the barbershop and the dry goods store as he passed by.

"Derringer!" He heard the challenge as he approached the saddle shop. His reaction was automatic. He pulled his Colt as he spun around and dropped to one knee in time to hear the report of the six-gun and the snap of the bullet as it passed over his head. He took dead aim and placed his shot in the middle of Gentry's chest. He watched him drop to be sure he had stopped him cold. Then he looked back up the nearly deserted street toward the lights of the saloon. Only two men came out of the saloon to look for the cause of the two quick shots. They remained there in front of the saloon staring down the darkened street for a few minutes. Then evidently seeing nothing, they went back inside. He had to decide what to do about the man he had just killed when he heard the voice behind him.

"Just drop that weapon on the ground, or the next shot you hear will be the last sound you'll ever hear." With little choice, Jesse did as he was told. "Derringer, I shoulda known it was you," Sheriff Warner Black declared. "You're on a killin' spree, ain't you? I just came from Doc Gregory's house after he sent word to me that he had to get the undertaker to come get the body of the first feller you killed tonight." He reached down and picked up Derringer's gun.

"Whadda you talkin' about?" Jesse responded. "This bushwhacker is the only man I shot, and if you got here in time to see it, you know he shot at me first."

"I can't say who shot first," Black claimed. "All I saw after I heard the shots was you down on one knee and him flat on his back. Ain't got no idea who shot first. Doc said you musta hit that other feller in the head with a hammer."

"It was a bottle," Jesse said, "and he pulled a gun on me before I hit him with it. Mickey Deal and everybody else in the saloon can tell you that. Hell, nobody dies from gettin' hit in the head with a bottle."

"That oughta make you famous then," Black said, still holding his six-gun on him. "The first feller to ever kill somebody with a likker bottle. I think you'd best spend the night in jail until I have a chance to find out what's what."

Derringer remembered then what John Walker had told him about the sheriff, that he was the blacksmith who was acting as sheriff until they found an applicant for the full-time job. "Sheriff, you don't wanna put me in jail. What I told you is the truth and I'm supposed to leave town Wednesday mornin' on the Union Pacific Railroad. We're pullin' outta here at ten o'clock 'cause there's a whole bunch of soldiers and surveyors and the general, himself, countin' on me to be at Crow Creek Crossin'."

Warner Black looked at Derringer for a few minutes, trying to decide if he could believe his side of the story, or if he was just being played. His only fear in his temporary position was that his inexperience might be taken advantage of and used against him. And Derringer looked like he might be the type to do just that. So he decided to play it safe and give himself time to find out the truth of the matter. "I think it's best if you spend the night in jail and we'll get all the facts straightened out tomorrow." Derringer started to protest, but the sheriff stopped him. "Ain't gonna do you no good to make a fuss about it," he declared. "You're goin' to jail and how long you stay in jail depends on what we find out tomorrow."

It was plain to see that he was not going to talk the sheriff out of that decision and to resist arrest would only make matters worse. "All right, Sheriff, I'll go to jail, but will you get in touch with William C. Cartwright at the Union Pacific office and tell him where I am?" Black said he would do that, so Derringer went back to jail peacefully.

It was a worrisome night for Jesse Derringer, for according to what Cartwright had told him about Union Pacific's progress in the construction of the new track, he could imagine the general had needed him months ago. Cartwright told him that the general and his surveyors had reached Crow Creek Crossing back on the fourth of July and they had platted the town on the fifth. This while the railroad tracks were some four months short of reaching that point. Cartwright said people were already gathered there and they elected a mayor on August tenth and decided to call the town Cheyenne in honor of the Indians there. Of concern to Derringer, however, was the fact that it was already the first week in November and the weather was getting colder every day. The challenge facing the railroad now, after Crow Creek, was the steep mountains of the Black Hills. He was not at all confident that the track could be laid when the winter struck hard. He was sure that the general wanted him to explore those mountain passes again to be sure they found the best way to build the railroad.

* * *

His concerns about getting released from jail were evidently not enough to keep him from sleeping, for he was awakened the next morning at around six o'clock when the sheriff brought him his breakfast. "Did you check with William Cartwright at Union Pacific?" Jesse asked when Black pushed his tray through the pass-through in the cell door.

"No, I ain't yet," Black answered. "They ain't open yet. Most likely won't nobody be there before nine o'clock. I'll go over there later on."

"We can't wait till later on," Jesse urged. "I've gotta get my horses and my stuff outta my hotel room and load 'em on that train before ten o'clock."

"I reckon you shoulda thought about that before you shot that feller last night," the sheriff said. "I told you I'd go talk to Cartwright, but you'll just have to wait till they open their office. Just set down and eat your breakfast and don't bother me no more."

In no mood to tolerate the sheriff's stubborn atti-tude, Derringer knew he had to do something. So he at-tacked the breakfast tray Black had brought him, cramming sausage, potatoes, eggs, and coffee down as fast as he could until he felt sufficiently stuffed. Then he stuck his finger as far down his throat as he could until he created the action needed to throw it all up. When he vomited it all back up, he heaved it on his cot and the floor along with the contents of the coffee cup, the tray, and the dishes. Holding his stomach then, he groaned, "You poisoned me!"

"What the hell's wrong with you?" Black yelled in disgust upon seeing the mess on the cell floor and the one cot.

"I'm sorry," Derringer moaned. "I'm sick. I musta drank too much whiskey last night. I need to lie down and my bed's messed up."

"Lay on the damn floor," Black replied, then reconsidered. "You through pukin'?"

"Yeah, I'm empty. I just feel sick as a dog."

"All right," Black said. "I'll put you in the other cell. And after you sleep it off, you're gonna clean that cell up." He got the key to the cell and unlocked it. "And you might as well forget about that business with the Union Pacific. You ain't goin' nowhere." Then he drew his sidearm and stepped back to give Derringer room to walk out of the one cell and into the other one.

Giving his best impression of an ailing man, Derringer shuffled out of the first cell and started toward the open door of the second one. When he didn't move fast enough to suit the sheriff, Black gave him a kick in the butt to encourage him. It was a bad decision on the sheriff's part because Jesse was hoping for any opportunity to react. And he reacted quickly enough to grab Black's boot and shove it straight up in the air; Black landed on his back with Jesse on top of him. Black's reflexes caused him to squeeze the trigger of his pistol, sending a shot into the back wall of the cell, but Jesse trapped his wrist before he could aim the weapon at him. The ensuing struggle for control of the firearm went quickly in Jesse's favor and he wrestled it out of Black's hand.

Jesse was on his feet at once, the sheriff's Colt Peacemaker aimed at Black's head. "Now, there's two ways this can end," he told the sheriff. "One way is you can be dead. The other is you're gonna be inconvenienced for a while, but you'll be alive. So what's it gonna be?" Black was still in too much shock to answer right away, so Jesse said, "I know you fired a shot, but nobody seems to have thought anything about it. I doubt they'll think much about a second one either." He continued to hold the pistol on the sheriff's head. "If you choose to live, get up from there and go in that cell. If you'd rather die, you don't have to bother to get up and I'll just make it quick."

"I'll get up!" Black exclaimed. "I'll get up, but you know you're makin' a helluva mistake doin' this."

"You might be right, Sheriff. Half the decisions we make are wrong. But this much I want you to know. I hit that one fellow with a bottle because he pulled a gun on me and I shot that other one because he took a shot at me first. And that's God's Honest Truth. Now, it's too doggoned important for me to make that train this mornin', instead of missin' it just so you can take your time findin' out that I told you the truth."

Black got up and walked into the cell. Jesse locked the cell door and went into the office to look for his gun belt and a few other things he thought might be useful. He strapped on his Colt .44 and put the other things on the sheriff's desk chair. Then he rolled the chair out of the office, into the cell room, unlocked the cell, and pushed the chair into it. To answer the sheriff's questioning expression, he said, "I thought you might be more comfortable in your chair. So sit." When

Black sat, Jesse took the two pairs of handcuffs he found in the desk and used them to lock the sheriff's wrists to the arms of the chair. Then he tied the rope he found around Black's waist and the back of the chair and tied it to cell bars. The last touch was a gag, fashioned from a hand towel. "You just try to relax and somebody's bound to come lookin' for you before dinnertime. I'm sorry about messin' that other cell up, but I couldn't think of any other way to do what had to be done. I don't blame you for what you're thinkin', but you're a reasonable man. When you start askin' around, you'll find everything I told you is the truth and this should be the end of it. We just don't have the time right now."

He closed the door between the office and the cell room, then took a look outside the front door before stepping out to a street that was still empty of people. His first stop was the hotel, so he hurried down near the railway station, went into his room to pick up his saddlebags and his rifle. He went to the stable next, where he was greeted good morning by John Walker. "Good mornin', John," he returned. "I came to pick up my horses."

John looked at his watch. "You've got plenty of time," he noticed. "You must be in a hurry to leave our little town."

"No," Jesse replied, satisfied now that no word of the shooting after he left the saloon last night had spread around town yet. "I just like to give my horses time to settle into gettin' shut up in a cattle car." He couldn't admit that he had half a mind to climb on his horse and ride out of town before somebody discovered the sheriff bound and gagged. It was a hell of a gamble, but there was a fair chance that no one would discover Black until close to noon. And by that time, the train would be fifty miles from there. "They told me it'd be a good idea to show up early to get my horses loaded and accustomed to the cattle car."

"You reckon you'll be back this way anytime soon?" John asked.

"I don't anticipate it anytime soon," Jesse said. *Or ever*, he thought. "I expect I'd better take my horses on over to the train. They'll be gettin' her ready to leave." He and John shook hands and he climbed up on Clem and rode back down the main street to the train depot. He stared at the sheriff's office as he rode past, thankful that he saw no activity there. When he got to the track, the train was standing at the station and he saw several men checking different things on the various cars, most of which were flatcars, loaded with lumber. There were two passenger cars, however. Cartwright had told him to report to the conductor, a man by the name of Gilbert Nolen. So he dismounted by a man who appeared to be checking the coupling between two of the boxcars. "Howdy," Jesse said. "Where would I find Mr. Nolen?"

"The conductor?" the man responded, and Jesse nodded. "He's up ahead at the passenger cars." And he pointed to a man wearing a conductor's hat.

"Much obliged," Jesse said, and led his horses up to

the passenger cars, where Nolen was standing talking to another man. He paused when Jesse stopped his horses and waited for him to speak. "Mr. Gilbert Nolen?"

"That's right," Nolen answered. "What can I do for you?"

"Mr. William Cartwright told me to report to you this mornin'," Jesse said.

"Are you Derringer?"

"Yes, sir, I'm Derringer and I'm lookin' for a ride."

"Glad to meet you, Mr. Derringer. We've reserved a whole cattle car for you and your two horses. I understand you're going to stay in the car with your horses. Is that a fact?"

"That's right," Jesse said. "They have to keep their eyes out for me in case I get nervous."

Nolen chuckled and said, "We can load your horses up right now, if you're ready. We're going to be ready to roll in about forty-five minutes." Jesse said that would be great, so Nolen turned back toward the man he had been talking to. "Carl, take Mr. Derringer back to that empty cattle car and load his horses up."

"Yes, sir. Mr. Derringer, just follow me," Carl Swanson said, and started walking back toward the caboose. Jesse followed as they passed cars holding ties, spikes, and various other things until they reached the cattle car. Carl opened the car and pulled the ramp out, so they could walk up into the car. "I think you've got everything you need," Carl said. The forward part of the car was filled with hay bales stacked to the ceiling. The rear of the car was set up for Jesse and his two horses to camp with hay covering the floor, and the ceiling and sides covered with canvas to protect against the rain and the cold. Carl showed him how to open a couple of windows in the canvas if he wanted more air or light. "Cold as it is already, I doubt you'll want much more than what will come through when the train's moving," he said. "We'll be making stops for water and wood, so you can let your horses out for a little bit when we do. And there's a water barrel and a thunder mug for you."

"We oughta be just fine," Jesse told him.

"Let me know if there's anything else you need," Carl said. "The last report we got showed they were making good progress laying down track. I think you might get a ride all the way to Cheyenne."

CHAPTER 4

As Carl Swanson had predicted, the Union Pacific tracks reached Cheyenne on November thirteenth. The next day, the first train pulled into Cheyenne carrying materials needed to continue the railroad on its path to join the Central Pacific Railroad. Arriving on that train in a cattle car carrying only three passengers was a newly hired Union Pacific employee by the name of Jesse Derringer. The other two passengers in the car were a gray gelding named Clem and a sorrel gelding that was called many names. At first sight of the bustling town, Derringer was not quite sure he was in the right place. The last time he was here at Crow Creek Crossing, now called Cheyenne, there were the same three travelers as today in his cattle car. But on that occasion, they were alone, looking at a peaceful creek with nothing to detract from that peace. Now, as he looked at the town through the slats of the car, he was overwhelmed by the size of it. William Cartwright had told him that the town was platted by the surveyors on the fifth of July and now, four months later, he was looking at a street housing dozens of businesses. And the somewhat primitive-looking storefronts seemed covered up with people. He was to learn later that day when he found the Union Pacific office that there were already an estimated four thousand people in the town. Newspaper editors back east were campaigning to call Cheyenne the Magic City, the Queen City of the Plains, since it had magically sprang up almost overnight.

As soon as the train stopped, he opened the door of the car himself and pulled the ramp out. He was leading Clem down the ramp when he saw Carl Swanson walking back down the line of cars to help him. He dropped Clem's reins on the ground and went back into the car to lead the sorrel out. "Doesn't look like you need any help," Carl commented as he walked up.

"Just thought you might be too busy to worry about us," Jesse replied. "I need to borrow a shovel to clean up a little after my horses. I tried to tell them to hold it till we could get outside again, but it ain't too bad."

Carl chuckled in response. "Don't worry about that. I've got somebody who'll be delighted to take care of it. Hope you enjoyed the trip."

"Wasn't bad at all," Jesse said. "It's still hard to get it in my mind that we traveled five hundred miles in less than three days. I 'preciate the ride." He looked over toward what appeared to be the main street in the town. "Do you happen to know where the Union Pacific office might be?"

"Yes, I do," Carl replied. "It's up ahead of the engine,

close to the bridge. Right now, it's still a tent. They ain't built the office yet. That's what that lumber on that flatcar is supposed to be for."

"Much obliged," Jesse said, and he climbed up into the saddle and rode toward the large tent that Carl had pointed to. Having worked for the general before, he felt it unlikely that Dodge would be in the office. He figured he would have to find him in the field, somewhere ahead of the existing tracks. But maybe whoever was in headquarters could tell him where to look for him. The conductor, Gilbert Nolen, called out to him when he rode past the passenger cars, and asked if he had enjoyed the trip. "Can't complain," Jesse called back, but didn't stop to expand on the subject.

There were several horses tied up to a rope stretched between two trees that served as a hitching rail in front of what actually appeared to be two large tents set up to form one large headquarters. Jesse tied Clem to the rope and pulled the flap back to enter the first tent. There were two men sitting at desks inside and both stopped what they were doing to stare at him. "Can I help you?" one of them asked, then before Jesse could answer, he said, "This is not the construction employment office, if that's what you're looking for."

"I've got a job," Jesse said. "I'm wonderin' where I might find General Dodge."

"What do you need to see General Dodge about?" the man asked. "My name is Clyde Woodcock. I handle most of the general's business in the office."

"I don't know, Mr. Woodcock. He just sent word that he wants to see me and whenever he sends for me, I always come."

Woodcock looked perplexed for a moment, then it occurred to him. "Are you Sergeant Derringer?"

"Well, I'm Jesse Derringer," he replied, "but I'm not a sergeant anymore."

"Yes, sir," Woodcock responded. "The general will see you!" He jumped up from his desk and hurried into the adjoining tent.

The man sitting at the other desk broke out in a great big grin and continued to stare at Jesse. They heard an exclamation from inside the other tent, then a few seconds later, General Grenville M. Dodge charged into the tent with Woodcock close behind. "Sergeant Derringer!" Dodge declared. "I knew if you passed through Council Bluffs, you'd stop in the Whistlestop Saloon for a drink of whiskey."

"Yes, sir, General," Jesse japed, "that's where I pick up all my messages."

"Did they take care of you like I told them to?" Dodge asked.

"Yes, sir, they sure did. I got off that train that just pulled into town, rode all the way from Council Bluffs, me and my horses, ready to go to work."

"Your timing couldn't have been much better," Dodge said. "I'm going to get on that train and take it about nineteen miles farther west to the end of the line just as soon as they unload the lumber for the Union Pacific office to replace this tent. And that's just going to be the start of the final building. I planned from the beginning for Crow Creek Crossing to be the division point for the Union Pacific Railroad. It's right here that the land goes gradually downhill for five hundred miles back east to the Union Pacific's starting point at

Council Bluffs. And to the west of Crow Creek Crossing it starts a serious climb to its highest point. And that's about two thousand and two hundred feet in just thirty miles from right here when we climb Sherman Hill."

"That's a pretty big climb up that mountain," Jesse had to comment, "especially in this kind of weather. I remember when we came through that mountain pass when those Indians were after us and it was a pretty good climb for a horse."

"You remember correctly," Dodge said, "and that's why we're only going nineteen miles on the train. That's where the track ends. We made good time all the way from Council Bluffs laying three miles of track a day until we came to this hill. I christened it Sherman Hill because it stands firm against aggressors. We didn't get halfway up it before the snow and ice got so bad that we're stopped cold. I'm getting ready to ride back there and give the formal notice to the construction gangs right now. I hate to do it, but I'm closing the construction down until the worst of this weather is done. Old Man Winter is showing us what a mean S.O.B. he can be. We lost half a load of crossties yesterday down the side of that hill that had to be snaked out of the valley with mules, one by one. I haven't announced a shutdown yet, but we can't do decent work in these wintry conditions. That's what I've got to do today. So are you ready to take another train ride?"

"Yes, sir," Derringer said. "My horses have been restin' for two and a half days. So I figured it was about time they worked a little bit, but I reckon I shoulda left them on the train. I guess I wasn't thinkin' when you said nineteen miles. It would be a lot quicker on the train, wouldn't it?"

"Yes it would," Dodge said, laughing heartily. "You might decide to look that hill over again when we get out there, so why don't you take your packhorse to the stable over on the other side of the track. A fellow by the name of Leon Draper owns it and he takes care of the Union Pacific's personal horses. You just tell him you work for me and he'll take good care of your horses. It'll be a little while before they get all that lumber for the office here unloaded, so you ought to have plenty of time to leave your packhorse and put your belongings in the hotel room I reserved for you. All paid for by the Union Pacific Railroad," he added when Derringer's eyebrows raised as if uncertain. "There's more than one hotel in town," the general went on, "but I recommend the Union Pacific Hotel. That's where I stay when I'm in town. It's safe to eat in the dining room, too."

"Whatever you recommend, General," Derringer said, "but I'm a little in the dark about what I'm gonna be doin' to earn my money. You say you're goin' out to the end of the track today to shut it down for three months, till the weather improves. What am I gonna be doin' for those three months? Are you gonna be here in Crow Creek Crossin', I mean Cheyenne, for three months?"

"No," Dodge answered. "I'll be back in Council Bluffs for most of the time because I can get more done there. But I'll be popping in on you from time to time, especially when the winter shows signs of letting up. Don't you worry about earning your pay. I've ridden with you long enough to know what kind of man you are and I'll be using your scouting skills for a long time after this winter."

After Derringer took his packhorse to the stable and got a room in the hotel, he returned to the tent to discover his horse was missing. Woodcock told him that his horse had been returned to the railroad station and put back inside the cattle car, along with the general's horse.

"The general's over by the train, watching them unload the last of the lumber. I expect you'll be leaving as soon as the last board comes off."

"I reckon I'd better get down there then, else I might get left behind," Derringer japed. "And the general's got my gray geldin' with him."

After a trip that took less than an hour, the engine rolled to a halt nineteen miles from the railway station at Cheyenne. Several men jumped to the task of opening the cattle car and dragging out the ramp so Derringer could lead his and the general's horses out. "Any problems?" Dodge asked as he hurried from the caboose to join him.

"No, sir," Derringer answered, "smooth as silk."

"I told you they would ride all right," Dodge said. "My horse always rides by himself in that car and there's never a problem."

"I reckon," Derringer replied, "but I wasn't sure about Clem. He ain't used to ridin' trains, so I thought he might be more comfortable if I took the ride with him." He also knew that on this particular train, the caboose was fixed up to be an office for the general to work in when he was out with the construction crews. So he didn't want to interfere with the general's office time.

They were joined then by a man wearing a heavy buffalo hide coat and hat. He was riding a Morgan horse and he stepped down to greet the general with a brief progress report. "We ain't laid another foot of track since you were here two days ago, General. This damn weather just keeps gittin' worse. I ain't sure now whether God's against layin' tracks all the way across the country or not." He paused only briefly to cast an inquisitive look at the man with the general before continuing. "We're tryin' to build the bed up the first real steep climb, but the ice and the snow just won't let us work the mule teams. The damn roadbeds we're tryin' to build keep washin' out before we can get the mule teams up that slope to secure 'em. It wouldn'ta done much good if they coulda got up there. Last night we got another two feet of snow."

"I don't know if God's against the Union Pacific joining up with the Central Pacific or not, Jack. But I think He's sent sign enough to let us know He doesn't want it done this winter. That's why we're shutting it down until we get weather you can work in," Dodge told him. Then he motioned toward Derringer and said, "This is Jesse Derringer. He'll be workin' with us to build this railroad. Jesse, this is Jack Tyler. He's the foreman of the construction crew working to climb Sherman Hill."

Tyler didn't extend his hand, giving Derringer only a nod, his first impression being a suspicion that the rugged-looking man was there to tell him what he was doing wrong in the construction of the tracks. Consequently, he responded, "Mr. Derringer, what do you do?"

"As little as I can get away with," Jesse answered. "I'm on the Union Pacific payroll, but the most I know about the railroad is trains run on the rails men like you build. I just do whatever the general tells me to do." He stepped toward him and offered his hand, which Tyler accepted at once.

Dodge had to chuckle at the introduction of the two men and the way Derringer handled it, so he explained to Tyler. "Jesse rode with me in the army as my scout. His job with the railroad will be to scout out the best routes to put down track. And I might point out that this pass you're working on was discovered by him and it's the only way we can get the railroad past these mountains." With the introductions settled, the general got to the business at hand. "I'm shutting down construction on this part of the railroad until we get a little better weather. I think it best to go with you to tell your construction workers, myself, so they'll know it's the official word and they'll still have their jobs when we can start back to work."

They climbed on their horses and Tyler led the way along the railroad tracks past the end of the last rails in place, where they found Tyler's crew of men waiting. Unable to work, they were gathered around several different fires and were so many that Derringer couldn't estimate the number. Tyler led him and the general to the largest of the gatherings, drew his handgun from his holster, and shot a couple of times up in the air to get everyone's attention.

The general got off his horse and climbed up on a

wagon to stand and address the crowd of workers pushing in to get as close as possible. Speaking as loudly as
he could comfortably manage, he told them that work
on the railroad would stop for three months due to the
wintry conditions. "You can all go home and if you report back here in three months, the Union Pacific guar-
antees you will still have your job. Tomorrow and the
day after that you can file by the office in Cheyenne to
collect the money you've got coming for this month.
I'm sorry to have to give you this news, but we can't
control the weather."

His announcement was met with a general groan of
disappointment, even though they were well aware that
the railroad could not be built under four feet of snow.
Most of the crew laying the tracts were ex-soldiers of
the Civil War and their homes were back east. "I ain't
sure I can go home and come back here in three months'
time," one man sang out.

"I know I can't," another man said. "I ain't made
enough money to buy a horse." There were many more
comments with the same complaint.

Jack Tyler climbed up on the wagon then to address
the issue. "The Union Pacific don't wanna stop construction for three months any more than you don't
wanna be outta work for three months. But there ain't
no use in bellyachin' about it. It's the weather that's
sendin' you home, not the railroad. Be back here in
three months and we'll lay these tracks over this hill.
You'll all receive pay through the end of this day, so
you might as well go back to Cheyenne. And you can
sign your name, or make your mark, and pick up your
pay tomorrow and the next day."

There was a stirring in the crowd of workers, accustomed to responding to Tyler's commanding voice, as they reacted to the railroad's decision to quit work. For those without a wagon or a horse, it meant a four-hour walk back to Cheyenne. It was a five-hundred-mile trip back to Council Bluffs, where most of them had hired on, with nothing but prairie or desert in between. But Council Bluffs was not home to most of them. So when a man considered adding the distance from there to Mississippi, Georgia, or Carolina, the natural response was, "Ain't no way I can get home and back in three months."

"Maybe I could make it, if I didn't stop when I got home and just turned around and came right back," one voice speculated. "This time of year, it don't make no sense."

"Don't make no sense a-tall," another agreed. "Hell, I'll walk back to Cheyenne, but that's as far as I'm goin'."

"Hey, Tyler," one voice shouted out, "are you expectin' us to unload those flatbeds and boxcars of all them crossties and timbers off that train?"

Tyler looked at the general and Dodge answered for him. "If you want to ride back to Cheyenne on the train, I expect you'd better."

Derringer looked at the general and wondered if he had really thought about the risk of leaving a trainload of track-building material from back east at the end of the tracks, unguarded for three months. Then he decided that Dodge felt the gamble was worth the little bit of goodwill it would buy with the workers.

"You heard the man," Tyler called out then. "Let's get that train unloaded. Might as well earn your last day's pay." The men responded and he led them back to the train to get the work done. Knowing it would take a while to unload all the cars, Derringer decided to ride beyond the end of the existing track to get a look at the pass he and the general had fled on that day in September 1865. That was over two years ago, but he could still picture it in his mind when he and the general rode out of that narrow pass. The trees at the base of the mountain had been cut down and the entrance to the pass had been built to a less severe incline. That much was obvious, even under the snow. If he had the time, he would have liked to make his way up the slope to get a look at the pass from the top again and what the other side of it was like. Evidently, Dodge had found it doable, or he wouldn't be laying the track up the hill.

"Like everybody else working for the railroad," he informed Clem, "we'll have to wait for the winter to let us explore the other side of the mountain." The gray gelding only snorted indifferently in response. He turned the horse around and rode back to watch the unloading of the train. It didn't take as long as he expected, since there were plenty of hands to do the work. And since there was really no reason to linger, the general decided to go back to Cheyenne right away. Jack Tyler loaded his horse into the cattle car with the general's and Derringer's horses, and like Derringer, he chose to ride with his horse. The construction workers scrambled to fill the two passenger cars, and when there was no room left to stand, they crowded aboard the flatcars and boxcars for the short ride to town. For those who had a wagon or a horse, the trip was going to be considerably longer, but they received no sympathy from those who found a place on the train. "Enjoy your walk, Lonnie," one fellow called out from his seat in the middle of the flatcar. "Give ya a chance to get better acquainted with that mule of your'n."

"I'm chargin' a nickel a piece for anybody who wants to ride in my wagon," Lonnie called back. "I'll make enough to buy a bottle of whiskey."

"Hell, there's liable not to be any whiskey left by the time you get there," one of the other men on the flatcar declared. "I'm gonna drink till I get drunk enough to last for three months 'cause I sure as hell ain't going to go home to Tennessee."

Derringer knew they were all japing, but he knew they were right about not being able to get back east and back in three months' time. *I doubt the town of Cheyenne can handle the gang of men that's about to descend on her,* he thought.

CHAPTER 5

Jeb Massey rode into town with four men late in the afternoon in time to see the Union Pacific train backing across the bridge over Crow Creek. He pulled his horse to a stop at the railroad tracks and took a look at the two streets he could see from there. "Boys," he announced, "we mighta found us a gold mine."

"I don't know about that," Lester Bostic responded, "but it looks like we found out where everybody is. And they're bringin' 'em in by the trainload." He pointed to the train when it pulled to a stop and all the construction workers jumped off the flatcars and emptied out of the passenger cars.

"Whaddaya reckon they're fixin' to do?" Ace Barnes wondered.

"Don't look like they're fixin' to do anything," Massey said. "They're just headin' to town. All those men gotta be workin' for the railroad, layin' the tracks. Maybe today was payday and they all came to town to spend their money."

"Maybe we can help 'em get rid of it," Sly Parker suggested.

"I'm kinda curious about that last car," Massey said, looking at the train again. "That caboose, ain't nobody come outta there. I bet there's a safe or somethin' in there where they keep the money to pay the workers."

They all turned their attention toward the caboose. "Wouldn't hurt to take a look," Sly suggested. "I ain't never seen inside one of them cabooses." His comment raised the interest of the other men, so they turned toward the end of the train and rode casually back to look at the caboose. Confident that all activity to do with the train seemed to be taking place at the other end where the engine was, they rode around the caboose putting it between them and the town. Massey took hold of the handrail and started to step up onto the caboose when he heard the voice behind him.

"Something I can help you gentlemen with?" They turned to find the imposing figure of Jesse Derringer, his rifle held ready to fire in front of him.

Not sure where he had suddenly come from, Massey paused but a moment to consider the risk. He smiled then and answered casually. "My friends and I have never seen the inside of one of these cabooses, so we was just gonna see if we could look in this one."

"I'm sorry but this ain't a very good time to take a look inside this caboose," Derringer said. "This one ain't like the regular ones on a freight train, anyway. It's an office for the construction boss and he said to keep it locked up, even though the payroll's all been paid and there ain't no money in the office."

"Too bad, Sly," Massey said, still smiling. "I reckon

we'll have to wait till we see a regular freight train before we can get to look inside a caboose." He turned back to face Derringer again. "You work for the railroad?"

"That's right," Jesse replied. "I work for the Union Pacific."

"Was you gonna use that rifle, if I didn't come down offa this step?" Massey couldn't resist asking.

"Yes, I was," Jesse replied frankly.

"Against five of us?"

"Matter of fact."

"Why? You wouldn't stand a chance. We could cut you down."

"I'm quick enough with this rifle to kill you and the fellow standing beside you, so I reckon it don't matter much to neither one of us what happens after that," Derringer said.

"Damn," Massey responded with a chuckle. "What's your name?"

"It don't matter what my name is. We ain't gonna be friends. Next time you see a freight train, ask 'em to let you look inside the caboose. I'm sure they won't mind."

"Right," Massey responded sarcastically, "we'll do that. Come on, boys, let's see what this town has to offer." They got on their horses under the watchful eye of Derringer. Not one of the five would hesitate to shoot him down, but not one of them was willing to risk taking that first shot when he already had a cocked rifle needing only the squeeze of a finger.

Derringer waited until they rode off toward town before stepping up on the caboose. He looked through the glass pane in the door and saw the general seated at his desk. When he rapped on the glass, Dodge looked up and, seeing who it was, waved him on in. "I heard a discussion out there," Dodge said. "What was that about?"

"That was five fellows who had an idea there might be something in here worth stealin'," Jesse answered. He glanced at the open safe beside the general's desk. "If you don't mind me sayin', sir, you oughta keep that thing locked while you're in the station."

Dodge shrugged. "There's never enough money in there to worry about," he said.

"It don't take much to get shot," Jesse said.

"Of course you're right," the general conceded, and reached down to close the safe. He motioned toward a chair and said, "Sit down, Jesse, and I'll tell you what I want you to do while I'm back in Council Bluffs."

"I hope it ain't layin' down more track up that hill," Jesse japed, "'cause I ain't got no snowshoes."

Dodge chuckled and replied, "When I form a picture of that in my mind, it's not a pleasant sight. No, you'll be pretty much free to do whatever you want while work on the new track is shut down. Of course, I expect you to stay in touch with Woodcock and Butcher in the Union Pacific office, but they'll be handling the construction of the company office. The weather shouldn't slow that down too much and we can get them out of that tent."

"I'd like to get a look at the country beyond that hill, if the weather lets up a little," Jesse said. "Accordin' to that map you've got, you're plannin' to head toward that little tent town on the Laramie River, right?" The general nodded, so Jesse said, "Wouldn't hurt to take a look at the terrain between Sherman Hill and there."

"Sounds like a good idea to me," Dodge responded. "I'm going back to Council Bluffs tomorrow on the train, so why don't you have supper with me tonight at the hotel? Woodcock and Butcher will be joining us."

"I reckon I could squeeze that in my busy schedule," Derringer japed.

"Let's go look the town over," Massey said when they left the caboose, "and see where we wanna light." They rode across the tracks by the railroad station, past the Union Pacific Hotel, and down the busy main street, which seemed to be filled with people. Even the side streets were crowded. They looked the saloons over as they made their way along the muddy streets. Even if there had been no signs, they would have been easy to determine because of the greater number of horses tied up in front of their doors. The one they picked to look over first was the one proclaimed to be Dawkin's. It seemed to be the most popular.

Inside, the saloon was what they expected. The long bar was filled with drinkers standing two deep, most of them having just jumped off the train. The tables were all filled as well, two of them with a card game in progress. "I'm tellin' you, boys, we found us a gold mine," Massey announced again. "Might as well take a look at some of the others, but I doubt they'll be any better than this one." With that pretty much to the other four men's satisfaction, they backed out of Dawkin's and moved down the street to get a look at what else the town offered. From one end of the main street to the other, they were well pleased with what they found. "The only thing better would be a brand-new bank," Lester said, when they stopped to stare in the window of a small shop. "And lookee here. Comin' soon, Cheyenne National Bank."

"Where's it say that?" Ace Barnes asked.

"Right there on that paper stuck in the window," Lester said, knowing Ace could not read nor write.

"Oh, yeah . . . I see it." Then he stepped back and looked at the shop. "In that little ol' shack. It ain't gonna be a very big bank."

"It ain't gonna be there, dummy," Tiny Thomas said. "That's the *Cheyenne Gazette*."

"The what?" Ace asked.

"Gazette," Tiny said, "a newspaper. *Gazette,* that's a French word for 'gossip.'"

"Right, that's what I figured," Ace said, then he whipped his six-gun out, spun it around real fast a couple of times before dropping it back in his holster. It was his way of demonstrating what really counted and that he was good at it.

The next saloon they came to was one called The Crossing. It was busy as well, but there was a little space at the end of the bar just vacated by two customers. So Tiny and Sly wedged into the empty space and expanded it to accommodate the five of them, causing some complaints farther down the long bar. There were no complaints from the drinkers standing next to the smiling Tiny Thomas, whose name was an outright contradiction. "Whaddaya drinkin'?" Benny, the bartender, asked.

"Whaddaya pourin'?" Massey asked, and nodded toward the bottle on the bar. When Benny told him it was corn, Massey nodded his approval. Benny poured five shots and Massey slid them down the line until they all had one. Then he held his glass up to propose a toast. "Here's to the firstest and the fastest, and to hell with the rest of 'em." They all tossed their whiskey back and slammed the glasses down for another. Unimpressed, Benny poured five more shots, which met the same fate as the first five. Massey put the money on the bar and said, "I'll buy the first two. They can pay for their own now. They might favor me, but I ain't their daddy." He watched Benny as he gave him his change for a five-dollar bill, his face still devoid of expression. "What's the matter, bartender? You act like you ate some meat that's turned bad."

"I just pour the drinks," Benny replied. "I ain't paid to entertain the customers. If you want entertainment, you can go next door to Vera's." He moved down the bar to wait on another customer.

"You see that, boys?" Massey responded. "That's what happens when you got more customers than you can handle. You don't have to try to win the customers' business."

"When are we gonna eat?" Tiny asked. "I don't want no more whiskey in my empty belly." Massey didn't answer him, having been distracted by a card game in progress at one of the tables and the amount of money in play. Tiny turned to the stranger next to him at the bar and asked him if there was any place close by to eat.

"If you ain't too particular," the stranger said, "you can get some grub at Vera's next door."

"Vera's, huh?" Tiny asked. "What is it, a family style eatin' place?"

"No, it ain't, unless you're talking about a family with half-neckid women walkin' around. Vera owns it and she cooks dinner and supper every day, but she keeps half a dozen sportin' ladies in the rooms upstairs. She calls the place Vera's Vineyard, but like I said, you can go in there and just get some dinner or supper. It ain't cheap. It'll cost you fifty cents, but lookin's free."

"Sounds more like eatin's twenty-five cents and lookin's twenty-five cents," Sly said, having heard the conversation. "I'm willin' to try it out if you are. Let's see what the other boys say."

The other three were in favor with only Massey and not that interested. "I'm hungry, too, but I'm comin' back here just as soon as I get through eatin'. And you boys can play with the women. The prettiest thing I've seen here so far has been the pile of money in the middle of that table over there. I aim to get in that game and walk out with that money one way or the other. Let's go right now. I wanna be sure I get back before that one feller cleans 'em all out." He was pretty sure the man he referred to was a professional gambler, so he figured he wouldn't be in any hurry to quit the game.

They walked out of the saloon, crossed the alley where their horses were tied, and walked into the two-story house bearing a sign that read VERA'S VINEYARD.

Lester read the sign aloud, causing Ace to ask, "What's a vine yard? That feller in the saloon said it was a vin-yard."

"It's a grapevine, Ace, where they grow grapes," Massey told him.

When they walked into the parlor, there were three women in various stages of dress sitting around on sofas. "Well, good evening, gents," one of the women greeted them. "Did you come to pluck a grape from the vine?"

"I came to eat supper," Massey answered her. "Just point me to the dining room and you can have these other four."

"You can have me later," Tiny said. "I've gotta eat before I fall down."

"All right, sweetie," one of the other women said. "Follow me." He and Massey followed her through a door to a hallway, and she led them to a dining room with a huge table in the center. There were a couple of men seated at the table eating. "Sit wherever you want," she told them, then yelled through the kitchen door. "Vera, you got two more fellows wanting to eat." She looked at Tiny and said, "My name's Lucy, if you're looking for me after you eat." Then she smiled at everyone at the table and went back to the parlor.

"Welcome, gentlemen," Vera greeted them. "Welcome to my vineyard. Have you come to pluck one of my luscious grapes from the vine?" She didn't wait for an answer but asked what they wanted to drink with their supper. When they gave her their choice, she said, "Coming right up. I'll get you fed and ready for anything else you've got on your mind."

Tiny was still in the middle of his supper when their three friends came into the dining room, but Massey was already finished. "The grub ain't bad he told them. I'm goin' to break into that card game next door, so don't hang around here too long. Get your business done, then get over there, in case I need you. That feller looked pretty slick."

"What?" Sly asked, his mind still on a plump woman named Rosa.

Massey ignored him. "Don't hang around here too long," he repeated. "I might need witnesses."

When he was in the saloon before, he picked out the player who was steadily getting fleeced, so he thought that might be an empty chair when he got back. He had him figured to be one of the railroad workers who just got paid. Of the four players left, two looked to be holding their own, one appeared to be losing, and the professional was clearly winning the night. So Massey stopped at the bar and bought a drink. Then he walked over to the table and said, "Looks like you've got an empty chair. Is this a private game, or can I sit in for a few hands?"

"Always room for one more," the gambler said, "if you've got cash to gamble with. We've agreed on a twenty-dollar limit."

Massey reached inside his coat pocket and pulled out a sizable roll of money and sat down. "That's a sizable bettin' limit, but I'll throw in the towel before I lose the family farm," he joked. He played conservatively for several hands before bluffing to win a pot. The gambler watched him carefully after that as the game went on. Massey noticed when his four friends returned from Vera's, but he made no show that he did. To him, however, it was the signal to bring the gambler down because it appeared the man was too sharp to be beaten at the game. Then, when it was the gambler's deal, Massey got a hand strong enough to challenge. It was time to make his move.

When Massey saw the hand he was dealt, he almost decided to play it honestly, for he had three tens, a queen, and a seven. He started the betting with ten dollars and no one folded. On the draw, Massey threw away two cards. The gambler smiled when he dealt him two cards, for he knew that Massey had three of a kind. So did the other three players, so no one folded. The gambler discarded one card and smiled at Massey. "You started the betting," he reminded him.

"That's right, I did," Massey replied, "and it's gonna cost you twenty dollars to see how I did on the draw." The next two players called Massey's bet, the other one folded.

When it got back to the gambler, he studied Massey for a few seconds. "I'm thinkin' you had three of a kind and you drew two cards. I figure you probably had two chances—draw two of a kind for a full house, or draw one for four of a kind. I don't think you drew either one, so I'll see your raise and raise you twenty more."

"The game suddenly got expensive, didn't it?" Massey said. "But I've really got a strong interest in seein' that card you drew. Here's your twenty and another twenty raise."

That was enough to discourage the other two players, so they folded and the bet was back to the gambler. He was sitting on an ace-high straight and he was convinced that Massey was trying to buy the big pot with a bluff. "I'll tell you the truth," the gambler said. "I'm not an unreasonable man. It doesn't look like you've got twenty dollars left in front of you. How much have you got left?"

"Eight dollars is all the cash I've got left, but I've got a watch and a pocketknife that's worth something," Massey replied.

"Like I said, I ain't unreasonable, so I'll see your raise and raise you seven dollars."

"I'll call," Massey said. "I wanna see that last card you drew."

"I'm afraid you picked the wrong hand to bluff on," the gambler said, and spread his ace-high hand on the table. "I was just plain lucky. There's the card I drew, the ace of diamonds. You said you wanted to see it." Quite a few men had gotten interested in that last hand of the game. No one noticed that the four who were the closest were the same four Massey had left the saloon with earlier. Massey spread his three tens, Jack, and a Queen on the table before him. The gambler grinned apologetically and reached out to rake in his winnings.

"Not so fast," Massey ordered. "You picked the wrong man to cheat, you slimy low-down crook. I wanted to see that card you drew again, because I already saw it come off the bottom of the deck." He looked at the other card players, who were gaping dumbfounded at him. "Kinda funny how many hands he won when it was his deal, weren't it?" He looked back at the gambler, who was as astonished as the other players. "I got suspicious after a few hands, but I saw that card come off the bottom this time. You think I'm dumb enough to try to bluff every cent I had on three of a kind? Hell, no, 'cause I knew I was the winner of this hand on account we don't put up with no cheatin' gamblers in Cheyenne." He reached out and raked the pile of money over to him.

Finally recovered enough to respond, the gambler put his hands up before him, palms out. "Now, hold on!" he pleaded. "That's a damn lie. I've not ever cheated in a game of cards and I sure as hell didn't cheat in this one."

"You no good rat," Massey spat. "Now you're callin' me a liar? That's something I don't allow any man to do. First you try to steal my money, then you call me a liar. You're packin' a gun—maybe we'd best settle this man-to-man." He pulled his coat away to expose his six-gun and glanced at Lester Bostic, who was now standing close beside the gambler. Lester nodded and patted his shoulder, which told Massey the gambler was wearing a shoulder holster under his coat.

Hardly able to believe what was happening, the gambler dropped his hands from in front of him and started to protest his innocence, but Massey drew his pistol and shot him in the chest. Pretending he was trying to help, Lester grabbed the gambler's arm with one hand while he pulled the revolver from the shoulder holster and let it fall to the floor as he made a show of helping him lie down. Then he moved away from the dying man.

"That's his mistake, goin' for that gun," Massey announced to the spectators. "He only left me two choices, go for mine or get shot. I didn't have no choice. It don't give me no pleasure winnin' a hand like this," he claimed as he picked up the money and stuffed it in his pockets.

"The bartender sent somebody to get the sheriff," a man standing near him said.

"Thanks for the warning, friend," Massey replied, "but I ain't got no reason to run. He went for his gun and I didn't have no choice."

In a few minutes, the sheriff arrived at the saloon, just having come from locking up a drunk who had assaulted a prostitute at one of the town's several brothels. Showing the effects of a man overburdened with the job of trying to enforce law and order in a town with more perpetrators than a sheriff and two deputies could handle, he made his way through the spectators. "Gimme some room, damn it," he ordered as he took a look at the body. "What happened here?"

Ready to answer his questions, Massey volunteered. "We was in a card game and I caught him cheatin'. He called me a liar and one thing just led to another, I reckon. Then he went for his gun, so I didn't have no choice. I went for mine and I got him before he could pull the trigger."

The sheriff didn't say anything for a moment as he stared at Massey, trying to decide if he could believe him or not. "What he said was the truth, Sheriff," Sly Parker volunteered. He pointed to the dead man on the floor. "He went for his gun first, but this feller was just faster."

"Anybody else see it?" the sheriff asked.

"I saw it," Tiny Thomas responded, followed immediately by Ace Barnes. They both claimed that the gambler had reached for his gun first.

"I reckon that's pretty much what happened, then." The sheriff looked over the customers crowded around, then back at Massey. "I ain't got any reason to hold you for any charges, but we don't like gunfights in Cheyenne, duels or any other kind."

"I understand, Sheriff," Massey replied. "I don't like 'em either, but this feller was fixin' to shoot me, sure as I'm standin' here, and I didn't have no time to run. I'm just lucky I'm still standin', I reckon."

"Yeah, I reckon," the sheriff responded. "Couple you fellers give me a hand to move him out on the porch. Benny!" he called to the bartender, "I'll send somebody back here to pick him up and take him to the undertaker." Tiny and Sly grabbed the unfortunate corpse and carried it out the front door, with the sheriff following close behind to make sure he searched the body for valuables.

Tiny and Sly went back inside to join their partners. "We weren't fast enough to go through that jasper's pockets before the sheriff got there," Sly said.

"That's all right," Massey replied. "He's gonna pay for all our whiskey and a couple of rooms tonight, if we can find a vacant room. There was that much and more in that one last pot. Let's go back to that first place, Dawkin's. I like it better than this one."

CHAPTER 6

Derringer and Jack Tyler joined Clyde Woodcock and Fred Butcher for supper with the general in the hotel dining room. They enjoyed a fine meal specially prepared for General Dodge, since he was taking the train back to Council Bluffs early the next morning. After the supper was over, Woodcock and Butcher went to the general's office in the caboose with him to discuss the plans for the Union Pacific office they were going to build there in Cheyenne. Since neither Tyler nor Derringer was involved in that project, they said good evening to them. Tyler was going to Council Bluffs on the train the next morning, but the evening was young, so he suggested a visit to a saloon for a couple of drinks before calling it a night. It seemed like a good idea to Derringer as well, so they walked down the street to the closest saloon, which was Dawkin's. Although most of the shops and businesses were closed for the day, there were still a lot of people in the streets. Most of them were railroad workers, but there were also drifters and out of work cowhands, as well as soldiers from the fort three miles up Crow Creek. Up and down the creek, they spotted campfires and occasionally the report of a firearm was heard. "I swear, Jesse, you'd best watch your back around here," Tyler commented when they both jumped out of the way when a man on a horse charged down the street at a gallop, firing his handgun in the air. "There's just more folks here than the town can hold."

"I can't disagree with you," Derringer responded. "I just hope to hell they don't burn the hotel down." He had his room paid for by the Union Pacific as well as his stable fees for his horses. He wasn't sure how long that was going to last, but he knew he could count on it for at least the next three months. He just started to comment that he was sure he'd get used to the chaos in the streets when Tyler interrupted.

"Look out!" Tyler blurted. "Here he comes again!"

Derringer looked behind him and saw the drunken fool charging back up the street, bearing down on them again. So they stepped out of his way once more. This time, however, Derringer turned his rifle upside down, holding it by the barrel. Then he stepped into the path of the charging drunk and, swinging the nine-pound Henry rifle like a club, he knocked the unfortunate man off his horse. When Tyler gawked at him in open-mouthed surprise, Derringer said, "I can stand a drunk and I can stand a fool. But I can't abide a drunken fool."

"I'll remember that," Tyler said, and they walked on

down the street toward Dawkin's Saloon, leaving the dazed drifter sitting in the middle of the street, wondering what had happened.

When they came to the saloon, they passed through a gathering of penniless drunks blocking the entrance. Having witnessed Derringer's method of dismounting the man from his horse, they quickly made a path for him and Tyler. Inside, the noisy saloon was filled with the thick, smoky breath of a room packed with whiskey drinkers. "We were lucky to find a place to have a nice quiet drink of whiskey after a big supper," Derringer remarked sarcastically.

"Maybe you oughta change your mind and get on that train back to Council Bluffs in the mornin'," Tyler said. "I ain't sure this town can handle all the people pourin' in here. Too many of 'em are the wrong kind of people the town wants to attract. And you know that sheriff and his two deputies ain't gonna be able to handle the trouble that's bound to come."

"I expect what you say is true," Derringer replied. "But the general's my boss and he said he wanted me to stay here. There ain't really nothin' I can do for him back in Council Bluffs, anyway. And since I ain't independently wealthy, I reckon I'll do what he says." While he was talking, he was watching four soldiers at a nearby table who appeared to be in the process of vacating it. So he moved over next to it and motioned Tyler to follow. "You fellows leavin'?" he asked one wearing corporal's stripes.

"Yep, we've gotta get back to camp," the corporal answered. "You want this table?"

"Yes we do, if you're leavin'," Derringer said. "Don't want to rush you."

"Ain't no problem," the corporal said. "We're about broke now, anyway, and we got a long walk back to camp. Come on, boys, let's let these fellows have the table." They all got to their feet.

"'Preciate it, Corporal," Derringer said, and quickly took possession of the corporal's chair. "Jack, if you'll go to the bar and buy us a bottle and a couple of glasses, I'll hold the table and pay you for it," he said to Tyler.

Over in the back corner, there was a party of five at a table with only three chairs. One of them noticed the soldiers walking out and the man who went to the bar for a bottle. He followed him with his eyes, then looked back at the table. "There you go, Tiny. Look over yonder," Massey said. "Go get them other two chairs from that table."

"I'm takin' these two chairs," Tiny said when he walked up to the table. It was not in the form of a request for permission.

"Help yourself," Derringer replied, realizing he had seen the big man somewhere before. He watched him as he walked back through the crowded room, holding a chair up in each hand, until he reached a table in the corner. It occurred to him then where he had seen him.

At just about the same moment, Massey was able to get a quick view of the man seated at the table when someone at a table in between pushed back away from his table. "You ever see that man before?" he asked Tiny when he sat down.

"I don't know," Tiny answered. "He looked familiar."

"He's the Union Pacific man we met at the train caboose this morning," Massey said.

Tiny's face lit up. "That's right!" he exclaimed. "The jasper with the rifle, said he was gonna get you and Sly before the rest of us got him. Well, I'll be . . . You wanna go get him now?"

"Go get who?" Sly asked.

"That Union Pacific jasper with the rifle," Tiny answered him. "Said he was gonna shoot you and Jeb before the rest of us shot him."

"Is that right, Jeb?" Sly asked. "We goin' after him?"

"That's the man, all right," Massey answered him, "but we ain't gonna go take care of him right now with all these witnesses. We don't want the railroad to send a gang of detectives and railroad police out here looking for us. Hell, we just got here. We need to take a little time to see where we're gonna make the most money. I know what you're thinkin'. That's right, I shot that no-name gambler. But we made it look like a duel and we made a little money on it. It ain't gonna make us any money if we cut this turkey down right now, is it?"

"I reckon that's right," Sly said. "Wouldn't make no money if we did that."

"Did what?" Ace asked.

"Hold up the bank with our hands in our pockets," Sly answered him.

"Why would we do that?" Ace asked.

"Damn it, Sly, don't get him started," Massey said, and Sly held up his hands to surrender.

Still confused, Ace said, "That sign in the window said they was gonna build a bank. There ain't no bank here yet."

"That's right, Ace," Lester told him. "Sly's just japin' us. Pay him no mind."

"I swear," Tyler said when he returned to the table with a bottle and two glasses. "I leave for two minutes and you let somebody walk off with half our chairs."

"You're lucky he didn't want three chairs," Derringer replied. "Did you see how big that fellow was? I might notta said nothin' if he'd wanted all four. Then we'da had to stand at the table to do our drinkin'. Next thing I know, you're likely to ask me to pay for my half of that bottle."

"I figure if you don't, I'll just toss one of these glasses over in that spittoon over yonder," Tyler replied, "but you're welcome to watch me drink." He pulled the cork on the bottle and poured two shots while Derringer pulled some money out of his pocket. "Do you know that fellow?"

"We met briefly this morning, but I don't really know him. I'm pretty sure I know he's somebody you'd best not turn your back on, though." He told Tyler about the brief meeting he had that morning with the five men behind the general's office on the train.

When he finished, Tyler asked, "And that's the same five men sittin' at that table in the corner?"

"Yep," Derringer answered. "The one with his back to the corner, facin' this way must be the boss. He did all the talkin' this mornin'." He poured them both another shot, then continued. "Now, I might be wrong. Those five might be a travelin' pack of Catholic priests.

But I think they're a gang of rawhide thieves who don't have any rules when it comes to what they want. And when you look at all the people pourin' into this town every day now, how many of them are outlaw gangs like the one sittin' at the table over there? I don't see how in hell the town's gonna make it. They've got a sheriff and two deputies charged with keepin' the peace. I don't see how they can do it." As if in agreement with what he said, they suddenly heard the sound of multiple gunshots outside on the street.

"Like you said," Tyler remarked. He was about to say more but hesitated when two men burst in the front door with weapons drawn. They walked over to the bar, where a large space was rapidly cleared for them as the drinkers retreated.

"Don't nobody move!" one of the men ordered. "Just go on with your drinkin' and you won't get hurt. Bartender, pour us a drink of likker."

"Don't be lookin' at us," the other man said. "Just mind your own business, if you don't wanna get shot."

Sam, the bartender, set two glasses on the counter and filled them. "Two bits," he said.

"Won't be no charge," the first man said. "We'll let you live if you don't cause no trouble. Ain't your life worth two bits?" he said, realizing then that the noisy saloon they fled to was now silent as a tomb. It was too late to try to do anything about it because the deputy sheriff walked in the door at that moment. Deputy Sheriff Cliff Crenshaw was struck by the silence as soon as he entered. Young but not inexperienced, Crenshaw knew right away that the Crowe brothers had taken refuge there.

"Arthur and Caleb Crowe!" Crenshaw demanded. "Drop your guns and step out here in the open with your hands up. I'm arrestin' you for the murder of Claude Johnson and his son, Chester." With the deputy's demand, the men standing in the crowded saloon slowly retreated from the two gunmen who had taken refuge in the crowd, now leaving them exposed to face him.

Standing firm with their six-guns still in their hands, the Crowe brothers took stock of their situation. "Who sez it were us who shot 'em?" Arthur, the older brother, asked. "There was a lotta folks arguin' out in the street."

"Ain't no use wastin' time," Deputy Crenshaw responded. "There's half a dozen people who saw you do it and saw you run in here. So drop your weapons, you're goin' to jail."

Arthur looked at Caleb and Caleb nodded his agreement, so Arthur said, "Look here, Deputy, there's somethin' that don't make no sense a-tall. There's two of us standin' here and ain't but one of you. And we don't wanna go to jail. So we're both gonna aim our six-guns at your belly button until you turn yourself around and walk outta here. Whaddaya think of that?"

Crenshaw was stunned when he realized the situation he had walked into. To turn and walk away would not only bring shame but also a shot in the back most likely. Enjoying the deputy's predicament, Arthur Crowe started to grin until he heard the distinct click of a Colt .44's hammer cocking right behind his ear. "If you don't drop those guns right now, I'll put a .44 slug into the back of your head," Jesse Derringer whispered loud enough for them both to hear. He put the barrel of his Colt under the back brim of Arthur's wide-brim hat and lifted the hat to cause the front brim to slide down over his eyes. Then he stuck the cold steel barrel on the back of Arthur's head. Arthur dropped his gun immediately. It was followed by Caleb's gun an instant later. "Start walkin'," Derringer said. "Jack, pick up those guns, will ya?"

"What about this bottle of whiskey?" Tyler asked. "It ain't half empty."

"Give it to the bartender to hold till we come back for it," Derringer told him. Tyler handed the bottle to Sam, picked up the two guns, then followed behind Derringer.

"I'm obliged," Deputy Crenshaw said quietly to Derringer as he stood aside, then stepped in behind the prisoners to walk beside him. Tyler walked behind them, carrying the two firearms.

"You wanna walk 'em on over to the jail?" Derringer asked.

"I'd appreciate it," Crenshaw said, so they walked the two brothers through the crowd of spectators, down the street to the sheriff's office and jail. When they got there, they found the other deputy back from a call he had answered, so the two deputies took over the job of locking up the Crowe brothers. Tyler left the two six-guns on the sheriff's desk and followed Derringer to the door. Crenshaw came from the cell room in time to catch them before they went out the door. "Wait up a minute," he called out. Talking directly to Derringer, he asked, "What is your name?"

"Jesse Derringer," he answered, "and this is Jack Tyler."

"Well, Mr."—he paused—"Derringer?"

"That's right," Derringer answered, "just like the little pocket pistol."

"Well, Mr. Derringer," he started again, "I owe you one helluva lot. You saved my neck back there in Dawkin's Saloon. That coulda ended a whole lot differently if you hadn't been there, and I wanna thank you for steppin' up to help law and order in Cheyenne. And thank you, too, Mr. Tyler." He almost forgot him. Back to Derringer, he asked, "Are you fellows gonna be in town for a while?"

"We work for the railroad," Jesse said. "Jack oversees the actual building of the railroad. He'll be leavin' Cheyenne in the mornin' to go back to Council Bluffs, but he'll be back in three months when construction starts again." He looked at Tyler and smiled. "Hopefully, right, Jack?" Tyler nodded and Jesse continued. "I'll just wait the winter out here in Cheyenne or close about. I've got a room in the hotel."

"Have you talked to Sheriff Warton about the problems we're havin' with the number of outlaws, drifters, and gunslingers we're already havin' here in Cheyenne?" Deputy Ray Cooper asked.

"Why, no," Derringer replied, surprised that he would ask. "I've not met Sheriff Warton. Why did you think I would have?"

"The way you stepped in and helped Cliff," Cooper answered, "I thought maybe you had talked to the sheriff about the citizens helpin' the sheriff's department out."

"No," Derringer said. "It was just a matter of helpin' a lawman out who was outnumbered. Seemed like the thing any responsible person would do."

"It does, don't it?" Crenshaw remarked. "That saloon was packed full of responsible men. How many of 'em stepped up to give me a hand?"

"I expect none of 'em wanted to be remembered for steppin' in on an arrest in case the prisoners had friends," Tyler remarked. "Afraid that'd put a target on their backs."

"Maybe it won't get as bad as we think here in Cheyenne," Derringer said. "If it does, you boys will have to do what that marshal over in Denver's done and organize a vigilance committee. They had an outlaw that was terrorizin' the town, so a bunch of 'em pulled gunnysacks over their heads and put a rope around his neck and strung him up on a pole." Crenshaw and Cooper exchanged a quick glance, having recently found out that Mayor H. M. Hook had already been talking to the other businessmen about that possibility if things got completely out of hand.

Derringer and Tyler left the jail then and returned to Dawkin's to claim their bottle of whiskey. The noisy saloon went almost quiet for a few seconds when they came in the door and went directly to the bar. "Here you go, gents," Sam sang out when he handed them the bottle. "And here's your money back as well." He put the money on the counter. "We were about to lose a deputy sheriff if you hadn't stepped up to settle things."

"Well, that's mighty generous of you," Derringer said. "Ain't that right, Jack?"

"Yes, sir, it surely is," Tyler replied, picked up the money, and gave Derringer his half. Then he poured a drink for both of them in the glasses Sam set on the bar.

They tossed those back and were considering one

more when a man got up from the table they had been sitting at when the two Crowe brothers rushed into the saloon. "Howdy, Mr. Tyler," the man said to Jack, and waited for him to recognize him. When Tyler hesitated, the man said, "I'm Wilbur Murray. I work on your track-layin' gang."

"Of course you do," Tyler responded. "I recognized you," he lied. "But I was tryin' to call your name to mind. I think the likker musta tied my mind in a knot."

"It'd be a wonder if you could remember everybody's name in a crew that big," Murray said. "Me and Jim Otis have been settin' over there at your table, holdin' it for you and your friend till you got back. There still ain't but two chairs, but like I said, we was just holdin' it for you."

"That was damn considerate of you, Wilbur," Tyler said. "This is Jesse Derringer. He's General Dodge's special scout. Jesse, this is Wilbur Murray. He's one of my construction crew. He and another one of my crew have been holdin' our table for us."

"Pleased to meet you, Wilbur," Derringer said. "That was mighty thoughtful of you and your friend." He glanced at Tyler and guessed he felt the same as he, so he said, "But I think we're about to call it a night. Is that right, Jack?"

"That's a fact," Tyler said. "I've got to leave early in the morning on the train and I need to get a little sleep tonight."

"So why don't you take this bottle of whiskey and you and your friend can just keep the table and enjoy a drink on Jack and me," Derringer directed.

"Why, thank you, sir, and thank you, Mr. Tyler," Wilbur responded. "This'll tickle Jim when I tell him."

"Come on, Jesse," Tyler said, "let's go back to the hotel." They thanked Sam again and walked out the door while Wilbur hurried back to the table with almost half a bottle of whiskey.

It was only minutes after Wilbur and Jim had tossed back their first shot of free whiskey when one of the five men sitting at the table in the back corner got up from the table and walked over to the two construction men. "Say, friend, maybe you can help me out here," Jeb Massey said. "I saw you talkin' to those two fellows that just walked out. My friends and I saw them help that deputy sheriff out of a real bad situation. And I've been rakin' my mind tryin' to think of that one fellow's name, but I just can't call it up. I ain't talkin' about the one that picked up the guns and followed 'em out the door. I'm talkin' about the one that stepped up behind them and stopped 'em cold."

"The one that picked up the guns was the feller we work for on the railroad," Wilbur answered. "He told me that other feller is General Dodge's special scout. Said his name is Derringer. That's his last name. He told me his first name, too, but I can't remember it. But his last name is Derringer. That one was easy to remember."

"Much obliged," Massey said. "You're right, that is an unusual name, ain't it? It puzzles me how in the world I coulda forgot it." After a minute or two more of friendly conversation, he walked back to the table repeating the name "Derringer" over and over to himself. When he sat down again, Lester asked him what he had learned. "I found out his last name is Derringer, like the pistol," Massey replied. "He couldn't remember his first name, but he said he was a special scout or some-thin' for General Dodge."

"Who's General Dodge?" Ace asked.

"He's the one who decides where the railroad is goin'," Massey answered him. "That's the reason that Derringer was snoopin' around that train caboose. That feller said the other jasper was the boss of the construc-tion gang and he's leavin' on the train in the mornin', headin' back to Council Bluffs. I hope that Derringer feller is leavin', too. I'd just as soon he didn't hang around."

"If he does, we just might have to take care of him," Sly said. "I'da liked to have took a look in that caboose they got fixed up like an office. You know there's a safe in that office. That damn snoop mighta cost us a big payday."

"I was thinkin' the same thing," Massey said.

"I reckon those two Crowe brothers would be mighty sore if they knew we was settin' back here watchin' the little show they had with that deputy and didn't even try to help 'em outta the fix they got theirselves into," Lester Bostic commented.

"Hell, them two Crowe boys ain't nothin' but hog-lot slime," Sly Parker said. "Jail's too good for 'em. And that goes double for their old man."

CHAPTER 7

Derringer was at the hotel dining room early the next morning to have breakfast with the general and Jack Tyler before they departed. "Jack tells me you two participated in an arrest last night with one of Sheriff Warton's deputies," Dodge remarked.

"Wasn't much," Derringer replied. "We just evened things up, so the deputy wasn't outnumbered."

"I don't reckon I need to warn you that the sheriff and his deputies are gonna have their hands full trying to keep law and order in this town, with all the unemployed men hanging around. I'll remind you that you're on the Union Pacific's payroll and not the sheriff department's."

Derringer had to chuckle. "You know me, General, I always stay away from trouble. That was Jack who decided to help the deputy last night."

"The hell it was," Tyler responded. "I just went along behind him to pick up the guns those two fellows dropped on the floor."

"You don't have to worry about me," Derringer told the general. "As soon as the weather lets up a little, I'm gonna ride back out to that Dale Creek Ravine, about three miles on the other side of Sherman Hill. I'd like to find the best route across those mountains, maybe up toward that little tent town they call Laramie City," he said, referring to an Overland Stage stop some fifty miles or so from Cheyenne but only about thirty miles from Sherman Hill.

"You'd better watch your scalp if you spend much time up in that territory," General Dodge cautioned him. "The Indians are still pretty hostile to the idea of our building tracks for the 'iron horse' right through their territory, the Cheyenne especially."

"You can count on me, sir," Derringer responded. "I'm always careful not to take risks."

The general laughed. "Not since I've known you and I've known you for a pretty long time."

After breakfast, Derringer walked them to the train station and the train pulled out as soon as the general was on board. He watched until the train was out of sight before walking directly to the stable to see how his horses were getting along. They had not been getting much exercise lately and he wanted to make sure they were ready to travel. Leon Draper was standing out beside his corral, studying the clouds hovering over Crow Creek. "Mornin', Jesse," he offered when Derringer walked up. "What you up to this mornin'?"

"I just thought I'd better make sure you ain't sold my horses," Derringer said.

"Matter of fact, there was a feller in here the other day, lookin' to buy a horse, and that gray of yours caught his eye," Leon said. "I told him that horse weren't for sale, but he took a look at him, anyway. He wasn't interested no more when he found out the gray wasn't shod. I told him I hadn't noticed that myself. He said he wasn't interested in an Indian pony. After he left with a dun mare I sold him, I went back in the stable and took a look at your packhorse. He ain't shod neither. How come you don't shoe your horses? Ain't you worried about their feet up in them mountains?"

"They ain't ever come to me wantin' horseshoes on their hooves," Derringer answered. "I always figured they handled some of the rocky places I've been in better without those iron bars on their feet. And barefoot horses seem to work okay for the Indians." He didn't explain the one big reason was because he spent so much time alone in Indian territory and he thought it sensible not to leave tracks of a shod horse. Winter or not, he didn't plan to lay around Cheyenne waiting for the snow to leave the mountains. He was even of a mind that, thanks to the weather, he might be able to count on exploring that ravine past Sherman Hill that they called Dale Creek Ravine. He went back to visit Clem in his stall with the packhorse and both horses came to greet him at once. He gave them both some attention and promised the gray gelding he was going to take them both on a little trip. When he left the stable, he told Leon that he was going to take a ride up to Sherman Hill, if the weather continued to lighten up a little in the next day or two. "So I'd appreciate it if you would make sure they got some grain today and tomorrow." Leon said he'd make sure they did.

The rest of the morning was a matter of killing time

until the dining room opened up for dinner. "Mr. Derringer," Cecil Humphrey, the dining room manager, greeted him when he walked in.

"Mr. Humphrey," Derringer returned the formal greeting to the young man and started toward a small table by a window where he had sat while eating breakfast.

"Beg your pardon, sir," Humphrey said, and motioned for him to stop.

"Cecil," Derringer replied. "That is your name, ain't it?" Cecil said that it was, so Derringer said, "Well, Cecil, my name's Jesse. Let's do away with the *Misters* and the *Sirs*. They just get in the way of my thinkin'. Now, what is it? You want me to sit somewhere else?"

"No, sir . . . I mean, Jesse. I wanted to tell you that the mayor, Mr. H. M. Hook, is eating dinner at the back table near the kitchen. He told me that he wanted to invite you to have dinner with him, if you came in today."

"He did?" Derringer responded, surprised. "Did he say why?"

"No, sir . . . I mean, Jesse. He just said to give you that message."

Derringer hesitated, wondering what in the world he and the mayor of Cheyenne could possibly have to discuss. *Maybe he knows I work for the Union Pacific*, he thought. *I'll just refer him to Clyde Woodcock or Fred Butcher.* "All right, I'll go see what he wants," he said, and went back to the table where Mr. Hook was sitting. "Mr. Mayor, I'm Jesse Derringer. Cecil said you wanted to talk to me."

"Yes, Mr. Derringer, I was hoping I could ask you to have dinner with me. Won't you sit down and join me?" This was the first look the mayor had of the general's special scout and he knew at first glance that the rugged individual had to be no other.

"I don't mind if I do," Jesse replied, "although I'm more accustomed to folks askin' me to sit somewhere else." He pulled a chair back and sat down. Noticing the mayor had only a cup of coffee in front of him, he asked, "Have you already ate, or just gettin' ready to?"

"No, I haven't eaten yet," Hook said. "I was waiting to see if you came in." He signaled to Rachael, the young daughter of the cook, Clara Bowden.

Rachael acknowledged his signal and went into the kitchen at once. She came back out almost instantly carrying the coffeepot. "You always drink coffee," she said to Jesse. "Mama's filling your plates. I'll be right back with them."

"Thank you, young lady," Jesse said, then turned his attention back to the mayor, waiting for an explanation for the invitation to join him for dinner.

"Jesse," Mayor Hook began, "I heard about the shooting in the street last night and the trouble that followed in Dawkin's Saloon that you were involved in." He hesitated until Rachael set their plates down before them and left again. "Jesse, we've got the makings of a great city here in Cheyenne. But right now, we've got big trouble with all the people who have flocked to Cheyenne this winter. As a result, we're at the mercy of the undesirable troublemakers and they're too many for our sheriff to handle. Already, there are too many shooting incidents like the one you were involved in last night and it's only going to get worse."

"Whoa! Hold up there, Mr. Mayor," Jesse interrupted.

"You're right about the trouble you've got, but I'm not part of the problem."

"I know! I know!" Mayor Hook exclaimed, holding his hands up in surrender, his knife in one, his fork in the other. "You misunderstood," he went on to explain. "I was told that you stepped in to help in the confrontation in Dawkin's and single-handedly captured the two gunmen and saved Deputy Cliff Crenshaw's life. Good Lord, man, I want to thank you and applaud you for your part in making that arrest."

"Oh," Jesse responded. "Well, you're welcome, I reckon. But I suppose there's a lot of men in town who woulda done the same thing."

"I agree with you partially," Hook said. "There are a lot of men in town who would like to help apprehend the outlaws and the gunmen but are afraid to risk being identified. You obviously didn't let that stop you from answering the call. So I wanted to tell you that some of the citizens in town and I have been talking about creating a vigilance committee to punish the outrageous crimes ourselves. It is already out of hand for the sheriff and his deputies. We feel that a hanging by the vigilance committee is in effect punishment by the town itself and not by any individual. I'm telling you all this because I want you to become a part of it." He paused then. "So, what do you say? Do you want to join the citizens of Cheyenne to defend our town?"

"Well, Mayor, let me say this. I think a vigilance committee is a damn good idea in your situation." The two deputy sheriffs had already mentioned the talks the mayor and the town people were having about that solution to their problem. "I have to point out that I'm not going to stay in Cheyenne very long. I work for the Union Pacific and I'm keepin' a base here for three months only until the railroad can move on to the west. And I won't be here all the time during those three months because it's my job to scout out the route ahead of the tracks, so as to avoid any construction problems. I just came from the stable to make sure my horses are ready for a scout that'll take me about a week, I expect. But when I'm in town, you can count on me to help if you call the vigilance committee out."

"I know you work directly under General Dodge," the mayor said. "But have you ever considered taking the job of sheriff?"

"No, sir," Derringer answered emphatically. "I ain't never hankered to be a lawman. I'm afraid I'm just not that much straight-up honest. I'd break the rules somewhere, I'm afraid."

"Well, I can understand how you feel, I expect," the mayor said, obviously disappointed. "But you'll be the first one we'll call on in the event of a need for the committee to move on someone, and thank you again for backing up Deputy Crenshaw."

"Glad I could help," Derringer replied. The mayor finished his dinner quickly then and got up to leave. He said he would pay for Jesse's dinner, but Jesse thanked him anyway and said, "The Union Pacific's pickin' up the bill."

Derringer took his time finishing his coffee before he got up to leave. He thanked Rachael for her attention and told Cecil he'd see him at suppertime. He started to open the door when someone opened it from the outside, so he stepped back and waited. A man of middle age or more walked into the dining room. He wore a heavy mustache and a black suitcoat to match. He also wore a sheriff's badge on his lapel. Derringer would not have guessed he was Sheriff Tom Warton had he not seen the badge. "Sheriff," he acknowledged as a courtesy.

Warton, on the other hand, had no trouble guessing the stranger's identity. "You must be Jesse Derringer, right?"

"Guilty," Derringer replied, "but only for being Jesse Derringer."

Warton chuckled in response. "I bumped into the mayor outside," he said. "He told me you and him had a talk about a vigilance committee."

"We did," Derringer replied.

"Good," Warton remarked. "He told me you said you would help out."

"I did," Derringer replied.

"Good," Warton repeated. "And I want to give you my thanks for the assistance you gave Deputy Crenshaw in the arrest of the Crowe brothers. He said he was in a bad situation when you stepped in."

"He was," Derringer agreed.

"Well, I'm glad to finally meet you and have this conversation," the sheriff declared.

"Me too," Derringer said. They shook hands and he went out the door. *I wonder if the mayor told him he offered me a job*, he thought, as he closed the door behind him.

Inside the dining room, Sheriff Warton said howdy

to Cecil Humphrey and commented, "I'm glad I finally got to meet that fellow. He's well-spoken for an army Indian scout."

Alvin Crowe walked into the sheriff's office later that afternoon. Sheriff Warton took a quick look at him and asked, "Is there something I can do for you?"

"I wanna see my boys," Alvin declared. "You got my sons in jail and I wanna see 'em."

"What is your name?" the sheriff asked. "There's quite a few prisoners in the jail right now."

"Crowe," he answered curtly, "the same as my sons. What you holdin' 'em for?"

"Well, Mr. Crowe, they were arrested for murder. I'm holding them for a court date and that might take some time before a circuit judge can get here." It occurred to him then. "Although it ought not take as long as it used to, now that we've got train service to Cheyenne."

"Who'd they murder?" Crowe asked.

"They shot a man and his son after an argument about where the man parked his wagon," Warton told him. Neither the victim or his son was armed and your sons shot both of them."

Crowe found that hard to believe. Neither Arthur nor Caleb was very bright, but they had more sense than that, he thought. "That don't sound like somethin' my sons would do." *Leastways not when anybody was looking*, he thought. "Can I go in the jail to talk to 'em?"

"Sure," the sheriff said. "You can go see 'em for about

fifteen minutes, but you'll have to leave that gun out here with me. You carryin' anything else? Take your coat off. How 'bout in those inside pockets?" Crowe unbuckled his gun belt and laid it on the sheriff's desk. Then he opened his coat up and held it wide for the sheriff to see he had nothing more. "You got a knife?"

"It's on my gun belt," Crowe said, and pointed to it.

"All right, you can go talk to them for fifteen minutes," the sheriff said, picked up a ring of keys, and walked over to unlock the cell room door. "Fifteen minutes," he reminded him as he walked into the cell room.

Inside, there were three cells; there were several prisoners in the first two cells but only the two Crowe brothers in the third. Alvin looked at the somewhat crowded occupants of cells one and two, his gaze met by expressions of boredom before he heard Caleb call out, "Pa?" He went on past to the third cell then.

"How come them other two cells are crowded and there ain't nobody but you and Arthur in this'un?" Alvin asked.

"'Cause me and Arthur are under arrest for murder, so we get special treatment," Caleb told him rather proudly. "Them other two cells are full of drunks and disorderly conduct turkeys. Ain't that right, Arthur?"

"That's right, Pa. They're holdin' us for a circuit judge to come take us to trial."

"What the hell's the matter with you two birdbrains?" their father reacted. "You talk like you've done somethin' to brag about. That sheriff out there told me you're in here because you shot a man and his son and they didn't even have a gun between 'em. I know ain't neither one of you got a lick of sense on account you took after your mama's side of the family. But I swear, I woulda thought even you would know better than to shoot unarmed folks when there's witnesses to see you do it."

"That sheriff didn't tell you like it really was," Caleb protested. "That man and his son had whips they used to drive them oxen pullin' their wagon. They like to run us over with them damn oxen, till we put a couple of shots under the feet of their lead oxen. So that's when they commenced to poppin' me and Caleb with them damn big whips they use. And those things sting like fire. So we showed 'em how to put that fire out. Ain't that right, Arthur?"

"We sure did," Arthur answered. "The only thing we did wrong was hang around too long. We shoulda took off as soon as we shot them two, but we didn't know somebody had already gone to get the sheriff. We'da still got away with it 'cause nobody but one deputy sheriff showed up and tried to arrest us. We had him buffaloed until that son of a gun snuck up behind us and stuck a gun on the back of my head. He's the reason we're in jail. There woulda been one less deputy in this town and we'da been gone if he hadn't stuck his nose in it."

"Who was it, the other deputy?" their father asked.

"His name's Jesse Derringer. He ain't even a lawman. They said he works for the railroad."

"Derringer? Like the pocket pistol?" Alvin asked.

"I reckon," Arthur said. "That's what it sounded like to me."

"Wouldn't nobody but a gunslinger have a name like

that," Alvin speculated. "Most likely that ain't his real name."

"He's a rough-lookin' critter," Caleb said. "He don't look slick like some of those fast guns. I don't know what he does for the railroad. But he's the only reason we're in jail right now, so I say damn him."

"You reckon there's any way we can get outta here, Pa?" Arthur asked then.

"Well, right now I don't know of any. If you're thinkin' about me breakin' you out, I can't hardly do that by myself. Maybe I can sneak you a weapon in that little window up there near the ceilin'. I'll have to get a look at it from the outside. I just don't know yet." There wasn't any time left to discuss it because Sheriff Warton opened the cell room door and told him the time was up. "I'll come see you again," he said hurriedly. "I'll do what I can do." When he walked back into the office, he said, "I 'preciate it, Sheriff. Can I come back again to see 'em?"

"Yes, you can come visit them as long as it's between dinnertime and suppertime," Warton told him.

Crowe got on his horse and rode off up the street for a couple of blocks before turning the horse into an alley and riding back down the street behind the buildings until he came to the back of the jail. He spotted the small window he had seen from inside the cell room and he was sure he could reach it if he stood on his saddle. He pulled his horse to a stop under the window and got up to stand in the saddle only to find there was a permanent grillwork in the window that was too small to pass even a large knife through. Disappointed, he dropped back down into the saddle and rode away.

I might not be able to get them out of there, he thought, since he was just one man alone in the endeavor. Then another thought entered his mind. *But maybe I can settle up with the S.O.B. who caused them to get caught.* "Jesse Derringer," he spat. "He ought not be so hard to find, even in this town full of people."

CHAPTER 8

"How come we don't go back to The Crossin' Saloon no more?" Tiny Thomas asked. "That woman that runs Vera's next door cooks up some pretty good grub."

"We don't go back there 'cause that's where I killed that jasper in the poker game," Jeb Massey answered him. "Over here, we ain't got no reputation. We're just five more of the strangers fillin' up this town."

"Tiny's right," Sly said. "That Vera woman set a pretty good table."

"It weren't all that good," Massey said. "Course, I had my mind on the food and not the half-neckid women that was—"

"Lookee yonder, comin' in the door!" Lester interrupted. "Alvin Crowe! I reckon he's come lookin' for Arthur and Caleb. But he ain't gonna find 'em in here."

"Don't let on that we was in here when they got arrested," Massey warned them. "He might wanna know why we didn't back 'em up."

"Hell, we don't owe them nothin'," Sly remarked.

"Just don't let on we was here," Massey said again. Then, since they were sitting around a table closer to the front door, and likely to be seen, he called out to him. "Alvin Crowe!" Crowe jumped and dropped his hand down to rest on his six-gun, thinking it a lawman. "We figured you might show up here. You lookin' for your boys?"

"Jeb Massey!" Crowe responded. "No, I found 'em already. They're in the jailhouse. I just come from there."

"Was that your two boys that shot a feller and his son?" Massey asked him. "We heard about it, but we didn't know their names. Arthur and Caleb, I'll swear, that's bad news. Set down and we'll buy you a drink. Tiny, borrow a chair from that table for Alvin. Sly, ask the bartender for another glass." Back to Crowe then, he asked, "They gonna let 'em outta jail anytime soon?"

"Hell, no," Crowe replied. "They've got 'em in there on a charge of murder and they're holdin' 'em to go to trial. They'll hang for sure. The sheriff said the man and boy they shot didn't even have a gun." He sat down when Tiny brought the chair, and immediately tossed the drink Lester poured for him.

"I swear, that's sorry news, Alvin," Massey said, and motioned for Lester to pour him another drink out of their bottle.

"I 'preciate it, fellers," Crowe said. He looked at Massey and shook his head. "Young boys, you'd think they'd have enough sense to wait till there weren't no witnesses around, if they was of a mind to shoot somebody. And they was took by one deputy that came to arrest 'em. They said they almost got away from him, but some hotshot joker stepped in to help him. He's the one

I'd like to find to give him a little lesson in mindin' his own business."

"You know who he is?" Massey asked when it occurred to him that it would be handy if Crowe was able to eliminate Jesse Derringer. He was afraid Derringer was going to be a source of trouble somewhere down the line.

"I know his name," Crowe answered. "Jesse Derringer is his name."

"Jesse Derringer," Massey repeated. "We know that name. We ran into him the first day we rode into town. He works for the Union Pacific. I'd advise you to be mighty careful when you go to stalkin' him. A dark night in a black alley is the best place to settle his bacon."

"I don't even know what he looks like," Crowe said. "I'm hopin' to get a look at him, but there are so damn many people in this town, I mighta seen him on my way over here and not even know it."

"That's sure 'nough a fact," Lester commented. "This town can't hold many more folks."

"It's a doggone good thing they got the railroad this far," Sly said, "else we'd all starve to death."

"That train that just left here wasn't carryin' anything but railroad ties, lumber, and iron rails to build the tracks when it came from Council Bluffs," Ace said. "I can't eat any of that stuff."

"The first passenger train will come to Cheyenne pretty soon," Massey said. "That'll have a mail car, too, and probably some freight for the stores." He didn't say it, but he was more interested in the train's return trip to Council Bluffs when that mail car might be holding the money to pay for that freight. He started to change the conversation in case the same thought might occur to Crowe, but paused when the door opened. "Well, Alvin, it's a good thing you decided to come in here, 'cause the man you're lookin' for just walked in."

Crowe froze. His hand dropped to grasp the handle of the Colt .45 he wore as he stared at the formidable figure of a man. "Derringer?" he whispered, barely audible.

"That's him," Massey answered softly, "Jesse Derringer. That's the man who sent your two sons to the gallows." Like him, the other four men in his gang were locked in on Alvin Crowe, silently urging him to take the shot.

Derringer walked over to the bar, his back to the table and the six men seated there in the midst of the crowded saloon. Crowe's hand tightened around the handle of his Colt, his eyes piercing the broad back of the man talking to the bartender as he slowly lifted the weapon from his holster. His concentration was broken for an instant by a boisterous laugh from another table and he became aware of the crowded saloon. Remembering then how stupid he had told his sons they were for murdering someone when there were witnesses to send them to the gallows, he reconsidered. He dropped the Colt back in the holster to the disappointment of Jeb Massey. Crowe turned back toward the table then and confessed, "I almost made the same dumb mistake my sons made."

"Yeah, you had us worried there for a minute," Massey said. "That woulda been a mistake. There oughta be better opportunities for you. I know he stays at the hotel and I reckon that's where he eats. Looks like he favors this saloon. Maybe he'll come back here after supper to have a drink before he turns in. You just have to wait for a chance, I reckon."

At the bar, Derringer was unsuccessful in his efforts to pay Sam for the bottle of whiskey he had donated in appreciation for saving Deputy Sheriff Crenshaw. "I got to thinking about that this mornin'," he said. It was a helluva nice thing you did and then I ended up giving it away to a couple of fellows I didn't even know. I felt like I ought to come back and pay you for it."

Sam chuckled outright. "No such a thing, Jesse. I never gave it a thought. Forget about it. You deserved something for acting when nobody else did."

"Well, I appreciate it, Sam, and I reckon I'll most likely see you after supper for a drink tonight." He turned away from the bar and went out the front door, noticing but ignoring the table of six men watching his every move. Without another word to Massey, Crowe got up and followed him out the door.

Once he was outside, Crowe looked up and down the busy street in an effort to see which way Derringer had gone. Finally, he spotted him, walking rapidly toward the hardware store, so he set in behind him, keeping pace but not closing in too close. He stopped in front of the barbershop when Derringer went into the hardware store. He waited there until Derringer came back out, carrying a box of .44 cartridges. When he saw him coming back toward him, Crowe panicked for a moment before hurrying into the alley between the barbershop and the bridle shop, where he waited until he saw Derringer pass by the alley. Then he hurried back to the street, searching cautiously until he caught sight of him again. Keeping the same distance as he had before, he followed him past the saloon and on up the street toward the stable. Thinking there might be a chance to catch him away from witnesses if he went into the stable, he increased his pace a little to close the distance between them. *What about the man who owns the stable*, he wondered then. He didn't know his name. He might have to kill him, too, to keep him from talking. Then, when they got closer to the stable, he saw Leon Draper out in the corral on the far side of the barn and stable. He was working to repair some of the rails around the corral. Crowe looked back at Derringer in time to see him walk into the back door to the stables before he got to the man working in the corral. "He never saw him," Crowe whispered to himself. "He don't even know there's somebody in his stables."

Crowe hurried to the back door, then stopped to make sure Draper was still unaware of his visitors. He considered his escape route. One shot, then out this door, then down through the grove of trees beside the stream. He would be gone before the owner got out of the corral. He eased the door open a few inches, just far enough to permit him to see the stalls along one side of the stable and the alley between them. *There was no one in the alley, so he must be in one of the stalls,* he thought. The trick was to sneak down the alley until he found the stall. So he drew his .45 and cocked it. Then he opened the door just wide enough to permit himself to slip inside. He paused to let his eyes adjust to the dark interior when the door slammed shut behind him and the gun was knocked out of his hand to land on the floor. Locked helpless by one powerful arm around his arms, he felt the cold steel of the gun barrel against his head.

"All right," Derringer told him, "you've been followin' me up and down the street since I left Dawkin's and now you caught up with me. So what the hell do you want?"

Lost in a complete state of shock, Crowe's brain was unable to function properly. All he could think to blurt out was, "You broke my arm!"

"I sure as hell did," Derringer said, still holding the heavy piece of lumber Leon used to lock the back door. "Who the hell are you and what were you plannin' to do with that pistol?" He kicked the weapon across the floor, in case Crowe tried to pick it up.

"You broke my arm!" Crowe repeated frantically, his brain still cluttered as he stared at his right arm, bending between his wrist and his elbow, where there was no joint. Aware now of the pain coming from his arm, he confessed helplessly. "You killed my sons," he accused.

"I don't know your sons," Derringer replied. "Who are you?"

"Arthur and Caleb," Crowe said, ignoring the question. "It weren't none of your business. It was between them and the deputy sheriff, but you stepped in behind 'em and caused 'em to get arrested. Now they'll hang, so you killed 'em, the same as, anyway."

Derringer just looked at him for a few seconds, trying to decide what he would do with him. "So you'd be Mr. Crowe," he finally said as the injured man slumped in obvious pain. "The acorns sure didn't fall very far from the tree." Seeing a bale of hay on the side of the alley, he said, "Sit down on that bale and I'll take a look at that arm." Unable to resist, Crowe sat down on the bale. "Now, let's get your coat off."

"Why? What are you gonna do?" Crowe protested, completely confused now.

"If you was a horse, I'd just put a bullet in your brain, but since you ain't, I'll see if I can't put that bone back in place. Your brain woulda been an awful small target to shoot at, anyway." He unbuttoned Crowe's coat when Crowe found it difficult to do with his left hand. Then when his disillusioned patient managed to pull his left arm out of the sleeve, Derringer took hold of the right sleeve and pulled it off the injured arm. The sudden action caused a howl of pain from Crowe. Derringer tried to pull the shirtsleeve up past the broken bone but it wouldn't come, so he drew his skinning knife and cut the cuff of the sleeve. Then he ripped it apart until it was out of his way.

"That was a good shirt!" Crowe complained.

"Oughta teach you a lesson," Derringer replied. "Don't wear your good clothes when you go to murder somebody."

"It weren't murder," Crowe protested. "I was fixin' to call you out to face me man-to-man."

"Oh, I don't know about that, Crowe. I've been called out a time or two and it was always in a saloon or outside in the open. I ain't ever been called out by somebody sneakin' in a barn or a stable behind me with their gun already out. I think I'd have to classify that as murder."

"What's goin' on back there?" Leon Draper called

out from the front of the stable. "I heard somebody yell."

"It's me, Leon, Jesse Derringer. That was Mr. Crowe you heard yell. He broke his arm. Come give me a hand and we'll try to set the bone back in place."

Leon walked back to the end of the stalls, puzzled to find Alvin Crowe sitting on a hay bale with Derringer standing over him. "Well, I'll be . . ." he started. "How'd he break his arm?"

"That two-by-six you use to lock the door," was all the explanation he got. "Come here and help me put this bone back in place," Derringer directed, so Leon walked over to the bale. "Grab his upper arm and hold it back." Realizing then what Jesse was going to do, Leon took hold of Crowe's upper arm and set his feet in position to resist his efforts. "All right, everybody ready?" Jesse asked. No one answered, but Leon tightened his grip and Crowe released a faint sigh of despair. So Jesse grabbed Crowe's right wrist and pulled with all his strength until he could feel the broken end of the bone pass beyond the other broken end. Then he let up enough to let the two ends settle back together. Looking at the arm, he could tell that the two ends were not perfectly mated, so he said, "Let's do it again." This time, they pulled the break apart over Crowe's seemingly dead body, for he passed out during the procedure. "Hell, that ain't half bad," Derringer said as he examined their work. "I've seen worse jobs than that in a field hospital durin' the war. You got some rags or something we can tie that arm up with and maybe make him a sling?"

"Yep, I've got plenty of rags that'll do for that," Leon replied, but he didn't go to get them right away. Instead, he stood looking down at the unconscious man on his stable floor, then he looked at the six-gun lying over against the side of the stall. "Jesse, who the hell is that?" He paused to look up at Derringer. "And what are you and him doin' in the back of my stable?"

"I was just going to check my packs to see what else I needed to take about a week's trip up toward the mountains tomorrow or the next day. His name is Crowe. I don't know as I've ever heard his given name. But that's his two boys, Arthur and Caleb, that Deputy Crenshaw put in jail for killin' a man and his son."

Leon didn't need any further explanation. "So he figures he owes you for the capture of his two boys and he came after you for revenge, right?"

"Well, he followed me in here with a drawn gun. I don't reckon that was just to make sure I paid attention to his complaint."

"You want me to go get the sheriff while you stay here and watch him?" Leon asked.

Derringer hesitated before answering, still debating the issue in his mind. "No, I don't think so. I don't know if I want to put him in that jail with his two sons or not. That broken arm is gonna be a good reminder for a while that it was a foolish thing he was trying to do. Let's get him bandaged up while he's takin' a little nap. Then when he comes to, I'll have a little talk with him. All right?"

"If that's what you think is best," Leon said. "I know I'd like to have him outta my stable before he decides to shoot somebody again. Are you gonna take him to the doctor?"

"No, hell, I ain't takin' him to raise. I think we'll bandage him up nice and tight and he won't need a doctor. He'll just have to let that bone heal up." He picked up Crowe's pistol then and emptied the cartridges out and put the gun back in the holster. When he did, the movement seemed to stir Crowe back to consciousness.

"My arm!" he blurted, and tried to sit up, but when he did, his right arm was in a sling and he couldn't put his hand on the floor to push himself up. "What the hell?"

"Your arm's broke," Jesse said, "but the bone's set and you're bandaged up. If you don't try to use it, it'll heal up. I shoulda just shot your sorry butt when you came after me, but I thought it woulda been a waste of a cartridge. So here's what you need to learn. You tried to dry-gulch me like a damn coward and you got a broken arm for your trouble. The next time the notion strikes you to come after me, you get a shot in the chest and another one in the head. I don't tolerate fools like you but once. It's best you remember that because there won't be any warning. So I just saved your life when I decided not to shoot you. All business is done between you and me, right?" When Crowe didn't answer, Jesse repeated it more forcefully. "Right?"

"Right, we're done," Crowe replied, his attitude a little more sullen now. "Let me outta here now."

"Ain't nobody holdin' you," Leon said, anxious to see him leave his stable.

He got up from the hay bale and stood for a moment before plopping back down. "I don't feel so good."

"Maybe you ought to go to Doc Bell's office," Leon advised. "Maybe he'll give you something to ease that pain. That's got to be hurtin' like hell." He turned aside and whispered to Jesse, "Why didn't you just shoot the son of a gun? That woulda took care of everything."

"Things don't always work out for the best," Jesse replied. He looked at Crowe and asked, "Where's your horse?"

"At Dawkin's Saloon," Crowe answered. "I'll be all right if I can get to my horse."

"I'll get you to your horse," Jesse said. "Can you sit in the saddle?"

"I think so," Crowe replied. So Jesse went to the stall where his horses were and saddled Clem. He led the gray gelding back to Crowe and he and Leon lifted Crowe up into the saddle. He told Leon he'd be back to leave his horse in a few minutes. Leon nodded, then shook his head slowly, finding it hard to believe the bizarre incident taking place in his stable had actually happened.

Since it wasn't that far to the saloon, Derringer walked and led Clem. When they got to Dawkin's, he helped Crowe off Clem and left him standing beside his horse, tied at the hitching rail. Before he rode away, he looked down at Crowe and said, "You'd best remember what I told you. If you ever come near me again, I'll shoot first and ask questions later." Crowe just stood there, his head down, holding on to his saddle horn with his one good hand, the picture of a defeated man. Derringer wheeled his horse and returned to the stable at a lope, halfway expecting a shot in the back at any second, even though he knew Crowe's .45 was empty. *I just did the dumbest thing I've ever done,* he thought. *I stopped the man who came to kill me and then I set him free.* "Maybe I need a new line of work," he told Clem.

Behind him, Alvin Crowe took a tighter grip than before on the saddle horn. He discovered that he was not feeling as bad as he was in the stable. *Maybe*, he thought, *the thing I really need right now is a drink of likker*. He released his grip on the saddle horn and stood without holding on for a couple of minutes. Satisfied that he could make it without stumbling, he stepped up on the boardwalk and walked very carefully into the saloon. As he had hoped, Jeb Massey and the boys were still occupying a table.

"What tha . . ." Sly Parker started when he saw Crowe making his way toward them through the crowded saloon. "Massey! Look comin' yonder." Massey looked where he pointed. "He's about to fall over and it looks like he's got his arm in a sling."

"Damn if he ain't," Massey said. "He musta fell off his horse." The others at the table saw what they were looking at then, so Tiny confiscated another chair from a nearby table.

"I thought he went after Derringer when he followed him outta here," Ace said.

"Looks like he musta caught up with him," Lester said with a chuckle.

"Set down, Alvin," Massey said. "You look like you fell off your horse. The way you lit outta here when Derringer left, we thought you mighta been thinkin' about settlin' up with him. What's wrong with your arm?"

"It's broke," Crowe replied.

"I swear," Sly said, "how'd you do that?"

"He done it with a two-by-six," Crowe answered simply.

"How the hell did he do that?" Massey asked. "Pour him a drink, Ace."

"He ain't got no glass," Ace said.

"Well, let him use yours," Massey ordered impatiently.

"Right," Ace responded. "Here, Alvin, you can drink outta my glass." Then he poured him a drink. Crowe tossed it back at once, having a great need for one.

"Who bandaged your arm up like that?" Massey asked. "That don't look like nothin' a doctor would do."

"Derringer," Crowe answered, and held his glass out for another shot of whiskey.

"I swear, Alvin, you ain't makin' no sense a-tall," Massey said. "You sure you ain't got a bump on your head, too? You sayin' he broke your arm with a two-by-six, then he bandaged it up and made a sling for it? You sure your arm is broke?"

"Yeah, I'm sure. I saw it. The bone was bent up where it ain't supposed to bend. He set the bone. It hurt so bad I passed out."

Massey turned serious for a moment. "I reckon you're lucky he didn't kill you," he said. "You sure he knew you came after him to kill him?"

"Yeah, he knew it," Crowe said, "that's why he broke my arm."

"Why didn't he kill you if he knew you came after him to kill him?"

"I don't know," Crowe replied. "He said if I tried it again, he'd kill me."

"That don't make no sense," Lester said.

"Maybe he's one of them Bible-thumpin' religious nuts," Sly offered, "wantin' to forgive everybody for their sins." He thought about it for only a second or two before adding, "Except for the part about killin' him if he tried it again."

"One thing I guarantee you," Massey declared, "there ain't a religious bone in that man's body. I've been thinking about it and it bothers me when I know he works for the Union Pacific. They call him a scout. But the folks building the railroad are all gone, for three months anyway, and they left him here. What for? The only thing I know of that he's done after he surprised us at that caboose is to step in and arrest Arthur and Caleb Crowe."

"He ain't the only one left," Lester said. "There's two fellers that stayed here to build the Union Pacific building."

"They're in charge of gettin' the building up and takin' care of the train station," Massey said. "That don't count. Derringer ain't got nothin' to do with that. The more I think on it, the more I believe his main job is to keep an eye on us, and that could be trouble. I don't cotton to havin' that hungry lobo prowlin' around our campfire."

CHAPTER 9

Massey's comments about Jesse Derringer created a discussion among the gang of five men and their one injured acquaintance sitting around the saloon table. The more they talked about him, the more mysterious he became, especially when Sam, the bartender, told them that Derringer was a special scout for General Grenville Dodge. Massey and his gang had big plans for several robberies in Cheyenne, plus one train robbery as their final score. It was decided that Jesse Derringer was going to be a severe threat to their success and consequently had to be eliminated.

"That don't seem like a problem to me," Ace Barnes remarked. He got up from the table and whipped his six-gun from his holster and performed his little show of spinning the weapon on his finger to demonstrate his skill and his speed. It was a trick none of the others could do. He was anxious to put his skill up against that of Jesse Derringer. He didn't know how fast Derringer might be, but he knew how fast he was. He kept the names of four men in his memory, whose cold corpses were pushing up daisies. They thought they were faster than he. They found out the hard way. It was time the other four members of the gang showed him a little respect. "I think it's time I called Mr. Special Scout Derringer out," he announced.

"Are you crazy?" Sly responded. "You don't know nothin' about that joker. He might be faster'n greased lightning."

"I know he carries that Henry rifle most of the time," Ace replied, "and he don't wear a fast draw holster. And I know that I'm faster'n greased lightning. The hardest part might be gittin' him to face me man-to-man. Looks to me like he didn't even wanna face Alvin Crowe face-to-face. Hit him with a board when Alvin weren't lookin'."

Massey looked at Lester and they both shrugged in response, both thinking the same thing. Why not? It would be no great loss if Derringer was faster than Ace. On the other hand, Ace was pretty fast. It would be a hell of a thing if he could take Derringer out. So with a sense of nothing to lose and everything to gain, they decided to encourage Ace to call him out. "You sure you're ready to call him out?" Massey asked Ace. "There must be some reason the Union Pacific Railroad would pay a man to stay here in Cheyenne with nothin' to do. He might be quicker than a rattlesnake with a handgun, even if it does look like he favors that rifle."

"He ain't nothin' but another jasper that wears a sidearm to kill snakes and rabbits," Ace insisted. "I can tell a fast gun by the way he walks and the way he wears his holster. That feller is built too solid to move fast. His shoulders is too wide to let his hands drop to his hips quick enough to draw his gun. He might beat a feller like me if we was arm-wrasslin'. But I ain't aimin' to arm-wrassle him."

"You might be right, Ace," Massey said. "I reckon I ain't studied him the way you have. But I see what you mean. He is kinda wide shouldered at that. Looks like he druther fight with an ax." He paused to look over at Crowe. "Or a two-by-six, right, Alvin?"

Crowe didn't respond to the question. Well dosed with alcohol by that time, he was picking away at his bandaged arm and complaining that it was hurting. "I need to see the doctor," he slurred drunkenly.

"You oughta left that bandage alone," Tiny told him. "It'da healed up all right if you'da left it alone."

"I need to see the doctor," Crowe insisted. "It ain't tied up right."

Tired of messing with him, Tiny said, "Well, go to the damn doctor, then; he oughta still be open. It ain't even suppertime yet."

"I ain't got no money and I don't know where the doctor is," Crowe complained.

Tired of hearing him complain, Massey said, "Tiny, you and Sly take him down to the doctor's office and leave him." They both protested and said they didn't know where the doctor's office was, or if there even was a doctor in Cheyenne. "It's down near the dry goods store," Massey said. "I saw it when we first rode into town, a house with a white picket fence around it. When you get back, we'll go back to Vera's and eat supper."

"Come on, Tiny," Sly said, "let's throw him on his horse and take him to the doctor." They got up from the table and waited for Crowe to get on his feet. He struggled up from the chair but stumbled when he started to take a step. So Tiny caught him and hoisted him up to lie across his shoulder, then they walked out of the saloon and Tiny unloaded Crowe to lie on his belly across the saddle. They took him down to the picket fence with a sign that said HOLLIS BELL M.D. Sly tied the horse to the fence while Tiny carried Crowe to the doctor's front door, where he dumped him on the porch and yanked on a short rope that rang a bell. He didn't wait for the bell to summon anyone but turned around and walked back to the gate. "Don't you reckon we oughta tell the doctor what's wrong with Alvin?" Sly asked.

"You can, if you want to," Tiny replied. "I'm tired of messin' with him. If he's a real doctor, he oughta be able to figure out what's wrong with him. I'm ready to go to Vera's Vineyard." Sly made a face and shrugged, then they walked back up the street to the saloon.

"You take him to the doctor?" Massey asked when Tiny and Sly came back into the saloon.

"Sure did," Tiny answered. "You said take him to the doctor, so we took him to the doctor."

"Any trouble?" Massey asked.

"No," Tiny answered, "no trouble a-tall."

"He claims he ain't got no money," Massey recalled. "I wonder if he's got enough to pay the doctor."

"Don't matter," Tiny said, "we left his horse there. Let's go eat."

* * *

"Howdy, Jesse," Sheriff Tom Warton greeted him. "Mind if I sit down with you?"

"Not at all," Jesse responded. "Glad to have the company."

"What's Clara cookin' tonight?" Warton asked, staring at Jesse's plate and unable to identify it right off. When Jesse smiled and told him it was meat loaf and gravy and it tasted better than it looked, the sheriff pulled a chair back and sat down. "Sometimes it's hard to tell just lookin' at it," Warton said. "I have to admit that most of the time it's good eatin'."

"I reckon this is one of those times," Jesse said.

Warton looked around, searching, but then relaxed when he saw Rachael already coming toward him with his coffee. "Evening, Sheriff," she greeted him. "Glad you showed up. Mr. Derringer looked like he needed some company." She placed his coffee cup on the table. "The special tonight is meat loaf and gravy." When he made no objections to that, she left to fetch a plate for him.

"Leon Draper told me you had a little trouble with Alvin Crowe," Warton said. "Anything you need to tell me about?"

"It wasn't that much," Derringer replied. "I figured you had enough trouble on your hands, so I took care of it."

"Leon said you broke his arm when he came at you with a gun," the sheriff said. "Then he said you set the broken bone and put his arm in a sling."

"It seemed like the right thing to do, since I'm the one who broke it. I expect I had a legitimate right to shoot him, since that was what he had in mind to do to me. But I think he's most likely got that notion out of his system. He was just not thinkin' straight 'cause his two sons are in jail."

"He's in jail with his two sons right now," the sheriff said. When Jesse looked genuinely surprised, Warton figured he didn't know about that, so he told him. "Doctor Bell found Crowe on his front porch, passed out drunk, and his horse was tied at Doc's front gate." Seeing even more signs of surprise in Jesse's expression, Warton continued. "Doc said you did a passable job settin' that bone, but he put a splint on it and a new bandage. Said he would have given him some laudanum for the pain, but he was too drunk for it to do him any good. He didn't have any money and Doc didn't want to mess with his horse, so he sent for me. And Crowe's in jail on a drunk and disorderly charge. I put him in the cell with his two sons."

"I apologize for addin' to your problems, Sheriff," Derringer said. "I bandaged Crowe up pretty good and took him back to his horse. When I left him, he was standin' by his horse and I thought he was gonna be all right."

"I wish to hell you had shot him, instead of just breakin' his arm," the sheriff said.

Derringer shrugged, surprised. "Well, I told him that was what I was going to do the next time he came after me with a gun." He paused when Rachael brought Warton's supper and warmed up their coffee. When she left, Derringer asked, "You have any idea yet on when you'll get a circuit judge over this way to try Crowe's two boys?"

"No, I don't," Warton replied. "And that's another thing I don't understand. We've got the railroad here now, so why the hell can't they send a judge on the train? He could come all the way from Omaha in two and a half days."

"I don't know," Jesse said. "Maybe it's because those judges ride a circuit, so they hold court in several different towns in a week or two. If they come to Cheyenne, there ain't no towns between here and Council Bluffs. Like I said, I don't know, but it might be that it ain't worth it to them to spend five days ridin' on a train and get paid for one trial. And I know I don't have to tell you that it's just gettin' worse with all the people pourin' in here every day. You're already talking about a vigilance committee—you might wanna set up some kind of court system, too."

"The town council has already talked about that very thing," the sheriff told him, "and it ain't gonna happen. The town ain't got the money to support all the prisoners we'd have to house and feed. We ain't got anybody to try 'em, anyway. The best way to handle crime is to capture the ones who do the crime and hang 'em as soon as we catch 'em. That oughta discourage some of the wild ones from shootin' up the town."

"I reckon so," Derringer replied, but he was thinking how disappointed General Dodge would be to think his queen city of Cheyenne used "gunnysack" gangs to enforce law and order. In spite of that, he had to agree with the town council to do what you had to do to keep the peace.

Sheriff Warton didn't linger over his supper because he had to help Ray Cooper, one of his deputies, pull a handcart back to the jail, loaded with supper for his prisoners. Derringer offered his help but Warton said he and Cooper could manage it. So he remained at the table long enough to finish another cup of coffee before retiring to his room for the night. He had decided to ride up toward Sherman Hill in the morning, since the bad weather had let up just a little. With that thought in mind, he decided to treat himself to a shot of whiskey before going to bed. So he thanked Rachael for her excellent service and told her to tell her mother that he really enjoyed her meat loaf and gravy. "Thank you, kind sir," Rachael said with a little curtsy to boot. "You're such a sweetheart to say that."

"That's me, all right, a sweetheart," he responded with a chuckle. He was not burdened with illusions that young women found him attractive. He knew for a fact they did not. It made it easier to have a casual conversation with a woman. "I'll see you for breakfast," he said, then went out the door to the street and walked up to Dawkin's Saloon.

"Evenin', Jesse," Sam greeted him when he found some room at the bar. "Whiskey?" Jesse nodded.

When Sam poured his drink, Jesse said, "If this keeps up, Mr. Dawkins is gonna have to hire another bartender to help you out."

"Ain't that the truth?" Sam replied, then went down to the other end of the bar in answer to another customer's banging his glass on the bar for another shot.

"Look what just walked in." Sly reached over and poked Lester to get his attention.

"Where?" Lester asked.

"End of the bar, near the front door," Sly answered.

Lester nodded, then turned to inform Ace that Jesse Derringer had just walked in the saloon. Ace immediately came to attention. "Where?" he asked.

"End of the bar close to the front door," Lester said, then he winked at Massey, who had become alert to something going on.

Massey nodded in return, then he commented, "Walks in like he owns the place, don't he?"

"It's time he found out who owns the place and who don't," Ace declared. He got up out of his chair and stood there a few seconds while he made sure his gun belt was settled just right on his hips. Then he drew his .45 and checked the cylinder to make sure it was fully loaded. Satisfied, he returned the weapon to his holster and lifted it and let it drop back a couple of times to make sure nothing was restricting its movement. Ready then to match his skills against any man's and especially Jesse Derringer's, he pushed his way roughly through the crowded room until he stood at Derringer's back. "Hey, you big jackass, move the hell outta my way!"

Derringer turned to look at him and recognized him as one of the five drifters he had encountered at the train. He immediately realized what he had in mind and he had no intention of accommodating him. "I'm sorry, friend, I didn't know I was standin' in your space." He looked at Sam then and said, "Sam, you shoulda told me I was standin' in this fellow's space." Sam's only response was a worried look. Back to Ace then, Derringer said, "I'm sure the rest of these fellows won't mind taking a step to the side, so I can move out of your space. Will that be all right?"

Ace was dumbfounded, but he was determined to call the man out. "You smell like a railroad man. I don't like a railroad man."

"Is that a fact?" Derringer responded. "You can tell I work for Union Pacific just by the smell? You must be a regular bloodhound."

"I don't like your looks, either," Ace said, rapidly becoming desperate for insults.

"You know, I ain't particularly happy with 'em myself, but I got used to 'em after a while. Besides, what are you gonna do about it, right? I expect it took you a pretty long time to get used to yours."

"You dumb jackass!" Ace finally roared. "I'm callin' you out! Right here, right now!"

"Is that what you want? Why didn't you say so? I could have saved you a lot of time. I'm sorry, but we can't have a gunfight because it's now against the law in Cheyenne. If we had a gunfight, they'd put the winner in prison and I don't wanna go to prison."

Far past the limit his underdeveloped brain could tolerate, Ace demanded, "You're wearin' a gun, so get ready to use it, 'cause I'm gonna shoot you down right where you're standin' if you don't." The crowd of spectators backed away to create a space for the gunfight.

"Now, that ain't a good idea," Derringer said. "See, that would be outright murder and they'd hang you for that. This crowd right here might even do it. Just string you up by the neck. Hell, you're too young to go out that way. So why don't you go back to your friends over there and have a drink. Here, you can take mine. I'll buy you a drink." He took the glass Sam had just filled off the bar and handed it to Ace. It was too much for the simpleminded gunslinger. He slapped the glass out of Derringer's hand and reached for his six-gun. It was one move too many with the same hand because Derringer was quick enough to grab Ace's right hand just as he started to pull the weapon. Ace reacted by pulling the trigger while the gun was still in the holster, resulting in a bullet into the calf of his leg.

Ace yelled in pain and reached for his leg and would have gone down had Derringer not grabbed the back of his collar with one hand while he pulled the Colt out of his holster and shoved it in his belt. Once the weapon was secured, Derringer supported him while he limped back to the table where his four friends were sitting dumbfounded. "I believe this belongs to you," he said as he released Ace to drop in the chair, his gaze aimed directly at Massey. "He's a little too green to be allowed to play with guns." He pulled Ace's gun out of his belt, causing a reflex reaction from all four, their hands automatically dropping on their weapons. Derringer paused a moment to say, "I swear, you boys are wound tighter than a cheap pocket watch." He went on then to break open the cylinder in Ace's gun and empty the cartridges out on the floor. Still directing his comments to Massey, he said, "Might not be a bad idea to just let him carry that Colt without any bullets in it until he gets a little more responsible attitude about carryin' a weapon." He smiled at Massey and added, "You and I know that guns ain't playthings."

Massey smiled back at him, fully understanding the

meaning of his message. "That's right, Derringer," he said, "guns are best handled by those who know what to do with one."

"I see you know my name," Derringer said. "I don't believe I caught yours."

Massey chuckled. "I didn't throw it," he said.

Derringer grinned again. "I'll just call you by the same name these other four do. So, Boss, I reckon you know where the doctor's office is. I expect he'll wanna cut that lead outta Junior's leg."

"You devil!" Ace blurted.

"Shut up, Ace!" Massey ordered.

"My apologies, Ace," Derringer said. "I shoulda guessed your name was something like that." Back to Massey then, he asked, "What brings you and your men to Cheyenne, Boss?"

"Curiosity," Massey replied. "We just wanted to see what the attraction was that was drawin' all the people to a place that wasn't nothin' but a creek crossin' before the railroad got here."

"How long you figure on stayin'?" Derringer asked.

"Till my curiosity gets satisfied," Massey answered bluntly. "What the hell? Are you with the sheriff's department now?"

"No, I'm still with the railroad," Derringer answered. "Like you, I'm just curious about what kind of business you boys are in."

"Why don't you just tell him the truth, Jeb?" Sly finally blurted, having grown impatient with the game going on between him and Derringer. "We're likker inspectors and we've got a whole lot more work to do before we're finished with this town." His remark brought a couple of guffaws of laughter from Lester and Tiny, but a hard look from Massey.

"That's right interesting work, Jeb," Derringer commented, emphasizing the name, Jeb. I won't take up any more of your busy time. Don't forget to take care of Ace. He looks like he's hurtin' pretty bad."

"Don't you worry about Ace," Massey replied. "We'll take care of him." *And we'll take care of you, too, Dead Man,* he thought. That much he was sure of. He wasn't certain what Jesse Derringer's role was as far as law enforcement in the town of Cheyenne, or if he even had any role in it. But he felt convinced more than ever that Derringer was going to prove to be a problem for him and his gang. So it was better to get rid of him to prevent any problem he might cause. He also knew that the man was dangerous. He was going to have to be taken by surprise by more than one shooter to make sure. Massey watched him as he turned and walked back to the bar. The temptation to pull his weapon and shoot him in the back was almost overpowering, but he knew, if he did, he and his gang would be finished in Cheyenne. He needed a plan for an outright assassination. Calling him out for a gunfight was no good because it would cause the law to come down on him and his gang.

It was Sly who came up with the assassination plan. At least he planted the idea for the final plan. Later that night when they had all visited Vera's Vineyard and they were sitting around her kitchen table, only Ace was missing. He was on a cot in the room they were renting, his leg bandaged after Doc Bell removed the bullet from his calf. "Too bad it ain't his birthday," Sly commented when the subject of Derringer's assassination came up again. "We could send him a cake with a stick of dynamite in it." They joked about the idea, but it caused Lester to think about it after the conversation moved back to the subject of Vera's Vineyard and the grapes on her vine.

"Maybe it ain't his birthday," Lester suggested, "but why don't we give him a birthday cake?" No one paid any attention, but he continued anyway. "We know he's got a room in that hotel, but we don't know which room. If we was to get Vera to bake a cake for us, I bet somebody could take that cake to the hotel when we knew Derringer weren't there. They could tell the hotel clerk it was a surprise birthday cake and they wanted to slip it in his room while he was out. I'll bet the clerk would be tickled to do it, so we could go to the room with him, to place the cake on his bed."

"What good would that do?" Tiny asked. "What are we supposed to do with the cake?"

"Nothin'," Lester said. "Sometimes you're slower than Ace. What that does is tell us which room he's in without none of us havin' to ask. So when we kick that door in after he's gone to bed, we empty our six-guns into his butt. It would take about two minutes and we'd be out of that hotel before anybody knew what happened." He paused, then added, "Except Derringer, and he ain't gonna be too happy about it."

"I swear, Lester, you mighta come up with a sure-fire plan," Massey said. He started thinking about the possibility of success and what weak points Lester hadn't thought about. "What about the one who takes the cake to the hotel? The clerk could tell the sheriff who brought the cake."

Lester hadn't thought about that. "Hell, we can pay somebody to do it and tell us the room number," he said.

"Yeah, but he could tell the sheriff who paid him to take the cake and give us the room number," Sly said.

"Not if he had an accident after he told us the room number," Lester said.

Massey nodded his agreement and said, "That'd work, but what about Vera? She could tell the sheriff she baked a cake for us."

"Vera ain't gonna tell on us if we pay her a nice price for the cake," Lester said, "and tell her what would happen to her if she told anybody."

"I like it," Massey said. "I think it'll work and it will take care of Jesse Derringer in about two minutes, with nothin' to tie his killin' to us. Anybody got any objections?" No one voiced any reluctance to the plan, even the part where the delivery man is eliminated. "Good, I'll talk to Vera in the mornin', so she can bake that cake and have it ready to take to the hotel. And we'll pick out the lucky sacrifice who's gonna deliver that cake for us. Then Mr. Derringer is gonna have one helluva nightmare tomorrow night."

CHAPTER 10

"A birthday cake?" Vera questioned. "Whose birthday is it?"

"Nobody you know," Massey said, "and keep your voice down. I don't want nobody to know about this but me and you."

She lowered her voice, fully surprised that the emotionless outlaw would ever think of doing anything to honor someone's birthday. "Hell, you can tell me," she said. "I ain't gonna tell nobody."

"You don't understand," he told her. "I don't want you tellin' anybody about the cake, not any of your girls, or anybody else. It's so important to me that nobody but me and you know about the cake that I'm willin' to pay you fifty dollars to make it and keep your mouth shut about it. It don't have to be a real fancy cake, just a cake, that's all, and keep it a secret, like your life depended on it. Can you do that?"

Her expression turned deadly serious. "Yessir, for seventy-five dollars, I'll take it to the grave with me."

He smiled and nodded. "Seventy-five it is then. I want it before dinnertime today." She nodded her okay. So he went back upstairs to tell the others that the cake was on order.

"You want me to go down in front of the saloon to pick out a drunk to take the cake to the hotel?" Lester asked.

"No," Massey told him. "Wait till we can give him the cake to take at the right time, so he won't have a chance to tell anybody else about it."

Tiny Thomas shook his head in amazement about the elaborate execution plan for Jesse Derringer. "I swear, Jeb, why the hell don't we just set up an ambush for that jasper and shoot him down? If we're careful, won't nobody know it was us that done it. He'll be just as dead and nobody else would have to know anything else about it. And we wouldn't be out seventy-five dollars for a cake we ain't even gonna get a slice of."

Sly didn't wait for Massey to answer. "You see, Tiny, that's why Jeb is the leader of this gang. That Derringer is hard to trap and some of us might get shot in the process. Jeb knows the best way to make sure Derringer is stopped cold is to catch him in his bed and kill him like a firing squad."

"Yeah, I reckon," Tiny conceded. "But if it was just me, I'd hide in an alley and wait for him to walk back to the hotel. Then I'd put a couple of shots in his back and go out the other end of the alley. He'd be dead and wouldn't nobody know who done it."

"That does seem like the simple way to kill a man," Sly declared, "but there's a reason to do it like Jeb says."

"That's right," Massey said when he detected a hint of doubt in Sly's response. "And the reason is, the man will be stopped cold and none of us will have to worry about gittin' hit with a return shot. So that's the way we'll take care of him."

Close to the same time the complicated assassination was being discussed, the target of that assault walked into Leon Draper's stable. "Mornin', Jesse," Leon greeted him. "I was expectin' you right after breakfast this mornin'. You get off to a late start?"

"Mornin', Leon," Derringer returned. "Yeah, I know I said I was gonna ride outta here this mornin', but I decided to wait till tomorrow. To tell you the truth, I might not make it tomorrow. I'm thinkin' about givin' this spell of rain a little time to pass over us. I better not wait too much longer, or I might get too used to sleepin' indoors. And when General Dodge gets back here, I expect I won't even see the inside of a tent except when I report to him."

"Cliff Crenshaw was in here this mornin'," Leon said. "He said they was gonna let ol' Alvin Crowe outta jail tomorrow. So you better watch your back. You made him look like a damn fool, so I don't expect he's feelin' very kindly about you."

"Oh, I don't know about that," Derringer said. "I think somebody put that notion in his head about comin' after me. I believe he's decided it ain't the right thing to do. Besides, it made it possible for him to spend some time visitin' his sons. Did Crenshaw say anything about gettin' a trial scheduled for Arthur and Caleb?"

"He said they ain't heard a word on when a circuit judge might be able to come over here to try them two," Leon said. Derringer didn't say it, but he was thinking about a very real possibility that the two Crowe boys might get a visit one night from the Cheyenne vigilante committee. And the sheriff would be inclined to open the cell door for them. Derringer told the sheriff and the mayor that he would join the vigilantes if he was in town when the call came, but it was not something he was keen on participating in. "I reckon we'll do what we have to do," he declared. "But right now, I think it's about time the dinin' room opened up for dinner, so I'll see you later, Leon." He gave the big gray gelding an affectionate scratching behind his ears, then headed for the hotel. As he entered the street entrance to the hotel dining room, he paid no attention to the rather scruffy-looking drunk heading for the front door of the hotel. Walking with a determined shuffle through the hotel door, he carried something in a paper bag that required both hands.

With a wary gaze, Julian Burnett, the room clerk, automatically assumed the man, an obvious drunk, was not aware he had walked into a hotel. Still, he patiently asked, "Can I help you?"

"Yessir, you sure can," the drunk blurted, attempting to sound important.

"What's in the sack?" Julian asked.

Speaking with a slight lisp, the drunk replied, "Well now, I can't tell you that unless you can keep a secret."

"I'm afraid I'm going to have to ask you to—"

"It's a birthday cake," the drunk interrupted. "And it's gonna be a surprise to the birthday boy." He set it on the check-in counter and opened the bag, so Julian could take a peek inside.

Julian looked in and said, "It is a cake. What are you doing with it? Did you steal it?"

"Hell, no! Do I look like a cake thief?"

"No, you look like a drunk," Julian had to say, his patience already exhausted.

"Hey, you got no call to say that. I'll have you know I'm on an important business deal. A feller, I can't tell you his name, is gonna give me ten bucks to take this surprise birthday cake to"—he paused and looked around the empty lobby as if afraid someone might hear before continuing—"Mr. Jesse Derringer's room."

"Derringer?" Julian exclaimed, amazed. "That cake is for Jesse Derringer?"

"It sure is," the drunk replied, looking all around him again to make sure there was no one nearby to hear. "But it's a surprise and the feller payin' me to deliver it wants me to put it in his room, so he'll be surprised when he finds it."

Julian couldn't suppress a chuckle when he pictured the rugged individual that was Jesse Derringer. Somebody was having some fun with him. "All right," he said, "I'll put it in his room and I won't tell anybody about it. He's not in his room right now, so it'll be a good time to do it."

"No, sir," the drunk replied, and picked up the cake again. "The man payin' me said you might say that.

And he said he ain't gonna pay me my ten dollars if I don't put this cake in his room myself, and place it on his bed just like he showed me to do." Beginning to have some concern at this point, the drunk turned a pleading face to Julian. "Please, mister, I need that ten bucks. You can watch me the whole time I'm in the room. I ain't gonna bother nothin'."

Julian hesitated. He didn't like the idea of letting the unkempt cake deliveryman into one of the guests' rooms, but he didn't want to spoil someone's surprise, either. "All right," he decided. "You can go with me to Mr. Derringer's room and I'll put the cake in the room just like you say you want it. You can stand in the door and watch me and that'll be the same as if you placed the cake yourself."

The drunk hesitated while he tried to think if that would be any different than if he actually took the cake in the room. He decided the man paying him wouldn't have any way of knowing if he went in the room or not. He looked at the clerk, impatiently waiting, and nodded rapidly. "All right, I 'preciate it, but if he asks you if I took it in the room, you tell him I did. Okay?"

"Okay," Julian answered. "Come on and we'll go down the hall to his room." He led the drunk through the door to the first-floor rooms. "Who's the man who's paying you to deliver this surprise cake?" he asked as they walked down the long hallway.

"I don't know what his name is," the drunk answered, "but I've seen him goin' in and out of the saloon."

"I'm sure I'll find out when Mr. Derringer gets his surprise," Julian said. "Here we are, room six." He knocked on the door to make sure and, when there was no response, he inserted the key and unlocked the door.

"Number six," the drunk repeated to himself.

"That's right, number six," Julian said as he opened the door. "Now give me the cake and you stand right here and tell me where you want me to put it."

The drunk slid the cake out of the sack and placed it carefully in Julian's hands. "Be careful," he said. "Whoever baked it put it on a plate with a crack in it. I reckon they didn't expect to get the plate back." He watched anxiously while Julian walked into the room. "He said to put it right in the middle of the bed, so he can't miss it when he walks into the room."

"I hope he doesn't come into his room in the dark and flop down on the bed," Julian japed, knowing Derringer would most likely be in and out of the room a couple of times before dark. "It's not a very fancy cake."

Julian locked the door and walked with the drunk back to the front door. "Thank you, sir," the drunk said, "and remember, don't tell nobody before he sees it."

"I won't," Julian told him, while trying to imagine the look on Derringer's face when he found a cake sitting in the middle of his bed. *General Dodge's scout*, he thought. *I didn't think he had a birthday. I would have thought the general found him growing on a cactus somewhere.*

Milton Rice hurried away from the hotel, repeating the room number over and over to himself, afraid he might forget it. He was already grateful that he remembered the name of the man whose room he was being paid to deliver the cake to. "On the first floor," he recited, "room number six." He wished the man had told him to meet him at the saloon after he took the cake, instead of down by the creek behind the train station. He began to worry then. What if the man didn't show up? Then he reminded himself that the man wanted the room number. "So he'll be there," he reassured himself. "He told me ten dollars. He might try to get me to take less, but I ain't tellin' him the room number unless he pays me the ten bucks he promised."

He almost stumbled when a root sticking up in the middle of the path snagged the hole in the sole of his boot. Maybe it was a reminder that with ten dollars he could have new soles put on his boots and still have money left to buy a bottle. On the other hand, ten dollars would buy him whiskey to last him a little while, not as long as it used to, but long enough to save him from begging for enough to buy one drink. He tried to ignore the wet spot in his sock that told him the root had opened the hole in his boot sole wider than it had been. It crossed his mind that his wife could say, "I told you so," if she could see what he had come to since she went back to her folks' place in Kansas. That was too long ago for him to care now. His remorse was ended for the time being, however, when he saw the horse by the creek and his benefactor sitting on a log, waiting for him.

Lester Bostic got up from the log when he caught sight of Milton coming down the path. He wasn't surprised. Ten dollars was too big a reward for a drunk like Milton to pass up. So he tossed the last of the three cigarette butts he had rolled while waiting for the drunk to appear and went to meet him. "Well," he asked, "did you get the room number?"

"Yes, sir, I did," Milton answered. "Have you got my ten dollars?" Lester didn't say anything. He just reached in his pocket, took out a roll of paper money, and peeled off two five-dollar bills. He handed them to Milton, whose cautious attitude immediately disappeared. He looked at the two fives and immediately reported. "Mr. Derringer is on the ground floor in room number six. If you're thinking about surprisin' him on his birthday, it's the third room from a door at the end of the hall that goes outside, I think. I don't know for sure because that hotel clerk led me back out the front door."

Now Lester was the surprised one. "Outstandin', you did a damn good job. As a matter of fact, you did such a good job, I'm gonna double that money we agreed on." He reached into his pocket and brought out the roll of money again. He peeled off a ten-dollar bill and gave it to Milton.

Milton was overjoyed, scarcely able to believe Lester's generosity. He could buy a new pair of boots with that, if he wanted to. "Thank you, mister. I never caught your name."

"Lester Bostic," he said. "You're welcome. You earned it."

"Thank you again, Lester. If you ever need any more errands run, feel free to call on me. My name's Milton

Rice, and don't worry about me keepin' my mouth shut. I ain't one to let my mouth run off with me."

"I'll remember that, Milton. Good doin' business with you."

Milton folded his twenty dollars up and put it in his pocket, then turned to head back up the path, never hearing the cocking of the pistol or the shot in the back of his head. Lester walked casually over to the body and got the twenty dollars out of Milton's pocket. "At least you died happy, Milton. I figure I owed you that." He climbed on his horse and rode up the creek a couple hundred yards before heading back to town, in case someone heard the shot and came down the path to investigate.

"Do you want some more coffee, Mr. Derringer?" Rachael Bowden asked, since he was still sitting at the table after he had finished eating.

He looked at her as if it was a major decision. "You know, Rachael, I believe I will. I think I'll sit here and drink one more cup of coffee."

"Was there something wrong with your dinner, Mr. Derringer?"

"No, goodness, no," he quickly responded. "It was mighty good. You can tell your mother that. I'm just not in a hurry to move, unless I'm in your way and you wanna clean up this table or something."

"Oh, no, indeed, Mr. Derringer, you sit there as long as you want to. I'll get you some more coffee."

"You know, Rachael, I'm a little older than you, but not so much older that you should call me Mr. Derringer. My name's Jesse. Why don't you call me that?"

She laughed and replied, "All right, I'll call you that. Now, That, would you like a slice of pie with your coffee?"

He shook his head slowly. "No, I'll just have the coffee and a little more respect for your elders." She laughed and went to get the coffeepot.

While she was in the kitchen, Julian Burnett came into the dining room, on his way to get a cup of coffee. When he saw Derringer sitting there, he stopped and said, "Mr. Derringer, how are you, sir?"

Somewhat puzzled by his unusually cordial greeting, Derringer responded, "I'm fine, Mr. Burnett, how are you?"

"Couldn't be better," Julian answered with a broad smile. "Special day for some people, I guess."

Still wondering what was going on with the young desk clerk, Derringer replied, "I reckon so, them that have a date with the hangman or something better." Julian lingered, still smiling. Derringer was saved by Rachael's return.

"Here's a fresh cup of coffee, Jesse," she said. "We knew Julian would be in looking for his afternoon cup, so Mama just made a fresh pot."

"That's right," Julian said. "Those of us who are hooked on coffee have gotta have it. Right, Mr. Derringer?"

"It's Jesse," Derringer said, "and I can take it or

leave it." He looked at Rachael then and asked, "Is it all right with you if I take this out and sit on the front porch to finish it?"

"Sure is, if you'll bring the cup back when you finish," Rachael said.

"I'll bring it back," he said, and got up and went out the door before Julian came out of the kitchen. *I didn't know that boy was tetched*, he thought. *It's a wonder they let him work at the desk.*

He sat down in one of the rocking chairs on the front porch of the hotel and watched the crowded street while he finished his coffee. He hoped Rachael had not gotten the wrong impression of his asking her to call him Jesse. It just seemed that he had been around Cheyenne long enough to be on a more friendly basis with the people he was constantly in contact with. It occurred to him that he had no close friends or family. His younger brother, Dan, and his wife, Shirley, and their young'uns back in Omaha were the closest thing to a real family. But when he visited them right after leaving the army, although the visit was pleasant, they were obviously frightened to think he might want to settle in with them. He grinned to himself when he remembered how they attempted to hide their relief when he said he couldn't stay. "Well," he sighed, and got up from the rocking chair, "that's as much deep thinkin' as I wanna do. Too much will weaken the brain." He walked back in the front door of the hotel, past the check-in desk where Julian was back at his post. The young clerk grinned at him again and made a motion of proposing a toast with his coffee cup. Jesse returned the salute with a nod of his head, thinking, *He must be drinking something stronger than coffee in that cup.*

He returned his empty coffee cup to the dining room and Cecil Humphrey took it from him. Cecil thanked him for bringing it back. He complained that some customers left them out on the porch after they emptied them. Derringer commiserated with him and said it was inconsiderate of them. He decided then to go to his room and clean his rifle and his handgun, something he had reminded himself to do before leaving town in the morning.

When he opened the door to his room, his eyes went automatically to the one chair in the room and the Henry rifle propped in the corner behind it. Satisfied to see it was there, he turned toward the bed then and was stopped cold by what he saw. It looked like a cake, sitting right in the middle of his bed. "What the hell . . ." he started, and took a quick look around the room. Nothing else was different. The bed had been made and the cake was sitting on top of the blanket. He figured he must be in the wrong room but immediately thought better, for his rifle was there and his saddlebags were on the back of the chair. *Maybe the dining room made me a cake,* he thought. But what for? He took a closer look at the cake and realized there was some writing on it, almost too small to notice, since it appeared to have been scratched in the icing with a sharp object. He bent down close over the cake and read *Happy Birthday.* "Uh, oh," he said, "somebody's gonna be disappointed. They delivered the cake to the wrong room." He decided he'd better tell Julian Burnett about it right away because somebody might be waiting for the cake to celebrate. "Or I could just keep the cake and eat it myself," he japed.

He picked up the cake and took it back to the lobby and placed it on the desk before a grinning Julian Burnett. "Somebody took this to the wrong room," he said. "It's somebody's birthday and they put it in my room."

Julian's grin turned into a look of surprise. "No," he said, "that cake's for you."

"Hell if it is," Derringer replied. "It ain't my birthday. They took it to the wrong room."

"No, what I'm telling you is the man who brought it here said that it was for you. Jesse Derringer, he said, and he went with me to make sure I put it in your room."

"That don't make a bit of sense," Jesse said. "Who brought the cake to the hotel?"

"I didn't know the man," Julian answered. "Nobody I've ever seen before, but he looked like one of those drunks that hang around the saloons. He said he was promised ten dollars to deliver it and that's why he had to make sure it went to your room."

"Who promised him ten dollars?" Jesse asked. "Who sent the cake?"

"He said he didn't know who the man was that gave him the cake." He shrugged and declared, "I guess somebody wanted you to have some cake. You might as well enjoy it."

"I don't think so," Derringer said. "Anybody who goes to that much trouble to keep it a secret must want you to eat a piece of cake pretty bad. I suspect that cake must be loaded with some kind of poison. I'm not gonna eat any and I don't advise you to, but you're welcome to it, if you feel lucky."

"I declare," Julian uttered, "as much as I like cake, I guess I'll pass on this one." He shook his head, truly disappointed.

"Do what you want with it," Derringer said. He still couldn't understand why anybody would send him a cake. It sure as hell wasn't his birthday.

CHAPTER 11

"Are you sure that drunk you picked out took that cake to Derringer's room?" Massey asked Lester as they lay around the campfire Tiny had built. They were all a little grumpy about having to leave Vera's to camp out on the creek below town. This, even though they understood well enough that with what they planned that night, they couldn't very well go running back to Vera's at two or three in the morning. Even Ace understood that would be a bit obvious.

"Yeah, I'm sure," Lester insisted. "How many times are you gonna ask me that? Listen, I'm telling you that feller was so excited about doin' that job for me. He was hopin' to do any other jobs that I needed done. He liked the money I paid. Yes, sir, Mr. Jesse Derringer is in room number six on the first floor. And the quickest way to get to his room is to go in the back door to the hotel, which will take you to the long hallway. We pass by two rooms before we get to number six. I bet we don't spend five minutes gettin' in the hotel, doin' the job, and out of the hotel."

"And that drunk doesn't know your name?"

"I didn't say that," Lester said, which caused an immediate frown on Massey's face. "To be honest with you, I have to admit that we introduced ourselves. His name is Milton Rice and I told him my name." Massey started to explode. "Just before I put a .45 slug in the back of his head," Lester continued. The other men listening to his report broke into an uproar of laughter.

"You . . ." Massey complained. "I oughta shoot you for that." Then he joined in the laughter with the others. "All right, the plan is simple enough. We'll wait till he's had plenty of time to get to sleep, about two or three o'clock in the mornin'. Ace, you can't move too good with that leg, so you'll take care of the horses when we go in to do the job. That's all there is to it. Nothin' complicated about it, just get in, do the job, and get out."

"Doggone it, Jeb, I oughta be in on the shootin' of that sidewinder," Ace complained. "I owe him for that bullet he put in my leg."

"We might have to run outta that hotel pretty fast," Massey told him. "So it'd be better if you stayed with the horses."

"The hardest part is gonna be what to do after the saloon closes and we got all that time to kill before two or three o'clock," Sly said.

"That's what Vera's gals are for," Lester said.

"I'll be damned," Massey responded. "I don't want none of you layin' up with none of them whores. When it's time to go, I don't aim to have to go around draggin' your sleepy butts outta the bed. It ain't a bad idea to get a little sleep if you can, but get it in a bed by yourself, so you really get a little rest. That's the reason we moved out of that room at Vera's and set up this camp by the creek."

"Shoot," Sly said, "I've about run outta that money we got from that bank job in Omaha, anyway. We're gonna have to make another score pretty soon, or we'll be like the rest of these drifters hangin' around here."

"We sure rode a long way to find out they ain't even got a bank in Cheyenne," Tiny said.

"Yeah, but that sign in the window said there was gonna be one comin' soon," Ace reminded him.

"That don't do us a whole lotta good right now, does it?" Sly commented.

"Quit your bellyachin'," Massey said. "There ain't no bank here yet, but that don't mean there ain't no money bein' made. And I've got a couple of places I've been thinking about that oughta be a pretty good payday. Let's get this troublemaker out of the way first, then we'll pick the place for our next withdrawal."

"Well, I ain't had no dinner yet," Lester complained. "I was workin' while the rest of you boys was stuffin' your faces."

Tiny, who was in the process of picking his teeth with a matchstick he had put a point on with his knife, held up a shred of beef he had extracted from between his teeth. "Here, Lester," he said. "Maybe this'll hold you till you can get something at Vera's." He flicked the shred in Lester's direction, but it fell several feet short.

"If that had landed on me, I'da gave you the same thing I gave Milton Rice," Lester told him.

"You'da had to wait till I turned my back on you," Tiny responded.

"Let's not have no fightin', now, ladies," Massey scolded. "Save all that foolishness for Mr. Derringer tonight. Go on and get you something to eat, Lester. I'm gonna take a little walk up to see the mayor to see how business is gettin' along. I'll meet you back at Dawkin's." They all understood his reason. The mayor owned Cheyenne Merchandise, the largest store in town and one of the possible targets for the gang to hit. Massey's purpose in visiting would be to see the way the store was set up, where the money was kept for daily transactions, and where the office was. He would want to know if the big money was in a safe and how many people worked in the store, in case it would be best to rob it in the daytime when the safe might not be locked.

Massey was looking around in Cheyenne Merchandise when someone came in the front door and hurried through the store to the office behind. "Mr. Mayor!" the man exclaimed as he went in the office door. "Somebody found a dead man over near the creek. He'd been shot in the back of the head."

"Who was it?" The mayor asked. "Anybody we know?"

"No, he said it looked like one of them drunks that hang around the saloons."

"Well, what are you telling me for?" the mayor asked. "Why didn't you tell the sheriff?"

"The fellow who found him went to tell the sheriff. I thought you'd wanna know, since we've been talking about the crime here in town and what we can do about it." There were several other customers who overheard the man's announcement and they naturally gathered at the office door to eavesdrop. Massey took advantage of it and joined them.

Seeing the little crowd of nosey customers gathered outside his office door, Mayor Hook got up from his desk and came out to disperse them. They all backed away, except one. Massey remained standing right beside the door. And when the mayor walked past him, Massey took a quick look inside the office and spotted a safe beside the desk. The safe was open. Massey moved quickly back with the spectators then to hear the mayor calmly telling them that he was sure Sheriff Warton and his deputies would investigate the murder in short order. When a couple of the customers went out to the street to see if they could see a body being hauled to the undertaker, Massey joined them. When they discovered there was nothing to see, they went back in the store, but Massey walked back up the street to the saloon.

He found everybody but Lester at what had become their usual table, so he stopped at the bar long enough to get a shot glass from Sam before joining his men. "What was the noise outside?" Sly asked.

"Some jasper yellin' for the sheriff," Massey replied. "They found Lester's friend, Milton, with a hole in the back of his head. I guess he weren't lyin'."

"What about the general merchandise store?" Tiny asked.

"Easy pickin's," Massey said. "He's doin' a helluva business. There's one big cash drawer at the front counter where the two fellers he's got workin' for him do the business. And the office is in the back. He's got a safe, but it was open. Might be best to wait till we're ready to leave and hit it in the daytime, so we don't have to mess with openin' that safe."

"Maybe on a Saturday afternoon," Sly said.

Derringer spent most of the afternoon working on his weapons and picking up a few items he had forgotten to buy before he left for the high country in the morning. When it was time for supper, he left his room and entered the dining room through the hotel entrance, which was in the middle of the hallway his room was on. When he walked in the dining room, Cecil looked up, and seeing who it was, uttered a quick, "Good evening, Jesse." Then he turned around and hurried to the kitchen door and called Rachael.

Rachael came out and stood beside Cecil and they began singing, "Happy birthday to you. Happy birthday to you. Happy birthday, dear Jesse . . ."

That was as far as they got before Rachael broke down in a fit of giggles and Cecil couldn't finish without her support. Never changing the emotionless expression he came into the dining room wearing, Jesse said simply, "It ain't my birthday."

"Are you sure?" Rachael asked between giggles. "You mighta forgot what day this is."

"I was born on September the tenth, thirty years ago," he said. "I remember because I was there when it happened. Now if you'll excuse me, I'd like to get something to eat." He walked around them and went into the kitchen. When Clara turned from the stove to look at him, he said, "Mrs. Bowden, I'd like to have my supper now and I'd like to have a cup of coffee with it, please, ma'am."

"Why, certainly, Mr. Derringer. Is something wrong?"

"No, ma'am," he said. "I was just afraid Rachael might get it mixed up and take it to the wrong table." Then he gave her a big grin and winked. "And the name's Jesse."

She understood what was going on then and smiled. "I'll fix your plate and bring it to you, myself, with a cup of coffee, Jesse."

"What did you do, go tell my mama on me?" Rachael teased when he came out of the kitchen. Cecil had already retreated to his station by the front door.

"My supper is too important to trust to somebody who gets as mixed up as you do," he answered.

"Are you sure you didn't just forget it was your birthday and you're ashamed to admit it?" She chuckled. Obviously Julian had shared the cake story. She got serious then. "Have you found out who sent you the cake yet?"

"No, I haven't got any idea." He gave them a tired smile then.

He went on to enjoy his supper as much as if it was his birthday and he told them so. "Maybe I'll change my birthday to this date from now on."

"Oh, no you don't," Rachael said. "'Cause I'm writing this down on the calendar, September tenth, Jesse

Derringer's birthday. If you're anywhere near Cheyenne on that date you better come to the party."

"Might as well forget it," he told her. "I'll make it a point not to be here on that date."

"What a sourpuss," she said.

Before he finished, Sheriff Warton came into the dining room and, seeing Jesse, came over to join him. He told him about the body found on the path between the creek and the town. Jesse asked if he knew the man's identity. "No," Warton said. "There was still a little bit of snow on the ground down there under all the trees, so there were tracks, footprints, and hoofprints. But it didn't look like there were more than one or two people. The dead man looked to be one of the drunks hanging around town. Whoever shot him put a bullet in the back of his head. Ain't no tellin' why. I doubt the poor beggar had anything worth killin' him for. And the man that shot him had a gun and a horse. Don't make no sense, does it? The no-name section of our new cemetery is gettin' filled up faster than I'd like."

"You're right, it doesn't make much sense," Jesse had to agree. "Just a case of downright meanness, I reckon."

"Cliff Crenshaw said you were plannin' on leavin' town tomorrow," the sheriff said.

"That's right," Jesse replied. "I've been plannin' to leave for the past couple of days and I've changed my mind every time because of the weather. I might make it tomorrow mornin'. I plan to be gone for only a week or maybe two, depending on what I find up through those mountain passes. I'd like to have something to tell General Dodge when he comes back here to continue that railroad."

"Well, I hope you have a good trip," Warton said. "We like havin' you around, so don't stay away too long."

"Thank you, Sheriff, I appreciate that," Jesse responded. He knew the sheriff was all too desperate for anyone with a gun on the side of law and order. "I think I'll go and have a couple of drinks of whiskey and then I'm gonna turn in and maybe leave before breakfast. I ain't makin' no promises to myself."

He got up from the table and Rachael walked him to the door. "You're not really mad at Cecil and me, are you, Jesse?"

"Not a bit," he replied. "I know all about children and their games."

"You dog," she said, and punched him on the shoulder with her fist.

"Don't make me call your mother again," he teased as he went out the door.

He left the hotel and walked through the street still busy with strangers, even though it was already into the evening hours and most of the shops and businesses were closing. Soon, nothing would be open but the saloons and the houses of prostitution, like Vera's Vineyard. When he got to Dawkin's he noticed the usual drunks hanging around in front of the door and he thought of the one who was murdered. He wouldn't have known one was missing, if he hadn't been told. He went inside and paused to look the room over, especially taking notice of the table in the back corner that had become the nightly headquarters for the gang of five drifters. He found himself hoping they would be missing tonight, having decided to move on. But that was not the case. They were all present and it appeared they all had their eyes on him, especially Ace, his leg bandaged and a crutch beside his chair. *I probably should have gone to another saloon tonight,* he thought. But he felt at home in Dawkin's now and had gotten to know Sam pretty well. Besides, he never was one to go out of his way to avoid trouble.

"Evenin', Jesse," Sam greeted him when he walked up to the bar. He set a glass on the bar and poured Jesse's drink without asking his pleasure.

"Evenin'," Jesse returned. "I see your five best customers are still in town. They don't seem to ever run out of money, do they?"

"No, they don't," Sam replied. "The way I had it figured is, I think they'll eventually run out of money, then they'll hold me up and leave town."

"Wouldn't surprise me a-tall," Jesse said, then tossed his drink back.

Sam filled his glass again when he put it back on the bar. "I reckon I'll find out tonight if I was right or not."

"Why do you say that?" Jesse asked. He was aware of all eyes at the table focusing on him, but there didn't seem to be any trouble coming to a boil. *So maybe they've decided to leave me be*, he thought. Although he had to admit that Ace seemed a little more tense than the other four.

"They're leavin' town in the mornin'," Sam answered. "That Massey fellow told me that when they came in tonight." He could see that the news surprised Derringer, so he continued. "They've already checked out of that room they were renting at Vera's next door. Massey said they got their horses outta the stable this afternoon and made a camp down by the creek. Said they might come back after they pay a visit to some friends they've got at an Arapaho village about a dozen miles from here."

Jesse took his time to consider that possibility before he tossed his second drink back. To begin with, he couldn't believe any Indian village would have the likes of Massey and his gang as friends. When Sam got busy with other customers, his mind lingered on Jeb Massey and his boys. They appeared to no longer have any interest in him. That was a good thing, but it surprised him. *Maybe they heard about my "birthday" and that's why there's no challenge*, he joked to himself. He was tempted to delay his trip to the mountains again just to see if Massey really left town. *Maybe they've just run out of money.*

"All right," he finally announced. "That's it for me tonight. I'm goin' back to the hotel and goin' to bed. I'm plannin' on gettin' up early in the mornin' and takin' a little trip and I'll see you in about a week."

"Take care of yourself," Sam told him as he paid for his whiskey and walked out of the saloon.

Overhearing Sam's comment to Derringer, Massey made one of his own. In a quiet voice that only his companions could hear, he said, "Right, Derringer, have a nice little nap." He turned his attention to the plans for the rest of the evening then. Both Lester and Sly were in favor of robbing Cheyenne Merchandise right after the assassination of Jesse Derringer.

"You know we're gonna wake up the whole town when we take care of Derringer," Lester said. "Everybody's gonna come runnin' to the hotel. Won't nobody be watchin' that store. We might as well clean it out while the sheriff and his deputies are at the hotel."

"The fellow that owns that store lives in a house right behind it," Massey said.

"Then we can give him the same as we're gonna give Derringer," Sly said. "It'd just be his bad luck if he shows up in his store."

"We'd still have the problem of openin' that safe," Massey said. "If we wait and hit him in the daytime, the safe will most likely be open. And you know they most likely dump the cash drawer in the safe at night, too."

"Doggone it, Massey," Lester argued, "all it takes is one person to see us take care of Derringer. Then if we show up here again on a Saturday afternoon, there'll be a rifle shootin' at us from every window. Besides, there's probably some dynamite in that store and we could open that safe with that."

"I still think it would be an easier job in the daytime," Massey said. "But, on the off chance some night owl does see us, you might be right about the town people shootin' at us if we came back after tonight for a daytime job. What about you and Ace?" he asked Tiny. "Whaddaya think?"

Tiny shrugged his shoulders. "Whatever you wanna do," he said. Ace just shrugged.

"We'll just see how it goes tonight," Massey decided, "see how the town reacts and decide then, all right?" That seemed to satisfy everybody, so they remained at

Dawkin's until later in the evening. Then they retired to their camp by the creek, where most of them decided to get a couple hours' sleep before visiting the hotel.

It was twenty after two according to Massey's pocket watch when he decided it was time to act. He had not slept, hadn't even tried because of the fear of over-sleeping. He nudged Lester and Sly with the toe of his boot. Both of them became alert immediately, having slept only in short snatches. Only Tiny and Ace were snoring in deep sleep and had to be shaken to wake them. "It's time to get movin'," Massey said, "so get saddled up and check your rifles. We're gonna put so many holes in this coyote that you'll be able to read the newspaper through him."

"I swear, Jeb," Ace pleaded, "we can tie our horses, so they don't run off when the shootin' starts. I wanna be in on the shootin'."

"I already told you, Ace," Massey said. "You might have to calm them horses when they hear all the shootin' we're gonna do. And when we're done, we're gonna be runnin' for our horses and you can't even walk fast with that gimpy leg."

"I'll put in a couple of bullets for ya', Ace," Tiny said.

"Come on," Massey urged, "we're wastin' time."

"What if he has to get up in the middle of it to take a leak?" Lester japed. "You want us to stop shootin' till he gets back in the bed?"

"Put enough holes in him and he won't have to get up to go," Sly said.

They climbed on their horses, leaving their pack-horses tied by the stream, to be picked up on their escape straight up the creek. Massey led the column of riders up through the trees until reaching the road into town. It was a clear, moonlit night, although the moon was already getting low in the sky as the silent column of assassins walked their horses behind the buildings leading up to the hotel. When they reached the back of the hotel, they dismounted and led the horses up closer to the grassy area near the outbuildings. Ace took charge of the horses then. Not a sound came from any part of the hotel. "Tiny, you're tall enough to look in those windows on the ground floor. Go over to that side and count to the third window from this end. That's the room he's in. Maybe you can see if he's in the bed." Tiny nodded and started toward the building. "Third window," Massey repeated. The big man nodded.

CHAPTER 12

They watched from behind a smokehouse as Tiny crept along the side of the hotel until coming to the third window. He was just tall enough to get his chin level with the windowsill, so he stood on his tiptoes beside the window, then slowly eased over until he could look in the window. He remained there for what seemed a long time to the four anxiously watching from the smokehouse. Finally, he turned and hustled back to report. "He's in the bed, sleepin' like a baby," Tiny said.

"All right," Massey said. "Let's go send him back to where he came from. Sly, you got that steel bar? I expect they keep that door locked at night. See if you can get it open without wakin' up everybody in the hotel. If we can't, we'll have to shoot him through the window and that'll be a whole lot harder and give him a chance to roll off the bed. And I don't want him to get any chance to get to his guns."

Moving as quietly as possible, the four men hurried across the backyard of the hotel to reach the back door.

Lester, the first to get there, carefully tried the door-knob and found to his surprise that it turned and the door opened when he pushed it. "It ain't locked," he informed the others with a whisper after opening it only an inch or two, thinking it possibly a trap.

They all hesitated for a few seconds, then Massey whispered, "They must leave it unlocked, so the folks who don't like to use the chamber pot can go to the outhouse. Go ahead and push it open," he whispered then, and stepped back beside the door in case he was wrong.

Trusting him, Lester pushed the door open wide. The faint screech of the hinges sounded like the screech of a hawk to the intruders entering the dark hallway. They paused, huddled against the wall, in case the noisy hinges were as loud as they sounded to them. When the hallway remained dead silent, they crept along the wall, the only light that shone through the open door, until they reached the third door. Then, just to be doubly certain, Massey struck a match so he could see the number six on the door. He blew the match out and clutched his rifle tightly in one hand while he slowly turned the doorknob and pushed. He was not surprised when the door wouldn't open. "Everybody ready?" he whispered. They all responded, so he looked at Tiny and said, "Open the door."

The others backed away to give him room. Then Tiny took one big step toward the door and kicked it wide open with his boot, leading the assault into the room and firing the first shot into the sleeping occupant. It was followed by an explosion of gunfire as round after round was fired into the defenseless body that jerked and quivered under the blanket ripped with bullet holes. There was only the light of the muzzle flashes of the rifles, but there was no doubt the job was done. "That's enough!" Massey shouted to be heard over the gunfire. "Get the hell out of here right now!" Their escape counted on the slow response from anyone in the hotel. Sly was the first man out of the room. He made it to the open back door in the hallway before being struck down by a shot in the back. Tiny followed him and caught a shot in his chest when he tried to turn around and run back into the room.

"It's a trap!" Lester yelled, and hurried to the window with Massey right behind him. Fortunately, the window opened easily, so he stuck his head out and, seeing no one outside, scrambled out with help from a push by Massey, who was in a panic to follow.

Back at the head of the dark hallway, where he had sat with his Henry rifle, waiting for the attack he decided wasn't going to come, Derringer got up to give chase. Knowing he had to hurry, he checked his room first and saw right away that the other two had gone out the window. He knew that he would have had a good chance to get all four of them if he had shot them when they came in the back door. But his conscience wouldn't let him kill them until after they proved they had come to kill him. The bed they left shot to pieces served to prove they had not come to pay a friendly visit. Too bad he was left with three to chase. He would have liked to close the door on this chapter of his life. Cocking his rifle as he ran, he went out the back door into the yard, where he saw the two men running for their horses and another one on horseback.

The man on the horse saw him and started toward him, firing his handgun at him. Derringer recognized him as the one called Ace seconds before he knocked him out of the saddle with a shot from his Henry. Thanks to Ace Barnes's attempt to stop Derringer, Massey and Lester had time to get on their horses. "Grab the other horses!" Massey shouted, and they both grabbed the reins of a horse and galloped out of the hotel's backyard, leading Sly's and Tiny's horses.

With no concern for the fully awakened hotel coming to life after the barrage of gunfire, Derringer was in the process of calming Ace's horse, since his horse was in the stable. It took a few minutes to corner the frightened buckskin gelding, but he managed to finally, then he climbed aboard and rode after the would-be assassins. He started the buckskin in the general direction his two targets had taken, hoping the horse could follow the other four horses. The moon had disappeared by then and it was a dark trail he sought to follow. It led behind the buildings on the main street, but then he lost it right away when it came out on the road. It was too dark to see which tracks were fresh and which were not. He realized he was wasting his time riding around in the dark, but he was not willing to give up on tracking the two assassins down. He would wait until morning and try to pick up their trail. It should be a trail left by a small herd of horses, since they took the other two men's horses. And they must have had some packhorses. He admitted to himself that there was a slim chance of success, but he was determined to give it a try. It was not the first time someone had tried to kill him, but the fact that they had attempted such a brutal plan to totally destroy him made him want to return the sentiment.

The business with the mysterious birthday cake had started him thinking. He wondered what the purpose for the cake could actually be. Then when he remembered that the man who delivered the cake insisted on taking it to his room, instead of just letting Julian take it, he wondered why. Then it struck him that the delivery man now knew what room he was in. And when a drunk turned up dead, it occurred to him that the drunk was the man who delivered the cake. He had felt pretty sure then that he was going to have visitors.

He turned Ace's horse around and rode back to the hotel. It was well lit up by that time, with a lamp glowing in almost every window. He went to the back of the hotel and tied the horse there while he went inside to tell the sheriff what happened, if he hadn't figured it out yet. "Damn, Derringer!" the sheriff exclaimed when he turned to see who had come into the room. "I'm tickled to see you. Julian said this was your room. So I figured those two in the hall out there were your doin'." Jesse nodded. "That one out in the backyard, too?" the sheriff asked, and Jesse nodded again. "You got any idea why they decided to execute you like that?" He pointed to the destroyed bed.

"They didn't like me?" Derringer asked, innocently.

"That was my first guess," Deputy Sheriff Crenshaw offered. He was standing by the window holding a piece of a small mirror that had been shattered by a ricochet. "Now you got nine years bad luck, too."

"I didn't break the mirror," Derringer said. He looked

at the other man in the room, Bob Wolfe, the night clerk. "I wasn't in the room when it got broken."

"It's a good thing you weren't," Bob said. "I was asleep on the cot in the back of the office when it sounded like the whole building was blowin' up. Don't you worry, I can move you to another room. It'll be upstairs. Is that all right? General Dodge said to take good care of you."

"'Preciate it, Bob. That'll be fine," Derringer said.

"The three dead men are part of that gang that's been hangin' around Dawkin's Saloon," the sheriff said. "I've been wonderin' when we were gonna see some sign of real trouble outta them. Why did they come after you? Was it all because of that little affair you had with the one they called Ace? Why did they make such a big execution out of it, instead of just a simple shot in the back?"

"I can't say for sure," Derringer replied. "I have had a little run-in with them before." He told the sheriff about the stand-off at the caboose of the train as well as the incident with Alvin Crowe and his sons. "They were friends of those five men. By the way, I expect one of those five was the killer of that drunk you found with a hole in the back of his head." Then he went on to tell him about the birthday cake business.

"I reckon I should say I'm sorry you've had to deal with those five outlaws," the sheriff said. "But I'm glad three of 'em are dead and the other two have left town. Too bad they got away with it, but my jurisdiction ends at the city limits."

"Mine doesn't," Derringer said. "I think I'll see if I

can pick up their trail when it gets daylight. I don't expect much, but I think it deserves a look. I was already plannin' to do some scoutin' up toward the end of the railway, but I think I'll see if I can pick up their trail instead. We didn't get any rain or snow last night, so maybe the tracks are still there."

"I think you ought to count your lucky stars you got by this trap," the sheriff said. "You better watch yourself if you pick up their trail."

"I'll do that, for sure," Derringer said, and turned to meet Bob Wolfe coming back with a new room key. "Thanks for your trouble, Bob."

"Weren't no trouble a-tall," Bob replied. "Room twelve upstairs, right on top of this one. Feller that was rentin' it died last week."

Crenshaw looked at Derringer and chuckled. "You oughta feel right at home there, Jesse."

Bob stood there for a moment longer before he said, "I was gonna help you move your stuff to your new room, but I don't see anything here. Did those men who shot up the room steal your belongings?"

Derringer laughed then. "No, most of my stuff is at the stable with my horses, since I was all ready to ride out in the mornin'. I didn't have anything left in the room but my saddlebags and I'm gonna take them with me. But thanks for offering."

"You goin' without no sleep?" Crenshaw asked.

"I caught a couple hours earlier before I moved out to wait in the hall," Derringer said. "I'm seriously thinking about waitin' till Clara gets cranked up in the mornin' and get something to eat before I head out, though." As soon as he said it, he knew he wouldn't wait that long before going after them. They had put too much distance between him and them already and he couldn't afford to let them put more. He had to figure they were bold enough to think they could execute him in such a wild matter, then return to their camp and no one could prove they had anything to do with it. There would be no witnesses to say so.

Now that the whole execution plan had blown up in their faces, there were only two of them left and they had to run. But where would they run to, he had to wonder? Cheyenne was in the middle of nowhere. There were no towns of any size within hundreds of miles. They could have fled in any direction and that's why he knew he had to be at the place where he lost them tonight at first light in the morning. With that settled in his mind, he said, "I'll bid you gentlemen good night now. I'm going to catch a couple hours' sleep before daylight."

He surprised himself by actually sleeping for a couple of hours and when he awakened, the darkness was just beginning to fade away. So he got up from the bed and pulled his boots on. He had not bothered to undress, so he strapped his gun belt on, pulled on his hat and coat, picked up his saddlebags and rifle, and went out the door. He went down the steps to the back hallway. And when he walked past the door to the dining room, he tried it but found it locked and there were no sounds that would indicate Clara had even started breakfast. So he continued down the hall past his old room, which was still a mess, but at least the bodies of the two men he shot were gone. He knew Leon would be at his stable by five and he could probably get a cup of coffee there. "Easy, boy," he said upon approaching the buckskin horse he had left tied at the corner of the smokehouse. The horse gave no sign of resentment after having been tied there for a couple of hours. "I couldn't take you to the stable while I was sleepin', but it wasn't that long. And if I'd tied you to the water trough in front of the hotel, somebody woulda stole you. So we're goin' straight to the stable and you can get water there." The buckskin made no move to resist when he got in the saddle and they went up the street to the stable.

When they rode up to the stable, they found the barn door open and Leon inside with his small stove already cranked up with a coffeepot on it. "Good mornin'," Jesse called out as he approached the open door, so as not to startle him.

"Jesse?" Leon returned, not recognizing the horse. "Is that you?"

"Yep," Jesse replied. "I need to pick up my horses and leave this one with you. He needs some water, so I'll put him in the corral for you."

"Where'd you pick up that horse?" Leon asked. "Has it got anything to do with all the shootin' I heard in the middle of the night?"

"Matter of fact," Jesse answered, "you oughta recognize him. He was here in the stable with the other horses you were tending for those five gentlemen that were stayin' at Vera's."

"I swear, I knew they musta been up to somethin'

when they come and got their horses and said they was gonna camp down by the creek. What did they do?"

"Well, for some reason, they tried to shoot me, but their plan didn't work like it was supposed to and three of 'em got shot and two of 'em got away."

"Well, I'll be . . ." Leon responded. "So that was what all that shootin' was. I reckon you musta been mighty lucky."

"I reckon I was," Jesse said. "I hope you put enough water in that pot to sell me a cup of it."

"I reckon I did," Leon replied. "I filled it up, just like I always do. But I charge five dollars a cup when I sell it. So I reckon I'll have to give you a cup." He paused and grinned. "But only if you tell me all the details about that shootin'."

"I've got to get my horses saddled and ready to ride," Jesse told him. "I've gotta see if I can pick up the trail of those two that got away and see if there's any chance I can catch up with 'em. I'll tell you all about it while I'm drinkin' that expensive coffee."

With his horses ready to ride, they drank a cup of coffee that Jesse decided was about the rankest he had ever tasted. The weakness of it suggested to him that it had been boiled with the same grounds as the pot before this one. He thanked Leon for it anyway, and climbed on Clem just as the first rays of the sun broke through the trees. Leaving the stable, he rode straight to the spot on the road where he had given up the search. As he had hoped, there were tracks from the four horses that were definitely fresher than the older tracks on the road. They had to be the right tracks. He was able to follow them for the short distance they were on the road before they left it and rode down through the trees to the creek. *This was where they made their camp*, he thought right away. He didn't have to search very long for the tracks that told him which way they left the creek. He watched the tracks very carefully, thinking they could have run in any direction because there were no towns close to Cheyenne in any direction.

He stopped to be sure when the tracks seemed to be heading in the direction of the train station, then as he continued he wondered if they were thinking about returning to the hotel looking to settle with him. Surely, he thought, they were going to leave their small herd of horses somewhere before they came after him again. But when the trail reached the railroad tracks, they turned to the west and followed the train tracks toward Sherman Hill. *They're heading for the mountains,* he thought. Then it occurred to him; there was one town close to Cheyenne he had not considered—Laramie City. At least that's what they were calling the little tent town on the Laramie River near the Overland Stage Line route. He reprimanded himself for not having thought of it before. The one time he had been to Laramie City had been when he was riding for General Dodge during the Indian Wars. It was a tent town then with no permanent buildings. But that might likely have changed, since it was known that the railroad would soon be there. Laramie City would more likely be the destination for a couple of outlaws on the run for the same reason they were attracted to Cheyenne. Thinking back, he tried to estimate how far Laramie City was from Cheyenne. Somewhere around fifty or sixty miles as best he could recall and not a particularly easy trip, starting with Sherman Hill. *That's where they're heading,* he decided when their tracks continued to follow the railroad west. *Their plans having been blown apart in Cheyenne, they're going to start over in Laramie,* he told himself. With a little bit more to go on now than tracks that might get lost at any creek crossing, he continued on, hoping to overtake them before they reached Laramie. He looked up at the sky to check the weather. It looked favorable with a few clouds in a mostly clear sky. There were probably more clouds over the mountains but no sign of a real snowstorm.

Due to the construction of the railroad tracks, Massey and Lester had a wide path to follow out of Cheyenne in the middle of the night. It was still difficult with all the extra horses they were determined to hang on to, Derringer speculated. They did not stop to rest their horses until they reached Sherman Hill, which was about nineteen miles from Cheyenne. They were forced to rest them at that point because of the difficult terrain from that point onward to Laramie City. They were obviously concerned about a possible posse coming after them, being unaware of the sheriff's attitude when it came to his jurisdiction. He could only guess if they had any concern for him tracking them. He was sure his two horses were ready for a rest, too, so he brought the smoldering fire back to life and fed it some wood to revive it. Then he went to the stream to fill his coffeepot. While it was boiling, he cut some strips of bacon and a couple of large crackers to fry in the bacon grease and dust with brown sugar and he would call it breakfast. When he finished eating, he cleaned up his coffeepot and frying pan and put them back in his packs. Trusting Clem to alert him if he had any visitors, he sat down with his back against a tree and closed his eyes for a little while. Laramie City was still a good thirty miles away, so he would be stopping once or possibly twice before he reached it. There was no telling what condition the trail up the hill was in after the heavy snows. Dale Creek Ravine, a wide valley the engineers were going to build a massive trestle across, would be his next concern. He would have to cross that before climbing up in the hills to Laramie City. That was his last thought before drifting off to sleep.

CHAPTER 13

He was awakened by the sound of Clem snuffling around him and nudging his leg. When he opened his eyes, he had to blink several times before he realized he was covered with a light blanket of snow. His first thought was that there would no longer be any tracks to follow. He looked up at the sky and decided it had just been a small snow shower and didn't look like a heavy cloud cover. "Doggone it, Clem," he told the horse, "why didn't you wake me up when it started to snow?" He put his arms around the horse's neck and let the big gray gelding pull him up to his feet. "Hell, I don't need the tracks, anyway. They're on the way to Laramie City and I know how to get there." He saddled Clem and loaded his packs back on the sorrel and headed for the Laramie River. Once he struck the river, he could follow it to Laramie City.

* * *

It was the middle of the afternoon when he came to the stable at the end of the main street through the middle of Laramie City. There were quite a few horses in the corral, but since he could not identify them, he started to pass them by. "Howdy," a man sang out from the stable door, however, evidently seeing him pause a few moments. "You need to stable your horses?"

"Howdy," Derringer returned. "I don't know for sure. I might. It depends on whether the two fellows I'm trying to catch up with stay in town tonight. Two strangers leave a bunch of horses with you today?"

The man's smile faded immediately as if suddenly worried. "As a matter of fact, they did," he said. "They was sellin' horses and I bought five horses off of 'em, fair and square, cash money."

Derringer smiled. "Don't worry, I didn't say they were horse thieves. I hope you made a good deal. I'm just trying to catch up with them."

The man relaxed at once. "Glad to hear you say that. I got 'em for a mighty good price, so for a minute there you had me worried. Them two fellers said they was gonna go buy a drink of likker with some of the money I paid 'em. I don't know where they went. There's two saloons in town now. One of 'em's called The Baby Doll Saloon. It's the newest one; the other one is Moyer's Saloon." He paused to look over his shoulder as if making sure no one heard him. "Most of the town folks call it the Bucket of Blood Saloon, on account of that's where most of the gamblin' and the gunfights happen."

"'Preciate the warnin'," Derringer said. "I'll be real careful if I have to look in that one." It occurred to him then to ask another question. "Is there a town marshal and a jail?"

"Yep, we got a town marshal. His name's Big Steve Long and him and his two half brothers own the Bucket of Blood."

Derringer gave that a moment's thought before he asked, "And you say that's where most of the gambling and shooting happens?"

The man nodded slowly and answered. "Big Steve does most of the shooting." Derringer nodded slowly then. He thanked him for the information, gave Clem a nudge, and continued riding down the main street.

Many of the shops and businesses were still working out of tents, but there were also some buildings made with logs and a couple built with lumber from a sawmill. The Bucket of Blood was partially a wood-framed building with a huge tent on the front. He wondered if the town would soon be overrun with people when the railroad came like Cheyenne had been. He realized that he had to make a decision as to what he was going to do when he found the two men. He was not a lawman. He admitted to himself that he was coming after them because they had tried to kill him. So his mission was simply to find them and kill them, but somehow it didn't seem like the civilized action to take. If he captured them, he would take them back to Cheyenne and they would surely be lynched by the vigilance committee. But if he shot them without giving any warning, it would be judged as premeditated murder. He had given no thought toward taking them back to Cheyenne. He didn't want the bother of it. He wanted it finished wherever he found them.

His first stop was The Baby Doll Saloon because it was the first one he came to. Looking up the street, he could see that the other saloon was quite a bit busier than The Baby Doll. He had a notion that it was the place Massey and his partner would more likely be attracted to, but he thought he might as well check on The Baby Doll to verify his assumption. The saloon was small enough for him to see the whole room from the doorway. So he stood in the door and scanned the small crowd of patrons for only a minute before turning around and climbing back on his horse. Then he proceeded on to the Bucket of Blood.

He pulled his horses up beside two other horses, both of which had a packhorse attached with a rope from the saddle. They had to be the horses he followed because of the obvious signs of a recent hard ride. He dismounted, pulling his Henry rifle out of the saddle scabbard as he did, checked to make sure there was a round in the chamber, then looped his reins over the rail. As he stepped up on the boardwalk in front of the door, he realized that he had still not decided the question of kill or capture, unaware that the decision was not his to make.

He opened the door and stepped inside, pausing there to survey the crowded barroom. It was for only a moment, however, before the noisy din of the saloon was penetrated by the cry of a startled man, followed by the sharp crack of a Colt .45 and the smash of a window behind him. With no time to think, Derringer raised his rifle and fired one shot that struck the man he recognized as Lester Bostic in the chest. Knowing another shot was coming, he dropped to one knee while he levered another cartridge in the chamber and fired at the same instant he heard Massey's shot pass over his head. Standing alone now, since all those who had been around him had scattered to take cover, Massey looked down at the hole in his shirt. He staggered a few steps backward and tried to raise the .45 again, but it dropped out of his hand and he sank to the floor. "Derringer," he uttered as he dropped.

When there were no more shots fired, the buzz of conversation began again, but all eyes were on the ominous stranger standing at the front of the saloon. "What did he say after he got shot?" someone asked, one who had been standing close enough to Massey to hear him speak before he dropped.

"He said Derringer," a man who had been standing right beside him answered.

"Derringer?" another man questioned. "Hell, it was a Henry rifle."

"Somebody better go get Big Steve," someone else said. It was unnecessary, however, for the big town marshal walked into the saloon through the back door, having heard the shots fired.

"What happened here, Roy?" the marshal asked the bartender. "Who's the feller with the rifle?"

"Ain't got no idea," Roy answered. "He just walked in the door a few minutes ago and that feller over yonder pulled his gun and shot at him." He pointed to Lester's body. "He missed, so the feller with the rifle shot him." Roy pointed to Massey's body then. "Then that feller pulled his gun and took a shot at him and he missed, so the feller with the rifle shot him, too."

"You know who they are?" Big Steve asked.

"No," Roy said. "The two dead ones just hit town this mornin' and that feller just now showed up. It 'pears they all knew each other, but they was strangers to me."

"All three strangers, huh?" Big Steve replied, and he walked toward the front door to confront Derringer. "What's your name, stranger?"

"Jesse Derringer," he answered.

"Derringer," the marshal repeated. "Like the pistol?"

"Yeah, like the pistol," Jesse said.

"Well, Derringer like the pistol, I'm the town marshal and I'm gonna have to ask you for that rifle."

"What for?" Jesse asked. "You heard what the bartender said. All I did was walk in the door and the first one pulled his gun and shot at me, so I shot him in self-defense. Then the other one decided he'd take a shot at me and he missed, so I shot him. Everybody in here can tell you the same thing. Both men were shot in self-defense."

The oversized marshal seemed perplexed by the stranger's calm attitude. After a brief pause, he said, "Like I said, I'm the town marshal and I'm gonna have to take that rifle while you're in my town."

Deadly calm, Derringer said, "I'm afraid not, Marshal. I'm a law-abiding man, but I haven't been in your town an hour yet and already I've been shot at twice. I think I'd best keep my rifle to protect myself." It was obvious to Derringer that the marshal was accustomed to total authority, but he also knew he was not willing to risk giving up his rifle. "I don't plan to stay in your town very long, so I'll be on my way right after I find something to eat."

Not at all accustomed to being challenged, Big Steve wasn't ready to accept defeat. "There's also a matter of some money for damages here. Somebody's got to pay for that broken window behind you."

"You'll have to see if that first body over there has any money on him. He's the one who broke the window." He pointed to Lester's body. "And I expect there's a bullet hole in the door somewhere that the other fellow is responsible for. Both of my bullets are in the bodies, so they didn't do any damage to the building. So I'm pretty sure I didn't do any damage at all." He paused a moment, then added, "Unless you folks are cannibals and you figure I've spoiled the meat."

Big Steve was at a loss for something to say and he was very much aware that he was being made to look like a fool by this stranger. The only card he had left to play was the fact that Derringer had said he was leaving town right after he got something to eat. So he said, "All right, but don't let sunset catch you in Laramie City and don't come back."

"Whatever you say, Marshal." He turned halfway around, not feeling he was willing to completely turn his back on the marshal, and eased himself outside. He climbed up into the saddle and turned Clem away from the hitching rail to go back the way he had ridden into town.

When he had popped in to take a look at The Baby Doll Saloon, he had noticed a small sign that said EATS. He figured there was no restaurant, so he decided to gamble on the saloon because he was feeling pretty hungry and anything would be better than the bacon and hardtack he had in his packs. His gamble paid off because he was able to buy a sizable bowl of beans and rice and chopped beef for twenty-five cents plus a nickel for a cup of coffee. He was able to appreciate the luck that rode with him that day, especially when both Massey and Lester were too startled to take their time and shoot straight. By any odds, Massey should have been able to kill him when he returned Lester's shot. He was also happy that he had not had the burden of transporting those two outlaws all the way back to Cheyenne. He felt good enough to buy a drink of whiskey after his supper. And when the bartender asked if he wanted another, he answered, "I reckon not. The marshal ordered me to get out of town before sundown and I wouldn't wanna make him mad."

"Where you headed?" the bartender asked, not really interested.

"Cheyenne," Derringer answered, "so I'd better get started."

He didn't take much notice of the three men seated at a table by the door because they came in right after he did. They, on the other hand, had taken unusual interest in the stranger they had seen in the Bucket of Blood, who handled a Henry rifle so well. "Derringer, he said his name was," Curley George commented. "Wonder if that's his real name, or just one he calls hisself."

"Maybe he carries a Derringer," Red Pickens said. "But it's outright obvious that 1860 Henry is his choice of weapons."

"He didn't act like he was worried about Big Steve, did he?" Curley said. "Kinda told him straight out that he wouldn't be handin' that rifle over to nobody."

Coy Moffat chuckled. "He talked like he didn't know where he was, or if he ever heard of Big Steve Long. You reckon he just rode into town to kill them two fellers? He might be a deputy marshal."

"More like a bounty hunter, I'd say," Curley said.

"Nah," Red disagreed. "If he was a bounty hunter, he'da took them two bodies with him to collect the bounty. He's just a paid killer. Hell, them two fellers just rode into town and he showed up the same day, walked in the saloon and shot both of 'em. Most likely already been paid to go after 'em, or maybe just paid half of his money. Now he's ridin' right outta town again, on his way back to collect the other half of his pay. He told Sid he was headin' to Cheyenne. I'd like to wait till he collects the other half of his money, but I don't wanna ride all the way to Cheyenne to get it."

"I swear, you've convinced me," Curley said. "Let's follow that sidewinder and see if he's totin' enough money to buy a drink at the Bucket of Blood."

"Even if he's broke, he's ridin' a good-lookin' gray," Coy reminded them. "That packhorse looks like it's in good shape, too, and that Henry rifle's worth some money. I always wanted me one of them rifles."

"We're gonna have to cut the cards to see who gets that rifle," Red declared. "Shoot, there ain't no tellin' what that boy might be carryin' in them packs."

"I sure would like to see that, myself," Curley said, "but we better be careful how we handle that coyote. You saw the way he cut them two strangers down when they tried to ambush him when he walked in the saloon. He looks big as a bear, but he reacted quicker'n a bobcat when that first feller shot at him."

"Yeah, but his quick reactions ain't worth a dime if that feller hadn't missed," Red pointed out. "Let's don't make him up to be something he ain't. One bullet in the back really slows down a gunslinger's reactions." He looked from Curley back to Coy and asked, "Whaddaya say? We goin' after him?"

"Suits me," Coy answered. "We gotta do something. I'm down to my last dollar."

"I'm ready," Curley said. "If he's goin' to Cheyenne, he'll be headin' down the river. We'd best not let him get too far ahead of us before he leaves the river. There's a couple of trails that head in the direction of Cheyenne. We need to see which one he takes."

"As late in the day as it is, he ought not ride very far before he stops to camp for the night," Red said. "So we ain't gonna be ridin' half the night to get back here." They got up from the table and walked outside The Baby Doll where they stood in front and watched the lone rider and packhorse following the path beside the river until the image began to become smaller and smaller. "Better not let him get too far ahead," Red advised, "in case he takes some cutoff we don't know about." So they climbed on their horses and set out after him, holding their horses to a walking pace that looked about as fast as the pace they saw him walking. After about a quarter of an hour with no sight of Derringer, they increased their pace until they got a glimpse of him through the trees ahead, so they reined their horses back to let him gradually disappear again. Then they tried to hold that pace with one of them loping ahead occasionally to catch sight of their prey before falling back again.

They continued this procedure until the sun began to sink below the hills before them and the shadows began to deepen in the trees on each side of the path. "When the hell is he gonna stop to make his camp?" Coy complained. "When that sun drops below that mountain behind us, it's gonna be dark as sin."

"It looks like we might be comin' to some kind of water up ahead," Red said. "He'll most likely stop there. It's about the first place with water since we left the river."

Up ahead of the three outlaws, Derringer maintained a steady pace, only reining Clem back to slow down occasionally to see if the riders were still following him. He was first aware of them after leaving Laramie City. He had ridden about two miles when he looked behind him to see if his packhorse was all right. It was just a quick glimpse of a rider before it disappeared. He wondered if someone was overtaking him or following him. Either one could spell trouble, so he reached into his saddlebags and found his shaving mirror. He slowed his pace then, holding the mirror in front of him until a faint image came into view. It was not very clear but he was sure it was a horse and rider and it backed away again. So he was not being overtaken, but he was being followed. Since he was riding toward the east, he had to be careful to use the mirror when there were tree limbs shielding him and preventing a flash of sunlight from reflecting from it. Consequently, he never got enough of a picture to tell if it was one rider following him or more. He guessed that whoever it was probably would wait for him to make camp before planning to surprise him. And judging by the increased density of the trees about a quarter of a mile ahead, there was probably some source of water and a place to camp as well. He was sure when he reached it, he would remember it, having just passed it on his way to Laramie earlier in the day. The first thing he had to determine was how many he had to deal with, so while he still had a little distance between him and the camping spot, he turned off the trail and rode up the slope beside it.

It was already getting dark in the trees on the slope as the sun sank lower in the west, so he climbed up the slope until he found a good spot to tie his horses. After he tied them, he went back down the slope, looking for a place where he could watch the trail. He didn't have to wait long before they showed up. There were three of them and he noted that they had no packhorses. *They're intending to use my packhorse*, he thought. *Looks like supper's going to be late, boys. I'm glad I already had mine.* They were slowing down as they approached the creek ahead of them. He could hear them talking, but not well enough to know what they were saying, even though he was keeping pace with them as he moved beside the trail on foot. The sun finally dropped out of sight behind them, leaving them in total darkness.

"Where the hell is he?" Curley whispered. "I can't see squat. Is he fixin' to stop?"

"I don't know," Red answered. "I can't see him either. He's gotta be down there at the creek, most likely takin' care of his horses. We'd best just wait right here until he gets through with the horses. I expect he'll make him a fire pretty quick."

"I hope he makes a good one," Coy said. "There's a little bite in that wind."

The lone man on foot, watching them from the trees close to the trail, was frankly puzzled by their hesitation. When they were three against his one, why didn't they rush the creek in an attempt to surprise him? He had no way of knowing the reason was because they had witnessed the incident in the Bucket of Blood when two other men had attempted to surprise him and paid a dear price as a result. So all four men waited, until the three assassins decided Derringer must not have stopped to make camp.

"You reckon he's just gonna ride all night?" Curley wondered. "He's gotta stop and rest his horses or he's gonna be on foot."

"Well, we can't stand here all night," Red declared. "One of us oughta go on down to the creek and see what he's doin'." When neither of his two companions seemed too keen about the idea, he said, "Hell, I'll do it." He climbed back on his horse and began a slow walk toward the creek. After a long few minutes they heard a shout from him. "He ain't here! Come on!"

They got on their horses and went on down to the creek. When they did, Derringer came out of the trees and trotted down the trail after them. His rifle in hand, he could have easily shot both men in the back before they had any idea they were in danger. But he was reluctant to kill three small-time bandits outright, even though he was sure they held no reservations when it came to killing him. He would not hesitate to kill if he was attacked, but if he could find a way to get rid of these three without having to kill them, that would be his choice. At the moment, he was not sure how he could accomplish that.

He hurried along the path, and as he did, he realized what a foolish chance he was taking. He was on foot, stalking three men on horses, and he was not certain he could quickly find his own horses if he needed them in a hurry. When he approached the creek, all three men were sitting on their horses in the middle of it. So he stepped off the trail into the cover of the trees again, so he could get close enough to hear what they were going to do.

"He's crazy," Curley George declared. "There ain't no better place to camp than right here. He's gonna break his horses down and break ours down, too. He's crazy," he repeated, "and I'm sayin' to hell with him. I'm goin' back to Laramie City."

"Curley's right," Coy Moffat said. "That man's bad news. I say we go on back to town. It was a good idea, but that feller's dangerous."

"Well, I say it's still a good idea," Red replied. "I ain't turnin' tail and runnin' just 'cause the man ain't got enough sense to stop to rest and water his horses. You two go on back. I'm gonna catch that buzzard and I'll buy you a drink at the Bucket of Blood and let you admire that Henry rifle."

"Now you're as crazy as he is," Curley said. "You keep after him tonight and he'll break your horse down, too."

"I ain't goin' after him tonight," Red told him. "I'm gonna stay right here tonight, get me some shut-eye and rest my horse up good. Then tomorrow mornin', I'm gonna hit the saddle early and I'll likely catch that crazy sidewinder walking beside his horse. So how 'bout it? Wanna change your mind now?"

"Shoot no," Curley said. "Come on, Coy, we'll stop to water the horses at the river and be back in town before the saloon closes."

"See ya later, Red," Coy said. He and Curley turned their horses back toward the way they had come. "Hope he ain't waitin' up ahead somewhere to ambush you."

Red smiled as he watched them ride away, satisfied that he had what he considered a damn good chance of catching this rattlesnake probably by tomorrow afternoon. There would be no three-way split with his two partners. He really hoped that when he caught up with him, he wouldn't find that gray horse he was riding with a broken wind. The rattlesnake he had in mind withdrew from the trees by the creek where he had been watching and started walking back on the trail behind the two outlaws, who were soon out of sight in the darkness. He was going to count himself lucky if he found the two horses he left tied on the side of the slope.

Red had enough with him in his saddlebags to boil a small pot of coffee to go with some beef jerky, and his bedroll was behind his saddle. So he built a small fire on the creek bank and tied his horse down near the water's edge where the dun gelding could drink water and graze on the grass and small plants. After he ate his meager supper, he spread his bedroll down under a rise in the creek bank, in case he had any visitors during the night. It took a little while, but he eventually dozed off to sleep.

He slept like a rock, awakened in the morning by the sunlight filtering through the branches of the trees overhead and the sound of birds chittering to each other near the water. He lay there for a few minutes, reluctant to get out of his bedroll, until he reminded himself that he had a good ride ahead of him. With no thought of coffee before he got in the saddle, he picked it up only to discover there was no horse to put the saddle on. Stunned for several moments, he then told himself to calm down. His horse had somehow gotten loose and would not be far away. But then he discovered boot tracks in the soft sand at the water's edge, tracks that were bigger than tracks left by his own boots. He was struck by the thought that he had been lying there asleep and defenseless while someone had walked into his camp and stolen his horse. They had left him unharmed, which he could not understand. It had to be the man he was stalking. If it was an Indian, he would not have awakened and his scalp would be gone. He put his hand up on top of his head to verify it, thinking maybe he was dead but just then aware of it. He had never been dead before, so he wasn't sure. He quickly rubbed his chest and stomach to make sure he could feel his body and grasped his neck with his hand to make sure his throat wasn't cut. By all indications, he was alive. But then another thought caused him to look all around him to see if the man they had followed was watching him just before his execution. He was relieved to find he was alone but maybe twenty or twenty-five miles from Laramie City and on foot. He was not a smart man, but he realized his options were reduced to one. So he picked up his saddle and started walking back to Laramie City. His saddle would make it only halfway back before he would reluctantly abandon it.

He placed it behind a sizable tree and tried to cover it with dead branches and leaves. After he trudged on for about fifty yards, he stopped and turned around, so he could get a good look at the place where he had hidden the saddle. He was immediately distressed to discover that he was not sure which tree was the one he had chosen. Then he realized that he might not recognize this particular segment of the trail to be any different from a hundred other segments.

CHAPTER 14

Due to the unforeseen delay in Derringer's trip back, he arrived in Cheyenne with barely enough time to make the hotel dining room before it closed for supper. So he made no stops when he reached town before going to the dining room. His most urgent desire was for a good meal, since, except for a bowl of beans and rice, he hadn't eaten one since he had left Cheyenne. He tied his three horses beside the hotel and went in the outside entrance. "Evening, Jesse," Cecil Humphrey greeted him. "Welcome back."

"Thanks, Cecil," Jesse responded. "I'm glad I made it before you closed. I didn't miss it by much, did I?"

"Even if you didn't, you coulda knocked on the door and I expect Clara would see that you didn't go without your supper. We all felt pretty bad about our little birthday joke after we found out you coulda lost your life on account of that birthday cake. When the sheriff told us you had gone after the rest of that gang that tried to kill you, we were afraid we'd never see you again. Rachael and Clara were really upset about it."

Jesse was genuinely surprised by Cecil's confession. He hadn't given their little prank much serious thought at all. "I wish you and the women would just forget about it. I knew you were just japin' me and I didn't pay any attention to it a-tall." He saw Sheriff Warton sitting at a table near the back and the sheriff was waving his hand to get his attention. "There sure weren't no hard feelin's, if that's what you're worried about. I see the sheriff wavin' his hand at me, so I reckon I'll go join him."

Rachael was coming from the kitchen when she saw him, so she immediately spun on her heel to go back and get his coffee while he sat down at the table. "Any luck?" Warton asked.

"I'd have to say so," Jesse replied. "Matter of fact, there was a lotta luck involved, startin' with the two of 'em leavin' here by followin' the railroad tracks to the west. I figured they were headed to Laramie City, so I quit trying to track 'em and just rode on to Laramie City and that's where I found 'em." He was interrupted then when Rachael put his coffee on the table.

"Mama and I are both glad to see you," she said. "We were afraid you'd never come back here after we serenaded you on your birthday."

"There ain't no other place here in town to eat as good as this," he responded. "I didn't have no choice." Seeing the question on the sheriff's face, he didn't wait for him to ask it. "She and Cecil thought it was my birthday when that drunk delivered the cake to my room, so they sang me a little song."

"Well, that was downright tacky, wasn't it," Warton replied, "after the way those killers shot up your room?"

"No you don't, Sheriff," Rachael stopped him. "He knows we were sorry before they shot up his room."

They were interrupted then when Clara Bowden came out of the kitchen with a plate of food for him. "I thought I'd better bring this out here before it got cold," she scolded Rachael. "Welcome back, Jesse."

"Thank you, ma'am," Jesse responded. "I'm glad to be back."

"We'll let you eat now," Clara said, but she was looking at Rachael. "Those two tables over near the window ain't gonna clear off those dirty dishes themselves." Rachael responded by rolling her eyes straight up at her forehead, then went over to clear the tables.

When the women had gone, the sheriff asked, "Did you find those two you went after?"

"Yes, I did," Derringer answered.

"You bring 'em back with you? Or did you leave 'em with that damn gunslinger they call a town marshal in Laramie City?"

"I didn't get a chance to do either one," Derringer said. Then he told him what happened when he walked into the Bucket of Blood Saloon. "Luck was with me. They both missed." He didn't tell him about the extra horse he brought back with him.

"Well, I'm just as happy you didn't bring 'em back with you," Warton said. "My jail cells are full. I swear, I don't know where I woulda put those two. I mighta had to rent 'em a hotel room."

"Have you had any word about a trial for the Crowe brothers?" Jesse asked.

The sheriff hesitated a moment before he answered. "We ain't heard a word, but it don't make no difference now." He stopped, reluctant to continue.

"Why's that?" Jesse asked.

"'Cause they were hanged yesterday after a vigilance committee found 'em guilty of murder," Warton replied.

"Is their ol' man still in jail?"

"No," the sheriff said. "We didn't have any reason to hold him any longer and I needed the room in the cells. I warned him that if he caused any trouble about the hanging, he'd be the next one the committee hanged. I'm afraid there's gonna be some more hangin'. The city council ain't happy with the situation the town's in and they ain't happy with the sheriff's department. But damn it, Jesse, I'm doin' the best I can, me and my two deputies. We get these wild drifters and cowboys, outlaws, and railroad construction workers, even drunk soldiers from Camp Cheyenne shootin' up the saloons. And one of my deputies goes in to quiet 'em down, they just laugh at him. Even when there's a shooting, we can't go in and arrest the shooter. Cliff tried to arrest a drifter that shot an unarmed man in The Crossing. His friends surrounded Cliff, picked him up and carried him out the door," Warton said. "Threw him in the street and told him they'd shoot if he showed his face in the door again."

"Sounds like you've got more than you can handle," Derringer said.

"I'm telling you all this because I went to the Union

Pacific office they've just about finished building. I talked to a Mr. Clyde Woodcock and I asked him if you could help out with law enforcement, since you're a Union Pacific employee. He told me that you didn't report to him or Mr. Butcher, either. That you reported directly to General Dodge and was more like a free agent paid by the railroad. He said it was strictly up to you if you wanted to help us out. But he said he hoped you would because they're havin' trouble with all the troublemakers, too." He paused a moment, then asked, "So whaddaya say? Can you give us a hand?"

"I reckon I could," Derringer said.

"Good, good," Warton responded enthusiastically. "I thought I could count on you. I told the mayor you were the kind of man who would lend a hand. Cliff and Ray are gonna be tickled to hear the news. I was afraid I was gonna lose both of them."

"I'm glad to help, Sheriff," Derringer said. "But I ain't but one man."

"I know," Warton replied, "but you'll give us a posse of four men to address some of these gangs that think they can do anything they wanna do in this town." He didn't express it, but he actually felt like adding Derringer was the same as adding two more men. "Cliff and Ray are both at the office, waitin' for me to get back. Why don't you come, too, when you finish eatin' your supper, and we'll talk about what we're gonna do."

"I just got into town," Jesse said, "and I had to come straight here before they closed. I didn't even take my horses to the stable yet. Let me take care of them first, then I'll come right over to the jail. All right?" That was fine with the sheriff, so he left to return to the jail and prepare for the coming night. Cecil turned the CLOSED side of the sign out after Warton walked out. With Jesse the only one left, Rachael came back to the table carrying the coffeepot and an extra cup. She warmed Jesse's coffee, then filled one for herself and sat down at the table to drink it.

"Mind if I join you?" she asked as she added milk and sugar to her coffee.

"I didn't until I saw how you ruined a perfectly good cup of coffee," Jesse replied. "I forgot you ain't fully grown up yet."

"I'm grown up all right, I just ain't got the insides of a timber wolf," she came right back at him.

"And you still ain't got any respect for your elders," he japed. "I was hoping that would improve while I was gone." She stuck her tongue out at him and put some more sugar in her coffee.

Seeing the pot sitting on the table, Cecil locked the dining room door and took a clean coffee cup off a sideboard where they were stacked. "Anything left in that pot?" he asked as he approached the table. Rachael told him there should be at least one more cup, so he filled his cup. "Ain't no sense lettin' good coffee get cold, settin' on the table. Is this a private party?"

"No, indeed," Jesse said, "set yourself down. It ain't gonna last long, though, 'cause I've got three horses I've gotta take to the stable before Leon goes home."

He was accurate with his prediction because the party lasted for about five minutes when someone came to the outside entrance and tried the doorknob. When the door didn't open, he started banging on it. "Somebody can't read," Cecil complained, and got up to take care of it. He slid the bolt back and opened the door just enough to tell the stranger that the dining room was closed. He pointed to the sign.

The stranger, a rough-looking individual who was obviously emboldened by alcohol, pushed the door open and glared into the dining room. "The hell it is," he blurted. "Them people are eatin' and I'm hungry."

"That's our last customer for the night," Cecil explained as politely as he could manage. "He got here before closing time."

"Now I'm your last customer for the night. You fed him, you can feed me, damn it. I'm hungry."

"The stove's already gone too cold to cook anything," Cecil attempted to make the insistent bully understand. "The leftovers have already been thrown out and there's no more coffee. The best thing for you is to go to The Crossing or Vera's Vineyard. They serve food until late at night."

His patience lost, the brute shoved Cecil backward and stepped inside the dining room. He dropped his hand on the sidearm he was wearing and said, "The best thing for you is to get your sorry butt in the kitchen and get me some food, or I'm gonna shoot this place to pieces."

Derringer had waited to see if Cecil would have any trouble with the obnoxious stranger before he offered any help. Now he was afraid he might have waited too long. So Derringer told Rachael it was time for her to leave. "I want you to go into the kitchen and stay with your mother. All right?" That was in case the belligerent guest actually pulled his sidearm before he could get there. With no thought toward questioning the tone of his voice, she got up from the chair and went into the kitchen. When she went through the kitchen doorway, he got up and walked casually toward the front door where Cecil was still asking the unwelcome guest to leave. It only served to make the stranger more aggressive.

"I'm gonna start by shootin' those lamps off the wall," the brute threatened, "one by one for every second I have to wait for you to go get my supper." Seeing Derringer coming toward the door, he waited until he was there before he turned to him and demanded, "What the hell are you lookin' at?"

"A damn fool," Derringer answered, and came up with an uppercut in the drifter's midsection that doubled him over to receive the left cross to his cheek, which spun him around to face the open door. With one boot planted squarely on the bully's backside, Derringer propelled him through the open door to land on his face on the dirt path outside the hotel. Then he walked out the door after him while the bully struggled to his hands and knees. Derringer pulled the pistol out of his holster. He picked the man's hat up from the ground, tapped him on his head with the barrel of his pistol, then crammed his hat back on his head. While the dazed brute remained on his hands and knees, Derringer opened the cylinder of his six-shooter and emptied it. Then he dropped it back in his holster. "This hotel is owned by the Union Pacific Railroad. We don't stand for any rude behavior in our hotel or dinin' room. I take it you didn't know that, so I'm just gonna give you a warning this time. If there is a next time, we're gonna have to get rough with you. It's for your own good that I'm botherin' to tell you this. You seem like a fairly levelheaded fellow. You just didn't know about the Union Pacific's policies, so I'm not gonna take you to jail this time." He reached down and helped him to his feet. "You go on back down the street to Vera's. You can get something to eat there late tonight. You'll like it better there, anyway." The brute just stood there, confused. "Go on," Derringer said, and pointed down the street.

"I'm obliged," the bully finally said, and wandered off toward the saloons.

Derringer stood there and watched until the man disappeared on the crowded street, then he turned toward the side of the building to go after his horses when he heard the voice behind him. "I wouldn't have believed that if I hadn't seen it with my own eyes." He turned back to see Cecil standing in the doorway.

"Me either," Rachael said, peeking over Cecil's shoulder.

"Shame on you, Rachael," Jesse scolded. "Things coulda gone a whole lot differently. I was just lucky. You shoulda been lookin' after your mama in the kitchen."

"Fiddle," Rachael replied with a giggle. "Mama's in the kitchen holding her shotgun. She doesn't need me." He shook his head and turned to go get his horses, hoping his little delay with the drifter hadn't caused him to miss getting to the stable before Leon closed. "We'll see you in the morning," Rachael called after him. He responded with a wave of his hand without turning to look at her. If he thought he had the time, he would have taken his saddlebags up to his room in the hotel. But he figured it had taken him too long to dispense with the bully. He hoped all his talk about the Union Pacific had impressed upon the man that he was tangling with the big railroad and not just the dining room.

Luck was still riding with him, however, because he reached the stable just as Leon was closing up to leave. "Jesse, I swear, you just caught me," Leon said. "I didn't expect you back so soon. I thought you said you might be gone for a week or two."

"I thought I might be," Jesse replied. "But I got some things done before I thought I would."

"I see you brought an extra horse back with you," Leon said. "How'd you come by that?"

"It's a long story I'll tell you sometime when the sheriff ain't waitin' for me at the jailhouse and you ain't about to be late for supper." He started taking his saddle off Clem. "Not a bad lookin' horse, though," he said, looking at the dun gelding. "Take a look at him and see what you think."

Leon looked the dun over and when he looked at his teeth, he commented, "You got a fancy-lookin' bridle on him. He didn't come with a saddle to match it?"

"Yeah, he had a fancy saddle, too, but a fellow was usin' it as a pillow and I didn't wanna disturb him."

Leon had to let that thought simmer a few moments before it came to a boil. "That sounds like you stole the horse," he finally said.

"It does, don't it?" Jesse replied. "Take care of all three of 'em like you've been takin' care of the gray and the sorrel and I'll appreciate it." He took the packsaddle off the sorrel and dropped it in the corner of his usual stall with his saddle. He took his rifle and his saddlebags and told Leon he'd see him tomorrow.

When he walked in the sheriff's office, he found the entire sheriff's department sitting around the room, Sheriff Tom Warton and deputy sheriffs Cliff Crenshaw and Ray Cooper. "I see everybody's here, Derringer japed. "Who's watchin' the town?"

"Nobody," Ray answered him. "We're hopin' they steal everything in the town, including the railroad, and maybe we'll have a chance to grow a nice little town here." He paused, then said, "No offense meant."

Derringer laughed. "None taken," he replied. "I can understand your feelings. We've got a bad situation here due to that three-month weather delay. But if you folks can hang in there till the railroad gets going again, it's bound to get better. A lot of this mob of people will follow the railroad outta town to make some other places hell. And Cheyenne might turn out to be that nice little town you're talkin' about."

"I swear, Derringer," Cliff Crenshaw joked. "You talk like a politician. You oughta think about runnin' for governor."

Sheriff Warton interrupted the japing when he opened his desk drawer, took out a deputy sheriff's badge, and tossed it to Jesse. "I'm officially deputizing you, so you'll have the authority to do whatever you have to do. Now, as far as watchin' the town, I think we oughta work in pairs and that'll be a lot better than one man walkin' the town alone, especially at night." He got three nodding heads in response.

"That sounds like a good idea to me," Cliff Crenshaw said, remembering the first time he met Jesse Derringer, when he walked into the saloon to arrest the

Crowe brothers and Derringer appeared out of nowhere to back him up.

"Makes sense to me," Jesse responded. "It's a good
idea to have somebody to watch your back. I notice
you've got two cots set up here in the office."

"You don't miss a thing, do ya?" Warton japed.
"Ray and Cliff have started sleepin' here in the office
lately, so they can respond quicker. There's too much
trouble in the streets late at night and we need to get to
it quicker."

"It doesn't sound too noisy in the back," Jesse commented. "How many have you got in the cells?"

"Twelve right now," the sheriff answered, "a body in
every bunk. They ain't makin' much noise, cause they're
still eatin' their supper. We had more than that last night,
but we released a bunch of 'em this mornin' after
breakfast."

"What did you do," Jesse asked, "let some of 'em
sleep on the floor?"

"Had to," Warton replied. "Some of 'em were so
drunk, they didn't care. I'm thinkin' about turnin' the
rest of 'em loose after they've finished eatin' their supper, so we can get the cells cleaned up."

"Yeah," Ray remarked, "I'm looking forward to
that."

Jesse looked at the sheriff and asked, "Is that why
you wanted my help?"

Warton chuckled. "No, I've hired a man to clean the
cells and do the other little odd jobs around here, like
pullin' that handcart back and forth with the prisoner's
meals."

"Since Jesse is General Dodge's special scout, maybe he can have the railroad lay a short track from the dining room down to the jail and we can ship their grub on a handcar," Ray suggested.

"I'll see what I can do," Jesse said good-naturedly, although he was aware of a hint of friction between himself and the young deputy. He could not imagine why. He had not had much contact with Ray Cooper, a capable-looking deputy, maybe a year or two older than Cliff Crenshaw. If there was friction between the two of them, Derringer didn't care enough to find the cause of it, or to eliminate it. A lot of people didn't like him. As far as he was concerned, that was their problem. He didn't need to be liked by everyone.

If Derringer had known the root cause of Cooper's dislike for him, he could have solved the problem immediately. In Cooper's mind, he was the logical choice to replace Tom Warton as sheriff of Cheyenne. It was obvious to Cooper that Warton's nerves were becoming frayed under the pressure of the number of people who had descended upon the town and the large percentage of whom were lawless. He felt certain that Warton was going to resign under the pressure and his fear at this point was that the city council would go after Jesse Derringer to take the job. It didn't help when Warton asked for Derringer's help and deputized him. And he was sick of hearing Cliff Crenshaw's praise of Derringer's accomplishments. This was the reason Cooper asked to patrol the town with the sheriff and let Crenshaw partner Derringer. The sheriff agreed to the pairing, although he had planned to partner with Derringer himself.

When Derringer asked how he planned to keep an eye on the whole town, the sheriff explained that all four of them would go about business as usual during most of the day. He just wanted to have four men to respond to any disturbance. The two-man patrols would be performed during the critical hours. The first shift would be when business and shop owners were closing for the day and counting the day's profits, as robbers took that time to strike. The next shift would be the late-night patrol when everything was closed but the saloons and the dance halls. "Those patrols are when we take a really close look at what's going on in the town, so hopefully we can spot trouble before it happens."

"The rest of the time, we just come runnin' when somebody hollers, or we hear a gunshot, right?" Cliff Crenshaw asked.

"Right," the sheriff answered. "There ain't much else we can do, except try to show more law enforcement in town and try to stop most trouble before it turns into a shooting." He paused to see if anyone had any more questions. "Well, I reckon that's about it. Me and Ray will take the late patrol tonight to start things off. Jesse, you and Cliff can take the early tour around town, and we'll alternate every other day."

"So that means Cliff and I need to get out there right now and take a walk around town," Derringer said.

"That's right," the sheriff said. "If you run into more than you can handle, fire a shot in the air and we'll come runnin'."

"Let's go, partner," Cliff said to Derringer, then picked up his rifle, put on his hat, and started for the door.

"Right behind you," Jesse answered, and followed him out. He couldn't help noticing the hint of a smirk on Deputy Cooper's face as he walked past him. *I must have said something that didn't set well with him,* he thought, *but damned if I can think what it might have been.*

CHAPTER 15

The sheriff's office was located close to the halfway point on the main street, so Jesse suggested that they start their walk back toward the south end of it. "Then I can drop my saddlebags off in my room at the hotel."

"I was gonna ask you if you wanted to do that," Cliff said. "They look like you packed 'em pretty full." So they headed back toward the railroad station and the hotel along a street still busy with pedestrians, even though many of the shops were already closed. Some of the street corners were gathering places for small groups of railroad construction men with no place to go to get out of the cold and little money to spend in the saloons. Most of them would retreat at sundown to the makeshift camps along Crow Creek of canvas tents and scraps of anything that could be used to insulate them against the cold nights. What little bit of money they had left was desperately guarded and used to buy food. These were the honest railroad workers who could not afford to go to homes back east and try to return to work in three months' time. "I'm always glad to get by this part of town," Cliff commented when they had passed the idle workers. "I can't help but feel sorry for those poor fellows, but there ain't nothin' I can do for 'em."

"No there ain't," Derringer remarked. "So you might as well put it outta your mind." He was in the process of trying to put it out of his own mind, so he didn't want to discuss it with the young deputy. They walked into the hotel to find Julian Burnett talking to Bob Wolfe at the check-in desk.

"Evening, gents," Julian greeted them. "I heard you were back, Jesse. You musta come in the dining room right after I left."

"Yeah, I got there just before Cecil turned the sign around," Jesse said.

"Cecil said you had to escort an unruly customer out of the dining room," Julian said. "I was just telling Bob about it when you walked in." When Cliff turned and gave Derringer an enquiring look, Julian asked, "He didn't tell you about that?"

"No, he never said a word about any trouble in the dinin' room," Cliff answered, and looked at Derringer, waiting for the story.

"We're patrolin' the town, but I wanna run upstairs and leave my saddlebags in my room," Jesse said. "I'll be right back," he told Cliff, and started to walk toward the stairs.

"If you don't take better care of that room than you did your old one, we're gonna have to charge you extra," Bob Wolfe japed.

Jesse turned halfway around but kept walking as he

replied, "If I find a birthday cake in my room, I'm not sleepin' in there tonight." He heard the chuckles as he went up the steps to the second floor.

When they left the hotel, Cliff asked about the incident that Julian had referred to, but Jesse told him it was just a minor misunderstanding by a fellow who had been drinking. "He wanted to eat and the dining room was closed. Once he understood, he went on his way."

That wasn't good enough for the young deputy. He wanted a blow-by-blow accounting of the entire incident. When Derringer was still not forthcoming with details, Cliff gave up and said, "I reckon I'll have to ask Cecil to find out what happened."

"It was just a quick little discussion," Derringer told him. "It happened so fast I can't remember what happened."

They walked back up the street, checking to make sure doors were locked, checked the front and back doors of the Cheyenne Merchandise building to see if the mayor had locked up securely. After the post office, they walked into Dawkin's Saloon, where a big card game was in progress. There were five players. Derringer knew only one, J. D. Clayton, who owned the sawmill. There were three strangers who looked like typical outlaws. The fifth player owned the barbershop, Cliff told him. "Any problems?" Cliff asked Sam, the bartender.

"No, don't seem to be," Sam replied. "They've been playin' about an hour, and ain't been makin' much noise. Clayton's the big winner so far, but one of those three strangers is doin' pretty good, too. They called him Swan. Lou Johnson ain't doin' too bad," he said, referring to the local barber. Sam looked at Derringer then and asked, "You keepin' company with the deputy tonight?"

"Yeah, I reckon you could say that," Derringer answered, and opened his coat, so Sam could see his badge.

"Well, I'll be . . ." Sam chuckled. "I never woulda figured that."

"It's just a temporary loan from the railroad," Derringer quickly informed him.

"That's what he says," Cliff remarked, "but I'm gonna talk him into takin' the job permanently."

"Everything looks peaceful enough in here tonight," Derringer said quickly to change the subject. "I suppose we'd best see how the other saloons are doin'. Right, Cliff?"

"Right, partner," Cliff said with a grin. "Let's go check the rest of the town." They walked out on the street again and headed toward The Crossing Saloon.

Like Dawkin's, The Crossing was busy but peaceful with a couple of card games in progress; both of them were made up of Cheyenne regulars and no strangers. So Jesse and Cliff moved on after talking to Benny Thacker for a few minutes. Then they continued on, checking the locked doors as they progressed up the street until reaching the end, where they visited briefly with Leon Draper at the stable. "Any chance you might be stayin' at the stable late tonight?" Jesse asked Leon.

"No," Leon answered. "Ain't got no reason to. Why?"

"I was just wonderin'," Jesse said. Then he asked,

"You have three strangers leave their horses with you all night?"

"No, I ain't took in no new customers tonight," Leon replied. "Was I supposed to? 'Cause if I was supposed to, they ain't showed up. You want me to stay open a while longer?"

"No," Jesse said. "Go ahead and close. If they ain't here by now, they ain't comin'."

They left the stable with both Leon and Cliff puzzled over Jesse's questions about the three horses. After they crossed over to the other side of the street, so they could check the two smaller saloons on their way back to the jail, Cliff asked a question. "What three horses were you talking about?"

"It was just a thought," Jesse answered, preferring to drop the subject. But when Cliff persisted, he said, "I was just wonderin' if those three strangers in Dawkin's were stayin' in town tonight or leavin'. That's all."

"Why?" Cliff wanted to know at once. "You got some reason to suspect them of something?"

"No, I don't," Jesse said. "I reckon they kinda reminded me of Jeb Massey and his gang, especially the one they called Swan. And we just got rid of Massey. I hope to hell we ain't pickin' up another one just like him."

Cliff laughed. "I don't think there could be many like Jeb Massey," he said.

"I reckon you're right," Jesse said. "It's this damn badge. I pinned this badge on me and I started worryin' about the town right away." They checked the other two saloons and both of them were busy, but with mostly serious drinkers who came to the saloon for whiskey and nothing else.

When they worked their way back to the jail, they made their report to the sheriff, with Cliff doing the reporting. "There were no problems, nothing unlawful going on in the streets even though there were still a lot of people in the streets. Vera's Vineyard and all the saloons were busy but peaceful."

"All right," Sheriff Warton said, nodding his head as he tried to think of something important to say. "That's good," he said when nothing meaningful came to mind. "So, Jesse, you and Cliff have pulled your patrol and you're free to go to bed, if you want to, although it wouldn't hurt to hang around for a while. Ray and I will take the late patrol tonight to see the town close down. You and Cliff will have the late patrol tomorrow night."

"How am I gonna sleep?" Cliff wondered. "My bed is this cot here in the office and you and Ray are gonna be sittin' around in here talkin'."

"I thought of that," the sheriff answered. "You and Ray can move them cots outta here and put 'em in the storeroom. There's room for 'em in there, if you move that big gun cabinet out here in the office and shove that trunk back in the corner. You or Ray can go in there and shut the door whenever you're ready to go to sleep. You'll think you're in a hotel room," he joked.

"I'm disappointed that there ain't room for three cots in that storeroom," Derringer remarked, obviously japing. "Lucky the hotel ain't that far away. I'll be here in a couple of minutes, if I hear a gunshot."

"We wouldn't wanna disturb your sleep," Ray said.

"You older folks need your shut-eye," he added, knowing the sheriff would go home to sleep. "I expect me and Cliff can handle any trouble during the late hours. Ain't that right, Cliff?"

"That's what we're paid for," Cliff answered, although a little less confident than Ray.

"That's what the late walk around town's for," the sheriff said, "to see if there's any sign of trouble heatin' up. Right, Jesse?"

"Hopefully," Jesse answered to appease the sheriff, although he was not convinced the sheriff's master plan to prevent trouble was worth squat. He was in favor of taking a late walk around town to take the temperature in the potential trouble spots. But he also believed it was impossible to foresee the explosion of a hot temper when mixed with a losing streak and a generous serving of alcohol. "I'll help you set up your bedroom before I say good night," he said, and walked into the storeroom to look in the gun cabinet. "There ain't that many guns in here." He took hold of the top of it and tilted it over. "If one of you will grab the bottom of this thing, we can carry it right outta here without unloadin' it."

Ray stepped forward at once to take hold of the feet of the cabinet, anxious to match the strength Derringer obviously possessed. Finding the cabinet much heavier than it appeared to be in Jesse's hands, Ray made a huge effort to keep his facial expression neutral as he lifted his end off the floor. Since it was a heavy cabinet, Jesse backed out of the storeroom right away and when they were back in the office, he asked, "Where do you want it, Sheriff?" The sheriff hesitated a few moments, having given the question no prior thought, oblivious to the veins that began to appear at the temples of Ray's face. Jesse noticed, however, so he said, "We might as well put it down while he's decidin'."

"Yeah, might as well," Ray said, and immediately eased his end back down on the floor. When Jesse didn't push the top up to stand the cabinet upright, Ray said, "I thought you said to put it down. Ain't you gonna stand it up?"

"No, it ain't that heavy with that end on the floor," Jesse replied. "Might as well wait till he makes up his mind."

"Put it over there against the wall behind my desk," Warton said then, and pointed to the spot. Ray took hold again and strained to make a smooth lifting of the heavy cabinet. As soon as it was up, Jesse backed quickly behind the desk until reaching the spot pointed out.

"You can set your end down and I'll straighten her up," Jesse said. Ray complied at once, lowering his end to the floor carefully. Then he backed away while Jesse tilted the cabinet to stand upright on the floor. Jesse looked back toward the stockroom door where Cliff was struggling to pull the heavy trunk through the door. "You need a hand, Cliff? That thing looks like it's heavy." Cliff said it sure was, so Jesse walked over and took hold of the handle on the other end of the trunk. "This is heavy. What's in it?"

"Ammunition," Cliff replied. They picked it up and carried it to the other side of the cabinet. "Now, we can get these cots out of the office."

"I'll let you and Ray take care of your beds," Jesse

told him. "I didn't know that bein' a deputy sheriff was such hard work," he japed.

"This is the real job of a deputy sheriff," Cliff joked back at him. "Did you think it was all the sanctified work of keeping the people safe? You have to do this part of the job, too. Ain't that right, Ray?"

"He's right," Ray replied. "This is what you're really gettin' paid to do."

"Well, there you go," Jesse said. "That's what you're really paid to do. But I ain't gettin' paid to be a deputy, so I ain't supposed to do manual labor."

"He's right about that," the sheriff said. "He's strictly a volunteer deputy, just goin' for the glory of upholdin' the law."

"I swear," Jesse japed. "I believe I'll have to go back to the hotel and think about that."

"Too late, partner," Cliff declared. "You've already taken one tour of the town as a deputy, so you have to stay on the job till you get an official release."

The carefree mood continued throughout most of the evening, which was very unusual for the Cheyenne Sheriff's Department. It was a rare evening when there were no drunken cowboys racing their horses down the main street, discharging their six-shooters in the air, or no explosions of a sudden gunfight in one of the saloons. Derringer hung around the office until it was nearly time for Warton and Ray to take the final walk about town. He said he'd see them in the morning and went to his room at the hotel to go to bed, leaving Cliff in charge of the office until the sheriff and Ray returned.

"Evenin', Jesse," Bob Wolfe greeted him when he

walked in the front door of the hotel. "I heard you were workin' as a deputy with the sheriff's department. I didn't know you were a lawman."

"I'm not," Jesse explained. "I'm just helpin' out a little while I'm waiting for the railroad to crank up again. I still work for the Union Pacific."

"You've still got about a month and a half before the railroad said they'd be back to start up Sherman Hill again, don't you?" the night clerk asked. "You gonna work for Sheriff Warton for another month and a half?"

"I don't know," Jesse replied, "I suppose." He turned away from the desk and started for the stairs.

"You in for the night?" Bob asked.

"Yep, unless I get a call to help the sheriff, or hear some gunshots," Jesse responded. "I ain't particularly sleepy tonight."

"Well, if you ain't gone to sleep by midnight and you're hungry, come back down to the office and I'll treat you to a slab of corn bread and a glass of buttermilk. My wife makes the best corn bread in this county. I don't care what Clara Bowden claims."

"Why, that's right neighborly of you, Bob. I 'preciate the offer. That sounds mighty temptin', the corn bread anyway. I expect you'd have to hog-tie me on the back of a wagon with a funnel in my mouth to get that buttermilk down my throat."

"I take it you ain't overly fond of buttermilk," Bob deduced. "Have you ever tried corn bread with apple cider?"

"No, I can't say as I have," Jesse replied, "but I can guarantee you it's one of my favorites."

"Good," Bob said with a chuckle, "twelve midnight,

in the office." He pointed to the office door behind the check-in desk.

"Twelve midnight," Jesse confirmed. "If I don't show up, you'll know I fell asleep." He turned then and went up the stairs.

Jesse had not been gone twenty minutes before Sheriff Tom Warton and Deputy Ray Cooper walked into the hotel. "Howdy, Sheriff Warton, Deputy Cooper," Bob Wolfe greeted them. "Are you lookin' for Jesse Derringer? He just went up to his room. You want me to get him for you?"

"No," Warton answered. "Deputy Cooper and I are just taking our late walk around the town and we stopped in to check on the hotel. Everything all right here tonight?"

"Yes, sir," Bob replied. "Everything seems pretty quiet tonight. Understand Derringer is workin' as a deputy for you right now."

"That's a fact," Warton said. "He's helping Ray, here, and Cliff Crenshaw."

"I'll bet you're glad to have him help out. I know I feel pretty secure now, with him right here in the hotel."

Ray Cooper rolled his eyeballs up at the ceiling. Unable to hold his tongue, he said, "Yeah, it's like a gift sent down from heaven."

Bob and the sheriff both stared at him, amazed by the comment. He just shrugged. "Well, hope you continue to have a peaceful night," Sheriff Warton told Bob. "We'll take a little walk up the street now." When they got outside in the street, Warton asked Ray, "Are you all right?"

"Yeah, I'm fine," Ray answered, and started walking. Warton shrugged then and started walking after him. He was about to say more but was distracted when the noise in Dawkin's Saloon suddenly grew louder and several men ran out the front door. One of them, recognizing the sheriff and deputy, ran toward them.

"Sheriff!" the man cried out. "There's about to be a shooting in Dawkin's. Some fellows in a card game are threatening to kill J. D. Clayton!"

They didn't hesitate. Both sheriff and deputy drew their weapons and ran toward the saloon. The noisy saloon they had heard before suddenly became quiet as they approached the door. They paused at the door to take a look inside before charging blindly into they knew not what. From the door they saw J. D. Clayton seated at the table, his back to them. On his feet, facing him, was a tall brute of a man wearing a three-quarter length greatcoat, opened now to reveal a silk vest and a gold watchchain, as well as a gun belt with an empty holster. The Colt .45 Army model revolver that normally rode in the holster was now pointed at J. D. Clayton.

"Hold it right there!" Warton commanded. "Holster that weapon! I'm sheriff of this town and I'm ordering you to put that gun in your holster."

"Damn," the man swore as if confronted with a minor inconvenience. "I ain't in the habit of takin' orders from anybody," the brute said, still holding the pistol on Clayton. "This sleazy dog has been dealin' off the bottom of the deck all night and now he's gonna answer for it. I'm willin' to give him a chance to see who's right, him or me. He can stand up and face me and we'll let our guns decide who's lyin' and who ain't. Stand up, you yellow dog!" he demanded of Clayton.

"Put the gun down," Warton ordered, "or you're goin' to spend a little time in my jail. We don't stand for gunfights in Cheyenne."

"But you do stand for cheatin' at cards. Is that the way it goes in this town?" He glanced at the two surly-looking companions with him. "That's what it sounds like, don't it, boys?"

"That's what it sounds like, Swan," one of the men answered, and they both got to their feet and drew their pistols.

"Looks like we're gonna have a real face-off, boys," Swan said, "with the sheriff and his deputy. Don't seem fair, does it? Three of us against just two lawmen." He looked back at J. D. Clayton. "How 'bout it, J.D.? You can stand up with the sheriff and his deputy and that'll make it three against three."

"I already told you I don't carry a gun," Clayton told him. "And I don't cheat at cards and you know it."

"All right," Swan said. "I'm tired of messing with you people. Sheriff, you and your deputy was just un-lucky to walk into the middle of my business. But if you holster your guns, and turn around and walk out of here, I'll let you live to see another day. And when I'm done, me and my friends will ride outta town. Now, that's the best deal you're gonna get and if you don't take it, me and my two friends are gonna shoot you down where you stand."

The sheriff hesitated, his hand shaking visibly. He

dared not look at Ray, for fear he might have already holstered his weapon. Finally he swallowed and said, "I won't do that. You're all under arrest. Drop your weapons."

"All right, you damn fool," Swan cursed. "You had your chance and that's the last one you're gonna get." J.D. heard the cocking of the three outlaws' pistols at almost the same time he heard the roar of the two shotgun blasts, which hurled Swan and one of his partners crashing into the third man. Dazed and confused, that man turned to defend himself, only to be struck down by two rounds from a Colt .44 in his chest.

In the deathlike silence that immediately followed the explosion of gunfire, all eyes in the crowded saloon turned to focus on the calm specter that was Jesse Derringer. He methodically dropped his Colt .44 back in his holster, broke the action open on the double-barreled shotgun, and extracted the two spent buckshot shells. The conversation trickled back into the shocked saloon in bits and spurts as Derringer returned the shotgun to the bar and thanked Sam for the borrow of it.

With the whole saloon returning to life again, one alone had not moved. J. D. Clayton remained seated in his chair refusing assistance from several who offered to help him up out of the chair. "Thanks," he told them, "but I think I'll sit here a while till I can recover my wits. During the shooting, something was spilled in my lap. I think it must have been beer." Most of the glasses had been knocked from the table, but no one pointed out the fact that there was no spilled beer on the table over J.D.'s lap.

As shocked as anyone in the saloon, Warton and

Cooper stood motionless for a brief few moments before they looked at each other in disbelief. Their guns not fired, they suddenly remembered to return them to their holsters. "You all right?" Derringer asked them.

"How did you know . . . ?" Warton started. "Where did you come from?" he asked, amazed that he was still alive. "We just came from the hotel and Bob Wolfe said you were in your room. How did you get here? How did you know we were in trouble?"

Jesse didn't answer the question. Instead, he asked one. "Damn, that's right. What time is it?"

"Hell, I don't know," the sheriff responded. "Who cares? How did you know?" When Jesse still ignored the question but looked around frantically, Warton looked at the clock behind the bar and said, "It's eleven-thirty."

"I've got to get back to the hotel," Jesse said, but knew he had to answer Warton's questions. "I just had a feelin' about these three drifters when Cliff and I were in here earlier. It looked like it could be the same routine Massey and his gang pulled off. But unlike Massey, they didn't stable their horses, so they weren't plannin' to stay in town. They were gonna do whatever they planned to do and then leave town. It was just a feelin', but it bothered me. I didn't wanna bother you with it when I didn't have anything to go on but a feelin'. But I got to thinkin' about it again tonight, so I decided to see if those three were still in town."

"I'm damned glad you did 'cause I don't think those men were bluffing," Warton said. "I think me and Ray were in a hot spot. One of us, or both of us, was bound to get killed."

"I'm glad I did, too," Jesse joked. "If I hadn't, that woulda left all the work to Cliff and me. And Cliff would most likely be put out with me. If you don't mind, I'll let you take care of the bodies. I need to get back to the hotel."

"No problem," the sheriff replied. "That's the least we can do after what you did tonight."

"You'da done the same for me," Jesse said. "See you in the mornin'."

He thanked Sam again for the use of his shotgun. "I needed something with a big kick. I'll bring you two shells to replace those two."

"Them two shells was on the house," Sam replied.

Jesse thanked him again, then he went out the back door, which was the way he had come in the saloon. *Twelve-midnight*, he was thinking. *I ain't had any apple cider or corn bread in quite a while.*

Chapter 16

Jesse was a little later for breakfast than he intended to be, due to his midnight snack of corn bread and apple cider, courtesy of Mrs. Bob Wolfe. He had figured that Bob had offered the invitation just as a common civility to a Union Pacific employee and a hotel resident. But he found that Bob really enjoyed the company. After he left and returned to his room to go to bed, he imagined Bob's job as the night clerk must be a lonely one. Being a person who had never considered being alone a particularly bad thing, and most times better than being with someone, it was hard to imagine himself so afflicted. He had no desire to give Bob a detailed account of the incident that took place in Dawkin's Saloon that night. He much preferred to enjoy his corn bread and cider. So when Bob mentioned that he had heard some shots from somewhere up the street, Jesse had responded with a simple remark. "Most likely from one of the saloons." And when Bob asked if he had heard them, Jesse answered that he had.

It was not so easy to bypass the matter when he got to the dining room that morning, however. For Cliff and Ray had both been in before him, so Cecil and Rachael were waiting for him, loaded with questions. His initial defense against their interrogation was a simple one. He told them he didn't remember anything about it because he had been sleepwalking, a habit he was often afflicted with. They didn't buy it and proceeded to tell him exactly what had happened, as told to them by Cliff and Ray, and his part was reduced to verifying or refuting what they had been told. He was forced to end the investigation when Rachael wanted to know how it felt to blow a man away with a shotgun. "It doesn't feel good at all and I oughta tell your mama you're wonderin' about things like that." Instead of feeling ashamed, she was delighted.

When he got to the sheriff's office, he found his fellow lawmen waiting to interrogate him about the night before. He expected it, so he was not blindsided as he had been in the dining room, but the questioning was still intense. He was caught by surprise, however, when Ray Cooper thanked him for saving his and the sheriff's lives. "We were goin' down," Ray told him, "the sheriff and me. I was just hoping I could get off at least two shots before they got me. But the sheriff and I talked about this after you walked in and settled everything and saved our butts. Even if we had gotten one shot off, we woulda both got shot then because we were both aiming at the one called Swan. The other two would have shot us, taken all the money, and hightailed it outta town. Then you and Cliff would have had to decide if it was worth chasin' 'em."

"I think you're being a little bit hard on yourself, Ray, and on the sheriff, too," Jesse told him. "You were outnumbered until I got there. It mighta been different if we had been standin' there, three against three. I was just plain lucky to get there in time. And I was lucky Sam had a shotgun under the bar loaded with buck-shot. I hadn't even brought my rifle with me and that's my weapon of choice. But Sam's shotgun was what I needed to blow them to hell away, so it was just luck. When I went in the back door of the saloon, I wasn't prepared for what happened. I should have come pre-pared. If I had started shooting with nothing but my .44 pistol, it mighta turned into a wild shooting match with all six of us firing in all different directions. No tellin' who would have come out on top, or how many specta-tors caught a bullet."

"I hear what you're sayin'," Ray insisted. "And I reckon I know why you're sayin' it. But the fact of the matter is, me and the sheriff shouldn't have walked in that saloon like that. One of us should have gone in the front and the other one in the back. We'da had a better chance against them than we did standin' there together like one big target. I just want to say you did one hell-uva job and I lived another day thanks to you. I hope I learned something from it." He extended his hand, so Jesse took it. He realized it was Ray's apology for the friction he had created between them.

Things settled down a little over the next couple of weeks in Cheyenne as far as outlaws the likes of Jeb Massey and Swan were concerned. But the idle population of the town continued to grow, so that there were more and more petty crimes like outright theft and burglary, drunkenness, and public nuisance. Derringer was not particularly happy with the job of hauling drunks out of the shops and breaking up bar fights. So he was pleased to receive a telegram from the Union Pacific office in Council Bluffs. It informed him that Jack Tyler would be arriving in two days and would need Jesse's services as a scout. The telegram said that Tyler would inform him about the nature of the visit. That sounded like the relief he needed from the Cheyenne Sheriff's Department and he'd be glad to see Jack Tyler. He was a good man. Jesse grinned when he remembered that last night before Jack went back to Council Bluffs on the train. That was the night he and Jack marched the Crowe brothers to jail after they had shot a man and his son. He decided he would fill his job as a Cheyenne deputy for one more day, since Jack was arriving in two. So he waited until the day Jack was arriving before he gave the sheriff the news.

Sheriff Tom Warton was not at all happy when Jesse showed him the telegram and informed him that his days as his deputy sheriff were over. When Warton tried to talk him out of quitting the deputy job, Jesse reminded him that he was on the Union Pacific payroll and he was merely a volunteer lawman for the town of Cheyenne. So Warton tried to persuade him to stay by promising to get him put on the town payroll. "Hell, Tom," Jesse told him, "I told you when I started that it would only be for the time the railroad construction was stopped. That time's almost over and you don't need

me anyway. You've got yourself two good deputies."
Warton admitted Jesse was right and thanked him for
making good deputies out of Cliff Crenshaw and Ray
Cooper.

"They're both gonna miss working with you, Jesse,
and I'm damned sure gonna miss having you work for
me," the sheriff said.

"Thank you, Sheriff, I've enjoyed working with you,
too." He took his badge off and handed it to Warton. "I
reckon I'll still be around if you need my help again. I
reckon it depends on what the railroad does with me.
I'm not even sure of that yet."

The train was not due until that afternoon, so Jesse
decided to spend some of the time he had with his
horse. He wanted to make sure Clem and his packhorse
were both in good condition and ready to travel. So
when he left the sheriff's office, he went to the stable,
where he caught Leon Draper mucking out some of the
stalls. "I expect you can take your time with this one,"
he said when he walked up to his stall. "I'll be takin'
my horses outta town for a while."

"How long you gonna be gone?" Leon asked.

"Don't know," Jesse answered. "Jack Tyler's coming
in on the train sometime this mornin' and I expect we'll
be leaving town tomorrow mornin'. You remember
Jack, don't you? He's the construction foreman over all
the track-layin' crews."

"Yep, I remember him. Rides a black horse. Where
you headin'?"

"Don't know that, either," Jesse replied, even though
he assumed it would be somewhere past Sherman Hill.

"Jack will tell me when he gets here." He took a good look at Clem and his sorrel packhorse, too. They both seemed to be in good shape, although he felt as if they both had spent too much time in the stable and needed a good trip to get them back in shape. Finding nothing that needed to be done, he told Leon he'd see him later when the train pulled in and they would stable Jack Tyler's horse.

After the stable, he walked down to the newly completed Union Pacific office to see what time the train was supposed to arrive from Council Bluffs. "Look out, Fred," Clyde Woodcock japed when Derringer walked into the office, "the deputy sheriff is here."

"Not anymore," Jesse replied, "I retired this mornin'."

"You retired?" Fred Butcher responded. "Or were you fired? I heard the sheriff thought you weren't pullin' your weight on the job."

Clyde continued the horseplay. "Yeah, I heard that, too. He said you weren't earnin' your salary."

Jesse just shook his head as if in pain. "I heard that if people don't have enough work to do, it'll turn 'em plumb silly. So I reckon I should have just walked over to the train station and asked Melvin what time that train is supposed to get here."

Clyde laughed and said, "It's supposed to get here at eleven. Melvin can probably tell you if it's on time or not."

"I reckon I'll go talk to Melvin," Jesse said. "It's been real educational, talkin' to you boys, though. Keep up the good work."

"Anytime, Jesse," Fred Butcher called after him as

he walked out the door. He chuckled, then he thought of the man who walked into Dawkin's Saloon and blew three killers away in the blink of an eye. He glanced over at Clyde Woodcock and remarked, "Kinda like petting a grizzly bear at a zoo, ain't it?"

Derringer walked on down to the little telegraph shack beside the railroad on the site where the railway station was going to be built. Melvin Owens, the telegraph operator and acting station master, saw him coming and went to the door to greet him. "Howdy, Jesse, what can I do for you?"

"Howdy, Melvin," Derringer returned. "What time are you expectin' the train in here?"

"She's due at eleven," Melvin said. "The last I heard from her, she was running right on time." He glanced at his clock. "If they ain't had no delays, she ought to be pulling in here in about twenty minutes."

"In that case, I think I'll just sit down on that bench over there and wait for it," Derringer said. And when Melvin asked if he was expecting someone on the train, he told him that Jack Tyler was supposed to be on it. Melvin asked if Tyler was back to start construction again. "No, I don't think so," Derringer replied. "I think most likely some more surveyin'." Derringer went over and sat down on the bench and Melvin returned to his desk. It seemed only a short time later when he heard the whistle, for he had drifted off to sleep. He dug into his pocket for his watch and saw that it was ten minutes past eleven. "Close enough," he decided, and stood up to watch the train come to a stop.

There were two passenger cars on the train, but he

was concentrating on the freight cars, especially the one stock car. He figured Jack was most likely in that car with his horse. When the train pulled to a stop, he saw Gilbert Nolen, the conductor, swing off the step to oversee the unloading of passengers and cargo. Right behind him, Carl Swanson stepped down and hurried back to the cattle car to open the door and place the ramp in position for Jack to lead his horse off the train. Of the few passengers who left the passenger cars, only one was conspicuous enough to attract Jesse's attention. Dressed in a long black overcoat with a fur collar and wearing a derby hat, he carried a leather suitcase. *Another gambler for Warton and the boys to worry about,* Jesse thought. His attention jumped back to the cattle car then when he saw Jack leading his black horse down the ramp and start looking around for him right away. He threw up his hand in welcome and waved it until Jack spotted him, then he walked to meet him.

"You made it right on time," Jesse said as they shook hands. "Any problems with your horse?"

"Not at all," Jack answered. "I think he's gotten to be a veteran train rider." He looked around him and said, "I swear, I didn't think they could get any more people in this little town, but it looks like more than when I left. And that ain't been but two months." Back to Derringer then, he remarked, "But you don't look to be any the worse for it."

"You wanna get checked in the hotel first, or take your horse to the stable first?" Jesse asked. "We've got time to do either one, or both, if we don't waste any time, and we can still get to the dinin' room before they close. Then you can tell me what this job is we've gotta do."

Jack said he wanted to leave his belongings in his room first, so they went to the hotel, where Julian welcomed him and gave him a room next to Jesse's. When they came back downstairs, they bumped into the man Jesse had assumed to be a gambler. He was coming in the front door, but he stepped back when he saw them coming out and politely held the door for them. "Thank you, neighbor," Jack said. Jesse nodded politely as well, but he still thought his first impression of the man was the correct one. When they walked Jack's horse up to Leon's stable a question occurred to Jack. "Tell me this, if this town is so overcrowded with people, why is it that I can get a hotel room and keep it for however long I need it? So can you, and I'll bet that fellow we just met gets a room, too. I'd think that hotel wouldn't have any vacancies ever."

"That's simple," Jesse said. "All these hundreds of people you're seein' ain't got the money to spend on a hotel room. The bushes down by the creek are full of folks who can't afford a hotel. The flophouses are filled up with those who can only spare a few dimes to rent a corner of a little room with half a dozen other renters. Take a walk upstairs in Vera's Vineyard and take a look at her rooms. It looks like an insane asylum."

"I guess that would be a good reason for it," Jack remarked. "But the hotel is doing all right and I reckon the dining room is, too."

"The hotel and the dinin' room are both doin' okay," Jesse told him. "And it's because it's owned by the Union Pacific and most of the hotel is rented to Union Pacific employees. I've got a room here, Clyde Woodcock has one, Fred Butcher has a room, the room clerk, the night clerk, Julian Burnett. . . ."

"I get it!" Jack interrupted. "All Union Pacific."

"Not all," Jesse said. "The city rents rooms, too. Both deputy sheriffs live in the hotel."

"All right, you made your point," Jack begged. "I won't ask you any more questions."

They had arrived at the stable at that point and Leon put Jack's horse in the stall next to Clem and the sorrel. "I take it we'll be pickin' 'em up first thing in the mornin'. Right, Jack?" Jesse asked.

"Well, let's say after breakfast," Jack replied. "I like to get a good breakfast before I start a trip that's gonna take some time."

"You know how long you're gonna be gone?" Leon asked. He directed the question at Jesse.

Jesse pointed at Jack. "You'll have to ask him," he said. "He ain't told me where we're goin'."

"I don't know how long it will take," Jack said. "I won't know until you tell me."

Jesse stared at Jack Tyler for a few seconds, then he said, "I thought you mighta been a little tetched in the head when you left here. Is there any chance you mighta got kicked in the head by a mule when you were in Council Bluffs?"

"Come on," Jack surrendered. "Let's go eat dinner and I'll explain the whole job to you." Directing his words to Leon then, he said, "Just know that we'll pick our horses up in the morning and we'll give you a better estimate of the number of days we'll be gone."

When they got to the dining room, both deputy sheriffs had already eaten and the sheriff usually went home for dinner when everything was peaceful in town. So Jack pointed to a table in the back corner of the room when Cecil met them at the door. Cecil remembered Jack and welcomed him back, then reminded Rachael that Jack Tyler was in charge of the actual construction of the railroad tracks. Rachael promptly informed Cecil that she already knew that, then extended a gracious welcome to Jack. When Cecil returned to his post by the front door, Rachael told them the choices for dinner that day and recommended the best bet. When she left to get their coffee, Jesse asked, "So, what's the reason for your visit?"

"The general wants to be sure about Dale Creek Ravine and wants me to double-check the map we laid out to reach Laramie City. That ravine is about three miles past Sherman Hill and we've got to build a trestle across it six hundred and fifty feet long and about a hundred and twenty-six feet high. The purpose of our trip is to make sure there ain't no other way to avoid having to build that trestle. He's gettin' ready to order timbers from Chicago to build it and he'd like not to have to, if the track can go any other way."

"I thought we'd already decided that was the best way to go," Jesse said. "Ain't nothing changed up there since he was here," he added with a hint of sarcasm.

"He's trusting you and me to take another look at it and confirm the map we've drawn up," Jack insisted. "And while we're at it, he wants us to determine the best route from there all the way to Laramie City."

"I've already done that," Jesse said. "I went up to

Laramie City a little while back and the way I went there would be the most direct route for the train to follow."

"How many days do you think it'll take us to go there and back?" Jack asked.

"Well, from Cheyenne to Laramie City it's about fifty miles, but it ain't an easy fifty miles. Then I don't know how many miles we're gonna take to confirm there ain't no better way than what we already know. We can ride up to Sherman Hill in half a day, but then we'll be in the Laramie Mountains and won't be able to make that gooda time. I expect it might be a week before we get back. So we're gonna have to buy some supplies to take with us. I hope you brought some money to get what we need for the trip. 'Cause if it's my treat, you ain't gonna be too happy."

Jack chuckled. "Well, I thought you had a better sense of hospitality than that. Don't worry, I brought the money to pay our expenses."

"Enough to pay for the whiskey we'll drink tonight before we turn in?" Jesse asked.

"Enough to pay for a couple of drinks each," Jack answered. "I don't want it to end up like the last time we went to Dawkin's the night before I went back to Council Bluffs."

"Why? What was wrong with that?" Jesse chided. "You even made a citizen's arrest and sent two murderers to jail."

"Are they still in jail?" Jack wondered.

"Nah," Jesse replied. "They hanged those two. Don't have to worry about them anymore."

Rachael arrived at the table with two plates of generous servings. "We're glad to have you come back to see us," she told Jack.

"I'm glad I came back," Jack said upon seeing the size of the servings.

Rachael smiled, pleased by his remark, then she asked, "Did Jesse tell you what he did one night when everybody thought he had gone to bed?"

Curious, Jack said, "Why, no, he didn't." Grinning then, he turned to look at Derringer. "What did you do one night when everybody thought you'd gone to bed, Jesse?"

"Nothing worth talking about," he said. "Better eat that food before it gets cold. We ain't gonna be eating like this for about a week."

"Ray Cooper said he walked into Dawkin's Saloon and shot three men who were holding him and the sheriff at gunpoint," Rachael declared. "Shot two of them with a double-barreled shotgun and the other one with his pistol."

Jack looked at Derringer and said, "Make that enough money to buy one drink of whiskey tonight before we go to bed."

"It was just one of those little situations that crop up once in a while," Jesse tried to explain. "You know how it is."

"No, I don't know how it is," Jack declared. "It seems to me that trouble just tends to search you out. I'm serious, Jesse, you need to find yourself another line of work."

"You're right, Jack," Jesse insisted, "and I already

have. I was working for the town as a deputy sheriff and I quit that job this mornin'. We'll get outta this wild town after breakfast tomorrow, out where the pure mountain air is stirred up fresh every mornin' by the Man Above and no man shall go hungry."

Both Rachael and Jack stared at him, amazed to hear the words come out of his mouth. Rachael was the first to comment. "Why, Jesse Derringer, how inspirational! I've never heard you talk like that before."

Jesse looked at them both, puzzled by their surprised expressions. He shrugged then and said, "That's where a Lakota Sioux injun said he was goin' right before I cut his throat."

"Damn you, Jesse!" she spat. "What a terrible thing to tell! You can get your own coffee!"

"Hell, he was gonna die anyway," Jesse pleaded. "I'd already shot him." She stormed off to the kitchen.

Jack couldn't help chuckling. "I swear, Jesse, you really know how to sweet-talk the women."

"I don't know what got into her," Jesse said. "It sure ain't like her to act like that."

In spite of what she said, she did bring them more coffee, although she told Jesse it was only because he was at the table with Mr. Tyler. When they finished dinner, they went to Cheyenne Merchandise to buy a list of supplies they had made while still sitting in the dining room. They had planned to take only one packhorse, since they were going to go to Laramie City and Jesse said there was a store there, if they saw they might run short on some items. But Jesse changed his mind and insisted they would be better off with two packhorses. He told Jack that he had another horse at the stable they could use as a packhorse. So they took the supplies to the stable and packed them in Jesse's packs, ready to load on the packhorses in the morning. The rest of the afternoon was made up of a visit to the sheriff's office to let them know Derringer was going to be out of town for a while, so he could not be counted on to help if he was needed. After that, Jesse and Jack went over the maps Jack had brought with him to see if there were any changes Jesse wasn't aware of.

When it was time for supper, they returned to the dining room where Jack was looking forward to his reception and anxious to see if Jesse would be allowed to eat with him. They found that Clara thought Jesse's quote was hilarious, considering the circumstances in which it was repeated. She told her daughter that Jesse was too naive to know it was offensive to her immature mind. To demonstrate to Jesse that no one was really angry at him, she playfully told him he couldn't eat until he told them another quote he might remember. He thought for a long time, raking his memory before finally coming up with one. "It was when I was in the army and we were hunkered down along a creek bank waiting for a party of twenty-some Cheyenne warriors to charge our position.

"Who said the quote?" Clara asked.

"It was General Dodge," Derringer said.

"Well," she asked impatiently, "what was the quote?"

"He said, 'Hold your fire till you can smell their stinkin' breath.'"

"Good Lord, that's terrible," Clara said, and headed for the kitchen. "Feed him anyway," she said to Rachael.

Jesse looked at Jack and shook his head, puzzled again by the women's reactions. "Well, hell, that's what the general said. I'll never understand how a woman's mind works."

CHAPTER 17

They rode out after breakfast the next morning, following the railroad tracks that extended past Cheyenne. Jack Tyler was especially interested in seeing what was left of the tracks and the materials after having been left unguarded for over two months. Much of the heavy timber used for the crossties had been dragged away, but there was quite a bit still there. The closer they got to Sherman Hill, the more Derringer noticed hoofprints around the stacks of wood. The tracks were all from unshod horses and some fairly fresh. It was not a good sign. He had hoped to avoid Indian sign altogether. If it was just him alone on this trail, he would not have been as concerned, for both his horses were unshod. They would be lost among those of the Indians. But Tyler's horse and the dun packhorse were shod, so he could only hope, with two unshod and two shod, anyone noticing might decide two Indians had stolen a white man's horses.

Their first stop was to rest the horses where the railroad track ended at the base of Sherman Hill. Jack was anxious to walk up the incline to the point where construction was called off. There were quite a lot of the track beds washed away, leaving gaping holes in the ground. While he was inspecting the damage done by the winter storms, Jesse took on the cooking chores. He built a fire and sliced some strips of bacon to fry while he filled the coffeepot from the stream. When the bacon was done, he cooked some hardtack in the bacon grease. When Jack came back down from the hill, Jesse told him, "Before you complain, I ain't no cook. But this'll hold you until we get over this hill. Then I'm plannin' to get me a deer to give us something decent to eat while we're roamin' around these mountains. If we don't see one before we get to Dale Creek, we've got a good chance of gettin' one there. When I came back from Laramie City a while back, that valley was covered with deer sign. I didn't want to stop and butcher a deer then when I was so close to Cheyenne. We've got some beef jerky if the bacon ain't enough for ya, but I'm hankerin' for some fresh venison."

"That's fine by me," Jack made a point in saying. "I ain't complaining." He was afraid that if he did, then he would get the job of cook and he didn't care for it any more than Jesse did.

After the horses were rested, they saddled up again and started up over Sherman Hill. Jesse led the way up into the mountains, retracing the narrow pass he had found when he and General Dodge had escaped from the Indians back in 1865. Although it was only three miles from Sherman Hill, it took almost an hour to make their way over the rocky hills that stood between them and Dale Creek Ravine. When they reached it, Jack stopped on the hill overlooking the ravine, looking straight across to the other side. In his mind's eye, he was trying to picture the trestle that had to be built to take the train straight across to the other side. "It's gonna be one helluva job," he uttered, but Derringer didn't hear him.

Derringer had his sights set on three deer far below that had just emerged from the growth of trees beside the creek. *Now, why are you three coming out of the brush this early in the afternoon?* he was thinking, having planned to hide by the creek at sundown when he would normally expect deer to come out of the woods and go to the water. A buck and two does—was this the valley's way of welcoming the railroad? When Jack pulled up beside him and started to ask a question, Derringer stopped him with a finger to his lips, then he pointed toward the three deer now beside the creek, drinking the water. Jack understood and remained silent while Jesse dismounted, pulling his rifle out of the saddle scabbard at the same time. The ravine had been calculated to be 217 yards from one side of it to the other. The three deer were at the creek in the middle of the ravine, cutting that distance in half, well within the range of the Henry rifle. He knew if he rode down into the ravine to get a closer shot, there was a good chance the deer would see him and bolt. So he handed Jack his reins to hold while he moved carefully down to a fallen tree a few yards below them to use to steady his rifle. He took aim at the largest doe and laid the front site of the Henry on a spot behind her front leg, drew a deep breath and held it. Only then did he lever a cartridge into the chamber, for he knew he wouldn't have much time. As he had anticipated, all three deer popped their heads up when they heard the metallic sound of the rifle loading. They bolted out of the creek, but it was too late for the larger doe, for Derringer's shot was already on the way. She tried to follow but stumbled when she tried to clamor up the opposite bank after the buck and the other doe.

He hurried back to jump on his horse and start down the side of the ravine. Riding right behind him, Jack was already looking forward to the fresh venison. When they reached the struggling doe, Derringer quickly ended her suffering with a shot to her brain. "I know we just broke camp back on the other side of Sherman Hill," he said to Jack. "But I'm fixin' to make a fire beside this creek and butcher this deer right now. I know how important this scoutin' party is for the railroad, but there ain't no hurry to get it done. And I know there ain't gonna be any changes in that map you've got with you. I've already scouted this line of mountains and there ain't any place you could build it that would be better than this pass and building that trestle. That being said, it is important to bleed and butcher this deer before the meat goes bad. We'll have to smoke some of it, but as cold as it is up here, we'll be eatin' fresh meat for three or four days." He looked back up at Tyler, who was still on his horse. "I know this is your scoutin' party, official business for the company and you're in charge. So do you wanna do something different?"

Tyler just stared at him for a moment before responding. "I don't believe I've ever heard you make a speech that long before." Then with tongue in cheek, he asked, "If I object to filling your belly before what I was sent here to find out, what would you do? Blow me away like you did those three drifters in the saloon?"

Derringer grinned, knowing Jack was japing him. "There's always that possibility," he answered.

"This was why you insisted on taking two pack-horses, wasn't it?" Jack asked.

"Turned out to be a good idea, didn't it?" Derringer replied. "There's a lotta meat on that doe, plus that hide. It woulda been too much to pack everything on one packhorse, especially if we was to happen to have to move fast." He paused to take a look up and down the creek before deciding. "Let's move upstream a little way. That looks like a better place for the horses up there a few yards."

Tyler got down and helped him pick up the deer and place her across the dun packhorse Derringer had come up with. When they got to the spot he had picked out, he pulled the carcass off the horse, took his rope and hung the deer carcass up from a tree limb. He cut the skin away, bled the carcass while he took care of the horses, and Jack gathered wood for the fire. As soon as the fire was glowing, there were small strips of venison roasting over it. Jack tended the roasting meat as Derringer continued the butchering. The different parts of the deer were cut into manageable portions and wrapped in the deer hide to keep it safe. When they had wrapped all the meat they could possibly eat before it went bad, they smoked as much as they could of what left. It was dark by the time they finished preparing their meat supply and time for supper, but Jack complained that he was too stuffed with fresh roasted deer meat to even think of eating supper. All he wanted to do was crawl into his sleeping bag and they could continue their inspection of the proposed route to Laramie City in the morning. "I'm gonna make some coffee," Jesse said. He had eaten his fill of venison as well, but he, unlike Jack, recognized what his true fill was and stopped eating when he had reached that point. "Don't you want some coffee?"

"Hell, no," Jack replied. "I can't put another thing in my mouth. How can you even think about drinkin' a cup of coffee?"

Derringer realized then that Jack Tyler had never had the opportunity to eat all the fresh killed meat he wanted and he had decided to take advantage of the occasion, thinking Jesse would do the same. He had to smile at his folly, but he felt sorry for him when he thought of the stomach cramps that might possibly follow. He hoped he hadn't cured him from ever eating venison again because he had enough to last them a week. "You go ahead and turn in," he told the suffering man. "I'll take a look at the horses to make sure they're good for the night and get a little more wood for the fire." Jack groaned in response.

Feeling pleasantly satisfied, Derringer sat close to the fire and drank his cup of coffee, listening to the sounds of the night. When they were interrupted by a frequent grunt from Jack, followed by an unpleasant breeze of human creation, he took his cup of coffee down to sit with the horses by the creek. It was cold, but it was peaceful. There was no snow on the ground, so he sat down on some leaves at the base of a large tree. Clem came to inquire, so he rubbed his nose and scratched him behind his ears. The gray gelding was satisfied to submit to the attention while Jesse held the cup in his other hand. Then Clem's ears stood up and flicked back and forth and Jesse figured the horse had detected a raccoon or a possum maybe. But when Clem suddenly pulled his head away from his hand and nickered, Jesse became alert. He dropped his cup in the leaves and cautiously stood up, pressed tightly against the tree trunk to avoid a double image. He scanned the creek bank, thinking Indians were coming for the horses, but he could not pick out any forms along the dark creek. He slid cautiously around the tree trunk for a little way, so he could better see his campfire and Jack's figure in his bedroll. And then he saw them, two dark figures converging on the sleeping man from two different directions. They were Indians for sure, that much he could tell. Probably Cheyenne, his first question was how many? His next thought was, if there were more than two, were the others closing in around him at the same time they were stalking Jack?

He dropped down to the ground and stared intensely at the dark woods around him. He could not see any movement of human bodies in any direction surrounding him. So he had to conclude that there were only two. And instead of slipping in and making off with the horses, they had decided to kill the sleeping white men, enjoy a feast of fresh meat, and ride away at their leisure with the white man's horses and possessions. *Makes sense to me,* Derringer thought, *but I'd better get moving because they're getting close.* He crawled up the bank, wishing he had his rifle, but it was with his saddle back at the campfire. Consequently, he wanted to get a little closer, so his handgun would be more reliable. Suddenly, both of the Indians were close enough for him to make them out clearly. They were armed only with bows and each one had an arrow notched ready to be released. If he had his rifle, he would have simply dispatched them both to the Happy Hunting Ground. But with his Colt .44, he needed to be closer still, just as he was sure the two Indians needed to be close enough to clearly see their two targets. He thought of Jack lying unsuspecting that his life was in the balance and he prayed that he wouldn't suddenly wake up before he got close enough to take care of both Indians. Finally one of the Indians stopped and signaled the other one, who was nearly as close to the campfire as he. He made a sound like a night bird to attract the other Indian's attention, then he held up his hand with only one finger extended. They both stopped then and Derringer thought, *He's telling his partner there ain't but one body by the fire.* He couldn't gamble with Jack's life any longer. "Hey!" he yelled, "I'm over here!" And he pumped two rounds into the startled man's chest with time left to turn and fire another fatal round before the second Indian could turn and release his arrow.

It was a frightening wake-up for Jack Tyler, who became entangled in his bedroll when the shots from Derringer's .44 split the cold wintry air. "Jesse!" he called out, "we're under attack!" He frantically searched for his gun, which had managed to get lost in the blanket he was still tangled up in. "Jesse!" he called again.

"It's all right, Jack, everything's all right." Derringer tried to quiet him down. He thought there were only two Indians in the attack, but he wouldn't know for sure until he scouted the area around the creek. "Let me check on these two Indians and make sure they're dead."

"I heard three shots," Jack said. "Did you miss one?"

"No, there weren't but two that approached the camp. I shot one of 'em twice." He checked the two bodies and found that they were both dead. *What a waste*, he thought, *two young men. I wish to hell you'd picked somebody else to help you commit suicide.*

When he went back to the fire, he found Jack standing there with his gun in hand, but he still had part of his bedroll wrapped around him tied in a knot. "I expect there are two horses tied around here somewhere. I'm gonna take a quick look. I'm pretty sure those two young bucks were out to steal some horses and take some scalps. I doubt they're with a party of braves. Might be a good idea not to make too big a target of yourself till I get back, though, just to be safe. He gave a little chuckle and japed, "Then we can set that blanket on fire to see if we can get you outta your bedroll."

"That might be funny to you," Jack said, "but I was sound asleep when you started shootin'. It sounded like you were shootin' at me."

"I'll sound off when I come back, so you don't take a shot at me," Derringer told him, and went back to the horses. He untied Clem and jumped on his back, then he started down the creek, scouting both sides of it. After about eighty yards, he gave up and turned Clem around to scout upstream. About fifty yards past the place where the horses were tied, Clem raised his head and whinnied. Derringer heard the answering whinny twenty yards ahead of him. The two horses were tied securely to two separate limbs of a willow tree. They both were fitted with Indian bridles, made with a rope. Derringer left the ropes tied to the willow and removed the rope bridle. When he returned to the other horses, the Indian ponies followed him. "Jack," he called out, "I'm comin' back."

"Well, come on," Jack answered, surprising him because he was at the creek with the horses.

"Whaddaya doin' down here?" Derringer asked. "I thought you'd be back by the fire to stay warm."

"I'm watchin' our horses, in case you ain't right about those two bein' alone," Tyler said. "I see you found the two horses. You plannin' on keepin' 'em?"

"No, I've got no use for 'em," Jesse answered. "They followed me back here. They ain't worth the cost and the trouble to take care of 'em. I just didn't wanna ride off in the mornin' and leave 'em tied to a tree to starve to death or feed a bear."

"Jesse Derringer's got a soft spot," Tyler crowed. "How much will you give me not to tell anybody about your soft spot?"

"Not one skinny dime," Derringer said, "but I might have to kill you if you do tell anyone." Tyler was not sure he was joking.

Satisfied that the two would-be horse thieves were the only threats in the ravine that night, they managed to get a decent amount of sleep before starting out again in the morning. The two Indian ponies followed along behind them, which seemed to bother Jack Tyler, even though Jesse told him the two strays would eventually decide there was nothing to be gained from the two white men and their four horses. Then they would heed the call of their ancestors and realize they were born wild and would return to that way of life. After he said it, he thought maybe he should try to remember it and repeat it to Clara and Rachael if they ever asked him to remember a worthy quote.

Having already verified the absolute necessity for the trestle across Dale Creek Ravine, Tyler's secondary purpose for the trip was to see for himself where his crews would be laying track on into Laramie City. Derringer was leading him to Laramie City on the same trails he had used before when going to that town. They were the same trails that he and the general had decided to be the best route for the train to take. Consequently, it was the route drawn on the map Tyler carried. "It's looking like a waste of your and my time, so far," he said. "When you look at these hills and valleys, it's plain to see there ain't any other way to get there with a train."

"You sayin' you wanna turn around and go back to Cheyenne?" Derringer asked.

"No," Tyler replied. "They told me to follow the map all the way to Laramie City, so let's go the whole way. I'd hate like hell to find out later on that there was some reason the tracks had to be rerouted just before entering the town."

"I doubt that could be the case, but it won't hurt to make sure," Derringer agreed. "I expect we've rode these horses enough this mornin' to owe 'em a rest. But if we stay on this trail for about three more miles there's a nice place to stop and cook some deer meat. Whaddaya say? Can you stand another meal of venison, or have you sworn off it for good? Because I've still got bacon in those packs."

"You wouldn't be japing me about that venison if you knew how much I suffered last night," Jack said.

"Oh, I know you suffered a plenty—I suffered a little myself," Jesse replied when he remembered the reason he left the campfire and went to the creek to sit with the horses. He realized just then that it might have been the thing that prevented the loss of their scalps. He chuckled at the thought of it.

"What's funny?" Tyler asked.

"Nothin'," Jesse replied. "I was just thinkin' about all that deer meat we've got to eat."

"Well, let's ride on to that creek you're talking about and cook some more of it," Jack said. "Only this time, let's just cook enough for dinner."

"Fair enough," Jesse agreed, and stifled another chuckle.

They continued along the trail they had been following until they came to the creek that Derringer had recommended for their midday meal and horses' rest. Tyler agreed that it was a nice camping spot, with water, grass, and plenty of wood for a fire. "Did you camp here on your trip back from Laramie City?" Tyler asked.

"No, I didn't," Derringer answered. "It was too early then. That dun packhorse oughta remember it, though. This is where I got him."

"Whaddaya mean?" Tyler asked.

"I mean this is where I got him," Derringer answered, thinking now that maybe he shouldn't have mentioned it, having experienced Jack's tendencies to worry.

"You got the horse here?" Jack pressed. "How did you get him here? Was he runnin' wild or something?"

"No," Jesse answered. "I mean yes, he was running wild."

"You're telling me a tale. Why don't you want me to know where you got that horse?"

"Because you get a little nervous over some things, but if you have to have the truth, I'll tell you the truth. I stole the damn horse."

"I figure you for a lot of things," Tyler said, "but I never figured you for a horse thief." He looked truly disappointed.

As a rule, Jesse Derringer didn't care what anyone thought about him, good or bad. But Jack looked so disappointed that he would do such a thing. So he said, "It was either steal the horse or shoot the owner sleepin' by the fire to stop him from coming after me." He saw a gleam of hope in Jack's eye, so he knew he was going to have to tell him the whole story. So he told him about the three small-time outlaws who followed him out of the saloon and tailed him all the way to this creek. He told him that two of the three gave up here and returned to Laramie City. The third camped there, planning to get on his tail again the next day.

"So you came back and instead of shootin' the fellow in his blanket, that soft spot took over and you stole his horse, so he couldn't catch you and you wouldn't have to kill him."

"No," Derringer protested. "I stole his horse so he

would have to walk twenty miles back to Laramie City thinkin' about how I coulda put a bullet in his brain instead of stealin' his horse. He wasn't worth shootin'."

Tyler thought about it for a few minutes before it occurred to him. "Ain't it kinda risky for us to go to Laramie City where that fellow is, and the other two that were with him, too?"

Derringer thought for a moment. "Well, you might think so, except the fellow I stole the horse from don't know for sure who stole his horse. He might wonder if it was me, but he didn't see me take the horse. And his two friends, well, they don't think I ever saw them. They ain't got no idea that I doubled back and got behind 'em. I'm not sure I'll recognize them, if they're still hangin' around that little town. It was pretty doggoned dark by the time I got close enough to hear part of what they were sayin'. And they were sittin' on their horses in the middle of this creek right here. Besides, drifters like those three don't usually hang around any town too long. There ain't much in the town right now to hold 'em," he said. He shrugged then and said, "It's your call. It don't make no difference to me whether we go there or not."

CHAPTER 18

Tyler decided he would not be following General Dodge's orders if he turned around just short of Laramie City and returned to Cheyenne. So after they ate some roasted venison and the horses were rested, they rode the rest of the way into the former tent town. It didn't take long for Tyler to get a good look at the town. They rode up and down the short street that was referred to as Main Street. Since it was around suppertime, Derringer asked Tyler if he wanted to go ahead and make camp and cook more venison or if he'd like to buy some supper cooked by a woman and have a drink of whiskey afterward. "I ate a bowl of beans and rice, mixed up with some chopped up beef in The Baby Doll and it was pretty good eatin'. I wouldn't be afraid to try that lady out again, if you want something besides deer meat."

"I might at that," Tyler answered right away. "I'm gonna tell you the truth, Jesse. I got so sick on all that deer meat I ate that I'm afraid it won't take very much more of it to make me sick."

"I noticed you didn't eat very much this mornin' or at dinnertime either. We'll just tie up in front of The Baby Doll and see what that lady's got cooked for supper." He didn't confess to Jack that when he cut some of the meat for dinner, he wondered if it was going to start to turn sooner than he anticipated. He was glad they had smoked a great deal of it, but he hated to waste so much of it.

They tied the horses out front and went into the saloon. Since Derringer was the kind of man who was easy to remember, Sid, the bartender, recalled his name as soon as he walked in the door. "Mr. Derringer," he greeted him when they walked up to the bar.

"Howdy, Sid," Derringer returned. "You remembered my name. You looked surprised when I walked in."

"You remembered mine," Sid came back. "I was surprised when I saw you come in." He didn't care to tell him he was surprised after Red Pickens and his friends asked him where Derringer was heading when he left town.

"We got that straightened out," Derringer said. "This is my friend Jack Tyler. I didn't ask you the last time I was in here, but what is the lady's name who does the cookin' here?"

"Cora," Sid replied, "Cora Welch, same last name as mine."

"Oh, so she's your missus?"

"That's a fact," Sid said.

"Well, you're a very fortunate man," Derringer said.

"When I was in here before, she cooked up some beans and rice with some beef and it was good eatin'. Jack and I would like to try some of whatever it is she's got on the stove tonight."

Sid chuckled. "Red beans and rice with sliced ham and hot biscuits," he said. "You want some?"

Derringer looked at Tyler and Tyler said, "We do."

"Set yourselves down at a table then and I'll tell Cora you want some supper," Sid told them. "I reckon you want some coffee." They said they did, so he went to the kitchen door to give Cora the order, then he poured two cups of coffee and delivered them to the table. "Your grub will be out in a minute." As he predicted, the food arrived in the hands of a miniature little gray-haired woman who set the plates down before them, then returned to the kitchen without saying a word.

They both dug in without testing the quality of the meal but found out that it was very tasty. To Derringer, it was not only a meal but also a test of the woman's ability to cook. When they finished, they went up to the bar to pay for the meal and have a drink of whiskey. "Say, Sid," Derringer began, "do you suppose I could talk to your wife about some meat?"

The bartender was suspicious. "Why do you want to talk to her about meat? She's kinda busy right now."

"Here's the thing, Sid," Derringer went on. "I've got about thirty or forty pounds of deer meat outside on a packhorse. I killed and butchered the deer last night and I'd like her opinion on whether or not it's still good. I have an idea she might know better than me. It was still fine when we cooked some of it for dinner, but I'd like to have her see if it would be all right for her to cook."

Sid chuckled. It might have been the last thing he would have expected to come out of the rugged-looking man's mouth. "I expect she would. I'll ask her." He walked over to the kitchen door and gave his wife the message. Back at the bar Derringer could tell by Sid's motions that she was not inclined to, but finally she came out of the kitchen and walked back to the bar with her husband.

She had to arch her head way back to look into Derringer's eyes. "What is it you want?" she asked, although Sid had told her.

"First, I wanna tell you I admire your cookin'," Derringer said. "So I'd consider it a big favor if you would take about two minutes to take a look at some fresh deer meat I've got outside on my packhorse."

"I'm glad you thought your supper was all right," she told him, "but I ain't buyin' no deer meat. I've got somebody who supplies most of the meat I cook."

"Yes, ma'am, I'm sure you do. I ain't trying to sell you anything. I just want you to tell me if this deer meat is close to turnin'."

She looked at him in disbelief, then looked at her husband to try to determine if they were playing a trick on her, for which she had no time. Sid's facial expression was as puzzled as hers. Looking at Derringer again, she decided he seemed sincere. "All right, but just for a minute. I've got biscuits in the oven." He turned at once and led her out the door, then he went straight to his packhorse and started untying one of the deer hide bundles. When he was able to open it far enough to expose a large portion of the meat, he stood aside to let her examine it. She stepped up to the horse and looked at the meat. "When did you butcher it?"

"Last night," he said.

She pulled the hide back farther. "I shoulda brought a knife with me," she said, and he quickly drew his knife and handed it to her. She sliced off a small piece, looked at it closely, sniffed it, then tasted it. "Ain't nothing wrong with this meat."

"I didn't think there was," Derringer said. "But I wanted to see if you would serve it to your payin' customers."

"Sure I would," she responded, "if I had some venison, but like I said, I ain't buyin' no more meat right now."

"Would you take it if I gave it to you?" Derringer asked.

"Course I would," she replied, still waiting for the catch she knew had to be in the gift. "Why on earth would you want to give it to me?"

"Because I know me and my partner ain't gonna eat but a small portion of that fresh meat before it turns bad and I'd be throwin' about forty pounds of fresh meat away. I'd rather give it to you, if you can use it. If you don't want it as a gift, maybe I can trade you something for it."

"Like what?" Cora asked.

"Maybe no charge for me and my partner's breakfast in the mornin'," he suggested. When she looked as if he was trying to trick her and asked him how many mornings he was talking about, he said, "Just tomorrow's. We'll be leavin' town after breakfast."

"Mister, you've got a deal," she exclaimed. "Can you take it around to the back door? We've got a spring box in the stream back of the saloon. It'll stay cool in that for a good while."

He took one of the hide-wrapped bundles off the horse and asked, "Have you got room in your spring box for two of these?" She was pretty sure she did, so he handed Tyler one and he set the other one on the ground while he tied up his packsaddle again. Then he picked the bundle up and she led them back through the saloon and out the back door.

"I thought we couldn't buy no more meat right now," Sid commented when they walked past the bar.

"I didn't buy any," she answered him, "but the special for breakfast tomorrow is gonna be venison and grits."

No one passing by showed much interest in the transfer of the deer meat to Cora Welch, but the principals involved in the trade caught the attention of three men standing outside the Bucket of Blood Saloon. "It's him!" Curley George suddenly exclaimed.

"Who?" Coy Moffat asked.

"Derringer!" Curley blurted.

"Where?" Red Pickens responded at once at the mention of the name.

"Down yonder," Curley said, "in front of The Baby

Doll! Standin' by his horses, talkin' to that little woman that cooks in there and some other feller." All three of them automatically moved over closer to the front of the saloon in order not to stand out. "What are we hidin' for?" Curley said. "He ain't never seen us. He don't know we was tailin' him."

"He might notta seen you and Coy," Red said, "but I ain't so sure about me. That looks like my dun geldin' he's using for a packhorse."

"I don't think so, Red," Curley said. "If he was the one who stole your horse, you wouldn't be here. If he slipped into your camp and caught you sleepin', he'da shot you sure as hell. And he wouldn'ta had to sneak out with your horse."

"Curley's right," Coy said. "You saw the way he cut them two drifters down in the Bucket of Blood. That devil ain't about cuttin' nobody no slack."

"I hear what you're sayin'," Red replied, "but I still say that looks like my horse."

"I expect it does," Curley argued. "I expect it looks like a helluva lot of dun horses, since they all look pretty much the same."

"I know one thing," Coy commented, "he don't know who he's dealin' with here in Laramie City. Either that or he's crazier than a yeller jacket corked in a bottle. Big Steve ran him outta town the last time he was here. Maybe we oughta go tell Big Steve that Derringer's back in town."

"I'm gonna go take a look at that horse," Red decided when Derringer and Tyler followed Cora Welch back into The Baby Doll. He walked down to the saloon to look at the horses tied at the rail. Curley and Coy didn't hesitate to follow, secure in the false impression that Derringer had never gotten a look at them. Red went straight to the horse and walked all the way around it. Suddenly he stopped and blurted, "That's my horse!"

"What makes you so dad-gummed sure?" Curley said. "He looks like a hundred other dun horses."

"'Cause he's the only one wearin' that fancy bridle that matches the saddle I had to ride halfway back to pick up after I walked back here to Laramie City."

His statement was enough to silence both Coy and Curley, and all three men stood staring at the dun gelding in a mild state of shock. "You boys seem mighty interested in my horses," a voice sounded calmly behind them. The three turned at once to discover Derringer standing on the short piece of boardwalk in front of the saloon. He held his Henry rifle in both hands, cocked and ready to fire. A few feet away, Jack Tyler stood, his hand resting on the handle of the six-gun in his holster.

A pregnant moment of silence followed before Red summoned the courage to make the accusation. "This here dun horse belongs to me," he finally charged.

As Curley and Coy had argued before, Derringer replied, "You mean to say that horse looks like one you own, right?"

"No, I mean to say that is my horse 'cause it's still wearin' my hand-tooled bridle that matches the saddle I bought with it."

"Well, that explains the problem then," Derringer said. "Looks like you're the victim of some real hard luck. I bought that dun about a week ago from a Cheyenne Indian at the end of the train tracks. Paid him twenty dollars for the horse. It might be worth a little more than that, but the Indian didn't care. He just wanted to get some money for it. The bridle came with the horse. I thought it was kinda tacky, but since I was just gonna use it for a packhorse, I thought, what the hell?" He watched the reactions on their faces, concentrating primarily on that of Red Pickens. He was not overly concerned about the other two men. To this point, they had shown no interest beyond those of a couple of spectators. He was ready to move against Red should he show the first indication of retaliation. He was aware of Jack standing there with him, but he was not counting on his actions in what could amount to a face-off, depending upon Red's response.

"The fact of the matter is, that's my horse," was all Red could think of to say, "and I want him back."

"The fact of the matter is, that used to be your horse," Derringer replied. "You musta lost him somehow, you ain't said yet, but now you want him back? Are you wanting to buy the horse? 'Cause if you are, he ain't for sale. I need him for a packhorse. That's the reason I bought him." He maintained his calm exterior while he watched Red twisting in utter frustration. "I paid twenty dollars for that horse, but I found out he's worth a lot more. So if you want him back, I will sell him to you for a hundred and twenty dollars. And I'll buy another horse at a reasonable price."

It was too much for Red's simple brain to handle. Almost to the point of reaching for his gun, he finally said what he knew to be true. "I know damn well you slipped into my camp on the trail to Cheyenne and stole that horse while I was asleep."

"What were you doin' on the trail to Cheyenne?" Derringer asked.

"Mindin' my own business!" Red roared.

"Sounds to me like you oughta be keeping a better eye on your horse," Derringer said. "The horse is for sale for one hundred and twenty dollars or make your best offer."

"You son of a . . ." Red started while reaching for his six-gun, only to double over in pain when Derringer's rifle shot slammed into his chest. Derringer immediately cranked another cartridge into the cylinder and waited for a move from either Curley or Coy.

Both men put their hands up, palms out. "We ain't got nothin' to do with this," Coy said as they backed away. Then he whispered to Curley, "If Big Steve's in town, he'll come a'runnin'. Let's hang around and see what happens. He's already run Derringer out of town once."

Derringer turned around to find Jack Tyler standing seemingly in shock, his eyes and mouth wide open. "Let's go in and have that drink, Jack," Derringer said. "We'll have to wait till somebody comes for the body and I'm sure the town marshal will have some questions. Jack," he repeated when Tyler didn't respond the first time.

"What?" Tyler finally reacted, and Derringer repeated the need to go in and have a drink. "Right," Jack said. "Let's have a drink of whiskey."

His manner was enough to concern Derringer, so he asked, "What just happened, Jack?"

"What do you mean?" Tyler asked.

"What did you just see?"

"He went for his weapon, but you were faster and you shot him," Jack said.

"That's a fact," Jesse told him. "He drew his weapon first." He shook his head and thought, *I need a better witness*. There were other spectators who might have seen the incident, unfortunately two of them were Red's two friends. *Oh, well, I had to bluff my way out of town last time. Maybe I can do it again,* he thought. "Come on, we'll go inside and wait for the marshal to get here."

They went back inside the saloon and ordered a couple shots of whiskey. Sid poured the shots, but he also offered some advice. "The whiskey's on the house as part of the payment for all that deer meat," he said. "But it might be a good idea if you and your friend weren't here when Big Steve Long gets here."

Tyler nodded his head in complete agreement, but Derringer replied, "'Preciate your advice, Sid, but we've got no reason to run. That fellow wanted one of my horses and when I wouldn't give it to him, he reached for his six-gun. I had no choice but to shoot him. I figure the law oughta be on my side of the argument. I don't even know that fellow and he comes up and picks a fight with me."

"His name was Red Pickens," Sid told him. "He was one of three no-good drifters that have been hangin' around Laramie City for a couple of weeks."

"Yeah, there were two other fellows with him, but they didn't want any part of his argument," Derringer said. He didn't tell Sid that he was well acquainted with Red and his two friends. "I think it best if we just sit down in here and wait for the marshal to show up, so he can get the straight story on the cause of the shootin'. So pour us another shot of that whiskey and we'll go sit down at that table in the back of the room and wait for the marshal. Then we can give him the whole story." Sid shrugged and poured two more drinks. "Come on, Jack," Derringer said, and they picked up their glasses and went to the empty table at the back of the room. Derringer sat down with his back to the wall, facing the front door. When Tyler started to sit down opposite him, Derringer stopped him and said, "Sit over here, Jack." He indicated the chair on his left, so Tyler sat down in that chair. Then Derringer laid his rifle on the right side of the table, pointing toward the door, a new cartridge already in the chamber.

They both tossed the shot of whiskey back and Tyler finally found his voice. "Maybe that bartender had the right idea," he began. "It might be the smart thing for us is to leave this place before that marshal gets here. It looks like somebody had to go somewhere to find him. If he was in his office, he woulda heard the shot. As far as the railroad through here, I don't really have to see any more than I've already seen. So why don't we leave while we've got the chance?"

"I can't tell you what to do," Derringer said to him. "But I don't have any choice. I have to stay to defend myself. That fellow I just killed followed me last time I was here with the intent of killin' me. His two friends were in on the plan to kill me, but they gave up before he did. So I'm pretty sure they're gonna tell the marshal that Red Pickens didn't draw on me. And that's all that crooked town marshal's gonna need to justify my hanging. And I'll tell you one thing more, he's gonna play hell tryin' to hang me." He looked Tyler in the eye and said, "So do what you think is best for yourself and no hard feelin's either way."

Tyler just gave him a tired smile before he responded. Then he said, "I reckon I might be the only witness who saw him draw first, so I guess I'd better stay here with you. Growin' old and feeble ain't all it's cracked up to be, anyway."

"I knew I had you figured right," Derringer said. "We'll be all right just as long as we always handle this town marshal the same way we'd handle a rattlesnake." He had no sooner said it when they heard the noise increase from the spectators gathered in front of the saloon that announced the arrival of Big Steve Long. The noise level dropped again while they imagined Long was getting answers to his questions. Shortly after, he appeared in the doorway of the saloon.

All the conversation inside the saloon ceased when he stepped inside, ducking his head slightly to avoid bumping it on the head jamb of the door. With his revolver in hand, he took only a couple of steps before stopping to scan the room for the man he sought. The crowd in the saloon parted, leaving a clear path between the marshal and the two men at the back table. "I thought I made it clear to you the last time you was here that you ain't welcome in my town," Long said. He indicated with his pistol for Derringer to get on his feet.

"Maybe you ain't noticed, Marshal," Derringer responded, "but this rifle I'm restin' my hand on is aimed at you. It's hard to tell, you bein' so tall, but I'd have to guess where my bullet would strike you if I squeezed the trigger. Maybe in the belly, maybe in the crotch— like I said, hard to tell. Maybe you're wonderin' if there's a live round in the chamber. Well, I'll be honest with you. When that fellow outside reached for his gun, I cut him down before he cleared leather. Then I cranked another round into the chamber in case one of his friends decided to shoot me. At least, that's the way I remember it, so all it needs is the touch of my finger. But what if my memory's wrong and I didn't cock it again after I shot him? Then you'd have the advantage, instead of me. So are you a gambler? I am, and if you aim that pistol straight at me, I'm gonna pull this trigger and then we'll see if I cocked my rifle or not."

Long hesitated, unaccustomed to being challenged by anyone and concerned that he might be confronting an insane gunman. He felt strongly that the maniac knew there was a live round in the chamber of that Henry rifle, or he wouldn't have the brass to tempt him to shoot. He was not a fan of fair gunfights and although he had participated in many confrontations, he had avoided all in which he had not held the advantage. Looking into the deadly serious eyes of the man called

Derringer, he was not at all confident he would come out on top. In fact, the more he thought about it, the more he feared his best result might be no better than a tie. "All right," he said, "I'm a reasonable man. I'll hear your side of what happened outside. I'll holster my gun and you clear that rifle and hand it to me."

"You holster your weapon and I'll eject the cartridge from my rifle, but I'll not hand over my rifle. I'll leave the chamber empty and we'll decide what actually happened out front. That's what you want, isn't it? The true facts?"

"That's what I'm after," Long declared, "the true facts." He dropped his revolver into his holster while watching Derringer crank out the live round that had been in the chamber. "What about the rest of them?" He knew all Derringer had to do was close the lever and there would be a new cartridge in the chamber.

Tired of playing the game with the marshal, Derringer said, "I'm not going to empty my rifle. Here are the facts and all you need to know. The last time I was here Red Pickens followed me for over twenty miles, trying to dry-gulch me. When he finally made camp for the night, I slipped in and stole his horse, so he couldn't come after me. Must have made him mad because he came after me today. If I had wanted to kill him, I could have done it while he was asleep, but I just wanted to stop him from coming after me. So I took his horse. Today I offered to sell the horse back to him, but he reached for his gun and I had no choice. I had to shoot him. If those two partners of his told you any different, you oughta put them in jail for lyin'."

"Even if all that was true, you still showed up here again after I warned you not to come back here again and I can jail you for that," Long said, thinking once he had him in jail on any charge, he could take out his vengeance any way he wanted.

"Maybe this is where I should interrupt you here, Marshal," Tyler spoke up. "It's my fault that Mr. Derringer is in Laramie City today. My name's Jack Tyler. I'm the superintendent in charge of building the tracks for the Union Pacific Railroad. During the early part of the coming year we were planning to come through Laramie City. Mr. Derringer is the chief scout for the Union Pacific and I asked him to take me here to see the layout of the land around the town. We thought our business here was finished and planned to return to Cheyenne in the morning after breakfast here. Cora is cookin' us some venison we shared with her. I can assure you that General Grenville Dodge will appreciate any cooperation we receive from the officers and citizens of Laramie City. But if the town prefers not to become a Union Pacific station, we do have alternate routes to bypass Laramie City."

Big Steve Long wasn't sure if he could risk any trouble with the Union Pacific or not. He knew the mayor and the principal merchants were counting on the railroad coming through Laramie City. Even he and his partners, Con and Ace Moyer, in the Bucket of Blood Saloon were counting on the railroad to bring the business to make them all wealthy. It suddenly struck him that he would be very unpopular if he caused the railroad to bypass Laramie City. Not only that, but the land he and his half brothers, Con and Ace, had forced the homesteaders to sign over to them would be worthless. "I tell you what I'm gonna do, Mr. Tyler," he suddenly decided. "I'm gonna forget what I told Mr. Derringer about stayin' out of Laramie City. Come back to see us. You're welcome and the railroad is welcome here." He turned around and walked out of the saloon.

Everyone was surprised, but none more than Sid and Cora Welch. "I swear, I don't know if I believe what I just saw. Big Steve Long just backed down and walked away," Sid said. He turned to Derringer and said, "You mind your back. Big Steve don't back down to nobody."

Derringer looked at Tyler, who was sitting there with a self-satisfied smile on his face. "A well-polished lie is mightier than the sharpest sword," he said, "or something like that." He thought he should let Tyler enjoy it for a little while before he burst his bubble. "That was good thinkin', Jack. You bought us enough time to get us out of town alive." When Tyler looked confused, Derringer said, "Sid's right, Big Steve Long ain't likely to back down to anybody and he sure as shootin' ain't a forgivin' man. He doesn't want to do anything to keep the railroad from coming through Laramie City and he's got plenty of witnesses who heard him welcome us to town. Once we leave town, however, there won't be any witnesses to tell what happened to us on our way back to Cheyenne. My guess is that he'll try to make it look like we were jumped by Indians. So he'll bring a bow and a couple of arrows to leave stickin' out of our bodies. But the railroad ain't got this far yet, so there ain't no telegraph to tell Union Pacific what happened to us."

Tyler shook his head, disappointed. "I swear, I didn't think about that."

"Maybe not, but you did save my butt from possibly goin' to jail, or from gettin' shot in the back when we walk outta this saloon, or from anything else in front of witnesses. So that was smart thinkin'."

CHAPTER 19

"What happened?" Curley George asked Big Steve Long when he came out of the saloon without Derringer. "Ain't you gonna arrest him?"

"No, I ain't arrestin' him," Long answered, speaking loud enough so most of the people hanging around the front door could hear him say it. "It was a fair fight. Red Pickens drew first."

Curley and Coy Moffat looked at each other in total disbelief, then Curley said, "I can't believe you let him go. I told you me and Coy would say Red never went for his gun."

"Shut up!" Long told him. "You and Coy follow me." He walked away from the saloon and they followed him.

When he crossed the street and headed toward the jail, Coy said, "Whoa! Now wait a minute! What are we headin' to the jail for? We ain't caused no trouble here."

"Just shut up and keep walkin'," Long told him. "I ain't arrestin' you. Although I was thinking about it, but now I've got a use for you two saddle tramps." He led them inside the jail and in spite of what he said, they could not rid themselves of their feelings of discomfort. "I've been watchin' the three of you, wonderin' when you was gonna run outta money and I was gonna have to run you outta town."

"We ain't broke yet," Curley said.

"No, but you're gittin' close, ain'tcha?" the marshal asked. Curley didn't answer, so Big Steve continued. "How'd you like to earn a hundred dollars apiece for a little job you'd most likely do on your own for nothin'?"

Curley relaxed then and a grin broke out on his whiskered face. "I reckon we're available right now, ain't we, Coy?" Coy answered with a grin of his own. "Has it got anythin' to do with that Derringer feller?" Curley asked.

"I'd do it myself," Long replied, "but it's important that I'm seen around town when somethin' happens to Derringer and that Union Pacific feller, so it don't look like it's got anything to do with the town. So that means you need to let them get away from town before you hit 'em. If you do it right, it'll look like the work of injuns."

"You want us to scalp 'em?" Coy asked.

"I hadn't thought about that," Long said. "I've got a couple of arrows I was gonna give you to stick in 'em, but scalpin' 'em would be better. Hell, scalp 'em and stick the arrows in 'em, too."

"How we gonna shoot them arrows?" Coy asked. "You got a bow?"

"No, I ain't got no bow," Long responded. "You don't need no bow, just stab 'em with the arrows."

"I ain't sure you can stab somebody hard enough to get that arrow in deep as one shot with a bow," Curley said.

"Yes, you can," Long insisted. "I've done it before. You just have to get a good grip on the arrow and slam it in as hard as you can."

"I don't know," Coy said, still with some doubts. "I ain't sure I could do it. Maybe that feller with him, but Derringer looks like a pretty stout man to wrassle."

Long and Curley exchanged glances, then Curley said, "We'll shoot him first, Coy. Then we'll stab him with the arrow."

"Oh. All right."

"Okay, we've got a deal," Big Steve said. "You bring me their two scalps and I'll give each one of you one hundred dollars, cash money." They said they understood. "They said they're leavin' in the mornin' after breakfast at The Baby Doll Saloon," Big Steve said. "Remember, you don't do the job until they're outta town."

"Do they serve breakfast at The Baby Doll Saloon?" Coy asked.

"No, they don't," Long said impatiently. "Cora's just cookin' breakfast for them two because they gave her some fresh deer meat."

"Oh," Coy said. "Right."

"You boys would do well to find their camp tonight and keep an eye on it. Because even if they're sayin' they ain't leavin' till after breakfast in the mornin', they just might try to sneak outta here tonight. And if they do, you better be ready to go right behind them. If you boys do a good job on this, I'll have some more work for you to do that oughta keep you in spendin' money for a good while," Long told them. That served to kindle their enthusiasm for the assassination of Derringer and Tyler as well as an association with Big Steve Long. Their attitude satisfied Long; however, his plans included the death of the two of them as soon as he had proof of Derringer's death.

Back in The Baby Doll Saloon, Cora had inspected all of the bundles of venison that Derringer had given her and she informed him that she had not thrown out any of it. She told him that she was going to put all of it in the spring box, even that which she planned to take out to cook for their breakfast. When he hesitated for a moment, she insisted. "I told you I would fix breakfast for you and Jack and I meant it. And then I'm gonna cook up a venison and rice bowl to sell for dinner. That's something my customers don't get a chance to have."

"I'll bet that venison and rice bowl is mighty good," Derringer said. "But I need to talk it over with Jack and decide if it would be smarter for us to pull outta here tonight. I think your husband thinks like I do when it comes to your marshal's intentions." He glanced at Sid nodding in agreement. Then he looked at Tyler and asked, "What do you think, Jack? You wanna wait till daylight tomorrow mornin', or do you feel better about leaving tonight and hope to get too big a lead on anyone following us?"

"Doggone it, Jesse, I don't know. I feel better going with your judgment. Whatever you think best."

"Well, here's what I think we oughta do." He looked over at Sid, who was listening with great interest. "Sid, would you be all right if we was to set up camp tonight on the other side of that stream your spring box is in? I notice there's grass by that stream and we could tie the horses in the trees down below your place."

"Why, of course it would," Sid replied. "You're welcome to camp anywhere back there you want to. I own all that between here and the river, two blocks wide. So you stayin' tonight?"

"No, we're leavin', but I'd like for the marshal to think we're stayin' just like we said we would. And I think he's plannin' to come after us when we leave, him or somebody he sends. So I think somebody's gonna be keepin' an eye on our camp to make sure we're here in the mornin'. That being said, I think we'd best get that camp set up before it turns hard dark." They said their good-byes to Sid and Cora and thanked them for their help. "I'd ask you for one more favor, Sid, if you wouldn't mind. I'm gonna build a campfire down on the side of that stream. I know you gotta tend the bar. But do you know anyone you trust you could send down to the stream to put some more wood on the fire? Say about nine or ten tonight?"

"He sure does," Cora interrupted. "I'll go put some wood on your fire."

"We wouldn't wanna put you to the trouble, Cora," Derringer said.

"Nonsense," she replied, "no trouble at all. I don't want Sid to leave the bar. That would be too noticeable.

I can slip out the back door and run down there and put some wood on the fire and be back before anybody knew I left the kitchen."

"I declare, Sid, you sure married a genuine keeper. Thank you, Cora. Come on, Jack, we wouldn't likely find a better place to camp, if we did wanna spend the night. We could sit right there and see anybody approaching our horses. Too bad to waste it, but it would be to our advantage to get a good head start on whoever comes after us.

Jack hesitated, then asked Cora a question. "When we ate supper, you put some kinda yellow fruit-like thing on our plates. That was one of the best things I ever tasted. What was that?"

She laughed. "You mean you never had a pickled peach before?"

"No, ma'am. I never have. It sure was good. I'm sorry I won't get a chance to try another one of those." She laughed delightedly as she walked them out the back door, and when they passed the pantry, she reached in and brought out a jar of pickled peaches and gave them to him.

"Don't you eat this whole jarful at once," she warned. "You might make yourself sick." He was still thanking her when they went out the door.

They left the saloon and rode their horses down behind it, and by the light of the setting sun they took the saddles off the horses and led them into the trees. On a rope between a couple of trees close to the stream, they tied all four horses. Then they gathered some wood for the fire, picking a spot beside the stream that could be seen from the street about fifty yards away. They made a show of making their beds, using their saddles for pillows. Then they sat by the fire, listening to the noise from the saloons on the street above them until darkness made it impossible to pick out definite objects on the street. They stacked some firewood for Cora to find close to the fire, then picked up their saddles and went into the trees to saddle the horses.

The two men standing by the corner of a hog pen some thirty yards behind the Bucket of Blood Saloon peered at the campfire glowing close to sixty yards away. They had not risked getting any closer, afraid they might be spotted. But they were close enough to see Derringer and his partner bedding down for the night until finally it got so dark they couldn't make them out anymore. Their campfire was still strong, however, so they imagined they were crawling into their blankets. "There ain't no use in us standin' out here in the cold any longer," Curley said. "They've gone to bed."

"Looks like," Coy agreed. "Ain't no sense in standin' out here all night while they're layin' down there sleepin' away."

"You know what Big Steve told us," Curley reminded him, "make sure they don't try to slip out durin' the night. It ain't that late yet. Let's go back to the Bucket of Blood and have a couple of drinks, then we can check on 'em later." They went back to the saloon and sat around until Roy said he was closing up and poured one last shot for the few remaining customers.

"Ain't no sense in both of us checkin' that camp again," Curley said. "Tell you what, I'll flip you to see who goes back out there to check on 'em."

"All right," Coy agreed. "Let's go around back and flip it there where it can land flat." They walked out the front door of the saloon and went around to the back of the building where some steps had been built, leading to a second floor the owners called the Bunkhouse. There was a small stoop at the foot of the stairs and this is where they chose to flip the coin. "All right, you flip it and I'll call it in the air." Curley pulled a quarter out of his pocket and showed it to Coy to prove it wasn't the same on both sides. Then he flipped the coin and Coy said, "Heads." It landed heads up, causing Coy to giggle.

"Best two outta three," Curley said immediately.

"You lose," Coy answered, and started up the steps where he and Curley each rented one of a dozen cots. "Now, don't be late, you hear?" he chided him.

Coy was just about to drift off to sleep when Curley returned. "You didn't watch 'em very long," he declared.

"Didn't have to," Curley replied. "They ain't goin' nowhere tonight. When I got to that hogpen where we was before, that fire had just about died out. So I decided I'd get a little bit closer to make sure they were still there. But just as I started, one of 'em got up and put a lotta wood on the fire, about enough to keep it goin' for a good long while. They ain't plannin' to get up until it's time for breakfast."

"Maybe we oughta go down to The Baby Doll Saloon in the mornin', if that woman really is gonna cook Derringer some deer meat for breakfast. I'd enjoy havin' some of that fresh meat," Coy declared.

"I druther slip down there to that camp while they're layin' in their bedrolls and put a bullet in their brain pans and be done with 'em," Curley said. "Big Steve is worried about the railroad bypassin' Laramie City if we kill them two here in town. If he had half a brain, he'd know that the railroad's comin' here no matter who gets killed here because this way is the one that costs them the least money to build."

"You know that and I know that," Coy agreed, "and Big Steve is still tryin' to figure out how to tell his right sock from his left one. But you can count on one thing for sure. If you don't do what he tells you to do, he'll shoot you down and say you drew on him. So crawl on your cot and let's get some sleep. We'll be trackin' Derringer in the mornin'."

While Coy and Curley were participating in a chorus of snoring with five other cot renters over the Bucket of Blood, Derringer and Tyler were following a trail familiar to Derringer now. As soon as a good hard dark had fallen around Laramie City, they had picked up their saddles and walked into the trees by the stream to ready their horses for travel. Derringer took the short shovel he carried on his packhorse and shoveled some more loose dirt on the ring he had cleared around their fire, hoping to eliminate any tendency the fire might have of spreading. It was a calm night with the promise of a new moon. It would have been unlikely that the fire would spread if left alone, but he didn't want to take the chance. After making sure there was plenty of firewood left for Cora, they had freshened up the fire and led their horses down the stream. The stream had taken a wandering course, but it eventually led them to the river. Once they were there, they were able to climb on their horses and follow the river until they reached an intersecting path that Derringer knew well by then.

Now, with the light of a new moon, they made good time as they approached the creek that had become the favorite camping place to stop and rest the horses. Once the horses were taken care of, they built a fire and cooked some smoked venison to eat with some coffee and hardtack. With no idea how successful their secret departure from Laramie City had been, they knew it would be to their benefit to catch an hour's worth of sleep, if possible.

"Do you think we got away from there without Big Steve Long knowing it?" Tyler asked, when they sat by the fire and ate the smoked venison.

"Yeah, I think we did," Derringer answered. "The fact that we made it down that stream and along the river without raising any sound of alarm tells me we weren't being watched that closely. Like we figured, that marshal didn't want anything happening to us while we were still in his town. I think we've got a big enough lead on them now that they might just figure it's too big a head start to overcome. I guess we'll see. We'll start out again as soon as the horses are ready." He paused then before japing, "I neglected to ask you, though, were you ready to leave? After all, this was your scout to Laramie City. Did you get all the information you were sent up there to find out? Or should we turn back and take a closer look at the terrain around that little town?"

"I reckon I've seen enough of the town to know that there isn't any reason not to run our tracks through there," Tyler answered him. He was well aware that Jesse was japing him. "But there might be a lot more things to find out about the town, if it wasn't for the fact that you seem to have enemies everywhere we go. So most of the places we go to, I only get to see them when I'm looking back over my shoulder on a galloping horse." His comment brought a chuckle in response.

As Derringer suggested, they took the hour nap. At least he did. Tyler found it a little difficult to actually close his eyes and go to sleep. Derringer assured him that, even had the posse discovered they were gone and left Laramie City at dawn, they would not catch up before the two of them left this creek.

It was actually quite a while after the breaking of dawn before Curley and Coy became aware that Derringer and Tyler were no longer in town. They only became suspicious after they walked past The Baby Doll Saloon around six o'clock that morning to find it still closed. A peek through the window told them there was no one inside but Sid and Cora. "Somethin' ain't right here," Curley astutely declared. "She's supposed to cook breakfast for them two this mornin'. That ain't nobody but her and Sid settin' there at the table and that camp looks empty."

"What the hell?" Coy blurted, at once thinking what Big Steve Long might do if Derringer was already gone. He went to the door and started banging on it.

Startled, Sid jumped up from the table and went to the door. Seeing who it was standing outside, he knew what Coy wanted. So he yelled through the closed door, "We ain't open till seven. What?" he asked when he couldn't understand what Coy was saying. So he unlocked the door and opened it partway. "We ain't open yet."

"Where's Derringer and that other feller?" Coy asked.

"How in the world would I know that?" Sid answered. "If you're wantin' whiskey, come back at seven, all right?"

"I don't want no damn whiskey," Coy fumed. "Where's Derringer? You was supposed to cook breakfast for him this mornin'."

"Well, that's the first I've heard about it," Sid responded. "We don't sell breakfast. Tell him to come at dinnertime." A shocked Curley George stood speechless during the exchange of words through the crack in the door. Then he uttered a crow-like sound and took off toward the camp by the stream in a dead run. Equally stunned, Coy took off after him.

Halfway to the stream, Curley verified that the camp was just as empty as it had appeared to be from the street. He slowed to a walk and looked around him to discover no real evidence that Derringer and the other man had actually spent any time there. Coy, puffing from his unaccustomed sprint, stopped to puzzle over the ring of loose dirt around the still-smoldering ashes. Then he walked on down to the stream where

Curley was looking around. Without glancing up from the ground, Curley said, "They didn't spend no time here last night. They musta left right after we went back in the saloon. They led their horses down the creek toward the river."

"But we saw 'em makin' their beds and gittin' ready to go to sleep," Coy protested.

"They was play-actin'," Curley said. "They knew somebody'd be watchin' 'em."

Coy still couldn't believe it. "Yeah, but you went back to take another look after Roy run us outta the Bucket of Blood and you said one of 'em got up and put some more wood on the fire."

"I saw somebody put some wood on the fire," Curley said. "But I reckon now it weren't one of them."

"Well, who the hell was it?" Coy demanded.

"I don't know," Curley responded. "It don't make no difference who it was. The fact of the matter is, we're in a whole lotta trouble if we don't catch up to them before they get back to Cheyenne. And right now we better get outta here before Big Steve finds out we got buffaloed by that blame Derringer again." They made a hasty retreat to get their horses out of the corral behind the Bucket of Blood and their saddles and packs out of the shed next to it. Working as fast as they could to make their escape before anyone else saw them leave town, their hope was that Big Steve Long would think they had left in the middle of the night.

The shops and other businesses were just beginning to show life again as they rode their horses along the backs of the buildings until reaching The Baby Doll Saloon. Then they left the buildings and went straight down to the stream again. Unlike the two men they went after, they were not hampered by darkness. So they could remain in the saddle and see well enough to follow the meandering stream. Hopefully, it made it possible to gain a measure of time on the two railroad men. But it was a meaningless gain, for after the short distance to the river, there was a distinct path beside the river that was easily read in the moonlight on the night just past. Once they reached the trail where Derringer and Tyler finally left the river, the two assassins held their horses to a demanding pace, one they knew they could not maintain for too long before resting the horses. It was the only way they had a chance of overtaking their targets before they made the fifty-mile journey back to Cheyenne. In fact, they decided that was a part of their plan, to sacrifice the wind of their horses in an all-out effort to overtake Derringer and Tyler. Then when they were dead, they would take their horses and turn their own wind-broken horses loose to become wolf bait.

The first sign the two assassins found that indicated their plan to overtake their prey was working was discovered at the creek where Derringer and Tyler had stopped to rest their horses and eat some breakfast. Some of the coals from their campfire still showed signs of life, even after being dowsed with water to put out the fire. Of even more significance was the fact that the dirt a few inches from the edge of the fire was damp. They could not be far ahead of them!

CHAPTER 20

"I think I'll stop and rest Clem a little bit on that creek down there," Derringer remarked as Tyler pulled up beside him when he stopped on the ridge overlooking Dale Creek Ravine.

"That's where you shot the deer on our way to Laramie City," Tyler said. "But we just rested the horses a short while back. Ain't it a little too soon to rest 'em right now?" Derringer didn't answer right away, so Jack shook his head, amazed. "You wanna go deer hunting again? Did you forget there might be a gang of outlaws on our tails?"

"We don't know for sure that there's anybody followin' us," Jesse said. "That's just what we speculated. And I'm pretty sure we've got over a half day's start on 'em if they are followin' us. Besides that, I never saw so many deer in one place before and I know you'd love some, if I got lucky." Jack still looked at him as if he'd lost his mind. Jesse went on, however. "You know the way back to Sherman Hill from here, don't you?"

"Yeah, I know how to get back to Sherman Hill," Jack replied.

"And when you get over that hill, you're right at the end of the railroad tracks. So you don't have to wait here with me," Derringer said. "And I can catch up with you before you get to Cheyenne."

"What about those two Indians you killed down at that creek when we camped there?" Tyler asked. "How do you know there ain't some more of their brothers lurkin' around this creek? Maybe you ain't the only one who knows there's a lot of deer in this valley. I know I'd feel a lot better if we stuck together till we get out of these mountains." Derringer looked to be at a loss for words to explain. So Tyler said, "Jesse, why don't you just tell me what's really on your mind? Because you've got me really spooked right now."

"Doggone it, Jack, I just have to find out a few things and I don't wanna risk your neck while I'm doin' it. You're right, I don't know for a fact that somebody is following us. But I've got a feelin' somebody is. And I aim to find out for sure because they can't be followin' us for any reason other than makin' sure we don't influence the railroad to bypass Laramie City. I don't know about the mayor, but I'm damn sure that town marshal is as crooked as they come. Him and Con and Ace Moyer own the Bucket of Blood and they're tryin' to take possession of all the land they can steal or kill for."

"You think it's really that bad?" Jack asked. "There seemed to be some good people in Laramie City."

"There are a lot of good people in the town, but they've got a problem they don't know how to deal with. And it's gonna come to the same thing Cheyenne has already started, a vigilance committee of the honest people and some public hangings. Sid Welch told me some men in town are already secretly talkin' about it." He shrugged and said, "But that's their problem. I'm concerned when it becomes my problem. And my problem is three men came after me the last time I was in Laramie City. Two of 'em gave up and went back. I coulda killed the other one but I let him go. And he still forced me to kill him. I've definitely got a feelin' there's somebody comin' after me again and I wanna find out who it is, so I can deal with them." He looked Tyler in the eyes and said, "I'm pretty sure it's me they want to get rid of and I don't want you gettin' in the way of a bullet meant for me. Hell, man, you're the superintendent in charge of layin' the track across the country. I don't want you to catch a stray bullet with my name on it."

"I can't ride off and leave you if you think there's a killer coming after you," Jack declared. "That wouldn't make me much of a man, would it?"

"It'd make you a smart one," Derringer said, unable to suppress a grin. "I'd have a whole lot more respect for your intelligence." They both chuckled. "I'll be honest with you, Jack. Fact of the matter is I feel a whole lot better on my own when I don't have to be concerned about what's happening to you. Whether it's one man or many, I trust myself to do what I have to do to survive. And that'll be easier if I know you're four or five miles away, closer to home. So do me the favor, okay? And I'll catch up with you later on."

Jack Tyler didn't know what to say. He preferred not

to fight whoever might be chasing them. But if there was no choice, he was not afraid to stand and fight. And if there was a fight on its way, he didn't like the image of himself being sent ahead with the women and children. He finally shook his head and declared, "I swear, Jesse, I just can't ride away and leave you to face whatever comes up over that hill behind us. It just ain't what a man that's worth his salt would do."

"Doggone it, Jack. This ain't a question of whether you're a coward or not. Hell, I know you're not. I just want you to get on up the trail and give me some room to take care of business. I can't say for sure how many are followin' us, but if I had to guess, I'd guess two, which I'm capable of takin' care of. I promise you, if it turns out to be a fifteen-man posse, I'll lead 'em straight to you. All right?"

Jack couldn't help laughing at that. "All right, I'll let you be the big hero and if you don't come after me by suppertime, I'll come back and bury what's left of you. Let's ride on down to the creek to see where you're gonna wait, so I'll know where to bring the shovel." He gave his horse his heels and led off down the side of the ravine. Derringer followed, hoping he hadn't damaged the man's image of himself. But he had a strong feeling their pursuers would possibly be Curley George and Coy Moffat and it was time to settle things with those two or spend the rest of his life anticipating a shot in his back.

When they reached the bottom of the ravine, Jack rode along the creek until he found the spot where they had camped and Jesse had butchered the deer. "You gonna wait here for 'em?"

"Yeah, or close by," Derringer said, "since our tracks are leadin' 'em here."

"Oh," Jack said, "I didn't think about that. I shoulda let you lead down the side of that slope." Something caught his eye then. "Damn, there's the bones of that deer." There were a couple of small birds pecking away at whatever the buzzards had left. He looked back at Derringer then. "I think I understand what you're tellin' me, so I reckon I'll get on out of your way just as soon as my horse gets through drinkin' water."

"I 'preciate it, Jack," Derringer said. "And take my packhorse with you, will you?" Tyler nodded and Derringer tied his packhorse to Tyler's with a short piece of rope. He pointed to an odd-shaped rock at the top of the ridge forming the other side of the ravine. "Follow that trail right up beside that rock, keep goin' in that direction and you'll strike Sherman Hill. I'll catch up with you before long."

"Right," Tyler said. "I know the way. You be careful, Jesse."

"Always am," Derringer replied, and stepped away from his packhorse. He watched Tyler as he ascended the opposite slope. *General Dodge would hang me if I got his construction boss killed,* he thought. He waited until Tyler had ridden out of sight. Then, impatient to settle the question of who might be following him, he stepped back up into the saddle and said, "Let's go, boy, we got work to do." He wheeled the big gray gelding around and climbed back up the slope they had just descended, intending to shorten the time between him and his pursuers.

He had ridden no more than five miles when his

suspicions about his pursuers proved to be accurate. Just after crossing a small stream that flowed down a narrow ravine, he pulled Clem to a stop when he spotted the two riders and their packhorse about a hundred yards distant, making their way across a barren stretch of rocky soil. He backed Clem a little farther back in the trees and watched. It was easy to see that it was as he had suspected. They had decided to sacrifice their horses to catch up to him, probably planning to abandon them once they had captured his and Tyler's. *Well,* he thought, *their plan almost worked.* All three horses were walking very slowly, their heads hanging low over the ground. He was just about to draw his rifle and shoot the two men off the suffering horses, but they both dismounted when one of the horses stumbled and threatened to fall. The riders were now walking between the horses and he couldn't risk a shot, since he might hit the horses. It occurred to him that the horses might have been grateful had he taken the shot. But they were close enough to the stream now to sense water, so they labored on toward the line of trees and he didn't want to do anything that might prevent them from getting to the stream.

They were close enough now to identify them as the two he had come to know as Curley and Coy, Red Pickens's partners and the two men who had chased him before. "Well, you finally caught me, boys. Let's see if it's worth your determination. But first, I need to get you somewhere you won't catch a stray bullet," he said to Clem then. He had to assume Coy and Curley would continue to follow the trail into the trees lining the ravine. So he left the trail and rode Clem back into the shallow ravine and followed the stream for about forty yards before dismounting and tying the horse there. Then he went back on foot to find a spot to welcome his posse. Nothing to do now but wait.

It seemed like an unusually long time but they eventually showed up. "I swear," Coy said, "I didn't think they was gonna make it." They dropped the reins and let the horses go to the water.

"They sure as hell wouldn'ta made it five miles farther to Dale Creek," Curley declared. "I thought they was both goin' down back yonder in them rocks."

"I sure thought we'da caught up with them by now," Coy complained. "They can't be that far ahead of us." He and Curley both lay down on their bellies at the edge of the stream and drank. Both heads popped up at the sound of the lever cocking the Henry rifle behind them.

"Congratulations," Derringer said, "you caught us. Do you wanna know what the prize is?" His first shot hit Curley in the back of the head, killing him instantly.

"Hold on . . ." were Coy's last words as he rolled over to catch Derringer's second shot in the chest. The two rapidly fired shots startled the weary horses but not enough to drive them from the water they so desperately needed. They continued drinking while Derringer propped his rifle against a tree and grabbed each corpse by their boots and dragged them away from the stream. Then he started taking the saddles off the two horses and the packsaddle off the other one. He hesitated but only for a moment before he took the bridles off as well. "I hereby set you free," he announced as he threw the bridles over on top of the saddles. *Maybe an*

Indian will find all this, he thought. Then he picked up the two arrows he found stuck on the packsaddle. *Wonder what he'll make of this?* He took a quick look through their pockets in case they had been paid before killing Tyler and him. "Evidently not," he announced. Then he looked through their saddlebags and their packs to see if they were carrying anything he might find useful. He took a knife and a whetstone and collected the weapons and left them in a pile while he walked back upstream to get Clem. When he returned to the three newly freed horses, he paused to look at them for a moment before he decided to put the bridles back on them. He tied the reins to a single rope and led them away from the stream. It took an hour, due to the weakened condition of the three horses he had captured, but he thought it was for the best of their benefit. When he got back to Dale Creek Ravine, he removed the bridles again. "All right," he said, "this time I mean it. I set you free again. You'll do a lot better by this creek than you would have by that scrawny little stream." He figured they must have understood what he meant because they made no move to follow him as he rode up out of the ravine, anxious now to try to catch up with Tyler.

He tried to imagine what pace Tyler would be maintaining and try to ask Clem for a pace a little faster than that. But he was not willing to submit his horse to the same abuse the three he just set free were subjected to. He and the gray gelding were friends. He wanted to keep it that way. Clem was comfortable with an alternating pace between an easy lope and a slow walk. It covered ground a lot faster than a steady walk. As he rode through the pass where the railroad tracks were going to come after leaving Sherman Hill, he thought about Tyler's remark about the possible presence of Indians hunting in those hills. He felt a little guilty about practically forcing Jack to ride through those hills alone. He frankly didn't anticipate the actual confrontation with Curley and Coy to come off without a shoot-out and he didn't want Jack mixed up in that. His thoughts were interrupted then by the flash of sunlight on a shiny object in a grove of pines he was about to ride into. Already thinking about the possibility of Indians in these hills, he immediately thought of Tyler, riding alone, thanks to his insisting that he did. Now with no idea of who or how many, he pulled Clem off the path and drew his rifle as he came out of the saddle. Leaving his horse out of sight in the middle of a group of pines, he ran back to take cover in a deep gully beside the path. With a clear shot at whoever came out of that grove of pines, he waited. There it was again, another flash of light as the sun reflected off a shiny object, this one closer to the end of the pine grove. He prepared to react. A band of Indians maybe, they could be riding to investigate the two shots he fired, but that was more than five miles behind him. Seconds later, three horses broke clear of the trees. Jack Tyler was on the lead horse. The two packhorses were behind him.

Tyler pulled his horse to a sliding stop when Derringer suddenly stepped out from behind a tree, his rifle cradled in his arms. "Jumpin' Jehoshaphat!" Jack blurted. "Jesse! Where did you come from? You scared the hell outta me."

"The question is, where are you goin'?" Derringer

asked. "I came pretty close to shootin' you when you came outta those pines."

"I was goin' back to see if you were all right," Tyler said. "I got to thinkin' that it mighta been more than you could handle by yourself, if it wasn't the two you thought it was. And you hadn't caught up with me yet."

"I ain't had time to catch up with you. I was on my way when I saw sunlight reflecting up through those trees a couple of times. I didn't know what it was. I thought maybe an Indian with a lookin' glass signalin' another one. Were you fiddlin' with a mirror or something?"

"Shoot no," Jack replied. "Why would I be fiddlin' with a mirror? I sure as hell weren't shavin'."

Derringer walked around the horses, looking them over when something caught his eye. He went back to Tyler's packhorse, then turned to him and said, "You left the flap open on this sack. I reckon the wind musta caught it a couple of times." He opened the flap to expose the shiny tin lid on the pickled peach jar. He reached in the sack and pulled the jar out. It was less than half full. "I swear, Jack, didn't you listen to what Cora told you about eatin' too many of those things at a time? I thought you mighta learned that lesson when I butchered that deer."

"I reckon I just got kinda hungry," Tyler said. "Did those two fellows ever show up?"

Derringer shook his head, feeling as if he was dealing with a child. "Yeah, they showed up. It was who I thought it would be. I left 'em layin' near a stream about five miles short of Dale Creek Ravine. Let me go get my horse." He walked back into the trees and returned on Clem's back. "There wasn't anything of theirs worth keeping but some guns and ammunition. I looked for some pickled peaches, but they weren't carryin' any."

"I was gonna share 'em with you," Jack claimed. "Those left in the jar are yours. I was hungry so I thought I'd just go ahead and eat my half."

"I declare, if you don't beat all," Derringer said. "Cora gave you those peaches. I don't have much of a taste for 'em, anyway. That one I ate at The Baby Doll Saloon will do me for the year. Come on, let's use up what daylight we've got left." He untied his packhorse from Tyler's and they headed toward Sherman Hill.

They decided to keep riding that night until they descended Sherman Hill and could camp at the end of the railroad tracks out of Cheyenne. The horses were up to it due to having not been pushed too hard for most of the day. They planned to take it easy on the horses the next day to make up for that late push. With only nineteen or twenty miles left to reach Cheyenne, they planned to leave before breakfast and ride straight into Cheyenne by dinnertime. So they camped by the creek and ate a big supper of smoked deer meat and slapjack. Derringer passed on the offer of a pickled peach and Tyler ate only two, with the comment that he was getting a little sick of them.

The night passed peacefully enough with the conversation centering mostly around what Tyler's plans were when they got back. "Are you gonna stay in Cheyenne now, since it's less than a month before the construction is scheduled to begin again?" Derringer asked.

"I have no idea," Tyler answered. "It doesn't make much sense to go back to Council Bluffs, then turn right around and come back to Cheyenne, does it?"

"Maybe they got a lot more plannin' to do and they need you there for that," Jesse suggested. "You being the big construction engineer and all."

"They don't need me for nothin' back in that office," Jack insisted. "They keep going over those maps, over and over, like something's gonna change. And, hell, nothing's gonna change in those mountains God put there. There ain't but one way to go that makes sense and that's through Laramie City. The only thing the Union Pacific has to worry about is who's running Laramie City. That town's as evil as Sodom and Gomorrah, and if the same thing happens to Laramie City that happened to Sodom and Gomorrah, these railroad tracks are gonna look like shoelaces."

"Now, that's the longest speech I've ever heard you make," Jesse said. "What happened to those two towns? What did you call 'em?"

"Sodom and Gomorrah," Jack said. "You never heard of 'em?" He could tell by Jesse's expression that he never had. "They were in another country. Both towns burned down." He was afraid he would embarrass him if he told him they were in the Bible.

"It wouldn't take a helluva lot to burn Laramie City down," Derringer remarked.

They saddled up and started out following the road beside the railroad tracks, stopping to water the horses when they crossed a creek about halfway to Cheyenne. They arrived in Cheyenne with time to make the dining room at the hotel before it closed for dinner, even after a stop at the stable to leave their horses. Derringer promised Leon he would tell him all about their trip to Laramie City later on, but they had to get to the dining room before it closed because they hadn't even eaten breakfast.

"Well, look who's back," Rachael sang out when she came from the kitchen and saw Derringer and Tyler at the door talking to Cecil. She stood there at the kitchen door, hands on hips, waiting for them to select a table. When Cecil engaged them in conversation too long, she turned around, went back into the kitchen, then returned holding two cups of coffee, impatiently tapping her foot. Finally, she announced, "I'm gonna pour this coffee on the floor if somebody doesn't pick a table pretty soon."

Derringer walked over to his usual choice of tables and said, "Then you woulda had to mop up the floor, Rachael. Sometimes I don't understand the things you do."

Ignoring his comment, she placed the coffee on the table and asked, "Where have you two been for the past several days?"

"Jack had to take a little trip up to Laramie City to check on some things for the railroad," Derringer said. "They can't build the railroad unless Jack okays it."

"I'll bet," Rachael remarked.

"Who's the fellow sittin' over by the window in the

city clothes?" Derringer asked. "I've seen him some-where before."

Overhearing him as he sat down, Tyler said, "We bumped into him coming in the hotel door when we were coming out. He was wearin' a long coat with a fur collar and a derby hat."

"Right," Derringer said, remembering, then, "he came in on the train with you." He and Jack both looked at Rachael. "Who is he, Rachael?" Derringer asked.

"I don't know much about him," she replied. "He said his name was Austin Birch and he ran the gam-bling operation in a big saloon in Omaha. I think he might be thinking about building a new saloon here in Cheyenne. He likes to pour syrup on his corn bread."

"But you don't know much about him, right?" Jack teased.

"Well, that's all I know about him," Rachael said, and went back to the kitchen to get their food. When she returned, her mother was with her, carrying a plate with corn bread on it.

"Glad to see you two gentlemen back in town again," Clara Bowden said as she placed the plate on the table. "I just feel better when you're in town."

"Is she talkin' to us?" Tyler japed, and looked to see if there was someone behind him. She included him but he was well aware she meant Derringer.

"I've been called a lotta names before," Derringer replied, "but I don't recall ever being called that before. Thank you, ma'am."

"Yes, ma'am," Jack said then. "Thank you, ma'am."

The stranger seated at the table by the window seemed quite interested in the conversation between the two dining room women and these particular customers. He finished his second cup of coffee, pushed his empty plate away, and removed the napkin from under his chin. Each move was unhurried and deliberate. He got up from his chair and walked over to their table. "Excuse me, gentlemen. . . ."

"Damn, that's twice in one day," Jack couldn't help interrupting.

The stranger paused to give Jack a polite smile, then turned his attention back to Derringer. "I don't mean to interrupt your dinner, but are you the man they call Derringer?"

"My name's Derringer," he replied.

"Would you mind if I had a word with you when you've finished your dinner?"

Derringer took a quick look at the man and decided if he was carrying any weapon, it would have to be one like his name, a pocket pistol. So he said, "You can talk to me right now if you don't mind if I keep on eating. Have a seat." Then remembering he wasn't alone, he asked, "Is that all right with you, Jack?"

"Sure," Jack japed. "But if it's got anything to do with a train holdup I'll have to be paid to keep my mouth shut."

"Don't mind my friend, here," Derringer told the stranger. "He's still comin' down off a high dose of pickled peaches."

Seeming not to be amused by the introduction, the stranger pulled a chair back and sat down. He turned all his attention to Derringer then and said, "My name is Austin Birch. I understand you work for the Union Pacific Railroad. Is that right?"

"That's right," Derringer answered, "we both do. What can we do for you, Mr. Birch?"

"I'll get right to the point," Birch replied. "I am going to build a saloon here in Cheyenne, bigger than anything that's here now. And I intend to feature gambling tables of various kinds from cards to dice. I'd like to hire you to work for me."

Derringer was surprised, having not expected anything of the kind, so he had to answer, "Doing what?"

"The same thing you do for the railroad," Birch replied, "taking care of trouble." Derringer was amazed. Seeing as much, Birch said, "You would be well paid, a good deal more than the railroad pays you, I'll wager."

"I certainly have to say I appreciate the offer, Mr. Birch," Jesse responded. "But most of what I do, or even know how to do, takes place on the back of a horse. And it involves goin' into country I've never seen before. I ain't sure I'd be much good hangin' around a gamblin' hall. It might get to closin' in on me and I might go crazy."

"I understand you sometimes work as a deputy sheriff," Birch countered. "Your work for me might be quite similar to that."

"That was just for a short while and I'll be honest with you, I was mighty happy when Jack, here, came out from Council Bluffs with orders from my boss to head up in the mountains to Laramie City."

"I guess I can understand your feelings about always working outside. Some men were born to answer that call. I'll leave it at this. I'll be in town for a few more days before I head back to Omaha. My offer is still open until I leave town if you change your mind." Derringer thanked him again for the offer. As he got up to leave, he said, "If I see you in Dawkin's Saloon before I leave, I'd like to buy you a drink."

"'Preciate the offer," Derringer said. "I enjoy a drink of good whiskey, even though I seldom have more than one or two."

"Yes, that's what I've heard," Birch remarked. "And that was another reason I was interested in hiring you. Good afternoon, gentlemen," he said as he walked away from the table.

"That's three times in the same day," Jack said softly so Birch wouldn't hear it. "I swear, he was really after you, wasn't he? Musta been talkin' to everybody in town about you. I reckon he didn't know I was available," he joked. "That sounded like the kind of job I'm looking for, except the part about taking care of trouble. But the part about hanging around a saloon all day, I could get used to that."

Derringer looked at him and slowly shook his head, trying to remember him when he first met him. No one could have convinced him that Jack, a hard-driving, no-nonsense construction superintendent, could play the part of the clown if the time was right.

CHAPTER 21

After dinner, Tyler said he was going to telegraph Council Bluffs and let them know the two of them had confirmed the route on the map of the railroad as far as Laramie City. After that, he said he was going to the hotel for a bath and a nap. Derringer said the bath and maybe a shave sounded like a good idea, but first he was going to check in with the sheriff to see how things were going in Cheyenne.

"We were just talking about you," Cliff Crenshaw said when Derringer walked in the door of the sheriff's office. "We were wonderin' if you were gonna be back anytime soon."

"Everything looks peaceful enough right now," Derringer said. "Still too many idle people hangin' around the streets, but it looks pretty calm."

"They're just restin' up for tonight," Ray Cooper commented. "And I think you oughta know about one thing. Alvin Crowe is back in town. He showed up with two more Crowes. I think they're his nephews. They look like they came out of the same flock as the two Crowes we hanged for murderin' that man and his son."

"I thought Alvin Crowe left town for good after I broke his arm," Derringer said. "What's he doin' back in town?"

"What the rest of the drifters are doin'," Cliff said. "But if I was you, I'd sure be keepin' a sharp eye out for him. He might be lookin' to take some vengeance out on you for his two sons' deaths."

"Why?" Derringer asked. "I didn't kill his sons. The vigilance committee can take credit for that and I wasn't even in on that deal."

"Yeah, but he might be thinkin' he can't take his vengeance on the whole town of Cheyenne, but you were the one who caused his boys to be arrested. And if they hadn't been arrested, they wouldn't have been hanged." Cliff shrugged. "It ain't fair, but it's liable to be the way he thinks."

"I don't know," Derringer said as he recalled what he thought was the last confrontation he would have with Alvin Crowe. "He seemed to understand that he got a broken arm, instead of a bullet in the head when he came after me. And I told him if he came after me again, I wasn't gonna be so considerate. I would dispatch his sorry butt to hell. He even said he was done with Cheyenne."

"Well, he's back," Sheriff Warton remarked, "and so far, they haven't caused enough trouble to get locked up. One of 'em got in a fistfight with another drifter over one of the gals at Vera's, but it settled itself before Ray got there to break it up. The Crowe fellow won. What was his name?"

"His name was Levi Crowe," Ray answered. "Pretty good-sized fellow. The fellow he whupped weren't a little fellow, but nobody wanted to file any charges. Said it was just a little tussle between two young studs. I wish they all ended like that, without somebody wanting to kill the other'n."

"You can say that again," Warton said. "We have to keep one of us at the jail all the time now because we've got so many we've had to jail for disturbing the peace. It would sure help us out if you would put on that badge again, since the construction on the railroad ain't started up yet. Whaddaya say?"

Derringer was afraid Warton was going to ask that of him. He didn't care much for the job as a deputy sheriff, but he found it hard to refuse to help when they were so desperate for it. "Sure, I'd be glad to help," he lied, "at least until construction gets started again on the railroad. But once that gets underway again, a good portion of the people will be driftin' outta town."

"We appreciate it, Jesse," Warton said. "I hope you're right about a number of drifters movin' on with the railroad." He opened his desk drawer and took out the badge that Jesse had returned.

Both Cliff and Ray grinned in welcome when Jesse pinned it on his vest, causing him to remind them, "This is just for the week or so until the general gets back." He paused, then said, "And it's on the condition that I get to take a hot bath and a shave before supper tonight. They let me and Jack Tyler in the dinin' room for dinner, but they didn't look like they wanted to."

"Why, hell," Ray replied, "we'd all appreciate that. In fact, we were gonna suggest it. Weren't we, Boss?"

They all laughed, including Jesse, whose last hint of comradery was when he was in the army.

"I've got to go back to the stable and clean out anything in my packsaddle that needs throwin' away or replacin'," Jesse said, "and clean my rifle. I picked up some other weapons that I need to check over, too. I couldn't take the time to do it when we left the horses there, or we'da been late for dinner."

"Sounds like you did more than just scoutin' the route of the Union Pacific," Warton said. "You musta run into some trouble. Indians?"

"Some Indian trouble," Derringer answered. "A couple of young bucks tried to steal the horses, but that ain't where we picked up the extra weapons. That was when we came back from Laramie City."

"You're lucky you didn't get yourself crossways with Big Steve Long again," the sheriff said. "Did you run into him while you were in that town?"

"Matter of fact, I did," Derringer responded. "Interestin' fellow . . . he ordered me out of town again."

"For what?" Warton asked.

"For shootin' a fellow named Red Pickens when he drew his weapon with the intent of killin' me," Derringer said. "He was one of three outlaws who trailed me the first time I came back from Laramie City. They never caught me. When Tyler and I went back there, this Pickens fellow drew on me, so I shot him. Then the other two tried to catch up with Tyler and me when we came back from Laramie City this time. They caught up with us short of Dale Creek Ravine."

"And that's where you got the extra weapons, right?" Cliff asked confidently.

"That's right," Derringer said, "so I'll see you after supper. All right?"

"That'll be fine," Sheriff Warton said, and walked to the office door with him. "Then we'll see what kinda night we're gonna be looking at." He stood in the doorway and watched Derringer walk away, toward the stable. *You can only be shot at so many times before that one time when your number comes up,* he thought. *I hope it doesn't come up before we get some of this mess of people out of Cheyenne.*

After answering most of Leon Draper's questions at the stable, Derringer took the weapons he had inspected and cleaned back to his room at the hotel. Then he went to the washroom and put some more wood in the small iron stove until the top of the little stove glowed red. He filled a large tub halfway full of water from the pump inside the washroom, using the metal bucket provided for the purpose. Then he filled the bucket again and put it on the stove. When the water in the bucket started to boil, he pulled it off the stove, using a towel to wrap around the handle. He poured the boiling water into the tub and stirred the water, testing the temperature. Thinking he needed another bucket of hot water, he repeated the procedure. And when his tub water felt warm enough, he took his bath. He shaved while still sitting in the tub of warm water. Then when he got out of the tub, he washed his shirt, underwear, and socks in his bathwater. When he was finished, he removed the two iron bars locking the tub in place.

Then he rolled the tub over on its axle to empty the dirty bathwater through the slats in the floor to drain into the ditch beneath the floor and run out from under the washroom. He put the two iron locking bars back in place. *Ready for the next guest*, he thought. *Downright amazing what inventions men come up with in the modern world*.

He put on his spare underwear and his one clean shirt and his extra socks and hung the clothes he had washed on wall hooks, the back of his one chair, and the hook on the back of the door to dry. When that was done, he took a look at his pocket watch and saw that it was almost time to meet Jack in the dining room. The mirror on the dresser, about the size of an open book, was bigger than his small shaving mirror. So he stepped up to the dresser to check his shaving job. *Not bad*, he thought, *better than it was, anyway*. He never expected to see a handsome face when he looked in the mirror, so he was never disappointed. He was satisfied just to see a face that wouldn't frighten small children. He grabbed his hat as he went out the door and went downstairs to the back hallway to enter the dining room through the inside entrance.

Tyler was already inside the dining room, talking to Cecil when Derringer walked in. "My goodness!" Cecil exclaimed. "Another stranger. You two aren't the same two who came in for dinner today, are you?"

Derringer and Tyler looked at each other. "There ain't that much difference," Tyler said. "Just look a little bit cleaner."

"That's a fact," Derringer agreed. "You can't wash

off ugly. Course you can't wash off beauty, either—this young lady can tell you that," he said as Rachael walked over to see what the conversation was about.

"Why, thank you, kind sir," she said sweetly.

"I was talkin' about your mother," Derringer said.

She gave him a playful punch on the shoulder. "Wait and see what kind of service you get tonight. It's a good thing you two cleaned up a little bit. After the way you showed up for dinner, we were gonna make you eat supper out back with the hogs."

"Hey," Tyler protested, "he's the one who made the remarks, not me."

"You'd better sit down if you want any supper," Rachael said, "and I'll get you and your friend some coffee."

"I always gave you credit for being a pretty smart fellow," Tyler japed as they sat down at the table. "I thought everybody knows you don't insult the people who cook your food or make your bed."

"Ah, she can take it," Derringer said. "I'm still payin' her back for that happy birthday stunt she and Cecil pulled on me. Did you wire Council Bluffs and tell them to come the hell on and let's get this railroad goin'?"

"I did," Tyler said, "and I got a wire right back tellin' me to come back there on tomorrow's train. I reckon I shoulda waited until tomorrow to wire them. Then that train settin' out there on the track would be gone and I'd have a couple more days here before it got back."

Derringer was a little surprised to hear him say that. "I thought you'd be anxious to get back to Council

Bluffs, especially since I got you in so many situations where you could get shot."

"It wasn't really that bad," Tyler claimed. "Oh, I admit, there were a couple of times when I thought I was gonna get shot, like that night when the two Indians were fixin' to plant a couple of arrows in my behind. But most of the time I kinda enjoyed roaming through the mountains where the railroad hasn't even gotten there yet."

"As you can see, I let Tom Warton talk me into wearing a badge for him again." He opened his coat to reveal the deputy badge on his vest. "I told him I'd come to the office after supper tonight. But whaddaya say we stop in Dawkin's after we eat and have a couple of drinks before you go. We can celebrate the fact that we got back alive."

"Sounds like a good idea to me," Jack said.

They enjoyed one of Tyler's favorite meals, meat loaf, which Clara had just happened to fix on his last supper before leaving town. "She's got an instinct about things like that," Derringer joked. "I told her you wanted fresh venison and pickled peaches, but she insisted you'd like meat loaf best."

"You ain't ever gonna let me forget deer meat and pickled peaches, are you?" Tyler asked.

"It's what I'll think about every time I hear somebody mention your name," Jesse replied.

When they had finished their supper, Rachael asked if they wanted dessert and one more cup of coffee. Neither man was particularly enthusiastic about it but Tyler asked what it was. "It's sort of a pound cake with pickled peaches in a sauce over it." She jumped back in alarm when both men recoiled in a fit of laughter, almost knocking their chairs over. "What? What?" she kept asking when both of them seemed consumed by laughter. Getting no answer from either of them, she quickly looked at her blouse and the front of her skirt to see if she had spilled food on herself. When she could find no apparent cause for their moment of insanity, she looked at Cecil, who had walked halfway back to them when he heard the laughter. She shrugged in answer to the question on his face.

Since they were both on their feet then, Jesse said, "Let's go get that drink of likker." Jack agreed, so they started for the door.

Rachael grabbed Derringer's arm and stopped him. "What happened?" she demanded. "What's so funny?"

"Nothin', really," Jesse replied. He figured Tyler might be embarrassed if he told her all about the deer meat and the pickled peaches. So he quickly told her, "I'll tell you the whole story later," speaking softly so Jack wouldn't hear him.

"Promise?" she asked, still clutching his arm. So he promised and she released his arm and he followed Tyler, who was already going out the door.

"Wait up, Jack," Derringer called after him. "I've gotta get my rifle. I've gotta go to the jail after we have a drink." If he was going to go on duty as a deputy sheriff, he always carried his rifle.

"Where is it?" Tyler asked. "In your room?" When Derringer said that it was, Tyler said, "I'll wait for you at Dawkin's."

* * *

"What's the matter, Uncle Alvin?" Jasper Crowe asked when he saw his uncle go suddenly tense, almost missing his mouth with his drink.

"It's him!" Alvin said. "He's the devil who killed my boys! I knew he'd show up here sooner or later!"

Jasper and his brother, Levi, took a long look at the rugged man casually carrying a Henry rifle as he walked into the saloon. "Jesse Derringer," Levi announced softly. "So that's him, huh? He looks like a real handful, all right. You shoulda come to get us before you went after him by yourself."

"Wonder if he'd mind if we was to paint a big old target on his back?" Jasper japed to his brother. "Sure would make it easier. Big as he is, we could knock him off without even comin' into town."

"Watch your mouth, Jasper," his brother said. "This ain't no jokin' matter to Uncle Alvin." Everything seemed like a joke to the younger brother and the fact that he wore a silver ring through the left nostril of his nose tended to confirm it.

"No, it ain't," Alvin Crowe said, as he rubbed his right arm where the broken bone was still healing, a constant reminder of his crushing failure to avenge his sons' deaths.

"I'm sorry, Uncle Alvin," Jasper said. "I didn't mean no disrespect to Arthur and Caleb. I'm just anxious to pay him back."

"We'll get a chance to catch him when he ain't in the middle of a crowded saloon," Alvin said. "I promised your daddy I wouldn't take no chance of you gittin' caught."

"Shoot," Jasper responded. "I don't see why we don't shoot him down right now and shoot anybody else who gits in the way."

"I swear, Jasper, sometimes you talk like you ain't got a grain of sense," Levi said. "Look at all the men in here that are wearin' guns and he's wearin' a badge. We wouldn't make it to the door."

"Levi's right, Jasper," Alvin said. "This ain't the time or the place. Leastways, we know he's back in town. For a while there I was afraid he was gone for good. We just have to keep an eye on him and pretty soon he'll give us the chance we're lookin' for."

As usual this time of evening, Dawkin's was crowded. As soon as he walked in Derringer spotted Tyler standing at the bar talking to Sam. So he didn't bother to look the room over. He just walked straight to the bar to join them. "Howdy, Jesse," Sam greeted him. "Glad to see you back in town."

"How you doin', Sam?" Derringer returned. "Don't look like anybody's missing. Does it, Jack?"

"Nope," Tyler replied. "The town's gettin' bigger every day."

"Jack was tellin' me the two of you had some high times up in Laramie City," Sam said.

"Is that a fact?" Derringer responded. "I ain't surprised. I think Jack would have liked to spend more time up there if he didn't have to get back to Council Bluffs. Ain't that right, Jack?"

"Sure it is," Tyler said. "Laramie City is a lot like Cheyenne was before the railroad got here, but they have a different way of doin' things than we do here. Here in Cheyenne, we've got a sheriff and his deputies to keep the peace and punish the people who commit crimes. In Laramie City, the sheriff is the one who commits the crimes."

"That don't sound like a very good system to me," Sam chuckled.

"The worst part of that is that Jack ain't just makin' a joke," Derringer said. "That's a fact. The sheriff's the biggest crook in town."

"Speaking of crooks," Sam said, "I don't know if anybody's told you, but Alvin Crowe is back in town."

"Yeah, the sheriff told me Alvin was back," Derringer said. "Has he been in here?"

"Every day," Sam replied at once, "and he's settin' at a table in the back right now with two boys that look just like the two the vigilance committee lynched. I don't know how the situation ended up between you and Alvin after he came after you and you broke his arm. But you didn't arrest him and now he's back. And the sheriff said he ain't got no cause to arrest him as long as he doesn't cause any trouble, and so far he hasn't. But I wanted to be sure you knew he was back and he ain't alone."

"I 'preciate it, Sam. I'll try to keep an eye out for him." Derringer looked back in the crowded barroom until he spotted Alvin at one of the tables. Their eyes locked, for Alvin was staring at him as well. Derringer thought that the trouble between them was finished when he spared Alvin's life in trade for a broken arm. Now he was back with two wild-looking young men who could pass for the two the vigilance committee hanged. *Maybe I should have shot him when he came after me in Leon Draper's stable,* he thought. *This is the crap you get when you go soft-hearted in this business.* "So, are you gonna pour me a drink or not?"

"Sorry," Sam said, and poured. "I got lost in the conversation."

"Put that on my tab, Sam." The voice came from behind him and he turned to confront Austin Birch smiling at him. "I told you it would be my pleasure to buy you a drink if I saw you in Dawkin's. I'm a man of my word. Sam, put Mr. Tyler's drink on my tab, too."

"Well, that's mighty sportin' of you, Mr. Birch," Derringer said. "Thank you very much." He paused while Tyler thanked him as well. Then he asked, "What shall we drink to? Your success in buildin' a gamblin' hall in Cheyenne?"

"Oh, I think we would need a finer Scotch whiskey for that toast," Birch said. "I'd settle for wishing me luck in this five-handed poker game I've agreed to play in with four of the scariest looking gentlemen I've ever seen."

They all chuckled, and Tyler said, "Let's drink to that. Hope you clean them all out and live to brag about it." They tossed their whiskey back and Birch returned to the card game. "He's some kind of sport, ain't he?" Tyler remarked.

"Yeah, I reckon he is," Derringer said, "but I ain't figured him out yet." They had another drink then and it seemed to cause sentimental thoughts in Tyler's mind. He suddenly wanted to tell Derringer how much it had meant to him to have ridden with him. Derringer liked Tyler but he didn't want to talk about "the good old days" of the past week. So he told him he would see him at breakfast in the morning. He was supposed to be on patrol with Sheriff Warton that night.

"Okay, partner," Tyler said, "duty calls. I'll see you in the morning. Just remember to keep some eyes in the back of your head." He nodded toward the table in the back where Alvin Crowe and his nephews were sitting.

Derringer went out the door and a couple of minutes later, the Crowes got up and left as well. Seeing this, Tyler walked out behind them. They walked down the street toward the jail but stopped when Derringer went into the sheriff's office. So Tyler stopped as well. The Crowes turned around and came back toward him. He froze while they walked past him, all three staring at him. He remained standing there, afraid to turn around in case they might be looking back at him. After a minute passed, he turned slowly around but they were gone. *Good,* he thought, *I chased them away.* He hurried on his way to the hotel.

CHAPTER 22

When Derringer walked into the sheriff's office, he found Sheriff Warton, Cliff Crenshaw, and Ray Cooper all there waiting for him. "First day back on the job and it looks like I'm late for the meeting," he said.

They responded with a chuckle, and Warton said, "Not at all. We've got plenty of time, so I thought it would be a good idea to have a little meeting. Now that you're back, we can go back to our two-man patrol that we were working before. So we'll start tonight with you and me, Jesse, working the early evening shift. And Cliff and Ray will close the town up for the night. Since you just got back in town, we thought it would be the kind thing to give you the early patrol so you can go to bed early."

"That is mighty thoughtful of you fellows. I have been missin' a little bit of sleep the last few nights. I'll be glad to see that bed in the hotel."

"Well, Deputy Derringer, are you ready to go?"

Sheriff Warton asked. Jesse said he was, so they left the office and set out on the normal circuit of the town, walking south toward the train station, then crossing over to the other side of the main street to the hotel. After checking in with Bob Wolfe, the night clerk, they continued north checking the locked doors. They had just passed the barbershop when they heard the shots. Two shots of different caliber, almost at the same time, which nearly always meant a duel. They came from Dawkin's Saloon, that much was certain, so Derringer and the sheriff ran to the saloon, where a crowd of spectators were already gathering. The sheriff and deputy pushed their way through the crowd to get inside. When they got inside, the customers who had cleared a lane for the gunfighters were now closing in around the table where the card game had been. The table was flipped over on its side with cards and cash scattered on the floor beneath it. There was a body lying on the floor in the painful process of dying. Standing on the other side of the upturned table, Austin Birch stood calmly waiting. The smile that greeted the sheriff and Derringer spoke of a confidence that he was in the right. "Mr. Birch," Sheriff Warton addressed him.

"Sheriff Warton," Birch returned pleasantly.

"You want to tell me what happened here?" Warton asked.

"I'd be happy to," Birch replied, "or you could ask any of these people standing around here who witnessed it." When Warton said he'd hear his version of it first, Birch continued. "This unfortunate man has been cheating throughout the entire evening. Finally he made the mistake that sealed his fate. He spread a winning hand that showed a diamond flush with an ace high. I was holding three of a kind, aces as a matter of fact, and one of them was the ace of diamonds. He seemed to be offended when I told him there were not two aces of diamonds in a deck of cards. He stood up and turned the table over and drew his revolver to shoot me, so I shot him instead. That pretty much sums it up. I think anyone here will tell you much the same story."

Derringer reached down and took the .44 out of the now-dead man's hand and checked it. "One round's been fired, Sheriff."

Warton looked back at Birch. "Looks like your story holds up. I see his .44. What did you shoot him with?"

Birch reached into an inside pocket of his coat and produced a small double-barreled pocket pistol. He held it up by the barrel, smiled, and said, "You have your Derringer. I have mine."

The sheriff nodded to let him know he caught it, then he asked, "Any of you men know who he is?" He directed his question toward the other three men who were in the card game.

"He said his name was Ralph," one of the three finally spoke up. "He was just a drifter that's been hangin' around town for a couple of days, playin' cards. I played cards with him yesterday and he came out ahead in the game. I remember that and I figured he was just ridin' a lucky streak, but Mr. Birch, here, caught him with his drawers down tonight."

"I have to apologize for not catching him yesterday," Birch offered. "And I admit I didn't really catch him tonight. He caught himself."

"One of you fellows gimme a hand and we'll tote him outta here," Derringer said, and he grabbed him under his arms. Another sizable man picked up Ralph's feet and the two of them carried the corpse out and left it on the porch for the undertaker to pick up. "I sent someone to tell James Durham he's got a body to pick up," Derringer told the sheriff when he came back inside.

Sheriff Warton had already questioned some of the witnesses and they all verified Austin Birch's account of the incident. So he told everyone to go back to their enjoyment of the evening and that he hoped Mr. Birch could avoid being challenged again. He told Sam and the owner, John Dawkin, that it was what it looked like. The victim was a cheat who got caught and tried to shoot the man who exposed him.

They left Dawkin's and continued up the street toward The Crossing Saloon and Vera's Vineyard. While they walked, Derringer asked the sheriff if he knew anything about the stranger called Austin Birch. "Not much," Warton answered. "He's a slick one, though, ain't he?"

"He talked like he was thinkin' about opening his own business here in Cheyenne," Derringer said. "And from the way he talked, it sounded like he wanted to build a big gamblin' hall. He offered me a job."

"Doing what?" Warton asked.

"When I asked him that, he said the same thing I do for the Union Pacific—take care of trouble. I told him that wasn't really my job description with the railroad, that I was a scout for the construction crews. I said this job as a deputy was a temporary job. I was just helpin' out until the railroad construction got started again. He still wanted me to think about comin' to work for him." He paused when it appeared that the sheriff was wondering why he was telling him all this. So he explained. "The reason I'm tellin' you about it is because I think you and the mayor and the town council might not want a big gambling house, saloon, hotel, and whorehouse all in one business."

Warton didn't really think that was something for him to concern himself with and he was more than a little surprised that Derringer thought about it at all. "I 'preciate your interest in the town, Jesse, but I don't have anything to do with the businesses that come here. I reckon if a man wants to build a business in Cheyenne and he has the money to buy the land and build the business, why, hell, it's a free country."

"I reckon," Derringer conceded. "I can't help thinkin' about the trouble all these extra people have caused you and the rest of the businesses here in Cheyenne. And now you might be gettin' close to a time when most of the gang of people that descended on the town will follow the railroad right out of town. I'd think the last thing you folks would want is a business big enough to bring another horde of the wrong kind of people back. That's all I'm sayin', and since it ain't none of my business, I'll shut up about it."

Warton was amazed. He was surprised that Derringer ever thought deeply about anything other than range and windage. "I'll tell you what," he said as they approached the door into The Crossing Saloon. "At the next meeting of the council, I'll tell them about your concern for Austin Birch's plans for the town."

Like Dawkin's, The Crossing was crowded with drinkers and card players, but everything was humming along normally, so they walked over to the bar to talk to Benny Thacker. They found a space big enough at one end of the bar to fit two more bodies, so they filled it. "Non-drinkers step away from the bar," Benny japed when he saw the two lawmen belly up to the bar. He walked up to that end of the bar. "I see you got your other deputy back, Sheriff. Howdy, Derringer."

"Howdy, Benny," Derringer returned. "Looks like business is good tonight. Any problems?"

"Not so far," Benny said. "We heard a couple of shots a little while ago. Anybody dead?"

"One fellow in a card game. He got caught cheatin' and went for his gun," the sheriff said. "The other fellow was faster."

"Who did the shootin'?" Benny asked. "Anybody we know?"

"Austin Birch," the sheriff answered. "You know him?"

"Yeah, sure do," Benny replied. "He's a slick one. He's been in here three or four times this week."

While the sheriff was talking to Benny, Derringer was scanning the crowd and his gaze happened to fall on the face of Alvin Crowe. He was squeezed in at the far end of the bar, staring back at him, his eyes never blinking. Derringer gazed at him for a couple of moments, looking for the two young Crowes who were with him at Dawkin's. He didn't see them anywhere. He looked away then, not wishing to play a baiting game with him. When there was a pause in the conversation between Benny and the sheriff, Derringer asked a question. "I see Alvin Crowe down at the other end of the bar." Benny nodded, so Derringer said, "I saw him earlier in Dawkin's. He had two young Crowes with him, but they ain't with him here."

"Oh, they were here, but they're next door at Vera's right now," Benny said. "I think that musta been the price Alvin had to pay to get them to come to Cheyenne with him. I feel sorry for those gals over at Vera's. Ol' Alvin shoulda just thrown those two in with the chickens, so they could chase them around all day." He cast a serious eye in Derringer's direction then. "Jesse, you better keep a sharp eye on what's goin' on around you, with those three in town. That ol' man has got it into his head that you killed his two sons, no matter how you try to tell him you just helped arrest 'em."

"Well, that's part of it," Sheriff Warton interrupted. "There's also the part about when he went after you to kill you and you broke his arm. You did that to keep from killin' him. Hell, you even set the bone. But he don't see it that way. The way he sees it you shamed him. You killed his two sons and you shamed him. To that twisted ol' fool, the shame's probably worse than losing his sons." Warton shook his head. "Jesse, you shoulda shot him in the head, instead of breaking his arm. He woulda been a lot happier if you had."

"I know you're right," Jesse said. "I should have shot him. I wasn't even trying to break his arm when I hit him with that board. I was just trying to make him drop the gun. I didn't know then what I know now. I thought he would appreciate the fact that I chose to spare his life when he tried to kill me and he'd be at peace with me after that."

"Well, I've told Ray and Cliff to keep their eyes open anytime they see Alvin and his two nephews in town, and don't you get careless," the sheriff said.

"Damn," Derringer said, "I should have stayed in Laramie City and trusted my luck with Big Steve Long." He shrugged and said, "We're just taking up space that a couple of payin' customers could be occupyin', so we might as well continue our patrol. As long as Alvin is in here, I know nobody will be taking a shot at me outside."

"I ain't so sure about that," the sheriff said. "We better check Vera's next door to make sure the Crowe boys are havin' the fun their uncle Alvin said they would have with Vera's ladies."

They walked out of The Crossing, then paused for a few minutes to make sure Alvin Crowe didn't follow them. Then they walked into Vera's Vineyard next door, entering the door that led into the "Vineyard" area, where they stopped and looked around the large room. On the many sofas and chairs, they saw young women talking to several men, but there was no sign of the two Crowe nephews. They were not approached by any of the women, since the women recognized the sheriff and his deputy. Finally, one of the older-looking women came over and asked if they were looking for someone. "We're not lookin' to arrest anybody," Sheriff Warton told her. "We just need to know that two young men named Levi and Jasper Crowe are still here. They're not in any trouble. Their uncle's waitin' for 'em next door and he wants to make sure they ain't run off and left him."

"Well, I can tell you that," she volunteered. "Those two pistols are upstairs with Thelma and Rosa. I think this was their first time in a place like this. I think this must be the first time they've been anywhere. The girls cut the cards to see who had to take the two of them upstairs before they ran all the other men outta here."

"Why?" Sheriff Warton asked. "Were they threatening your customers?"

"Goodness no," she said. "They got so excited, lookin' at all the girls, till they started whoopin' and hollerin', jumpin' on the sofas like they hadn't never seen decent furniture before. Some of our best customers started talkin' about comin' back some other time. So Thelma and Rosa hiked their skirts up and started up the steps and those two hound dogs went right up behind 'em. I'm afraid to go upstairs to see what they did up there, but it's been quiet for a good while and the building ain't rockin' no more."

"Doesn't sound like they'll be going anywhere anytime soon," the sheriff declared.

"Or maybe ever," Derringer said. "I reckon we can go ahead and finish walkin' the town now that we know where Alvin is and his two nephews have found something better to think about than dry-gulchin' Jesse Derringer." He turned to the woman and said, "Thank you, ma'am, for your help."

"Don't mention it," she said. "If I can help you on anything else, don't hesitate to call on me. My name's Lydia."

"Why, thank you again, Lydia. My name's Jesse. Pleased to meet you." She walked them to the door.

When they were back out on the street, Warton chuckled. "I thought for a minute I was gonna have to finish this walk-around by myself. You must like 'em a little older."

"Not really," Derringer said. "I just appreciated her help and tried to treat her like a lady. I don't expect she gets a whole lot of respect in her line of work."

"No, I expect not," Warton said, and dropped the subject. He didn't want to think Derringer had a soft side, if in fact he had one. It was bad enough that Alvin Crowe was back in town to cause trouble because Jesse had chosen to forgive him for trying to kill him. He much preferred the Jesse Derringer who blew two men away with a double-barreled shotgun and pumped two .44 rounds into the chest of the third man to save him and Ray Cooper. "Let's see what's goin' on in the rest of the town."

They walked their way back around the north end of town and Leon Draper's stable and completed the walk-around back at the jail. When they walked back into the sheriff's office, they found only Cliff Crenshaw. Normally Ray Cooper would have been there also, since they had prisoners in the cell room, so the sheriff asked where he was. "He said he had some personal business to tend to," Cliff replied.

"He ain't forgot he's got the late walk-around with you, has he?" Warton asked.

"No, sir, he ain't forgot," Cliff answered. "He said he'd be back in plenty of time for that." He wasn't sure if the sheriff or Derringer knew that Ray had been courting Rachael Bowden for several months. Tonight, he just wanted to spend some time with her after they closed the dining room and she stayed to finish the cleanup after sending her mother home. At any rate, Cliff wanted the sheriff and Derringer to find out about Ray and Rachael from him or on their own.

"You could probably use a little time at home," Jesse said to the sheriff, "especially since I've been gone a few days. Why don't you go on home? I'll stick around till Ray gets back, then I'll watch the jail while they're lockin' up the town. I don't have any reason to hang around that hotel and I ain't really ready to go to bed yet."

"I think I'll take you up on that offer, Jesse. My wife's starting to look like she's waiting for an introduction every time I show up at the house. I 'preciate it, although I can't say for sure that she does." He didn't linger long enough to let Derringer change his mind. "I'll see you after breakfast in the morning and I hope you won't have anything important to tell me." He went out the door.

As soon as the door closed behind him, Jesse looked at Cliff and asked, "Rachael Bowden?"

"Yeah," Cliff answered. "But how'd you know that? I just found out about a week ago."

"Hell, you'd have to be half blind not to notice the way those two eyeball each other," Jesse remarked right away, "especially when they think nobody's watchin' 'em."

"I swear," Cliff said, "we thought we had a secret. I wonder how many others know about it." He grinned when he thought how embarrassed Ray would be.

"Most likely everybody who eats regular in the hotel dinin' room," Jesse said.

"She picks at you more than anybody else," Cliff remarked. "I halfway thought she was shinin' up to you."

Derringer chuckled at the thought. "That's what my boss, the general, would call a diversion tactic. She likes to pick at me because she knows I won't think it's anything but that and anybody can take one look at me and know she ain't got any interest in me. And nobody notices the secret little glances she and Ray exchange."

"I declare," Cliff said, "I reckon that doesn't make you feel very good, does it?"

"Doesn't bother me a bit," Derringer replied. "I learned at a very young age that I wasn't sent down here to please the ladies. It's saved me a lot of time and money."

"Don't you ever have a hankering to spend a little time with a woman?"

"Why, of course. Don't every man?" Jesse replied. "If he didn't, then we wouldn't have any children. Every once in a while you run into a nice lady that ain't any easier on the eyes than you are. And nine times out of ten they turn out to be the most interestin'."

"You're talkin' like an old man," Cliff said, "and you ain't really but a few years older than me."

"Maybe they sometimes put an old brain into a young body," Derringer suggested. "And that's enough old wisdom for your young brain. So let's go check the prisoners to make sure ain't none of 'em died while we were in here yakkin'." He was aware that Cliff looked up to him for guidance. *We must be a perfect set*, he thought. *He's younger than his years and I'm older than mine.*

CHAPTER 23

Alvin Crowe bought one more drink of whiskey and downed it. He had been standing in the same spot at the bar, unable to think of but one thing. And that was the face of the man who had killed his sons. He had offered his brother Edgar's two sons a trip to Vera's Vineyard and fifty dollars each to accompany him to Cheyenne to assassinate the man, Derringer. There had been no sign of the man for two days. Then to have him suddenly walk in the saloon and stand at the bar, looking him straight in the eye, was a shock to his system. He wanted to draw his .45 and shoot him down, but he couldn't seem to make his hand move. Then suddenly Derringer turned and walked out of the saloon. Alvin wanted to follow him but couldn't seem to make his body move. It felt as if it was dead with no feeling except in his right arm, which suddenly ached where the break had occurred.

When he could feel his entire body again, he cursed himself for not having been able to do what he had come to Cheyenne to do. But Derringer was here now and he was a dead man! He left the saloon and went next door to find his nephews. Charging into Vera's Vineyard, he grabbed the first woman he saw and demanded, "Where's my nephews?"

The woman snatched her arm out of his grasp and glared at him. Then it struck her at once who he was talking about. "Levi and Jasper?"

"Yeah, Levi and Jasper," he blurted. "Where are they? I want 'em!"

"You're welcome to 'em," the woman said. "Take 'em home and put 'em back in their cages." She called to another woman on the other side of the room. "Thelma, where are the two monkey brothers? Their uncle has come to get them."

"They're still upstairs trying to talk Rosa into going home with 'em." She walked over to the stairs, stepped up on the first step, and yelled, "Rosa! Come downstairs!"

In a couple of minutes, Rosa came down the steps with both Crowes following along behind her, still trying to persuade her to marry one or both of them. They both stopped when they saw their uncle standing in the middle of the room, glaring at them. "Hey, Uncle Alvin, we was just gittin' ready to come lookin' for you."

"Like hell you was," Alvin spat. "You've had your fun, now it's time to do what we came here to do. Jasper! Where's your gun?"

Jasper slapped his hip, thinking he had it on. "Uh, oh, I left it upstairs!" He turned around and ran back up the steps.

"Don't worry, Uncle Alvin, he'll be all right as soon

as he gets his gun in his hand," Levi said. "Papa wouldn'ta let us go with you if he didn't think we could handle it."

"I found it!" Jasper exclaimed as he hurried back down the steps. He looked at Rosa when he passed by her. "You change your mind, you let me know and I'll come get you."

"I ain't gonna change my mind, you knucklehead," she answered.

"I'll come git you, anyway," he said, and jumped toward the door when Alvin gave him a kick in the seat of his pants.

Alvin hurried them along to the hitching rail in front of the saloon where they had left their horses. "Where we goin', Uncle Alvin?" Levi asked.

"We're goin' to the jailhouse," Alvin answered. When Levi asked what for, Alvin said, "'Cause that's where Derringer went. That's where they all went after they took that walk around town. They always go back to the sheriff's office. We'll ride down there and I'll take a look in the window to make sure he's in there. I'll hold the horses and you'll just step in the door and shoot him down and anyone else that's in there with him. You understand?"

"Ain't much to have to understand," Levi answered. "Ain't nothin' to it."

They rode down the street just past the sheriff's office and the two nephews waited with the horses while Alvin stepped up beside the window in the office and peered in. He was there! The man he hated! He was tempted to step inside and blaze away with his Colt .45. But he was afraid he wouldn't be able to run back and jump on his horse fast enough to get away, if someone on the street saw him. Better to stick to the original plan. Let the young men do the shooting while he sat in the saddle and held their horses. Then they would gallop away before anyone could stop them. He went back to his horse and stepped up into the saddle. "That's him in there. I've got your horses. Make sure your guns are loaded. Shoot him down, then come a-runnin' and we'll ride like hell that-a-way." He pointed toward the south end of town.

Totally unaware of the three Crowes right outside the office, Derringer announced, "I think I could use a cup of coffee. You want some? If you do, I'll make enough for two cups."

"Yeah, I could drink a cup of coffee," Cliff replied.

"Come to think of it, Ray will be back here in a little while, maybe I'd better make a full pot."

"Maybe you'd better," Cliff said, so Derringer picked up the pot and walked through the cell room to the pump beyond the third cell.

"Now ain't that nice?" one of the prisoners declared. "The good deputy is fixin' to make us some coffee." Derringer never got a chance to reply. He heard a thud, which he identified later as the office door banging against the wall as it was flung open. The explosion that followed was identified immediately as the rapid emptying of two six-guns. Derringer dropped the coffeepot full of water and ran through the cell room back to the office. His .44 in hand, he burst through the cell room door to find Cliff lying on the floor and the outside door open. Knowing there was nothing he could do to save Cliff, he ran out the door in time to see the three horses galloping away into the fading light. He fired three shots after them, even though he knew there was little chance of hitting any of them. Without his horse, there was no chance of giving chase, so he went back inside to see if by any miracle Cliff had survived the attack.

"Cliff, Cliff," he repeated as he rolled him over, looking for any sign of life, but he knew at once that he was gone. Blood was beginning to pool on the floor as it flowed from the many bullet holes in his body and face. Cliff's Colt Peacemaker was laying in the pool of blood, which told him Cliff had drawn his weapon even in the hailstorm of lead that came down on him. He felt Cliff's neck for any sign of a pulse, feeling angry and sick at the same time because he knew the storm of bullets was meant for him and he was responsible for Cliff's death.

This was the way Ray found him when he ran inside the open door, his gun in hand. "Jesse!" he exclaimed. "What? Who? Oh, my God!" he blurted when he saw Cliff's bloody body. "Jesse! Who did this?"

"I was in the back of the cell room when they did it," Jesse said, "and they were gone by the time I got back here in the office. They were already on their horses and gone. I got there in time to see them ridin' away, so I know there was three of them. It was dark and I couldn't see their faces, but I knew who it was, so I fired three shots at them. Don't think I hit any of them. I couldn't tell."

"Alvin Crowe?" Ray asked.

"Who else could it be?" Jesse answered. "Him and his two nephews. The damn fools, they didn't come after Cliff. They came after me. Cliff never had a chance."

"What happened?" Sheriff Warton exclaimed when he arrived, puffing from running all the way from his house. Jesse went over the whole incident again for him while Ray went back in the cell room to quiet the few men locked in the cells. When he came back in the office, he was carrying the coffeepot Jesse had dropped.

When Jesse saw it, he said, "It's all my fault. I should have let Cliff go make the damn coffee. It's me they came for, not poor Cliff." He clenched his teeth in anger. "And they got away with it. By the time I got outside, all I could see was three riders in the dark, ridin' like hell to get away, and me with no horse to chase 'em." He shook his head as if trying to shake the thought out of his mind. "I wish I could tell Cliff how sorry I am for messin' things up, but I swear I'll hunt those three down and make 'em pay for it." He paused a moment, then said, "For all the good that'll do Cliff."

Neither Ray nor the sheriff said anything for a long moment. They had never seen an emotional side on the hard bark exterior of the man, Jesse Derringer. Finally, Sheriff Warton tried to put things into the proper perspective. "This is just the way things happen, Jesse. It ain't your fault they went after the wrong man. It sounds to me like it was those two boys Crowe brought with him to do the shootin', if it was Alvin Crowe. And I expect you're right about that. They just blazed away at whoever they saw in here, thinkin' it had to be you. And even if they had sense enough to know Cliff was the wrong man, they woulda shot him anyway to keep him from identifyin' 'em."

"Be that as it may," Derringer said calmly, "it's my fault Cliff's dead because I let Alvin Crowe go free when he came after me. If I'da shot him, instead of breakin' his arm, Cliff would still be alive. So I'm goin' after those three, that's the least I owe Cliff."

"I'll go get James Durham to come to pick up Cliff," Ray volunteered, and immediately went out the door. He was not without feelings of guilt, but they were mixed in with the thought that he was lucky he had not been there with Cliff as he should have been. He preferred not to divulge that information to the sheriff and was glad Derringer had not mentioned it.

When Ray left to get the undertaker, Warton tried to reason with Derringer. He had just lost a deputy and he didn't want to lose another, even if Derringer was only a temporary deputy. "I understand how you feel," he said to him, "but I need you now more than ever. The town is still overrun with drifters of all sorts. I don't have to tell you that. I can't afford to take a posse out to look for those three, even if we knew where to look. I couldn't leave the town unguarded for that long. We don't even know which way they left town." When Derringer started to interrupt, he held up his hand to stop him. "I know you said they galloped off toward the south end of town, but that don't mean that's the direction they ended up in. So, Jesse, you've got no trail to follow, even if you are a helluva tracker. They did it and they got away with it and I don't expect we'll ever see them again. The best we can do is police the town as good as we can."

Derringer let him finish his appeal to him to forget about the tragedy, but he knew that he could not, so he calmly told him so. "I'm sorry, Sheriff, I know the situation's bad for you, but you know I'm not gonna be here but a little while longer. You need to go ahead and try to hire one or two more deputies right now 'cause I'm quittin' today." He pulled his badge off and placed it on the desk. "I'll help you clean up in here after they take Cliff outta here and then I'm gone. I intend to find Alvin, Levi, and Jasper Crowe and rid this earth of them for once and all. I hope there're no hard feelings."

Warton shook his head, disappointed, and sighed. "Of course not, Jesse, you've done a helluva job for me. I wish you good luck and you better be careful. I think you're dealin' with a den of snakes." He saw how anxious Derringer was to leave, so he said, "Ain't no use in hangin' around if you're ready to go. Durham sends his son with the handcart to pick up the body. And he usually brings mops and buckets to clean up any blood."

"Much obliged, Sheriff. I do wanna get started." He picked up his rifle and started to leave, but the sheriff stepped in front of him and extended his hand. Derringer stopped and shook his hand. "Good luck to you, Sheriff."

"The same to you, Jesse, and you'd best be extra careful," Warton said. He stood in the open doorway and watched Derringer walk away toward The Crossing Saloon or perhaps the stable beyond the saloon. *I don't know what he's planning to do tonight if he's going for his horses,* he thought. *Maybe he's heading for the saloon. That makes more sense.*

Actually, Derringer was starting his hunt right away, but he was not heading for The Crossing or the stable. He was on his way to Vera's Vineyard. He went in the door to the big reception parlor where he and the sheriff had been earlier. Hoping to find Lydia, he scanned the broad room where several women were engaged in conversations with customers, but there was no sign of the older woman who had introduced herself as Lydia. He figured it was just his luck that she was upstairs with a client, but at that moment she walked out of the kitchen area holding a cup of coffee. Seeing him, she smiled and came at once to meet him. "You're back, Jesse Derringer. I was hoping we would see you again, but I didn't expect you this soon."

"I've come looking for help," Derringer said, "some information, really, and I'd be glad to pay you for your time."

"I don't charge for conversation with my friends," Lydia replied. "Would you like a cup of coffee while we talk?"

The offer caught Derringer by surprise and he hesitated when he thought of what happened earlier when he had a desire for a cup of coffee. Then he realized that he would still like a cup of coffee, so he said, "That would be mighty nice of you. I could use a cup of coffee. Of course I expect to pay for it." He didn't want to impose on her graciousness.

"It's just a cup of coffee," she said. "We don't sell it in this room. Do you have so much money that you're trying to get rid of it?" she joked.

He wondered what such a charming and proper lady was doing in a place like Vera's. "No, ma'am," he answered her question. "But I'm hoping to get some information on some of your customers and I don't want you to think I'm wasting your time."

She studied his expression for a few seconds and

said, "You've got something serious on your mind, haven't you?" She didn't wait for an answer. "Come," she said, and led him into the little room he had seen her come from. It turned out to be a small room not much bigger than a large closet, but it had a stove and a table and chairs. She motioned for him to sit down while she poured a cup of coffee for him from the pot on the stove. Then she warmed her coffee as well and sat down at the table with him. "Do you want milk and sugar or do you like cowboy coffee?" Figuring she meant black, he said he'd take it just like it came out of the pot. "Now," she said, "what do you want to know?"

"I'm sure you've seen Deputy Sheriff Cliff Crenshaw in here from time to time," he started. "Well, less than an hour ago, two men walked in the door of the sheriff's office and shot him down."

"Oh, dear Lord," Lydia responded. "That was that big burst of gunfire we heard!"

"That's right," Derringer said, "and I'm pretty sure the two men that killed him are the two Crowe brothers who were in here earlier. The problem is they struck so fast that they got away before anybody could get after them. I've got to find them, but I don't know where to start lookin'. Accordin' to what you and the ladies that they were with said, they were two wild young men who did a lot of talking. I was hoping I could talk to the women who were with them to see if they remember anything they said that might help me find 'em."

"You need to talk to Rosa," she said. "She's upstairs now, trying to recover from those two wild animals. I don't think they ever shut their mouths the whole time they were here. You wait right here and drink your coffee. I'll go upstairs and get Rosa." She got up from the table and went upstairs. In a short time, she was back with Rosa and Thelma, too.

"Lydia says you wanna ask us about the monkey brothers," Rosa said. "What do you want to know? Did they really shoot Cliff Crenshaw down?"

"Yes, they did," Derringer answered, "and they got away before anybody could see where they went. So I don't have a trail to even try to track 'em. I was hoping they might have told you where they live, if they've got a hideout somewhere, or a camp."

"Jasper, the one with the ring through his nose, he was the youngest," Rosa said. "He ran his mouth all the time. The whole time he was in my room. What was it he kept sayin', Thelma? 'You're sleepin' with the Crows,' over and over. Then both of 'em would say 'sleepin' with the Crow Creek Crows.'"

"Crowe is their last name," Derringer said, "Levi and Jasper Crowe."

"Oh," Rosa said. "I thought they were talking about real crows. Jasper tried to get me to marry him. He said he'd hook a chain to that ring in his nose and I could lead him around with it. And he said I'd like their cabin on Crow Creek."

As soon as she said that, Derringer became even more attentive. "He said they had a cabin on Crow Creek?" West or east, he wondered. Crow Creek was a long creek. "He didn't happen to say which direction from Cheyenne, did he?"

"No, I'm sorry," Rosa said. "He said he was gonna

come get me, and his brother said he'd have to put me in a sack to sneak me by the soldiers because they'd wanna steal me."

Derringer was immediately alert. *The soldiers! Camp Cheyenne, three miles west on Crow Creek!* That didn't tell him how far, but it was past Camp Cheyenne and it would start him in the right direction. "Ladies, I can't tell you how much you've helped me." All three looked very pleased. "I would like to pay you for your time, if you'll tell me how much I owe you."

Thelma and Rosa looked at each other and shrugged. "Since we didn't do anything but talk, how about two dollars?" Thelma asked. Derringer reached into his pocket and pulled out a small roll of money and peeled off two dollars for Thelma and two for Rosa. They thanked him and went back upstairs.

He turned to Lydia then, his money still in hand. "Put your money away, Jesse. I told you I don't charge a friend to have a conversation."

"That's mighty nice of you, Lydia. I feel like I owe you something for being so nice to me, when I don't ever do any business in here a-tall."

"That's one of the reasons I like you," she said. "Have you got a little wife waiting at home for you?"

"Nope, that's one trap I never stepped into," Derringer said. "I reckon it worked out so bad for my ma and my pa that I didn't think it worth the risk. Besides, I don't think I'd make a decent husband. I was gone from home all the time, either trappin' or in the army, or like right now, scouting for the railroad."

"Have you got someone who comes to see you in your hotel room?"

"No, ma'am, I reckon I don't. I'm not a very inter-estin' person, I guess."

"Don't you ever think about keeping company with a woman at least once in a while?"

He shrugged and said, "Sure, every once in a while."

"What do you do when you think about it?"

"I try to think about something else," he answered.

She smiled. "Well, next time you think about it, why don't you just come to see me. I'll fix you something to eat in the kitchen and we'll take it out on the back porch and talk a while." He suddenly found himself confused, so he hesitated a moment to remind himself that he was talking to a prostitute. She must have guessed his dilemma, for she said, "Just some supper and some conversation between two friends."

He hesitated for only a moment more before answer-ing. "Thank you for the invitation. I believe I would enjoy that very much, if you're sure it wouldn't be an awful waste of your time."

She laughed, delighted by his concern for her time. "I don't really have many true friends here in Chey-enne and no gentlemen friends. It would truly be worth my while to be able to spend some time with a gentle-man friend."

"I think I oughta warn you, I ain't ever been con-fused for a gentleman."

She laughed again. "That's because no one has ever sat down with you for a casual conversation. I'm glad we've become friends. I hope you will be very careful if you go after those Crowe brothers and their uncle. They struck me as having the conscience of an alley cat."

"It's not the first time I've dealt with alley cats like those three," he told her. "They shot down a fine young man for no reason other than the fact that he was in the office. It was me they were after, so I've got to go square things up for Cliff Crenshaw." He paused for a moment, then thanked her once again. "I expect I'd better go now and get ready to head up Crow Creek in the mornin'." She offered her hand and he took it very carefully, so as not to treat it too roughly. Then he turned and walked toward the door.

"Be careful," she called after him.

CHAPTER 24

When he left Vera's Vineyard, he walked up the street to the stable on the off chance that Leon Draper had not gone home yet. It was past time when Leon usually closed the stable, but on occasion he stayed later for one reason or another. Planning to leave in the morning, he hoped he might get a chance to check on Clem and the sorrel but also what supplies he might have left in his packs. Since he paid for full care of his horses, they should be in their stall inside the stable and it appeared the stable door was closed as he approached. But the barn door was open and he could see a light through it, probably from the tack room. When he got a little closer, he suddenly heard a noise he couldn't identify. It was an irritating, scratching, screeching-like noise and he was at once concerned for Leon's safety. So he cranked a cartridge into his rifle and proceeded through the barn door with caution. As he came closer to the tack room, the noise became increasingly grating. He eased up to the open tack room door and peeked inside. "Leon!" he yelled. "You all right?"

Startled, Leon jumped off the stool he was sitting on, almost dropping the banjo he had been tormenting. "Damn, Jesse, you almost gave me a heart attack!"

"What the hell is that?"

"A banjo," Leon said. "I'm tryin' to learn how to play it and I can't get the hang of it. A feller in here last week traded me this banjo for takin' care of his horse and wagon, since he was short of cash. He showed me how to make a couple of cords, but I'm havin' trouble makin' it sound like it does when he makes 'em."

"I was hopin' I'd catch you before you closed up," Derringer said. "I've gotta leave town in the mornin' and I wanted to see what I've got in my packs. I was afraid you'd already gone home."

"I already been home for supper, but my wife won't let me practice on my banjo at home. She says the noise drives her crazy, so I came back to the barn to practice."

"Women have extra-sensitive ears," Derringer said. *And horses, too, most likely*, he thought, thankful that Clem was in a stall at the other end of the stable.

"You going after them boys that shot Cliff Crenshaw down?" Leon asked.

"You heard about that, huh? Yeah, I'm goin' after 'em and I may be gone for a good while 'cause I ain't got a trail to follow."

"That's a damn shame about Cliff," Leon said. "He was a fine young man. Warton's gonna be runnin' kinda slim with you gone, just him and Ray Cooper to keep an eye on the town."

"I can't let that foul deed go unpunished," Derringer declared.

"No, I reckon not," Leon agreed. "You need any help with your horse right now?"

Derringer said he didn't. He just wanted to see what he needed in the way of ammunition and supplies. "I won't leave till after breakfast, anyway, 'cause I'm sure I'll have to wait till Cheyenne Merchandise is open before I can buy what I need to take with me." He went to the stable then and spent a few minutes with Clem before checking the sorrel. Then he went through his packs to make a mental list of what he was going to have to buy in the morning. He had some deer jerky that was still usable, but he would need to buy a slab of bacon, coffee, crackers, and beans. If he was lucky, he might find some small game to supplement his food supply.

When he came out of the stable, Leon was waiting to lock up. "Sorry to hold you up," Derringer said.

"No trouble a-tall," Leon said. "I ain't especially anxious to get home to listen to all my wife's complaints about what went wrong today." His comment caused Derringer to remember Lydia asking him if he had a little wife at home somewhere. He smiled to himself and thought, *Like I said . . .*

As he walked back down the street, he realized it was most likely time for the sheriff or Ray to take the lock-up tour around town. Maybe they would walk it together. He felt a slight sense of guilt for walking out on them. But he felt it a bigger crime to let Cliff Crenshaw's murder go unpunished. And this was the only time he would have to find Alvin and Jasper and

Levi Crowe, for in about two weeks General Dodge would be back. He had lived on the Union Pacific payroll, so he felt they rightfully owned his time. When he passed the jail, on the opposite side of the street, there appeared to be no one in the sheriff's office, so he figured Warton and Ray were walking the town together. *That's best*, he thought, *but it's not going to be good for Warton's marriage*. He was going to have to go ahead and build up a competent sheriff's department. He looked forward to a peaceful night's sleep as he said good night to Bob Wolfe when he passed by the night clerk's desk on his way upstairs to his room.

"Mornin', Jesse," Cecil greeted him when he walked into the dining room right after he unlocked the door. "You must have a busy day planned," he commented when Derringer dropped his rifle and saddlebags behind the desk by the outside door.

"That's right," Derringer responded. "I've gotta take a little trip today, so I thought I'd best get it started with one of Clara's good breakfasts."

"We were really sorry to hear about Cliff Crenshaw's death," Cecil remembered to comment.

"Yes, Cliff was a good man," Derringer said. "I reckon we're all gonna miss him."

"Ray Cooper said you were there when it happened," Cecil said. "It musta been a terrible thing to see."

"I didn't really see it happen," Derringer replied. "I was in the back of the cell room when they busted in the office door and emptied their guns at him. They were out the door and ridin' away by the time I got outside. I was able to fire three shots at them, but I don't think I hit any of 'em. So I went back to see if I could help Cliff and he was already dead. And you're right, it was a terrible thing to see him shot full of holes."

"Good morning, Jesse," Rachael said, as she came out of the kitchen. "Terrible thing about Cliff Crenshaw."

"Yes, it is," Derringer responded. "We were just talking about that." Her voice was without the usual lighthearted cheerfulness. Granted, it was a sad occasion. But there was an accusing expression on her face as well. He predicted what her next comment would be.

"Ray said you were there when it happened."

"And you're wanting to know why I didn't get shot, right? Or at least make some effort to help him, right? Well, I'll tell you why. I wasn't in the office when it happened. I was in the back of the cell room filling the coffeepot with water when I heard two six-guns emptying as fast as they could be. I ran to the office as fast as I'm capable of runnin'. They were already gone. I ran out the door and saw them ridin' hell-bent for leather down the street. I fired three shots at them before they disappeared in the dark, the first two hopin' to hit one of them, the third shot hopin' to hit one of the horses. Then it was too dark to see them at all. There was no way I could have helped Cliff. Ray and I both should have been in the office with him. But when the attack happened, I was in the cell room and Ray was visitin' with you. If either one of us had been where we normally should have been, we would all three be dead. It happened so suddenly that I doubt any of us would have had a chance to shoot back. Cliff tried. I found his gun on the floor, but it hadn't been fired. I suspect he was already dead when he drew it." He paused and waited for any further comments or questions. When there were none, he asked, "Can I get some breakfast now? I've got a long day ahead of me."

Rachael spun on her heel and went to get the coffeepot. When she returned, she turned his cup up and filled it. "I'm sorry if I sounded like I was accusing you of not helping Cliff," she said. "I should know better."

"Don't worry about it," he remarked. "It's my fault, anyway. If I had killed Alvin Crowe when I should have, Cliff would still be alive. I ain't denyin' that."

Clara came out of the kitchen carrying his breakfast of eggs, bacon, and potatoes, with two freshly baked biscuits riding on top of the bacon. "I heard you were fixing to leave, so I wrapped a couple more biscuits up in a cloth for you to eat when you stop for dinner. There's a slice of ham in each one of 'em."

"Why, thank you most kindly, Clara. I'll surely appreciate that when I stop to rest the horses."

They left him alone to eat his breakfast. Rachael was very dutiful in making sure his coffee cup never emptied. But she was not her usual playful self and Derringer was certain it was because of a guilty feeling for having thought he might have failed to come to Cliff's aid. It caused no concern on his part. He was already thinking about more important issues that he might have to deal with, like how big a clan the Crowes might be. And he appreciated the opportunity to have a quiet breakfast. When he was finished and got up to leave, Rachael came over to ask, "How long are you going to be gone?"

He shrugged and said, "As long as it takes."

"Maybe a day or two?"

He smiled at her innocence. "I expect it might take a little longer than that."

Hearing him getting ready to leave, her mother came out of the kitchen to give him the two ham biscuits she promised. "Keep them wrapped in that cloth till you're ready to eat them," she said. He thanked her again and she watched while he placed them in his saddlebag. "You be careful, Jesse Derringer," she said.

"I intend to," he replied, then picked up his rifle and went out the door, only to meet Ray Cooper coming to breakfast.

"I shoulda known you'd be eatin' breakfast a little earlier than usual this mornin'," Ray said. "I figured I'd catch you before you left. I know you're determined to find those three, but how the hell do you know where to start lookin'? I'd be mighty surprised if you can pick up any trail you could say for sure was one they left last night."

"I'm glad you asked me that," Derringer said. "In case I don't come back, you can tell General Dodge what direction I left in. I'll be ridin' up Crow Creek, somewhere beyond Camp Cheyenne, to see if the three of them went home last night." When Ray asked how he knew where they lived, he told him about the visit with the girls at Vera's.

"Well, I'll be . . ." Ray responded. "I never thought

about talking to them. Damn! I wish I could go with you. I should have been in the office last night."

"If you had been, I wouldn't be talkin' to you right now," Derringer said. "They struck without any warnin'. So don't go blamin' yourself for not being there. There's only one person to blame and that's me for not shootin' Alvin when I should have. That's why I've got to go. You're needed here. This town is your first responsibility. Sheriff Warton is helpless without you."

"You be careful, Jesse, and good luck," Ray said, convinced now that Derringer didn't blame him for not being there to help Cliff.

He went straight to the stable, knowing Leon would already be open. He saddled Clem and the packhorse, lingering to talk to Leon only long enough to give Mayor Hook time to open his store. After buying the items he was short on and a couple of boxes of extra .44 cartridges, he set out on the trail to Camp Cheyenne, some three miles up Crow Creek. The name of the fort was now officially Fort D. A. Russell, named for a general killed in the Civil War. But most of the people in Cheyenne still referred to it as Camp Cheyenne, the name it was called when Colonel John Stevenson began building the fort and the nearby Quartermaster depot called Cheyenne Depot. The fort, still under construction, was presently the home of Company H of the Second Cavalry, whose men were very familiar with the trail to the town of Cheyenne. It was a well-defined road. One thing that puzzled Derringer was the possibility that the Crowe family would live anywhere close to the army fort. And if they did, surely the criminal element of the family must have a hideout somewhere else.

It had been some time since he had actually ridden up Crow Creek and he was surprised by the occasional homestead he passed along the way to the fort. These would be the people the merchants in Cheyenne depended upon after the railroad moved on up into the Laramie Mountains. He wondered if these settlers did any business with the army at Camp Cheyenne. He decided it worth his while to find out if there were honest members of the Crowe family who might provide some service to the fort. In less than an hour's time, he was approaching the fort and he found that there were already quite a few buildings around a large parade ground. With no real notion where to go for the information he wanted, he decided to go to the commanding officer's office, which he figured should be the building with the flagpole standing out front. So he rode straight for it. There was a sign in front of the building that identified it as Company H, Second Infantry Regiment. So he dismounted and dropped Clem's reins on the ground.

Company Clerk Corporal Raymond Stevens looked up from his desk when the door opened and a good deal of the light was blocked out by the rugged individual entering. "Can I help you?" Stevens asked.

"I hope so, Corporal," Derringer answered. "My name's Jesse Derringer. I'm a special agent for the Union Pacific Railroad and I'm trying to find a family that lives near the fort. They mighta done some business with the fort. The name is Crowe, like the creek."

Another corporal standing beside a file cabinet turned to look at Derringer.

The corporal looked amused. "Your name's Derringer, like the pistol?" he asked, and when Derringer said it was, the corporal asked, "And you're lookin' for a family named Crow, like the Creek?"

"That's right," Derringer answered. "The only difference is the name Crowe has an *e* on the end of it."

Corporal Stevens smiled. "Who sent you over here? Did Sergeant Striker over at Quartermaster send you over here?"

"Nope," Derringer replied. "I just rode in from Cheyenne and you're the first place I tried."

"You're serious, aren't you?" Stevens realized then. "I didn't mean to wise off, but Striker's always trying to put something over on me. I'm sorry, sir, but I don't know of anyone named Crowe that has anything to do with us in the orderly room. But you might ask Sergeant Striker over at the Quartermaster. They deal with civilian suppliers all the time.

Derringer started to thank him and leave when the other corporal spoke up. "I don't know about the Quartermaster dealing with some Crowes. But the mess sergeant buys cattle from time to time from some old man named Edgar Crowe. I was at the mess hall one day when him and some men drove about fifteen cows into the cattle pens. The mess sergeant said it was never more than ten or fifteen at a time." When Derringer showed an immediate interest, the corporal said, "Why don't you go ask the mess sergeant? Sergeant Cox, he can tell you about Mr. Crowe. Come on, I'll show you the mess hall." He went outside with Derringer and pointed to a building across the parade ground. Derringer thanked him and led his horses across the parade ground.

"It's gonna be a while before we're open for mess call," Sergeant Cox called out from the back of the kitchen when Derringer came in the side door of the mess hall.

"Just wanna ask you a question, Sergeant Cox. Corporal in the orderly room said you might know somebody I'm tryin' to find."

"Is that so?" Cox replied. "Who might that be?"

"A fellow named Alvin Crowe," Derringer said. "He's supposed to live on Crow Creek."

"Whatcha lookin' for him for? You a lawman or bounty hunter?"

"Neither one," Derringer replied. "I'm an ex-army sergeant who works for the Union Pacific Railroad now. I'm tryin' to catch up with two of his nephews who walked into the sheriff's office in Cheyenne last night and put twelve bullet holes in a young deputy sheriff who had never had any dealings with them before."

Interested, the mess sergeant asked, "How come you're the one goin' after 'em?"

"Because it was me they thought they were killin'," Derringer said.

"And you ain't no lawman? What do you do for the railroad?"

"I'm a scout for the man who's buildin' the railroad to connect with the Central Pacific," Derringer said.

The mess sergeant's eyes lit up when it dawned on him. "You're Derringer, right?"

"My name's Derringer," he said, surprised that the sergeant could guess. "How did you know that?"

"I came out here with General Auger when they built that bridge across Crow Creek. General Dodge sent General Auger to build this fort. Well, I'll be . . . I don't know no Alvin Crowe. I know a feller name of Edgar Crowe. He might be kin to Alvin. Chances are they're all from the same family and I'm pretty sure all the cows I get from him are rustled. But we need the beef, so we don't ask 'em where they get the cows. Crowe always has a couple of young men to help him drive 'em to the fort." He shook his head, amazed at the coincidence. "I ain't really got no idea where they live when they ain't out rustlin' cattle, though. You can imagine how closemouthed they get when you ask 'em anything. Wish I could tell you more, but I ain't never asked them where they call home."

"I appreciate what you have told me. At least I know I'm on the right track. I know they live somewhere on Crow Creek. I just don't know how far up this creek it is. So I'm prepared to keep looking until I find 'em. I think there's a good possibility that the two families might live in the same hollow somewhere. There might be a whole clan of Crowes along this creek somewhere. I'll just keep lookin' till I find 'em."

Sergeant Cox shook his head and said, "Man, you'd better watch your step. You might be steppin' into a hive of hornets or something."

"I'll do that, Sarge. Thanks again for your help."

CHAPTER 25

Derringer left Fort Russell on a trail that closely followed Crow Creek, thinking it unlikely that an outlaw family would build a house on the creek. It would be too easily found, so he figured he was looking for a strong stream or another creek that emptied into Crow Creek. He passed occasional streams of various sizes but none that looked strong enough to support one homestead, let alone supply enough water for two or more families. From what he had to go on, these were grown families, with each brother having fathered at least two sons who had grown into manhood. He tried to picture a family farm or ranch where two brothers had each built a house to raise a family and what that might involve. Maybe there would be boys and girls of various ages.

He suddenly realized that the picture didn't make sense at all. Wherever the Crowe family conclave was, it wasn't anywhere near Crow Creek. What he was looking for was a hideout used by the two brothers,

Edgar and Alvin, and their sons. The crazy ranting of Levi and Jasper Crowe that Rosa and Thelma told him about was nothing more than silly japing about their hideout near Crow Creek. He had wondered why Sergeant Cox had never heard of a family of Crowes living anywhere on Crow Creek and it was the same for Corporal Stevens in the orderly room. If there was a large family farm on the creek, the army would have known about it. The thought that crossed his mind now was the real possibility that when Alvin and his two nephews fled from Cheyenne last night, they may have headed for home, whatever direction that might be. And he was riding a senseless journey that might lead him to the origin of Crow Creek and nothing more.

With that disappointing outcome in mind, he looked for a good place to pull off the trail and rest his horses after what he estimated to be about five miles past the fort. He picked a spot where there was some grass on the bank for them to graze. When he had taken care of the horses, He gathered enough wood to build a fire, figuring he might as well make some coffee to go with the ham biscuits Clara had given him. He was sure that they would be enough dinner. He decided that as long as he had made the effort to ride this far up Crow Creek, he might as well continue on a few miles farther on the possibility of finding a hideout. More than likely, it would be a shack used by other outlaws as well as the Crowes, so it would pay to be cautious in the event he did find one.

When he was satisfied that his horses were rested, he saddled up again and set out once more following the path beside the creek. After maybe four more miles with nothing encouraging, he spotted a line of trees up ahead that led off to the north and would normally indicate a stream or creek. He nudged Clem to pick up the pace without realizing he had done so, his focus zeroed on the line of trees. When he reached them, he discovered they bordered a smaller creek flowing into Crow Creek. There was a trail no bigger than a game trail that followed the nameless creek. Alert now for what he might find ahead of him, he pulled his rifle out of the saddle scabbard and cranked a cartridge into the chamber. Riding along the path, he could see hoofprints that looked fairly recent whenever he came to a place where the bushes were not hiding the path. He felt certain he was going to find someone wherever this trail led. Whether or not it might be the Crowes was yet to be determined. He gently reined Clem to a stop when he heard a horse nicker somewhere up ahead of him. Clem answered the request.

Derringer decided to leave the path and cross over the creek, then continue on the other side. He had gone no farther than another twenty yards when he spotted the clearing up ahead of him and a small herd of horses grazing there between him and a roughly built log cabin. Beside the cabin, there was a fire burning and he spotted a man butchering what looked to be a young cow on the other side of it. He looked hard at the man but was disappointed that he did not recognize him. But then he reminded himself that the man could be Edgar Crowe, who he had never seen before. *I guess that's one cow Sergeant Cox won't get for the mess hall*, he thought. He decided he'd better go on foot from there, so he turned his horses around and rode back down the creek a little way. Then he tied them beside the creek and went back toward the cabin on foot. When he went around the horse herd, he got a good look at the cabin. It was little more than a shelter from the weather, with a fireplace for cooking and warmth. There was a door in the front and one small window in the back.

He hid behind a thick clump of bushes, where he got a good view of the door. After a little while, the door opened and a voice he knew he had heard before called out. "How 'bout it, Ed? You 'bout ready to cook some of that meat?"

"Yeah," the man doing the butchering answered back. "Get your lazy butt out here and get some of this on the fire." A moment later, Alvin Crowe walked outside the cabin with a homemade rack to roast meat over a flame.

Derringer smiled. *Sometimes you just get lucky,* he said to himself. He wondered then how many more were in the cabin. Was there just Levi and Jasper? Or were there more Crowes inside the tiny cabin? He had to know for sure, so he told himself to be patient.

Edgar Crowe turned away from the carcass he was butchering to yell at the cabin. "You better get your sorry butts out here and get somethin' to eat. You better put somethin' in your bellies beside that whiskey or you ain't gonna be able to eat."

In a few minutes, Levi came outside, followed by his brother, Jasper. "Hell, Pa, we was still celebratin' that deputy's passin'. Mr. Jesse Derringer hisself. Ain't that right, Jasper?"

"You got that right," Jasper responded. "Bam! Bam! Bam!" he blurted, pretending his hand was a gun. "I bet he was too heavy to carry to the graveyard 'cause he had so much lead in him."

"I told you they could get the job done," Edgar said to his brother.

"I just wish I coulda seen it," Alvin replied. "But we had to get away from there fast before anybody could do anything about it, so I stayed on my horse and held theirs ready to ride. It's a good thing, too, because somebody threw two or three shots at us. But we were gone from there before anybody could see which way we went. And I know Arthur and Caleb appreciate what their cousins did for 'em."

Derringer looked them all over closely to see what he had to deal with. Edgar was the only one wearing a gun, so he would have to be the first to be dealt with. The two sons would likely panic. He wasn't sure what Alvin would do. He thought about what he was about to do and he realized that he might wind up being judge, jury, and executioner. But he was not prepared for the risk involved in trying to take the three of them back for trial. They would be sentenced to death at any rate and that would mean a hanging by the vigilance committee. Why bother? Then he remembered what he had silently promised Cliff's body.

Alvin was the first to see what he thought was the ghost of Jesse Derringer as the specter walked slowly up out of the water in the creek, his rifle ready to fire. Terrified with fear, Alvin was struck helpless to move as he gasped the one word he feared most, "Derringer!" Edgar, having never crossed paths with the man before, reacted as he would against an obvious threat.

He reached for his six-gun, only to draw it halfway out of the holster before he was struck in the chest with a .44 slug from Derringer's rifle, which was reloaded instantly as Edgar's six-gun dropped to the ground.

Frozen, trancelike as their uncle Alvin, Levi and Jasper realized at that instant that the man they murdered was not Derringer. They both recoiled in reaction to their father's death. "You have a choice," Derringer said. "You can die here and now for the murder of Cliff Crenshaw, or I can take you back to Cheyenne for trial."

"Damn you!" Levi spat, and dived for his father's six-gun on the ground. When he did, Jasper turned and ran to the cabin.

Derringer put a round into Levi's side, reloaded while he turned and caught Jasper in the middle of his back before he could reach the door. "I was hoping that would be your choice," Derringer said. He turned his attention back to Alvin then. "I spared your life the last time you tried to kill me. I told you then, I don't give second chances. But I'm willin' to give you the same choice I gave the rest of your kin. I'll take you back to town and let the people of Cheyenne decide what to do with you or put you out of your misery right now."

Alvin remained motionless for a full minute, still seemingly in a trance. Then he said, "I'd appreciate it if you would end it now." The words had barely left his lips before the .44 slug ripped into his chest. Derringer turned his attention toward the log hut then, reasonably sure there was no one else inside, since there had been no shots fired from there. Still he had to make sure. A quick look inside with his rifle ready to fire told him

there was no one else. So as he would with any crip-
pled animal, he drew his Colt handgun and placed a
round in the back of each dying man's skull to end any
suffering.

He chose not to labor over the right or wrong of
what he had just done as he went back down the creek
to get his horses. It was an act that had to be done and
an evil that needed to be eliminated. It was just his mis-
fortune that fate had chosen him to be the instrument
of the elimination. He led his horses back to the cabin
and dropped Clem's reins to the ground while he went
inside the cabin to search it. Inside, he found the weapons, packs, and saddles all jammed into the small interior. So he gathered all the weapons and ammunition
belts and put them in a pile. He dumped all the packs
and saddlebags, looking for anything of value then.
After that, he examined the saddles and found two that
were in decent shape and worth something. He did a
quick search of the four bodies to make sure there was
nothing of value he was leaving behind, finding a small
amount of money on them. When his search was completed, he walked among the horses grazing in the
clearing and selected the best two in the herd. He put
the two good saddles on these two horses and divided
the pile of weapons, ammunition, and useful items into
smaller piles of four. These piles he dumped into four
sacks that had been on their packsaddles and he hung
two of the sacks on the saddles of the two horses he decided to take with him. He took the bridles off the
other horses so as not to hinder them in any way when
he left them behind.

When he was finished, he went over to the fire and

took a charred piece of beef off the spit Edgar Crowe had improvised and dropped it in the fire. Then he inserted the spit into a fresh slice of raw beef, even though it had not been that long since he ate the two ham biscuits. While that was roasting over the fire, he took a couple more cuts of the fresh meat and wrapped them in a piece of the cowhide to have for supper that night and breakfast the next day. These he found a place for on his packhorse. He pulled the rifles out of the two saddles he was leaving behind and strapped them to the rifles in the slings on the two saddles on the horses. When he was finally ready to leave, he took his roasted beef strip off the spit and ate it. After he put out the fire, he tied the two horses on a line behind his packhorse. With his left foot in the stirrup, he started to climb up into the saddle but hesitated when another thought struck him. He drew his foot out of the stirrup and went to the front door of the cabin where Jasper's body was lying. He drew his skinning knife from his belt and stuck his little finger through the silver ring in Jasper's nostril. Then he slit the nostril with his knife, releasing the ring. He wiped the ring and his knife on Jasper's shirt, then went to the edge of the creek to give them both a better cleaning.

With that done, he dropped the ring in his vest pocket, climbed up on Clem, and started back down the creek to its confluence with Crow Creek. He had considered remaining there at the cabin that night but decided he'd rather leave the scene for the buzzards and the wolves to perform their valuable services. He preferred to make camp for that night where he had stopped to rest the horses and eat his ham biscuits. It was a little early to stop for the day, but he preferred that to maybe a stop at the fort. It would leave him with a trip of only about eight or nine miles in the morning, which would make his arrival in Cheyenne in the midmorning. And that would be a better time since he would have a lot of explaining to do.

"Rachael, come here quick!" Cecil Humphrey called from the front window of the hotel dining room.

"What is it?" Rachael asked, still cleaning up after the breakfast customers.

"Look who's coming up the street from the creek road!" Cecil said, and pointed to a man on a horse, leading a string of three horses behind him.

Rachael went to the window and looked at the rider for a few seconds before she realized who it was. "Jesse!" she uttered. "It's Jesse, already back! I thought he was gonna be gone for days. Do you suppose he found those men who shot Cliff Crenshaw?"

"He sure musta found somebody," Cecil answered.

"I wish he'd made it back for breakfast," Rachael said. "Now, we're gonna have to wait till dinner to find out what happened. Where do you suppose he's going?"

"To the jailhouse, where else?" Cecil answered her. "Either that or the stable." They continued to watch until he pulled Clem over to the rail in front of the sheriff's office and dismounted. "Warton came out of the office to meet him," Cecil reported.

"You caught up with them, didn't you?" Sheriff Warton asked as he looked at the two saddled horses behind Derringer's packhorse.

"Yes, I did," Derringer replied.

"What's in the sacks hangin' on the saddles?"

"Their guns and things to let you know I'm tellin' you the truth," Derringer said. "I gave them a chance to surrender to me and come back here for trial, but they said no, so I shot 'em."

"Both of 'em?" Ray Cooper asked as he came out the door to join them.

"All four of 'em," Derringer answered, "Alvin, Levi, and Jasper, and their father, Edgar. I found 'em in a hideout on a little creek that empties into Crow Creek about twelve miles from here. If you wanna verify that, I can take you there or give you directions to the cabin, but I wouldn't wait too long because the bodies are lyin' right where I shot 'em down. If you lift the back jockey on that saddle on the chestnut back there, you'll find the name Edgar Crowe. He was the father of those two that murdered Cliff. That Winchester 66 has got *E. Crowe* scratched on the stock. I just noticed that when I was strapping a couple of their rifles together. I didn't check all four rifles. There may be another one with initials or a name scratched on it. I figured you'd wanna look over the stuff in those four sacks, so we can take those inside and I'll take the horses to the stable." He started to untie one of the sacks but paused when he remembered. "Oh," he said, and reached into his vest pocket. "I brought you this as a remembrance." He handed the sheriff a silver ring. "This is the ring Jasper Crowe wore in his nose."

"Damn," the sheriff swore, and almost dropped the ring. "You didn't have to bring a whole bunch of proof to show me. I believe you. If you say all four of those men are dead, then they're dead. End of story." He handed the ring to Ray, who grinned at Derringer as he examined it.

"Thank you, Sheriff, I appreciate that," Derringer said. "It didn't occur to me till I was halfway back here this mornin' that I didn't go to much trouble to prove those two fellows that shot Cliff were dead." They took the four sacks off the two saddles and carried them into the office and the sheriff and Ray started emptying them right away. "I'll be back in a few minutes," Derringer said, and went back outside to take the horses to the stable.

The few minutes Derringer estimated to spend at the stable was far short of the time it took to satisfy Leon's need for details of his trip. So by the time he returned to the sheriff's office, Warton and Ray had pretty much inspected all the rifles and handguns. They told him that one of the other rifles had the name *J. Crowe* scratched on the stock. "I reckon all this stuff belongs to you now, don't it?" Ray asked. He held up the Winchester 66 rifle he had been fondling for Derringer to see.

"I reckon you could say that," Derringer answered, "plus two pretty good horses. But to tell you the truth, when I caught those four, I figured I was acting as a deputy sheriff for the city of Cheyenne. So I attempted to arrest them and they refused. That bein' the case, I figure all the stuff belongs to the sheriff's department."

"That's mighty generous of you, Jesse," Sheriff Warton said. "Nobody could have found fault with you if you figured you were actin' alone, so all the spoils belonged to you."

"You sure you don't wanna trade that Henry of yours for this Winchester 66?" Ray had to ask.

"I'm sure," Derringer answered. "That Winchester's a fine rifle, but my Henry and me have gotten so used to each other that I think it'd be a mistake to trade. I think the Winchester might be better suited to you." He didn't share the main reason he brought all the weapons back to the sheriff's office was because he didn't want to own any of the weapons that belonged to the two men who shot Cliff Crenshaw. He still blamed himself for Cliff's death and he didn't want anything around to constantly remind him of that, even if the rifle wasn't used in the murder. He had even thought about throwing Jasper's and Levi's Colt six-shooters into Crow Creek but decided he didn't want to explain why they were missing.

"I don't know about you two, but accordin' to my stomach, it's about dinnertime," the sheriff announced.

"It is about that time," Ray said. "You and Jesse go ahead and eat and I'll watch the jail." He looked at Derringer and said, "I expect you're about ready for dinner, since you've been campin' for a couple of days."

"I ain't sufferin' for something to eat," Derringer replied. "I had a pretty big breakfast of fresh butchered beef, courtesy of Mr. Edgar Crowe. I can stay here while you two go to eat."

"Things bein' as quiet as they are for a change, why don't we just lock up and we'll all go to dinner," the sheriff suggested.

CHAPTER 26

"The whole sheriff's department is heading this way," Cecil alerted Rachael, "all three of them. Better make that all two of them," Cecil said. "I forgot, Jesse quit night before last." He continued to watch from the window. "Wait a minute, they stopped to talk about something. Now Jesse's turned around and going back the other way, but the sheriff and Ray are coming this way again."

"He musta forgot something," Rachael said. "I'll just pour two cups of coffee." She went into the kitchen to get the coffeepot.

Ray and the sheriff came in the door and said howdy to Cecil before going back to Warton's usual table, where they were met by Rachael, who was already filling their cups. "Good afternoon, gentlemen," she said. "Is Jesse gonna be along pretty soon?"

"I expect so," Warton replied. "He was comin' with us, but he said he remembered something he had to take care of first, then he'd join us."

"I'll wait to pour his coffee till I see the whites of his eyes," she said. "He likes to drink it hot. We saw him go by a little earlier, leading a string of horses. Did he catch up with those two men who killed Cliff?"

"Yes, he did," the sheriff said, "and I reckon you could say he settled the score for Cliff, but it won't bring Cliff back."

Thinking he should say something in Derringer's defense, Ray said, "Jesse gave them a chance to surrender and come in peacefully, but they refused it." Rachael wanted more details than that but decided not to press for more information, knowing she could get everything from Ray when there was just the two of them to discuss it.

He was not quite sure why, but Derringer was anxious to make a courtesy call before he went to the hotel for dinner. He gave the sheriff and Ray the excuse that he had forgotten to tell Leon Draper to give his horse extra grain today. As he walked up the street toward the stable, he stopped when he was in front of The Crossing Saloon to look behind him. He paused long enough to see the sheriff and Ray going into the dining room door. Then he continued on past the saloon and went into Vera's Vineyard.

"Jesse Derringer," Thelma pronounced dramatically when she saw him walk in. "You lookin' for Lydia?"

"As a matter of fact, I just stopped by to thank you and Rosa for your information on the two Crowe brothers who killed Deputy Cliff Crenshaw."

"Is that so?" Thelma responded. "Did you catch up with the monkey brothers?"

"I did," he replied, "and it was only because you and Rosa told me where to start lookin' for 'em. So thank you and thanks to Rosa, but I reckon she's occupied right now, since I don't see her here."

"Yeah, she's upstairs with one of her regular customers," Thelma said. "I'll tell her you said thanks."

"I 'preciate it," he said. "I kinda wanted to thank Lydia, too, but it looks like she's occupied, too."

"She just went to see her mother," Thelma said.

"Oh," Derringer responded, obviously disappointed. "I'm sorry I missed her. Will she be coming back?"

Thelma looked at him as if he was crazy. "Well, I hope so. She just went to the kitchen."

"I thought you said she went to see her mother," Jesse said.

"You feeling all right, Derringer?" Thelma asked. Then very emphatically she slowly stated, "She went to the kitchen to talk to her mother."

It still took a couple of moments before it dawned on him that Lydia was Vera's daughter. "Ohhh . . ." he finally drew out.

"You didn't know Lydia was Vera's daughter, did you?" When his only answer was a slow shaking of his head, she said, "Well, not many people do, I reckon. I'll tell her you're looking for her." She didn't wait for his response but spun on her heel and went through the door at the back of the room.

Not sure if he should retreat or stand his ground, he was too slow to decide for Lydia came back through the kitchen door ahead of Thelma. "Jesse," she sang out cheerfully, "were you looking for me?"

"I reckon I was," he answered, "but I can come back some other time if you're busy in the kitchen." He hesitated, then added, "With your mother."

"I'm never too busy to talk to you, Jesse. Do you mind coming into the kitchen? I was just fixing something to eat. Have you had your dinner? If you haven't I can just as easily fix two plates."

"Oh, I wouldn't wanna put you to that trouble," Jesse said at once. "I was just stoppin' by to thank you again for your help gettin' enough information for me to start out after those two Crowe brothers. Besides, I just came in off the trail. I shoulda cleaned up a little before I even stopped in."

"Nonsense, I'll take you any way you come," Lydia insisted. "It's no trouble for me. Mama does all the cooking. I just take what I want and maybe add something more if I want it. I would enjoy having dinner with someone for a change. Won't you please join me?"

"It'd be my pleasure," he said.

"Good!" She took him by the hand and led him into the kitchen past a grinning Thelma to face a surprised Vera Collins, who stood motionless, holding a large carving knife. "Mama, this is Jesse Derringer. He's come to have dinner with me."

"Jesse Derringer," Vera repeated. Having caught only a couple of glimpses of him from her kitchen door, it was like seeing him for the first time. She glanced at Lydia and said, "He gets right big when you see him up close." Looking back at Derringer, she said, "Welcome to the private quarters of Vera's Vineyard. You and Lydia get yourselves a plate of food and go into the private dining room and enjoy your dinner." She watched as Lydia filled two plates from the kitchen stove, then thought to ask, "You know that Lydia ain't one of my . . ."

"Mama!" Lydia interrupted her. "Jesse knows that. Don't you, Jesse?"

"Why, sure," Derringer sputtered, the fact being that he was not sure and assumed that she probably was. He realized that he was genuinely pleased to find that she was not on the menu in the "Vineyard" part of the house. She picked up the two plates and led him through another door to a small room with a table and chairs and a stove. He recognized it as the room she had led him to from the big parlor when they had coffee and talked before.

They took their time over dinner and Jesse experienced the same feelings of peace and comfort in her presence that had struck him the first time they talked. When he finally confessed that he had to report to the sheriff's office, since he had agreed to resume his temporary position as a deputy sheriff, she made him promise to call on her again. "You can count on that," he told her. He asked to go back out through the kitchen, so he could thank her mother for dinner, and Vera surprised him with a confession.

"I don't know if you ever found out or not," Vera told him, "but I'm the one who made your birthday cake."

"You know about that?"

"Everybody in town knew about the night they tried to kill you," she said. "I just want you to know I thought

I was baking a cake for a surprise birthday party. I made him pay me seventy-five dollars to bake him a secret cake."

"Please say you'll call on me again, even though my mother was part of a plot to kill you," Lydia pleaded.

"I reckon," he japed, " 'cause I already promised and I never break a promise. Now, you promise you'll let me know when you're ready for me to stop coming to see you."

"I promise," she said, and went up on her tiptoes to plant a kiss on his cheek.

He left to go to the sheriff's office then, thinking he could still feel the kiss on his cheek. *What the hell am I thinking?* he thought. *I'm acting like a damn-fool young buck going courting for the first time in my life.* He paused for a long moment to think about that. For most of his life, he had been unhampered by feelings of restriction that befell most young men in their younger years. And now, he was getting a taste of it at his age.

"I like it!"

company is caught in the crossfire of two rival mine owners who want to control the freight routes. Like it or not, Trace and Chaw are stuck in the middle of another war. And this one's going to be every bit as bloody—and maybe their last. . . .

**NATIONAL BESTSELLING AUTHORS
WILLIAM W. JOHNSTONE
and J.A. Johnstone**

**THE BEST OF ENEMIES
A Trace and Chaw Western**

First in a New Series!

Live Free. Read Hard.
williamjohnstone.net
Visit us at kensingtonbooks.com

On sale now, wherever Pinnacle Books are sold.

CHAPTER 1

The first thing the man felt was heat, heat from the unforgiving sun baking down. By the time he came around, it had already reddened his upturned face and blistered his lips.

The next thing he noticed was yet more heat, but this time it came from within himself, from below himself, as if from the earth on which he lay.

He forced his eyes open, just a crack at first. All he could see were stinging pinpricks of light through a gauze of pink that edged out to redness. Jagged, brittle snatches of memory drizzled back to him at the same time. And not a bit of it impressed him.

All this told him was that he had to be dead, given what he was recalling. He almost wished he had lost his ability to recall anything, so awful were the bits of memory, of what he had seen and lived through. Or had he?

Then sound flooded in and became more pronounced.

But at first, all he could hear was a whooshing and thudding.

With more effort than he bet he'd ever expended on anything in a coon's age, the man lifted his head. It wobbled on its feeble stalk of a neck. He cracked his right eye wider than its slit and saw bright, warm light, and little else. How on earth did he get here? And where was "here"?

All he could recall was fighting. Seems that's all he'd done since he was born. What did that mean?

Notions, facts, or perhaps they were fabrications, he could not yet tell, flitted in and out of his mind. He gritted his teeth and fought to keep his eyes open. There, he looked down along the length of his body and saw himself, stretched out on his back in the sun. His clothes looked sodden, must be sweat.

And then, as if someone had clapped their hands and awakened him fully, he remembered who he was. And from that revelation, it was a short jump to how he got here. Wherever "here" was. He figured in time that that, too, would come.

And then he remembered—the war. The war and the cursed Yankees who started it. And there he was, all laid out, baking in the sun, not certain how alive he was, or if he was on his way out. The latter possibility seemed the most likely, given the pain he felt, the light burning away at him, and the rush of memories flooding into his mind.

But right then, he figured he knew who he was, and that was pretty good. He was Chaw Dagworth, Private in the army of the Confederate States of America.

He glanced down at himself again as he struggled to

raise himself up onto an elbow. And if he was in the Confederate Army, then that meant his uniform would be gray. And if that was the case, why was it so sodden-looking? Ah yes, the fighting. The cursed, fool Big War Twixt the States, a protracted fracas, as his old colonel used to say, caused by Yankee bellicosity.

Chaw grunted and felt a stinging in various parts of his body that quickly gave way to lancing pains, as if someone were sliding knives in and out of his arms, his sides, his legs. What was happening? And then he knew that he wasn't seeing a sweaty uniform, he was seeing a blood-soaked uniform. And as soon as that dawned on him, the rest of his situation became as clear to him as a cool mountain stream.

As he shoved himself up, despite the constant throbbing all over his body, more memories came gushing on in. Uninvited, but there they were anyway. . . .

His company had been taking a ridge, below which was a hollow, what was it called? Deadeye Gap, that's it. And then he'd seen a bluebelly and had taken off after him. That's right, that bluebelly and Chaw got into it pretty good. For a Yankee, the man was brute enough. Must have had Rebel bark somewhere in the woodpile.

In fact, Chaw recalled shouting that at the man as they tore into each other, each giving as good as they got. That comment sure got that bluebelly riled. That foul Yankee had called Chaw a slave trader and a child killer and all manner of raw names, none of which was true. Chaw found this humorous, considering the Yank was a foul traitor and a child killer and a secret slaver himself!

Of course, Chaw had no way of verifying such, but

he didn't doubt that bluebelly was guilty of that and a whole lot more. He was a foul Yankee, after all, wasn't he? That alone was reason enough to pin the entire mess on him.

As he lay there, Chaw pulled in as much of a breath as he could—it wasn't a deep one nor was it clear. Sounded to him as if he was breathing through a ragged pig's bladder. That reminded him of home at pig killin' time, when the men folk back home used to inflate and tie off the bladders for the kiddies to bat around.

None of that much mattered now. He was likely dying and would as likely never see his poor old family ever again. Not Ma, nor Pa, nor Jube, nor dear old Daisy the hound.

Chaw grunted and swung his gaze slowly over to his left. What he saw somehow did not surprise him, although it should have. But he reckoned some part of him knew what he would see before he looked there. And what he saw did not fill him with satisfaction, as he had expected it should. Nope, seeing that dead Yank not but a few yards to his left only made Chaw Dagworth feel almighty awful.

Even if the man was a foul Yankee, that carcass left Chaw hollowed out inside, even more than before. Because it only meant that, as bad as he felt, that Yank was worse off. For he was already dead.

And so, that meant that Chaw had given away his own life, and for a cause that had become so muddied and confused for him and most of his fellow Rebs, most had, at one time or another, considered running off in the night. Even though it meant risking getting shot in the back. And now, here he was, surely about to die himself, and that was a raw, hard thing to take.

The Yank, in Chaw's brief glimpse of the man, and then on repeated forced looks, appeared to be in particularly rough condition. The Bluebelly, too, was sprawled out on his back, and he, too, was covered with what looked to be a whole lot of dried blood from gashes and rents in his once-blue uniform. He knew this because there were a few spots of blue wool still visible through the darkened blood.

Was this it, then? Nothing more than kill or be killed? How on earth, he wondered, would his death or the death of that foul Yank beside him, be helpful to the cause of the South, or the cursed North, for that matter?

Chaw closed his eyes a moment and worked to breathe a bit more. And he came to the conclusion that there wasn't a single scrap of usefulness in his sacrificing himself for the dang cause. No sir.

And then he heard a sound. From his left.

Chaw grunted and worked to angle his gaze back over in that direction. He blinked hard and opened his eyes again, forcing them wide. Couldn't be. He could swear he saw that foul Yank move!

Long before he opened his eyes, Private Fullcup Trace, of the Union Army, lay awake. Keeping his eyes closed on waking each morning was a lifelong habit, and something that, even in the much-abused state he knew his body to be in, he nonetheless maintained.

He found it beneficial to slowly, over the course of several minutes, allow himself to come around to full consciousness. In this way he could take account of who he was, what had happened to him, and where he was at that moment.

All of this came to him as he lay there, sipping air between parted lips. He knew who he was—Trace, he was called—for he became aware of such as if someone had whispered it to his mind.

But it also soon became obvious to him that his normal method of waking was not going to cut it this day. For memory reminded him in the harshest way just what it was that had landed him where he was, and in the state he suspected his body of being in.

First, he felt a thudding building within him. It started down low, deep in his guts, and rose as if it were marching right into his chest, and on up his gullet. By the time it wormed its way into his mouth and nose, he had begun to ache all over.

And then, the memory of the events leading up to all of this flooded into his mind. The lashing agonies that come with what surely were a thousand cuts, stabs, cracked ribs, broken fingers, and more thrummed with a sudden and searing pain over all his body. As bad as that pain was, it bowed down before the thudding of the cannonade playing out betwixt his ears.

With more effort than he felt capable of, Trace cracked open his eyes. The sunlight that had been there, awaiting this moment with supreme impatience, drove forward and inward. As Trace squeezed his eyes shut once more, although too late to avoid this fresh, raw wash of pain, it felt as if forge-fired daggers were jamming themselves like steel vipers into his skull.

An unbidden moan, low and fragile, was accompanied with a deluge of memories that flooded over him. And he knew without doubt where he was. The battle atop that cursed ridge above Deadeye Gap, it was called. They'd found that holdout Reb company they'd been chasing for weeks.

Those foolish Graybacks fought like cornered lions, with claws out and fangs slashing and with a hard pistoning of their gunfire that seemed to not let up. Trace recalled wondering out loud, with some of the other Union men, if maybe the Rebel soldiers truly didn't know that the war was all but over for them.

No, there hadn't been any surrender as such, at least not yet. But it was bound to happen soon. That's what they had all thought going into the latest fracas with the elusive, dastardly Rebs. The enemy numbers were raggedy and slowly dwindling, but they nonetheless fought at every turn as if they were freshly minted men.

Trace groaned again as the rest of the preceding events came back to him. He recalled how he had made his way down past the far side of the battle, chasing after a pair of Reb snipers. He knew from experience that they'd been looking to sneak up around to where the Northern Army was encamped. That would not stand.

Trace had gotten the drop on them, sure, but instead of letting him take them as his prisoners, they'd put up a fight. He'd expected that, anyway. He didn't recommend it to anyone, even a foul Rebel, but he could hardly blame them, now, could he?

As he fought, trading shots with the two snipers, Trace realized from the sounds of the battle above and behind him, atop that ridge, that the melee was not about to end in favor of these maddening rebels and the rest of their Southern ilk.

He was all but through with these two, having pinned them pretty well, despite being a lone soldier against two men. He had the landscape to thank, in part, for that, too. He had been able to position himself behind a boulder the size of a wagon while the two Rebs he'd been pursuing had found themselves at the bottom of a gulley with nothing but knee-height rocks and crusty pines no thicker around than a man's arm.

Then, he had touched finger to trigger and had been about ready to send those two Rebel curs barking to the netherworld. Despite how he felt about them and their cause, there was that flicker of a moment when he regretted ever being involved in this foul mess to begin with.

It had less, far less, to do with the individual solders, no matter the side, than it had to do with the cause each side fought for. And for all that, he knew that all these deaths could be laid at the feet of the leaders on both sides for their failure to keep talking, keep shouting at each other across the back room negotiation tables.

Trace didn't care how how angry they got or how many days or weeks or months or years it would have taken. All of it would have been breath and time well spent if it had saved a single life of one of the soldiers on either side. Instead, they had ended up fighting, either by choice or, as had proved the case, by force, to fight and die for their respective so-called causes.

And Trace knew he wasn't the only man in the Union Army who felt that way. And he had it on good authority that most Rebs felt the same darned way, too. Fat lot of good it had done any of them.

All of that flooded into and out of his mind in that whisper of a moment before he squeezed the trigger to take yet another Rebel man's life. And at that moment, a shot whipped by his head from behind him. It spun Trace's gaze hard over his right shoulder. At the same time, instinct drove him down to one knee.

There he spied yet another Grayback. This one, however, wasn't oblivious like his fellows. Trace had, after all, gotten the upper hand on those two Rebs down in their gulley, looking this way and that.

In recalling that day, however many days before, Trace now realized that moment could have well ended it all, and in eyeblink speed. But for some reason that crazed Rebel he'd seen over his shoulder, with his rifle aimed right at Trace's head, had decided not to shoot him.

What he did instead genuinely surprised Trace. The man had delivered that shot at him. And when he faced him, Trace saw that the Reb hadn't been far enough away to have missed him. Why hadn't I heard the rascal sneaking on up behind me? thought Trace.

As if in answer to the question of why echoing in Trace's skull, the Reb who'd shot at him from behind, and who held a revolver aimed right at him—he must have used his rifle to deliver that first, too-close-to-have-missed shot—shouted from about sixty feet away.

The Reb eyed him down the short barrel and barked, "I am a son of the South and as such I am too proud to shoot a man in the back, even if he is a foul, yellow, blue-bellied Yankee!"

By then, of course, Trace had his own gun aimed right at that Rebel's gut. He rose once more to a standing position. Behind and below his big boulder, he heard a voice shout to another, "Let's git gone back to the fight! That Yank's done for!"

That told Trace he didn't have much to worry about from those two. He could concentrate on dealing with this crazy Rebel. A man who had him dead to rights, but who made him turn to face him before he would shoot him was a crazy man. Or a man with a conscience.

Make that a Rebel with a conscience. He knew there were a good many of them because he'd learned a whole lot since he started in on this war, with all its marches and lousy, maggoty food, and surly officers and lack of leadership with brains.

He'd learned that most Rebs were just about the same as most Yanks. That was to say they were all just men. Men with wives and children and parents and cousins and friends and homes and farms, all of it.

And now here was one who wanted to fight him, face-to-face, fair and square. All right then, thought Trace. Let's get to it.

He rose back to standing height, keeping his rifle aimed at that man's chest, and said, "What's it going to be, Reb? We have each other square on!"

"Shut up and approach. We'll see how far you make it, you stinking Yank!"

And so they had advanced on each other, slow step by slow step, their respective barrels not faltering, their boot steps sure and well placed, their eyes never leaving the other's, their trigger fingers ready to dole out the last sound the other man would ever hear.

But neither man pulled a trigger. Neither man dared to be the first, apparently, for they each advanced and strode with caution and unwavering concentration right toward the other.

And then they were close enough to see the grime caked in the lines on their faces, to see that they each could use a real shave, a haircut, a month's worth of sleep, and the same of food.

"Enough!" growled Fullcup Trace, flinging away his rifle. He didn't care any longer.

They'd been staring each other down for long, long minutes, slowly circling, and the situation had grown more than tiresome. A vital need had grown in him that they fight like men, men who were unafraid to cower behind the false cowardice of a gun.

As Trace regarded the other man, the Grayback sneered, and he, too, sent his own gun spinning to the dirt. That's when things really began to head off into an interesting direction.

Again, as if by mutual unspoken agreement, the two men each sneered, their lips pulled back over tight-set teeth. Their eyes narrowed and growls crawled up out of their throats.

Arms drew up fast and their hands sought each other with clawlike fingers, fingers that closed on the other, on arms and chests. They balled wool tunics and at the same time jerked the other man this way and that, hoping to gain the upper hand.

They each gave voice to deep rage that, while directed

at the other man, really represented the anguish and frustration and fear and confusion they had each felt for the past couple of years of being forced to kill or be killed.

Propelled by a clot of such feelings fueling their man rage, the two men muckled onto each other hard and fast, neither uttering any sounds that could be recognized as words. Instead they were growls and barks and the utterances of seething anger.

They circled, breaking their holds, only to collide again, one arm grasping clothing or hair, it mattered not. The other was curled into a thick fist that drew back then drove forward like a sledge wielded by a railway man.

Their blows staggered each other, sent blasts of starlight even during the day before the receiver's sweat-riddled eyes. The punches and cudgel-like shots staggered each other, and yet neither man relented. Once they had agreed to brawl it out, neither man gave the other a moment's peace. Legs kicked, circled around other legs, seeking to trip.

Once, the Reb was able to use his momentum to drive the Yank backward. One of the man's blue-clad legs lay pinned beneath him, and the Reb knew something had happened to that bent knee. It had not broken, for the man would have yipped like a kicked dog, but nonetheless he knew something very painful had overtaken the man.

He grinned, his gritted teeth stained yellow and gray, as if to match his uniform, and he used the moment's pain to his advantage, jamming his own knee into the Yank's midsection.

But his hubris at finding himself atop the other was short-lived, for he had lost, for a moment, his accounting of the Yank's left arm. And as the Reb bent low to deliver a pulled-back punch, he left his own right side exposed.

The desperate Yank's left fist slammed into the right side of the Reb's ribs with the force of a hickory log being jammed, butt end first, into the man's torso, with deadly, unexpected momentum.

The blow shoved any air the Reb had in his chest up and out in a rush that ended in a wheeze. The worst of it for the Reb was feeling the sickening, sharp, lancing pain deep inside. He'd been down that painful road before and knew he'd just received a broken rib or three from that foul Yank.

The Reb collapsed to his left, falling off the pinned Yank long enough that the man in blue could roll to his left. Again, as if by mutual consent, the two men rose to their knees, facing each other, panting their rasping breaths. Hatred, directed at each other, glowed through their narrowed eyes, their chests working like bellows.

The Yank put little weight on his bum knee, for it pained him already and he knew it was swelling. He bet that something inside, the stringy bits in a man's body that hold flesh to bone, had torn or separated somehow.

The Reb raised his left hand and rested it against the right side of his rib cage. He knew it showed a weakness, a wound dealt by the Yank, but he had to do it. Trace probed gingerly and again could not help the sharp-drawn breath of limping forward. With the Reb sipping shallow breaths, they drove at the other. Now each was intent on furthering the damage he had already inflicted on the other man.

How long they fought, neither man knew. Not that either of them cared. The brawl had become far more than two enemies having it out to some sort of end. It was the long-pent result of years of hardship shoved on them each day by their superiors, by the weather, by other soldiers, by bad food and worse water, by unforgiving terrain, and by the long-forgotten reasons behind why each was told they must kill other men.

And so it went, for hours or days or weeks, neither man knew nor cared. At some point, one of them, neither could recall later which, tugged free his knife barely an eyeblink's worth of time before the other did.

Thus the fight went on, continuing with each man guessing the move of the other, growl for growl, punch for punch, kick for kick, driving knee for driving knee, butting head for butting head, lunging, snapping teeth for the same. And now was the deadly promise of honed steel.

The appearance of blades in their scar-knuckled, brawl-reddened hands kindled in each man a renewed fire, a burning rage to kill, and to not be killed. It was no surprise to either man that his opponent wore a sheath knife on his belt. Most soldiers did, and frequently these tools were brought from home, cherished items that a man regarded with as much or more fondness than his gun.

A hip knife was perhaps a man's most-relied upon possession. It was a tool he used many times a day.

Men shaved with them, used them to cut hair and trim beards, to skin, gut, and slice fresh killed critters for the fry pan or pot, from turtles to swamp rats to rabbits, and more.

A big-bladed knife also could be used to split lengths of branch wood for kindling, for sharpening sticks, for cooking and hewing stakes for tents. And as long as a man had a whetstone in his possibles sack, it could also be used to dig a cat hole in the steel-dulling earth, should a man care that much about covering his leavings with more than forest duff.

Occasionally, although the men agreed it was happening more and more as the war dragged on, these knives had begun to be used to defend one's life, and to attack a foe as well.

As each man, Trace and Chaw, lifted free his knife, a sneer rose unbidden on each face. Without warning, they rushed at each other, snarls of rage ripping from their mouths.

They fought with bedraggled bodies sporting blood-shot eyes, bruised and bloodied mouths from split lips and smacked noses, and sweat-plastered hair. They wore the grime of repeated slammings and rollings in the dust and churned soil of the small, scree-riddled plateau they each had been stomping and trampling and kicking and furrowing for hours.

They fought as beasts, coming together amidst howls and clouds of dust, slashing and driving, peeling apart and wielding keen blades afresh with each parry and thrust. Over and over they attacked, not seeming to lose the renewed, whetted appetite for blood they each shared.

Their thirst for killing clouded their usual individual sensibilities and they fought hard and viciously. They rarely fell apart without leaving hacked slices in the arms of woolen tunics, on through into the sweat-soaked long-handle underwear beneath, finally drawing blood in scarred skin befouled by war and hard living.

Cuts more than gashes, although there were plenty of those as well, covered each man's head, face, torso, arms, hips, backsides, and calves. It seemed to each man as if they were covered with the denizens of a huge hive of deadly hornets, for with every move they made, their bodies screamed from the constant, stinging pain of a thousand lacerations.

Over time, neither man knew how much, the welter of agony each found himself mired within began to take its due toll.

Each man, the Reb and the Yank, after hours of cutting and slashing, howling and colliding, clubbing and flailing at the other, hammer and tong, staggered backward.

Trace, the Yank, had no idea how he had managed to stay upright for so very long, as his knee had somehow endured far beyond ordinary pain.

When he had been able to steal a quick glance at himself, he had been shocked to see, through the slashed fabric of his trousers, that they were no longer showing any trace of blue. They were matted with a reddened black, and were sodden with sweat and blood. His own and that of the foul, determined Reb.

What had shocked him most was the size of his knee. It had swelled to what seemed the size of a man's head. The ragged trouser leg about it, although slashed, had also brought with it a cold dose of luck. The knee had been able to swell and not be constricted by the fabric itself, for good or ill.

The Reb, leaning against the boulder before which the Yank had begun the fight, felt his breath wheezing in and out of his damaged breadbasket and rib cage. He hated to admit it, but that Yank had delivered into his side one mighty wallop, a pummeling such that the Reb was certain he might never again breathe as a normal man.

That thought had been from who knew how long before. Before the brutality their knives had inflicted. Now the Reb was a gasping, wheezing mess.

It was all he could do, now that they had fallen back apart from each other once again, to maintain his tender hold on his knife. He glanced down at himself and saw nothing he recognized.

Not his right hand, nor the knife in its grasp. He knew there was a knife there somewhere, hidden under a thick, syrupy coating of red-black gore that streamed and sluiced in steady rivulets down his drooped arm. The hand and fingers were covered with their own slick gore, beneath which dozens of cuts screamed at once. As did his entire body.

Chaw glanced up once more, as he held his left hand to his right-side rib cage, the tenderest spot on his entire savaged form. "If I . . . look . . ."

He swallowed and licked his lips, his voice a cracked, croaking thing. My how he longed for a long sip of cool, clear water. "If I looked as bad . . . as you . . . Yank . . . I'd up and die already."

The Yank regarded the Reb while he leaned against

the trunk of a much-scuffed pine. What he wanted to say was: 'Of course you would! You're a weak-kneed Rebel!' But what came out, between huffing gasps was: "Could say the same . . . to you, Reb. . . ."

In all the time of that fight, neither man had done much more, sound-wise, than to grunt and shout sounds that were not words. But they did not much care. But now, hearing their voices, after hearing nothing but raw animal sounds from themselves, surprised each of them.

It also seemed to trigger something within each of them once more, yet another animalistic lunge to satisfy the unreasoning rage each felt at nearly being killed by the other.

They bolted forward, once more as if they had nodded in agreement with one another, and yet they hadn't. This did not slow them down, but the wearing, atrophying pain of the protracted battle had shown its strain as each man shoved up and away from the only things that were really keeping them upright—the boulder and the tree.

They lurched forward, staggering and eyeing each other through blood-flecked eyelashes, blinking and wheezing, their knives held halfway up in weak grasps. Each man with his eyes fixed on the other advanced. Paltry, feeble step by lurching, halting step, they drew closer, slowly, grunting and wheezing, bleeding and groaning.

And, as had happened since they began their attempt at mutual destruction, they each faltered within ten feet of each other, and the last thing each man saw was the other, his sworn mortal foe, sagging and collapsing. Eyes rolled back in heads, knees buckled, heads slopped backward on their weak stalks as their bodies slowly sank to the churned, bloodied earth.

Each man slopped to the side, then flopped sprawled flat on his back, but a couple of yards apart. Each still held his dagger in a death-clench grip, stiffened into place by the sticky, drying blood.

When Chaw Dagworth, private of the Confederate Army, came to, and as he gazed on what he assumed was a dead Yank not but a few feet to his right, a Yank he had apparently killed, the entirety of the brutal fight came back to him. And he did not feel one sliver of goodness about it, not one slender thread of pride or satisfaction in having laid low yet another Yankee soldier.

Instead, he thought about how evenly matched they had been. Too much so, it seemed, for it had been one heck of a fight. And as much as he had tried to outmaneuver that blue brute, the fellow had done the same to him, as if they were each reading the other man's thoughts.

How long had they fought? Had it been mere minutes? Hours? The way he looked and the way he felt, it surely must have been days, days in which neither man was aware of light or dark passing. When neither one broke away, despite the fact that they yearned for a drink of water so badly from their respective canteens.

But now, with the thought of water, the wetness of it touching his lips, cooling his parched, burning throat, now all Chaw could think of was water, of getting a sweet, sweet drink into himself.

Where was his canteen?

He looked down at himself, but no, it was not strapped about his chest as usual. Nor was the rest of his gear. Where was it all?

And then he remembered—he had shed the canteen, the blanket roll, his pack in the dried grasses at the base of the tree. That tree that somehow the Yank had ended up closer to than Chaw.

He glanced back that way, beyond the Yank, and Chaw saw he'd been wrong. For the man now looked not to be alive but dead. Deader than dead, as his old Pap used to say. If he could only get on over there, past the Yank, over to the tree, where his gear still lay in a heap. Get to that canteen.

Then he saw what he had assumed was trickery of his eyes, that cursed Yank was moving again. Yes, he was alive! His chest was rising, falling, rising.

Chaw could not understand two things—how the man could possibly be alive, for Chaw had convinced himself that he alone had survived the awful fight. And the second thing he could not fathom was why he felt relief, immediate and flooding through his mind, as he saw that Bluebelly breathe.

Hadn't he fought such men for years now? Hadn't he vowed over and over again that he would kill every Yankee he came across?

Chaw groaned and squeezed his eyes shut then opened them again, the dried blood cracking slightly about them. Back to the water, he thought. Concentrate on getting water or nobody, not you or the Yank, is going to live for much longer.

And then Chaw had what at that moment he knew

was the very best idea he had ever come upon in his whole life. He turned his head slowly painfully to the left and saw that massive boulder where the Yank had been standing when Chaw had first popped off that warning shot. And there, at the base was the Yank's own gear pile. And among it, not but a few yards to Chaw's left, sat a canteen.

He grunted, trying to shove himself over onto his left side, pinioning himself from behind with his bloody right hand. That's when Chaw felt his knife still gripped tight in his hand, He tried to let go of it but it stayed there, attached somehow to his palm.

He raised it and saw that it was glued to his hand, then he knew—it was blood, likely his own, thick and mostly dried, holding the knife there. The sight of it made his head and guts churn. He flopped back to the earth with a gasp from his wounded ribs, his wind pinched and painful.

Why hadn't he shot the cursed Yank when he had the chance? What stayed his hand? Surely it wasn't just not wanting to shoot a Yank, even in the back. He'd done it a few times before. Yeah, it left a sour taste in his gut and mouth and mind for days after, but then he'd seen a new atrocity committed on a Reb by a Yank, and he'd gotten over it right quick.

A few feet away, Private Fullcup Trace, of the Union Army, managed a good few pulls of breath and worked at trying to open his eyes all the way. Something not unlike what a child felt when he awakened with eyes half-crusted shut following a night's sleep.

But this was different, and something he'd not felt before, not in all his adult years. He scrunched his eyes and worked his cheeks until whatever it was freed up a bit, enough for him to force, then pop open first one eye, and then the second.

He tried to raise a hand, but neither wanted to respond. And then, with a bit more concentrated effort, he was able to twitch life into first his left and then his right. But the left felt heavier. He gritted his teeth and forced his eyes open wide. It was a mighty effort and he didn't want to let his mind trail down the path of finding out why. Not yet. First he had to find out what that new sound was, off to his left.

Instinct told him to keep his movements as quiet as he could, but for all that, he grunted as he worked to raise himself up onto his left elbow. He looked down at his left side and saw that his hand, a blood-crusted claw, was curled tight around what looked to be a knife. Yes, it was a knife, his hip dagger.

Trace looked at his fingers, but somehow could not make them do his bidding. He'd have to use his right hand, which seemed to be working all right. He again heard a sound from his left, and, reminded of why he had been roused in the first place, he looked over to the left.

The first thing he saw was the big boulder, and he recognized it as the one he'd been hiding behind . . . for some reason. What had it been? And then he saw before the rock a body, but it was moving, faced away from him, doing something. . . .

On seeing it, in a fingersnap of time it all came back to him and Trace recalled everything that had happened. Chasing those two Rebs, pinning them down in the draw, then being jumped and surprised from behind as he hid by the boulder.

He'd spun and seen that Rebel. He was a tall, rugged-looking, scruffy, gray-clad fellow who'd gotten the drop on him. But instead of shooting to kill Trace, he'd missed him, missed him with intention.

It had made no sense to Trace then, and it still didn't. Despite the fact that the Reb had shouted something about how he'd not resort to shooting a man in the back, even if that man was a lousy Yank.

Trace almost grinned at the thought of him being referred to as "lousy." He reckoned he'd been called a whole lot of things in his life, but not quite that. And then . . . then they had fought. Oh, how they had fought.

Hammer and tong, as the old timers used to say it. Neither man had been willing to give in, let alone give up. It had been the hardest, rawest, most brutal fight of Trace's life.

A hawk's piercing call from high-up sounded. Other than that, and the slight sounds the Reb was making—what was that fellow doing?—there was no other sound. Nothing. Not even battle noise. There should be that, at least. It was . . . Deadeye Gap, that's right.

Something seemed . . . not right. He should hear something, should feel something. But all he felt was . . . numb. As if he'd spent a week inside a whiskey bottle and still hadn't reached the bottom of the thing.

He looked around himself, down at his bloodied mess of a body, and saw his right leg, puffed at the knee. So much so, in fact, that it looked as though there were two limbs in that trouser leg. If I'm that bad off, why can't I feel it?

He squinted and tried to see what the Reb was up to, but the man was faced away from him, looking at the boulder, but doing something over there.

So why, thought Trace, can't I feel something, anything at all other than this fuzzy, sort-of numb sensation? And then a thought came to him: I must be dead. This must be what it's like to be gone. Or maybe in that limbo place, because I have not been sorted out yet by whoever was in charge up there. Or . . . no, can't be down there. Can it?

I'm stuck in this middle layer of whatever this was, neither dead nor alive. He'd read about this, he thought, or maybe he was just recalling it from his Gran's growled interpretations of the Bible. Either way, here I am, thought Trace. Dead or dying.

Had that Rebel bandit killed him? As bad as Trace was beginning to feel, it must be so. He must have been killed in the fight. He sure knew it was a fight for the ages. And yet, when you're dead, or nearly so, what did that matter? You might well have fought for some cause you believed in, sure, but when you're dead, what good is that cause to you?

Heady stuff, he figured, but the upshot of it was that Trace was convinced more and more with each second that passed that he was sitting, or laying down, on Death's doorstep. And the Rebel?

Trace wagered that if he himself were dead, it stood to some sort of reason that his licks had laid the Reb low, too. But then why was that rascal here as well? Must be he had killed the Reb at the same time the Reb had done for him. Must be that one of his licks managed to find purchase on the Reb's body, a blow that surely had laid low the man.

As memory trickled, then flooded in, so had his begrudging admiration for the Rebel. As with most of his kind that Trace had come across, he was a scrapper.

"Hey!"

Trace jerked as if slapped. What had that been? or who?

"Hey, you! Yank!"

Trace had heard that, hadn't he?

"Hey now, Yank!"

The voice had come from his left, He looked over that way once more and saw that the Reb was now facing him and looking his way. And he held a canteen below his lips.

At the thought of that word, Fullcup Trace felt a quick zing of something charge into him. Water. He would kill all over again for a drink of water.

"Yeah, I see you heard me."

Trace looked at the man once more. Was the Rebel smiling? Can a man smile when he's dead? Oh, but this felt all too confusing.

"You best do what I did and crawl on back there behind yourself. My pack's there, not but a few feet behind you, at that tree. Got a canteen there."

The words, somehow, leached through the gauzy, thick scrim that Trace felt covering over himself, and he knew that even if he were dead he had to try to act on those words. They were important somehow. For they meant there was water at the end of them, and even if he were well and truly dead, which seemed pretty likely to him, he sure could use a drink of water.

"Wake up now, man, and go get that water. We ain't through tussling with each other yet."

Trace glanced once more at the Rebel to his left, then shifted his body such that he looked to his right instead. Sure, there was the tree, it was the tree the Rebel had been standing before when Trace had been tipped off by that shot that should have, by rights, killed him.

But it hadn't, and now here he was, and the Reb was telling him he needed to go get water. If Trace was understanding all this correctly, that meant the Reb was telling him to go get the Reb's water. And that sounded like a trap. A trick. Rebel treachery.

But then it occurred to Trace that the Reb was drinking water, and it was Trace's water. His very own canteen. Why was he doing that? But did that mean that he trusted Trace? No, it only meant that he was thirsty.

All of this thinking amounted to nothing more than confusion for Trace. He glanced at the Reb's dropped gear at the base of that tree, not all that far from him, to the right, and he thought he could see the man's canteen. And the sight of it gave him an overwhelming urge for water.

He grunted and worked to flip himself over onto his right side. Even as he did this, he stuck his thick, swollen tongue slowly out of his mouth and touched his lips. He had to get to that canteen.

Ever since Fullcup Trace was a child, he could recall no time when he did not accomplish a thing once he set his sights on it. And that water waiting for him was no exception. He saw it and he wanted it and that was all there was to it. That and crawling on over there.

In his mind he was nearly there. But when he glanced quickly down at himself, he had only planted one elbow, his right, to the dusty earth. He still needed to get himself righted and angled so he could make it over there.

He squeezed his eyes shut and gritted his teeth and somehow he managed to get the top half of his body angled where it should be, aimed for that water. He made for it, somehow, and felt himself actually moving forward, slower, he was certain, than an ant. But then again, he was dead or nearly there, so why should he complain? He was moving pretty well for a dead man.

He almost laughed at this, but somehow he hadn't the strength. He moved forward with one elbow and then the forearm of his left arm. And there was that knife, still gripped in his locked fingers, and he couldn't figure out how to let go of it.

Maybe it was best he didn't. That Reb might be sneaking on over to ambush him at that moment!

Trace wondered about this and figured that as bad as that man looked, he wasn't going to be moving any faster than was Trace. And besides, he was nearly to that water.

Then he felt something down low that he hadn't felt before. It was on his legs. No, just the one leg, ah yes, he thought. That swollen right leg. It was paining him something awful.

Could that be right? If he was on his way to death, just waiting for someone to tap him on the shoulder, would he be able to feel that pain?

As he crawled, now no more than a few feet from that water, that leg began to throb hard. He groaned again, and let himself do it. It was a sound, after all, and that might lead to him being able to say something. Or to shout, should he need to call for help from one of the boys. They'd take care of that Reb, and right quick, too.

Trace saw it now, just ahead of him, jumbled with a small pile of gear that looked a whole lot like his own. He spied a bedroll and a pack, and leaning against the pack, a canteen, round and carved wood and bound with what looked like rawhide, tight and shrunk to fit. A strap handle of some sort of grimy cloth, knotted and looking as if it had been through a war.

At that thought, Trace did snort, just a bit. His lips split as he did so and he felt the stinging anew.

He brought his left hand up to grab that canteen which sat right there before his face, but that blasted knife was still part of his hand. He shifted his weight over to the left elbow and reached with his crusted, filthy right hand.

It was a shaking thing that looked like it should be attached to some old dead man. But it did the job, after a couple of grabs, and he felt that canteen jostle, heard the water inside, felt the promising weight of it—it felt more than half full.

He drew it to his face and leaned it against his nose while his fingers fumbled with the wooden bung. It was attached with a strip of string and he grunted and made a slight, squealing sound deep in his throat trying to get it dislodged.

When he finally was able to drizzle that soothing,

although warm, liquid onto his lips and into his mouth, he nursed on it like a feeding piglet, and he didn't care who heard hm. Never, never, never—and he could not be convinced otherwise—had anything in the history of the world tasted as good to anyone. Ever.

He sipped and slurped and guzzled and although he knew he really should ration that precious stuff, somehow he could not make himself aware, could not make himself do the thing he knew he needed to do.

Which was to ease off on the water and . . .

"Take 'er easy, Yank, or you're liable to get a gut ache and throw it all up again. Then where will you be?"

Trace paused when the man first began to speak. It reminded him of what he had forgotten, namely that he was not alone. He angled himself to face the man, finding it easier to move and maneuver now that he had been somewhat revived due to the water.

He saw that the Reb was still where he'd last seen him, over by the boulder. But now he was seated and leaning against it.

"Huh?" said Trace, surprised on hearing his own voice. "Huh?" he repeated, more to hear his voice falter. But at least he could still hear and feel.

All of his senses appeared to have been rejuvenated by the water. It was a lesson he'd long known, but as he'd experienced throughout life, it often paid to be reminded.

"I said to back off the water. Rest up!"

Trace let these words sink into his mind a moment, then said, "Why?"

"Got to take care of you . . ."

"Why?"

The Reb chuckled. "So I can kill you fair and square, that's why!"

"Don't count on it, Reb."

And so it went, with each man resting and occasionally nibbling on the canteen of his enemy. Remembering, in their fatigue, to look across the few yards toward the other, taking stock and planning just how he would, with very little strength and a body sliced and stabbed and broken and bruised and aching, renew his attack. That was about all they had strength for.

This kept up for hours, and the sun began its descent.

"Reb!"

"Yeah?"

"You got food in this pack?"

"Not much. Hardtack. Coffee. You?"

"About the same. No coffee, though."

"Have at it, Yank."

"You, too, Reb."

Neither man did much more for long minutes as the shadows grew. Trace had been able to pry the fingers of his left hand from around the handle of his knife. He still couldn't flex them fully, but they were moving bit by bit a little better than they had been.

Then the Reb said, "If we built a fire, we could have ourselves coffee."

"I don't have any coffee," said the Yank.

"I do, like I said. In my pack. But no flint nor steel."

"I have those."

"All right then," said the Reb. "Where?"

Silence, then Trace, the Yankee, said, "Best by that boulder where you are."

"Yeah. All right. Bring my gear?"

"I will," said Trace, trying to figure out how he was going to do that and get himself on over to the rock where the Reb sat with Trace's own gear. But he did it.

At the same time, the Reb managed to get himself up to his feet, although he leaned heavily on the rock, and worked to toe up tinder and duff from the ground.

The entire knobby plateau on which they sat was sparsely treed, mostly with low, stunty growth, but there was enough of that. There were also a few dropped branches, and a long, dead tree, brittle and dry. So finding fuel for the fire did not look to be a problem to two men used to scavenging for such on behalf of their respective outfits.

Trace managed to also get to his feet, although his swollen knee proved a painful hinderance to his being able to move any faster than a snail with no ambition. Still, he pressed on, dragging the Reb's pack and canteen and blankets, as well as the man's rifle, lugged by its sling, along with him so a return trip to the base of the tree would not be necessary.

Although they had spent the past few hours but twenty or so feet apart, the two men approached each other with slow caution and grim looks. Each once more held his knife, and Trace was relieved to see that the Reb looked about as bad as he did.

He'd wondered earlier, since the Reb was so chatty, at least compared with himself, that maybe the man wasn't as bad off as Trace felt.

He knew that wasn't a very charitable way to think, but after all, this was a man who was a member of a group he'd been told to hate, so much so that he must kill him. But at that moment, seeing the haggard Reb before him, a man who, when he'd had the opportunity to shoot Trace, had not done so, gave Trace a strange sense of calm and relief.

He knew then that, at least for the time being, however long that might be, they had reached a truce of sorts and would break bread and share coffee. After that . . . well, that was a bridge they would cross when they reached it.

Together they managed to kindle a fire and keep it fed. All the while, from opposite sides of the fire, the two men stole glances at each other, stern faces not slipping a bit.

They exchanged snatches of speech and answered the other's brief questions without much elaboration. Soon, it became apparent to each man that the other was tired. Dog-tired and bone weary, as Chaw's old Gramps used to say.

Darkness descended on them, and while they had dragged back to the fire enough snapped wood and half-rotted lengths and sticks and such, they knew they would be unable to keep it fed through the night.

Trace fought to keep his eyelids open. Finally, he sighed. "Am I safe?" There was a brief pause and he realized he had likely just awakened the Reb from a cat nap.

"Safe? From me?" The Reb chuckled. "Yeah, I reckon. As long as I am from you."

"Yeah, okay. Truce for sleep."

"Truce for sleep. . . ."